Abigail Cottage

By

Margaret West

I0628268

Abigail Cottage

ISBN 978-1-9079-6304-9

Published by
Hedge Witchery Books
www.hedge-witcherybooks.com

Dedication

This book is dedicated to Logan Ruiz Aguilar.

Acknowledgements

www.sharonbenjamin.co.uk from All Write.
Proof Reading Services, for quick and professional help with this book

Mimi Riser. **www.mimiriser.com**,
for her great Critique on this book

And last, but no means least. A big thank you to Lily Oak, for all her hard
work and determination in helping Abigail Cottage finally see the light of
day.

Prologue

Rossheith, Ireland 1814

"Please don't die, Abigail," Justin begged. The small bedroom with its cold, grey stone walls enclosed him. He felt suffocated, powerless in the face of certain death. He rubbed his cheek against her hand. It felt cool, although he saw the heat of her fever reddening her ashen cheeks. "I can't bear it if you leave me here alone."

"You won't be alone, Justin." Her words whispered through dry, cracked lips. "We have a beautiful daughter."

He dropped her hand and gasped in horror as the blanket covering Abigail, turned from beige to crimson as it became soaked with her blood. Desperation widened his eyes to a frantic plea as he looked at the midwife hovering nearby. "Can't you do anything for her?"

"Only God can save 'er now, sir," she replied, fixing her eyes on the silver candle holders beside him. "She 'as the typhus."

Justin dabbed at the sweat beading on his forehead with a handkerchief. He felt the heat inside his own body stir to boiling point. The room was airless, stifled by the heat of sickness. "But surely you can stop the blood? Her life is draining away before my eyes," he argued. He licked his lips and swallowed, grimacing as a thousand spikes pricked his throat when he swallowed. He needed water, but there was none in the house and he didn't have the energy to draw it from the well outside.

The midwife packed her grimy instruments into an old, filthy looking carpetbag. "I can't do nuffink 'bout that, sir. She's gone and dun 'erself a mischief pushing out the babe."

Justin glared at the dishevelled woman, who looked no better than an unwashed streetwalker. "Well, get a doctor then, you stupid woman." But deep in his heart he knew it was futile. The doctor was besieged by the dead and dying.

As the midwife shook her head, her grimy mop cap flapped across her dirt stained brow. "Can't. 'Es dead. Caught the typhus a few days ago."

Eyes that pleaded became eyes of the condemned as Justin looked at Abigail. If they were in London now they would have a doctor and he would not have to rely on this bedraggled mess for help. "So I must watch her die - again?" he whispered to the midwife.

"What, 'as she died afore then?"

Justin smiled at Abigail, lost for a moment in thought. He dabbed her glistening brow with a damp cloth. "Only we know the truth, don't we, my love?"

Abigail slowly rolled her head on the pillow and opened her eyes. A sly smile flitted across lips whitened with pain. "Yes, my love. Didn't I tell you that nothing will ever separate us? Not even death."

He picked up her slender hand, kissed it and squeezed his eyes tightly closed. The pain in his heart was excruciating. He couldn't bear the loneliness if she left him again. "Don't leave me, my love," he begged.

A soft sigh, as light as the evening breeze, whispered through Abigail's lips in response. Justin slowly opened his eyes. He knew it was her last breath and his heart exploded with misery. "Oh, no. My beautiful Abigail." Her beautiful sapphire eyes looked dully at the ceiling. The sparkle of life now gone. "I can't live without you," he wept and collapsed over her.

The midwife put the silver candle holders into her bag and let herself out of the cottage. "Come on, Clover," she said to the scraggy, brown mongrel dog waiting for her. "The master ain't goin' to last much longer. By the looks of it, the typhus 'as got 'im too. If we come back in a few hours 'e should be dead. I saw a nice silver pocket - watch on 'is waistcoat. That'll pay our rent and keep our bellies full for a while." A cough squeezed her lungs into a spasm and she grasped the wall to steady herself. "I need a good tug of gin. That'll keep the fever away. It thinks it'll ave me too, but I ain't goin' to let it beat me."

Justin sat up. He gently closed Abigail's eyes and, oblivious to the blood drenched covers, lay down beside her. The child beside them remained silent in its crib. He had no idea what to do with it. His fortune was almost gone, his London house sold. His friends had long deserted him. No one understood about his and Abigail's unique love, so he was ostracised and left to rot here in this god forsaken cottage. He swallowed and held his throat as the saliva burned the soft tissue of his larynx like acid. 'I can't do this again, my love. Not without you." Justin closed his eyes and allowed himself to drift away and moments later was himself engulfed in his own eternal darkness

***

"Hillseth, come on, we can't go in there. If we get caught, we'll face the 'angmans noose for sure," the young gypsy whispered to his brother.

"Look, Raydean, we've been 'earin' that kid cryin' for the past hour. Sumfink ain't right in that 'ouse. Let's just knock. We might earn a few pennies, if they need a runner to get 'elp."

Raydean sighed, knowing his older brother would get his own way — he always did. "Go on then – knock."

Hillseth tapped on the thick wood and frowned at his brother when the door creaked open. "Allo, anyone 'ome?" he shouted as he pushed it wider.

Raydean sensed danger all around them like a dark cloud waiting to engulf everything it touched. "Hillseth, don't."

"Stop worryin'. You'll go grey before your time." He went inside the dark cottage and called out again.

Raydean followed more cautiously, catching his breath in horror as his brother ran up the wooden staircase. "Just cause there ain't no candle burning, don't mean no one's ere,'" he called after him.

"Oh, there's someone 'ere all right." Coming down with a whimpering infant, Hillseth rushed outside the cottage. "Quick, run," he called over his shoulder.

Raydean followed and ran as fast as his legs could carry him. He had no idea why he was running, but he'd learnt over the years if his brother said do it, then he did and asked questions later. As soon as they were clear of the cottage and its grounds, Hillseth stopped running.

"It's all right boy, death can't run that fast," Hillseth gasped out, and hugged the crying child to him as he fought for breath.

Raydean walked backed to his brother, his brow furrowed in confusion. "Death?" he repeated. "I thought we were running from the people inside."

"What them? No, they went to their maker some time since. We ran from death itself."

"Are you bloody mad?" Raydean said and backed away from his brother. "We're told to stay away from the townies. That child could be carrying the fever. If we take it back, the whole band might get it."

Hillseth shook his head. "No they won't. Look at this." He took the blanket from the child's head and smiled.

Raydean's eyes widened in shock. "It 'as the hair and blue eyes of the Esor."

"Just like our mother told us. The whole bands goin' to be protected from the evil eye and disease all the time she's wiv' us."

"Are you sure it's a girl, 'cause if it ain't...?"

Hillseth pulled the cover down. "Look for yourself if you don't believe me."

Raydean glanced over the child. "That's all right then. Mother said that only the Esor women 'ad the gift of protection. Well, cover 'er up then before she freezes to death." He shook his head, wiping his running nose across his sleeve nervously. "I never believed the stories you know. 'Ow can such people exist? In fact 'ow can we be sure that she's even from an Esor? I mean her parents can't be no one special living out here. "

"'Well, it's obvious isn't it. If all the 'uvvers in the 'ouse are dead and she ain't, then she 'as to be protected by sumfing. She's a chosen one for sure. You ain't got to be no toff to get picked, brother. This little one's a good omen. I can feel it in me bones. She's goin' to bring us all good luck. It's well know the Esor favoured our band and as we found 'er it's up to us to give 'er a name."

"'Er 'ouse were called Abigail Cottage. I saw it written on the outside wall. We could call 'er Abigail."

"Ah, so your readin' lessons with Klareena 'ave come in 'andy afta' all. It could've said Bog's End for all I know," he sniggered. "Abigail ain't no Romany name, but then she ain't really one of us. It'll do, I suppose. I mean it ain't like we know any Esor names. Come on, I'm freezin'. Let's get back an' show off our new lucky charm."

Sixteen years later. . .

"Get your bags and be gone," Bethlas snarled, and threw a sack of clothes at the silver-haired girl, whose bitter laugh stung her to the core.

"You're just jealous, because your man managed to fill my belly with a child while yours remains barren," Abigail spat.

Bethlas clenched her small hands into fists, hating her adopted sister for destroying everything she touched. It was as though her great beauty was tainted with evilness so foul, it corrupted everyone she met. Especially men. And especially, her handsome, kind, but foolish husband. "You're pure evil. You don't care who you hurt."

Abigail gave a nonchalant toss of her silver, waist length hair as she picked up the bag. "I care about those who care about me."

"We loved you for sixteen years and this is how you repay your family? Everyone knows how many men 'ave tasted your wares. I bet you don't know who's fathered your bastard. You're just doin' what you always does, and it ain't goin' to work this time. That baby ain't my husband's child. Now get out, you slut," Bethlas screamed, and pointed to the door. "And don't you ever look towards us for sanctuary again."

Abigail's lip curled into a contemptuous sneer as she eyed Bethlas up and down. "I don't need you or anyone. I've got a real brick built 'ome to go to. What do you 'ave?" Her cold eyes grazed over the worn, panelled interior of the caravan. "This miserable old wooden box, pulled 'ere and there by an 'orse that should've died of old age a long time ago."

"That cottage won't be nuffin' but rubble by now. But you go there - pick about in the rubbish like an animal. I'm sure you'll feel right at 'ome." Bethlas gave a bitter laugh. "You've been nuffin' but bad luck since my stupid brother brought you to us. My mother said you was evil, but 'er 'eart was too big. She couldn't turn from you and thought 'er love would make a difference. Ha! What big joke that was."

"Innis was a madwoman," Abigail mocked. "Everyone knew it and laughed at 'er behind 'er back."

Bethlas' eyes widened in horror. Taking a step towards Abigail, she pushed her face within inches of hers. "My mother was a good woman. 'Er words were 'eeded and respected around 'ere.

She knew that you were no descendent of the Esor. You came from a seed spawned from in the depths of wretched darkness. Your real parents said they were 'usband and wife, but they were father and daughter, abandoned by anyone good. You're nothin' but incestuous filth. You're the one who'll be despised by decent people, not us."

Abigail's sapphire eyes narrowed in anger. "You're a lying, dirty gypsy. You're just jealous that your 'usband prefers me in his bed. He likes to 'ear my groans of passion at night, rather than your nagging. You ain't tellin' me to go. I was leavin' anyway. I ain't raising my baby wiv gypsy scum." Abigail walked slowly towards the caravan door, her head high, her back straight and proud. With one hand on the copper knob she turned to Bethlas. Her mouth bent into a cruel smile, which only emphasised the coldness of her sapphire eyes, flashed their venom like a snake striking out at its prey. "You say people will despise me, but your kind will always be 'ated. I'll be the one livin' beside decent folk in a proper 'ouse. You'll always be 'ere. Living in a rottin' box on wheels." Opening the door, she walked through, and slammed it closed behind her.

***

Justin sighed and looked out of the grimy windows of the cottage. He kept the crumbling wreck of a cottage whole through magic. Was it too much to ask for Adrinia, the shadow queen, to order her minions to clean it occasionally?

"Why can't you content yourself with your existence?" Adrinia asked.

"Because you know it isn't enough. I want to be with my wife," he ground out. "I feel incomplete without her. Not that you'd know how that feels."

Adrinia gave a long sigh. "Even a queen can get lonely, Justin."

"It's not only that. Look at me." He threw his arms wide, emphasising his shabby clothes, which barely covered his scaly body. "If it wasn't for the spells I barter from the night crawlers, I'd have to look like this for eternity. I used to be a handsome man. I don't understand why I look like this now."

"I don't think you look that bad. I…" she began and was cut off by a sharp rap on the front door. "Who's that?"

Justin frowned. "How do I know? I can't see through doors."

"Well, it won't answer itself," Adrinia said, as she disappeared into a dark recess in the corner of the room.

Justin quickly transformed himself into the young man he had been before his death, and opened the door. Words dried in his mouth when he saw familiar sapphire eyes staring back. The girl was almost the mirror image of his wife.

"Ello' mister, my name's Abigail. I was... um… well, this place was…" She sighed and put her bag down on the floor. "Look, I need a room. I can work for my board. I can sew, cook and clean. My parents owned this cottage. They died in 'ere when I was born."

It was as if fortune had just walked in and slapped him on the back. Justin opened the door wider and wished the cottage was nicer inside. "Did you say your name was Abigail?"

"Yes, mister. I was named afta' the 'ouse."

He could sense the infant growing inside her belly. Even though she took pains to conceal it. Now he could try out the transformation spell on her and bring his wife back to him. "As it happens I do have a spare room and as you can see, I'm in dire need of a housekeeper."

Abigail picked up her bag and stepped into the cottage. Her eyes scanned the small room and dulled in disappointment. "You'd better know I'm expecting a child. But it won't interfere with my work" she quickly added.

Justin smiled broadly. "No, I'm sure it won't interfere with my plans at all."

Chapter One

The wind howled and picked up the leaves on the floor, whipping them into a frenzied dance around her legs. Abbey ran through the dense forest oblivious to the sharp stones which sliced her feet without mercy. Her heart pounded against her ribcage, fighting to break free from its confines, yet she didn't dare stop. Her hands tore at the bushes blocking her path, ignoring the spiteful bite of the brambles as they clawed at her skin. He was coming for her.

Heavy footsteps crashed through the undergrowth behind her. She fled in the opposite direction. He mustn't catch her. Her whole existence depended on it. A scream of terror burst from her lips, as giant trees, gnarled through time, reached out to grasp her long, silver hair with their creaking branches. They worked for him now. His dark magic had given them life.

The sudden ring of a loud bell cracked like a whip. Screeching through the air, it drove back the trees into the cold darkness they had emerged from. Abbey ran. Sheer terror constricted her throat and it ached with screams she couldn't release. The ringing in the air grew louder and louder until she couldn't stand its piercing shrill. She dropped to her knees and put her hands over her ears. It was deafening. She couldn't think, couldn't see through the dense forest roof. Then just when she thought she could not stand it any longer, Abbey saw it. A bright light, full of rainbow colours, streaking intermittently through the foliage.

The colours seemed to call to her, softening the loud peel rattling her ear drums. She stood and ran towards it. Something deep inside her knew if she could just stand inside the rainbow she would be safe. She stretched out her hand, feeling the lights comforting warmth as she groped to touch it. Her fingers stretched, each joint separating. She was only inches away when she felt a sharp pain in her ankle. A scream tore though her lips when she saw a gnarled branch pulling her away from the light. The ground opened up beside her and Abbey felt herself dragged into it. Down and down she tumbled as the bell carried on its relentless peel.

Abbey opened her eyes and felt a trickle of sweat seep into them. The harsh sting as it hit her iris made her sit up. She quickly rubbed it. "What the hell..." she mumbled, as her alarm clocks' piercing call threaded its way through her consciousness. She reached over and switched it off. She smiled wryly. So that was the ringing bell in her dream. She thought a new flat, new job - a life - would end the relentless nightmare that plagued her. She had blamed them on her mother initially. As much as she loved her, the past few years living with such over-protective paranoia, had made life very awkward.

The nightmare had started on her sixteenth birthday. It was always the same one. A faceless man chasing her through a dark forest, and the rainbow light that could save her. Only she never quite made there. Her eyes flicked to her innocuous plastic alarm clock. That was a new addition to her dream. It was a shame its bell hadn't woke her up, rather than entering the nightmare and becoming part of it. Abbey closed her eyes. Every time she woke from this dream she felt a deeper sense of foreboding. It was like the man chasing her had become more and more familiar and ever closer to catching her. She now began to feel his presence in her waking moments, especially in the shadowy parts of a room. Those dark patches on walls and floors, although she knew were mere reflections of light, terrified her.

She sighed heavily and pulled back her duvet. Away from its warmth, the cold air in the room settled on her skin and caused it to erupt in protesting goose bumps. She grimaced and remembered her dressing gown was hanging in the bathroom. The room was ridiculously cold. The sooner she got someone to look at the heating system, the better.

As she got out of bed, Abbey tried to expel the irritation pricking her skin like sharp needles. The whole flat was going to pot ever since she allowed her mother to spear head the decorating. Nothing catered to her taste at all. It was her mother's, everywhere. She had only allowed her to do it to quell her devastation. She just couldn't accept her daughter had grown up. Heading for the bathroom, Abbey yawned as she turned on the shower. Exhaustion caused her muscles to ache and her head felt pummelled. She had to do something about the dreams. Maybe get some sleeping pills. Anything to stop the exhausting nightly chase. She closed her eyes and welcomed the massaging effects of the water jets on her neck and shoulders. How had she ever lived without this shower! Abbey reluctantly opened her eyes and washed. The traffic would be hell if she dithered any longer.

Now encapsulated in her long towelling robe and feeling a lot warmer, she made her coffee. Black, hot and strong. Her morning caffeine hit. She carried the mug into her bedroom and grimaced at her new, nicotine coloured curtains. They blocked out most of the light, even when they were open. They had to go, and soon. She put the cup down and opened her wardrobe to drag out a predictable work suit. Because that's what she was nowadays. Predictable and reliable. A friend to everyone, industrious work colleague and boring herself silly.

It was a feat on its own to manoeuvre her waist length silver- hair into a respectable French pleat. One day she'd get it cut really short. Whenever she thought the day was here, something would always hold her back. A flick of brown mascara, a smattering of coral lipstick, and she was ready to face the world. She smiled as she made her double bed. The only time she had shared a bedroom was at university. Susie Baxter had been her room-mate. A funny, sensitive girl, whose one fault was her constant inability to make her own bed. Tired of the untidiness Abbey offered the perfect solution. She would do it if Susie cleaned the room. It was the start of a truce between them that carried on for the three years they lived together.

It had been Susie's idea to visit a travelling fair outside the campus one weekend. They were supposed to study. But as usual Susie's mischievous nature got the better of her and Abbey found herself swept along with it. After they had walked around the bright stalls spending most of their weekly allowance, Susie spotted a small tent with a sign saying 'palm readings' in dodgy, black felt-tip-pen.

Susie pushed her towards the tent. "Go on, go in," she urged.

"No, it's all nonsense. You go in."

"I can't. My purse is as empty as Old Mother Hubbard's cupboard," she said, tipping it upside down to prove it. "You go in and I'll listen outside."

After another gentle shove, Abbey ducked into the tent. Once inside, a curtain of cheap beads gently swayed in front of her. She winced at the plastic clattering noise it made when she moved it to one side and walked through. In the semi-darkness, Abbey wrinkled her nose at the scent of burnt wood with a hint of perfume. Incense sticks had never been a favourite of hers. She swallowed and coughed as the dry air sucked the moisture from her throat. An old woman, dressed in an array of coloured clothing, looked up from where she was sitting. The cards she was just about to shuffle fell to the floor with a soft thud when she saw Abbey.

"I'm so sorry, did I startle you?" she quickly apologised.

The gypsy shook her head. "Not really. I knew you were at the fair."

Abbey frowned. How did she know who I am, never mind where she was? "Sorry, have we met before?"

The woman continued to stare. Her eyes like two little dark holes on her face. "No, we've never met. What can I do for you?"

A flutter of nervous anticipation filled Abbey's stomach. She'd never done anything like this before. How much were you supposed to give? "How much do you charge for a reading?"

"One gold coin."

She hesitated. Gold? She didn't have any gold coins. "I've got a pound coin. Will that be okay?" It was gold coloured – sort of.

The old woman bent down to retrieve her cards she sat up, her face expressionless. "It'll do."

She pointed to the wooden chair in front of her, and Abbey sat, placing the coin on the table. It seemed a silly amount. No one works for a pound. "Are you sure it's enough?" So much for the theory that you had to cross a gypsy's palm with silver.

The woman picked up the coin and held it tightly. "I never take more than I need. Give me your hand, child."

The woman grasped Abbey's extended hand. She stared at it intently. "Your path of life is not an easy one. But you've a task to perform that will test everything that you believe in. Trust in your intuition. It won't let you down."

Shifting anxiously in her chair Abbey frowned. "Sorry? I'm not sure what you mean."

The gypsy ignored her question as she ran her finger lightly down a deep line that ran from Abbey's forefinger to her thumb. "A battle against the light and dark side will be fought. It'll be fierce. Many will give their souls to save the child of the sphere carrier."

"Child of the what?" Abbey replied.

"A man, who has a symbol on his body like yours, is the only one who'll speak the truth to you. Words that sound like music when they are spoken will bind your spirit to him eternally. But deceit will tear you apart. He will hold more than your life in his hands when the time comes to reclaim what is his."

Abbey was still confused. Nothing the woman said made any sense. "What birth mark? I don't have..."

"The Fleur De Lis," the gypsy interrupted. "You have a birthmark shaped like a flower. The carrier of the sphere will have the same. Beware of the man with two faces. He'll do anything to have you. Remember, even pretty things can hide unspeakable evil. A crown sits in the same darkness as him. A queen. Take great care, child. Her wrath is fierce and swift if she's crossed."

Abbey felt her stomach churn. Whatever happened to meeting a handsome man and living happily ever after? A shiver of apprehension passed through her. She didn't like this reading at all and told herself that it was nonsense. Yet she could feel a horrible sense of foreboding. What if her future was mapped out and not in a good way? Was this what she had to look forward to? "Thanks, but I'd better be on my way now," she said, freeing her hand from the gypsy's surprisingly firm grip. Life is what you make it. No silly fortune teller was going to frighten her.

"Here, take your coin." The woman held out the money.

"No, I couldn't possibly take it," Abbey protested. "You gave me... um... well you told me..."

"Nothing that you won't eventually find out for yourself," she interrupted. "My name's Rizavoi Petulengro. I've a daughter called Rosa." Rizavoi's bony fingers pushed the coin into Abbey's hand. "Remember her name. You'll need her knowledge and wisdom one day."

Abbey quickly took the money, reluctant to prolong her stay. "Well, if you're sure." She quickly got up from the chair, happy to leave the cloying air in the tent. As she stepped outside her heart thumped uncomfortably in her chest.

"She's as mad as they come," Susie laughed and linked her arm through Abbey's as they walked away.

"Were you really listening? Remind me not to do that again. What a load of rubbish."

"I overheard, so it's not really classed as listening. I'm not sure it's all tosh. I mean you do have that Fleur De what's its name on your thigh."

Abbey shook her head. "It doesn't look anything like a flower. You're as mad as her. Come on, let's get back to the dorm, I've a stack of essays to write."

Even after all these years that silly prediction still bothered her. Susie had harped on about it for weeks. She even drew around the birthmark on her thigh one night to show that it was a flower. It didn't prove anything. Nothing else the gypsy had said made sense anyway.

After plumping the pillows, Abbey left the room and picked up her ever-bulging brief case. A nervous apprehension prickled her skin at the thought of going into the underground car park. She swallowed. *Stop it, Abbey*, she told herself. *You're being silly. Nothing is out to get you.* Walking to her car she tried to ignore the nervous flutter in the pit of her stomach. The early morning light magnified the shadows, making them look larger and more intimidating than usual. She shuddered. As a child, the shadows terrified her. She always felt as though something evil lurked in them.

Once inside her car, Abbey allowed her heartbeat to slow its frantic pace before she drove away. It was an irrational fear, she knew that. But recently it had started to intrude in her life. It had to stop, but she had no idea how to make it go away.

An hour and twenty minutes later, she entered the reception area of Hodder and Armstrong Solicitors, where she had worked for the past year. Fed up and frustrated with traffic queues and 'gung ho' taxi drivers, she walked wearily through the reception to her small office and dumped her bags down onto the polished desk. She needed a cup of strong coffee before she could face work.

The tea room was her sanctuary, the forever bubbling percolator her best friend. Abbey saw Janet hovering outside the door and she forced a smile of thanks as the receptionist handed her a stack of letters. She knew there would be nothing interesting in it. Just the usual boring cases that no-one else wanted. Coffee and letters in hand she went back to her office and her day was filled with tearful to angry spouses, which she had to either soothe or cajole; insurance claims and compensation disputes, nothing she could really get her teeth into. Abbey released her pen and listlessly watched it roll to the edge of her desk. She yawned and rubbed her eyes.

"When am I going to get real court work?" she complained to the empty room as she closed the file in front of her. Each time she had asked Mr. Morris, one of the three partners in the firm, his answer was always the same. "You need to deal with the mundane and master it first."

Abbey glanced at the round, brass clock on the wall. Six o'clock. She had missed breakfast, worked through lunch and looked as if dinner was going to be quite late too. *Work is taking over your life*, she told herself, just as her rumbling stomach voiced its complaint at not being fed.

Her chair creaked and groaned like an old woman as she sat up, she arched her back and stretched her tired muscles. Now would be a good time to have someone waiting at home to give her a nice massage. But her love life was tantamount to a disaster zone, so that wasn't going to happen any time soon. She had been out with a few men in her twenty-two years, but none had been serious. *It would be just my luck to die a damn virgin*, she thought. It wasn't as if she hadn't had chances to sleep with boyfriends, it just didn't feel right at the time. She wasn't a prude or shy, it's just her virginity was too important to 'give up' to a passing fancy. With that thought grating on her nerves, Abbey reached for her ivory handled letter opener. A gift from the Partners at Christmas. A wry smile tugged at her lips. The company had received a bucket load of them from a grateful client. So her present hadn't even been brought. *Is that all I'm worth, a damn freebie from a client?* She had asked herself that question all year.

She picked up each envelope and slashed it open, discarding the contents on the table with little interest. Then she saw one that did catch her eye. An envelope from McKinley and Acorn Solicitors. Abbey fingered the gold embossed edging with longing. She'd harboured a dream to work for them for years. But her limited experience didn't match their demanding criteria. It never would if she stayed here. "Now what do you want with me?" she mumbled and carefully sliced it open. She pulled out the thick paper and felt something drop into her lap. Abbey looked down and saw what looked like an old fashioned coin. She picked it up and turned it over. It was a silver half-crown. Her eyes widened in surprise at the date - 1816. As she contemplated its significance, turning it over in her hand, she frowned in annoyance when her vision suddenly blurred. She looked up and tried to focus on the brass wall clock, but her head began to swim as if she had just come off a merry go round. She swallowed down her nausea and tried to get up from her chair, but her limbs suddenly felt heavy, her hands numb and her head too heavy to hold up. With mounting panic she realised she couldn't move. The temperature of the room dropped and a shuddering coldness began to penetrate her clothes, winding through her body like a venomous snake, until she was sure the blood in her veins would freeze.

Abbey opened her mouth to call for help. She didn't know what was worse; the silly, soft hiss that escaped her lips or the knowledge that no one would come. She tried to call again, but her breath whispered through her lips and curled away in a column of silent, misty vapour. Terror froze her even more to the chair, as a dense mist began to fill the room. With it came the stench of rotting flesh and her stomach heaved in protest. Within the veiled depths of the mist Abbey saw dark shadowy shapes bending and swaying to a macabre song only they could hear.

A mournful wail echoed in the room. The hair on her body stood to attention, every nerve screamed at her to run, but she was powerless to do anything, but watch the mist edge towards her and embrace her like a long lost friend. Abbey's heart thumped in terror and she squeezed her eyes tightly closed to blot out the dancing shadows that reached out to her. She sensed a cold darkness surround her. Its inky depths swallowed her whole and just when she felt she would be lost in its foul stench forever, a different odour filled her nostrils. Its bitter, acrid taste choked her, she gasped for breath as it filled her lungs, expelling the clean air. She couldn't breathe, every cell in her body was slowly suffocating and she knew in that instant, she would surely die.

Then, as if by magic, it was all gone. The fear, pain and biting cold that froze her veins vanished like smoke in the wind. Even her eyes, sealed firmly shut, no longer bothered her. Someone was there, beside her. She could feel their presence, it was familiar – yet not. "Who's there?" she whispered.

Soft lips covered hers in response. The kiss was long and deep. Filled with passion and longing. It ignited something inside Abbey. An urge to give all she had. The lips moved from hers and nibbled her ear lobes, nape and face. The barest whisper of a masculine voice told her how much she was missed. His words filled with a love that she had waited a lifetime to hear. Her body tingled with anticipation. Warmth flooded through her, every nerve became hyper sensitive to his fingers as they unbuttoned her shirt and cupped her breast through her lacy bra. She wanted this, needed him – had to have more.

Desire flooded her senses and she drowned in a mirage of different emotions, yet through it all, a light shone at the edge of the darkness surrounding her. Her mind, foggy with desire tried to disregard it, but something deep inside her recognised its familiarity. The light made her feel safe. Suddenly everything seemed less appealing. It was as if she had greater clarity than ever before. The darkness became cold and cloying as its tentacles wove around her. The hands that touched her were icy cold. Devoid of humanity. Desire fled, leaving nothing but emptiness in its wake. "Leave me alone," she pleaded.

"Excuse me. Miss Newlands, are you feeling all right?"

Abbey's eyes flew open. Her head was cradled in her arms and she stared at her desk in confusion. She sat up and her hands immediately flew to the front of her shirt. Relief flooded through her when she realised that it was firmly buttoned up. She looked at Janet and saw her concern. "Um… yes, thank you. I must have dozed off," she stammered, and felt her face flush with embarrassment. Had she spoken? Given a hint as to what she was dreaming? She swallowed and grimaced. Her throat felt dry and scratchy as though she hadn't drunk for a week.

"Are you sure? I was just passing your office and heard you making the strangest noise. I thought you were ill."

Abbey wanted to die of embarrassment. She'd had an erotic dream, in the day, in her own office. Was she that desperate for a man? "Actually I don't feel all that well. I think I'll go home," she stammered.

"I'm not surprised. You haven't eaten all day. The job isn't worth your health you know," Janet scolded as she left the room.

Abbey massaged her forehead as a dull throb settled behind her eyes. She looked at the coin on her desk. The dream felt so real. Her body still tingled from the intimate caresses of her dream lover. She put her fingers to her lips. They felt slightly swollen, as though she had been thoroughly kissed. But that was impossible of course. She must be over tired. Her mind was playing tricks on her. Abbey got up from her desk and picked up the letter, she still hadn't read it. Maybe it would tell her something about the coin.

She read the letter and was shocked by its contents. Someone called Abigail Hortense Mooreland had left her a large sum of money and a property in Rossheith. It seemed McKinley and Acorn had been searching for her for a long time. She put down the letter, her brow furrowed in consternation. Her father was an internationally recognised architect. Her family quite easy to find. Her mother would enlighten her. Nothing escaped her. She rarely spoke about her childhood. So maybe Abigail Mooreland would open her up a bit. Abbey's hand trembled as she dialled their number. Although the room was warm, she still felt horribly cold.

As the line connected, she remembered that Mooreland was her mother's maiden name. But she didn't remember an Aunt Abigail. She clicked her tongue in frustration when a recording of her father's voice told her to leave a message. She quickly replaced the receiver. This was a question that could not be left on an answer phone.

Chapter Two

"I'm off then, Janet," Abbey hurried out of the main door. She gave her jacket pocket a quick tap and felt the coin's hardness through the thin material. Instinct told her to throw it away. It gave her the creeps. But her curiosity over ruled it. What did it mean? Her mother would know. She was sure of it. After all, it was her mad relation who had passed it on.

"Goodnight, Miss Newlands," Janet replied. "I hope you feel better soon."

As Abbey hurried into the underground car park, she felt the familiar sense of apprehension build inside her. Shadows confused her. They distorted their subjects, and made them seem larger or smaller at will. Her rational self explained they were just harmless reflections of light. But it wasn't what they were that bothered her; it was what she believed was concealed within their dark depths that terrified her. A shaky sigh hissed through her lips as she got into the car and pressed the central locking button. Only when she was fastened into her seatbelt, did she feel safe enough to breathe more calmly. She pulled out of the garage determined not to look at the dark shadows looming behind.

Driving through the hectic London traffic, Abbey pondered the letter in her bag. *Why would a woman I've never met leave me so much money and her home? Why was nothing left to her mother or other relations? Did she have no children of her own?* Sadness crept over her. All her life she had been loved. Her mother, father and grandfather showered her with affection. They were like the fixtures and fitting of her life. She could never imagine them not being there.

Abbey pulled into the underground car park of her building and grimaced as she stared out of the windscreen. More shadows. Tonight they looked darker than ever. She closed her eyes and took a deep breath. When she exhaled, Abbey counted to ten, opened her eyes and got out of the car. *Be calm*, she told herself as she locked it. *Nothing is here, you'll be fine.* Her heart thumped against her rib cage as she strained her ears to hear the slightest noise. But all she heard was the echoing click of her own heels, which mocked her every fearful step.

Once inside the sanctuary of her flat, Abbey angrily threw her bag onto the floor. This irrational fear was getting ridiculous. She blamed her mother. If you teach a child to be scared of spiders, they'll grow up being terrified of them. With her mother, her fear was the shadows and now that phobia was passed onto her. Abbey kicked off her shoes and scanned the room for her slippers. Spying them wedged under the sofa, she slid across the floor in her stocking feet to recover them. "Warmth at last," she sighed, as she slipped them on and went into the kitchen. Whoever invented laminate flooring ought to be shot, she told herself crossly. It was a cold, hard, unwelcoming material. She much preferred carpets.

Abbey opened the fridge and took out a roasted chicken drumstick, all that remained of yesterday's packed lunch, courtesy of her mother. Abbey looked at it and felt her appetite wane as she inspected its frigid, wrinkled skin. "You're a small price to pay for independence," she told it, and picked up the phone and dialled her parent's number. She listened to the ring tone, half expecting the answer phone to click in. When her mother's enquiring voice echoed down the line, she was pleasantly surprised. "Hi, mum. It's only me. How are you?" Abbey waited for the twenty questions her mother was bound to fire at her. Was she warm? Had she eaten? Were the doors locked, the alarm on...it was endless. Her mother always expected the worst from every new and different situation.

"I'm fine, dear. Is everything all right?"

Abbey sighed. That was a double edged question. Her mother's impersonal enquiry barely hid her anxiety. What calamity was she waiting for? "Everything's great. I'm going to start redecorating the flat tomorrow," she said and dropped the chicken into the pedal bin beside her. It wasn't fit to look at, never mind eat.

"Oh no, was my colour choice that bad? I'm sorry you didn't like it."

Abbey felt a moment of guilt. Her mother had spent weeks with the interior decorator. "No, it's not bad at all," she lied. "I just prefer more pastel colours, to your bright ones."

"It's okay dear; you can tell me I'm rubbish at interior design. Your father does all the time. We're just about to have dinner, but I can hold off if you want to join us? Maybe I can help you choose the new colours."

Abbey shuddered at the thought. Her mother had wreaked enough damage on her flat. "No, you go ahead and eat. I've already got my dinner in the oven," she lied again. "Actually, I'm calling about a letter I received today from McKinley and Acorn solicitors." Abbey frowned and pulled the phone from her ear at her mother's high - pitched scream of delight.

"Jonathon, come quickly! Our daughter's got a position with McKinley and Acorn."

"So you've finally done it!" her father's questioning voice boomed down the line.

Abbey drew her brows together in annoyance. "Daddy, I didn't say I had a job with McKinley and Acorn, I said I had a letter from them. I wish mother would listen to the whole of the conversation before she goes off on one of her mad turns. Put her back on, will you." Drumming her French polished nails on the worktop, Abbey waited impatiently.

"Oh, I'm so sorry dear," Harriet apologised. "I just heard the name and assumed. What do they want with you?"

"Well, it's a bit confusing really. They say a deceased relative left me some money and a little cottage in Rossheith. That's in Ireland by the way," she added.

"It's obviously a mistake," Harried replied quickly. "We've no connections there. If I were you I'd just tear it up and forget all about it."

Abbey paused, surprised at her mother's response. She wasn't someone who would disregard something as huge as this. "Don't be ridiculous. The letter *is* for me. I was supposed to get the inheritance years ago, but they couldn't trace me. Don't you think it's a bit strange? After all, our name's quite well known. We don't exactly live incognito. Maybe they're just rubbish at finding clients," she added. "Anyway, the legacy's from Abigail Hortense Mooreland. And if I'm not mistaken,

Mooreland's your maiden name!" Abbey frowned at the silence which followed. Why didn't she answer?

"Mooreland?" Harriet suddenly repeated.

"That's right. Is she a cousin of some sort?" When the line remained silent again, Abbey tapped the receiver with her finger. "Hello… Mother, are you still there?"

"You're not to reply, Abbey, do you hear me? Nothing good can come from that legacy."

Abbey shook her head in confusion. So her mother did have connections in Ireland. Why had she lied? "Mother, you're not making sense. You either know her or you don't."

"I know who she is," Harriet replied slowly.

"Then fill me in. She's left me a tiny cottage, not a mansion in the sun. You never know, it might be my destiny to be a country lady," she teased, trying to lighten the mood.

Abbey heard a rattle, which sounded like the phone being dropped onto the floor at her mother's end. She strained to hear the muffled conversation which followed, but it was too hurried and whispered. When her father's voice came onto the line she jumped as though she had been caught eavesdropping.

"Listen, sweetheart, I know it's a little late, but can you come over? We need to talk about this legacy."

"Is everything all right?"

"Yes, your Mother's a bit upset. It's been a long time since we heard from…" he paused and coughed to clear his throat. "Well, from that side of the family," he finished. "So I'll see you in about half an hour then?"

Abbey groaned inwardly. The last thing she wanted to do was go out in the cold again. But she had to get this settled otherwise she wouldn't sleep a wink. "Okay, I'll see you later." She replaced the receiver and chewed thoughtfully on her bottom lip. What's so bad about Abigail Mooreland?

She hurried to the bedroom and pulled off her work clothes. With no time to shower, she quickly tugged on a pair of jeans and a jumper. Threading her arms through the sleeves, she shuddered as a sudden icy blast of air froze her exposed skin. Abbey's accusing glare fell on the window. But it was closed tighter than Methuselah's mouth. She yanked the jumper over her head and pulled it down. The flat was like a damn sieve. At the weekend she would make sure every draught was found and plugged.

Then, without warning, the hairs on the back of Abbey's neck stood to attention. She nervously looked around the room. Her mother always told her to trust her intuition and it was telling her at the moment that she was being watched. She frowned. Being four storeys high, with nothing but open fields around her, any peeping tom would have to have a long neck or a large pair of binoculars that could see through blinds.

Abbey dismissed the silly thoughts from her mind as she continued to get ready. But when a strange smell, a mixture of gone off meat laced with perfume, filled the room, she paused, her nose wrinkling in distaste as the bitterness of the scent filling her throat. By the time she had fastened her jeans it was intolerable. Abbey staggered as her head swam. She clutched the bedside table, sick to her stomach, as the room whirled around and become a blur of coloured shapes. Just when she was sure she would faint, her head cleared and the scent was gone. Abbey sat on the bed unsure what had happened. She lay back as her body became bone crushingly weary. But as she began to close her eyes, she was almost blinded by a brilliant white light that filled the whole room.

Abbey cried out in pain and sat up covering her eyes. It had to be a power surge in the electrics, because every light in the room was on and shining so brightly it hurt. The shock of it cured her sudden lethargy immediately. Her head cleared and she was back to normal instantaneously. That'll teach her to try and function on fresh air. The lights in the room dimmed to a more manageable glare and she got up, dragged out her French pleat and brushed her hair. A shudder went through her at the cold chill still lurking around her legs. Something she would soon remedy with nice thick carpet. But then she heard something she couldn't explain away — the faintest whisper of her name being called.

Abbey spun around in the empty room. "Who's here?"

No one was there, she knew that. But someone had definitely called her name. "Hello?" she called again. The lounge remained ominously silent. Abbey reached for her heavy sheepskin jacket and folded it over her arm as she pushed on her trainers. She was rattled. Things had got too bizarre today for her liking. She had to get a grip before she drove herself insane.

***

The front door closed with a soft click and immediately the shadows in the bedroom began to grow. They filled it with an impenetrable darkness that blotted out the dim glow of the bedside light as they merged together. A door opened in the centre of the shadow and Justin Montgomery stepped through into the bedroom. His thick, wet lips, retracted into a contemptuous sneer as he looked around. Frustrated beyond measure, he kicked out at the shadow helpers grovelling around his feet.

"What the hell just happened?" he said angrily. "One minute I'm blending with Abigail's consciousness, becoming one with her body and then I'm suddenly blinded by a ferocious light and almost pushed back into the underworld. How many more setbacks must I take?" His frown deepened as another shadow began to grow to his left.

"Patience, Justin," Adrinia replied as she stepped from it. "You knew there was a spell shielding her from you. It was probably just the tail end of it refusing to submit to your will. You worry too much. Abigail needs to come to you. She can't be pressured, otherwise your metamorphose spell won't work."

"I know," Justin snapped as he wandered over to the bed and ran a filthy hand over the white linen sheet, turned down over the duvet. The yearning to lie within its clean folds, with Abigail beneath him, tormented his thoughts. His lust only served to enhance his anger further and he glared at Adrinia. "Why are you here anyway?"

"You know me. Always curious."

"Nosey, more like it." Justin fixed his bulbous eyes on a shadow helper. "Stay here and watch over my queen. As for you," he turned his malevolent glare onto Adrinia. "Stay away from her. Abigail isn't like the others. She can sense our presence in the shadows."

"Don't be so foolish, Justin," Adrinia replied. "I'm the queen of the shadow people. She can't sense anything about us unless I allow it. Shadow dwellers have been around since the sun first rose in the sky. Mortals have never known that we exist within them and they never will. They are too simple to see beyond what their eyes tell them."

Justin bit back an angry retort. He wouldn't have to put up with her for much longer. Once Abigail came home, he would have the only woman he needed. Adrinia was becoming like a dripping tap, annoying and hard to fix. "Just do as I ask… please." He emphasised the please, knowing his patronising tone would annoy her. "She *is* different from the others. I can feel it."

"Yes, if you insist," Adrinia replied in a bored tone.

***

Justin stood in the lounge, oblivious to the cobwebs that covered the ancient furniture and the smell of decay caused by the rotten timbers which held the two hundred year old cottage together. This was his home now. The mansions and servants were long gone, along with his money and title. When Abbey had failed to return to him on her sixteenth birthday, despair had swallowed him into a terrifying darkness. Days, months and years turned into one long torment, with only Adrinia for company. If it hadn't been for the reveal spell on the coin, she would still be lost to him.

He knew she was different from birth. She had a light in her sapphire eyes that all the others lacked. Hiaxzel, the demon of subterfuge, saw Abbey was different too and told him to get her mother to make a will and enclose the coin with the reveal spell on it. Nothing stayed lost forever if the reveal spell was used. All he had to do was make sure that the will reached the right legal man. He would then make sure Abbey got her inheritance – and him.

Adrinia was right too, not that he'd admit it to her. Over the years, the previous Abigail's he'd spell bound had begun to change. They were too promiscuous, hard and unfeeling. Nothing like his dear wife, whose gentle nature had charmed him from the start. He tried so hard to get her back. But each time was a miserable failure. He knew there was a penance to pay for altering the laws of nature maybe that was it. All the other Abigail's, made in her image, were his cross to bear along with the cruel fact his wife would never return to him. How deep that loss rankled him. But now he had Abbey. Someone to love and who would eventually grow to love the real him, without all the spells and potions.

Her body was unsullied. He felt a warm flush of lust envelop his body at the thought. A virgin. Something he had never experienced, even with his wife. There would be no other man's child in Abigail's womb when she came to him. He would never be second best again.

Justin grimaced with distaste as he looked out of the grimy window. It was a long time since he had touched anyone clean. He had to make do with slaves sent by Agrat-bat-mahlaht when the need took him. She might be one of Satan's wives, but she wasn't one for cleanliness with herself or her offerings. Abigail's virginity was like a cleansing balm to his festering body and he wanted her desperately.

Abbey had to love him. The alternative of spending eternity with Adrinia sent a shiver of horror down his twisted spine. She wasn't even real to the touch. Her body was just a vague shimmering darkness, which possessed a sharp tongue that cut deep into his patience. She may be a queen, but Abigail was a goddess. Nothing Adrinia did could match that. Justin took a deep breath and released it in a loud hiss. The curls of air which followed reminded him how cold and empty the cottage was. But Abigail would soon bring the warmth back. To his heart as well.

Justin turned and faced the empty room, his smile sly and insidious as he gazed at the squalor around him. The cottage needed more up to date, comfortable furnishings. A larder full of fresh food and most importantly, a bed fit for a queen. His forked tongue flicked out of his mouth salaciously. Silk sheets. Her body looked soft and delicate. It needed gentle persuasion to give up its secrets. His loins began to ache when he thought how close he had come to possessing her. Before the light had almost blinded him. "Soon my love," he whispered. "Soon you will feel me within you and you will cry out my name in ecstasy."

Justin staggered slightly and gripped the rotting window frame as the ground below his feet heaved. A terrific crack rented the air as the floor imploded and filled the room with sharp wooden splinters. Then, like poison spewing from a canker, a stream of shadow demons poured from the hole.

"Welcome, welcome, welcome," he greeted, throwing his bony arms wide. "It's time. My queen's arrival is imminent and there's much to do."

Adriana, hidden in the darkest shadow of the room, sucked in her breath and exhaled in an angry hiss of injustice at Justin's words. "I'm the only queen here, Justin Montgomery," she whispered. "I think he needs a reminder of that, don't you Aslow?" She stroked the dark shape nestled in her arm and smiled. "It was hard enough getting rid of Justin's slut of a wife. The soul seekers asked a high price to entomb her soul. I wonder how much they'll want for his precious Abigail."

Chapter Three

Jonathon's hands shook as he replaced the receiver. "Abbey will be here in about half an hour. We have to tell her the truth."

Harriet's hand trembled as it flew to her mouth. Her eyes were bright with despair as she looked at her husband. "I don't think I can," she whispered.

Jonathon eyes softened, pleading for understanding. "We haven't got a choice. It'll all come out as soon as she speaks to that solicitor. We must tell her our side of it first."

Harriet fumbled in her sleeve for the tissue she had put there earlier. "Don't you think I know that?" She wiped her nose and tucked the tissue back up. "I've expected this day to arrive for years and now it's here, I'm terrified."

Jonathon sighed, pulled Harriet close and kissed the top of her head. "It'll be okay. Abbey will understand. I'm sure of it."

Harriet clung to him before she reluctantly let go. She wished she could believe that. But she knew Abbey too well. This would devastate her. Everything she believed in, her memories of them as a family would all be erased in a few sentences. She'd see their silence as a horrible betrayal. They allowed her to believe they were her parents, when all along her real ones were dead. "I hope you're right," she replied.

Harriet took a deep breath and exhaled as she looked around the room. "We've got to be more prepared. If Abbey knows about the cottage, then *he* knows her every movement." She saw his look of impatience and sighed. "Don't start. You and I both know what lives in that cottage and now he wants our daughter there too. Well, it'll happen over my dead body. There can't be any shadows in the house tonight. I'll not give his helpers an easy place to hide."

Jonathon shook his head, his face a mask of irritation. "Oh, stop it. Your nonsense isn't helping. It'll scare Abbey witless and we need her on our side."

Harriet felt her own suffocating fear raise its ugly head. She swallowed deeply and pushed it back to where it always lingered, waiting to erupt and stifle her life. So long as her husband refused to believe her, she was in this alone. But even if he did, she knew they weren't strong enough to fight Justin Montgomery. She needed help. But who would believe her, when she couldn't even convince her husband? "Abbey needs to be afraid. It's the only thing that'll save her now."

Jonathon gripped Harriet by the shoulders. His face contorted in frustration as he looked into her eyes. "For god's sake listen to yourself. Demons don't exist. Shadows are just tricks of the light. You've let this neurosis ruin your life for years. Do you really want it to blight our daughters too?"

Harriet lifted her head, her eyes hard and defiant. "I have to warn her. She can't be left oblivious to it all. Abbey needs to protect herself. Why won't you believe Justin exists? He's killed every woman who ever loved him. Now he wants the one thing we love more than life."

Jonathon's arms dropped to his side in despair. "Your sister, Abigail, died in child birth. Abbey's father, Morgan, had a heart attack. There's nothing supernatural in that."

"And the women before my sister? My mother, grandmother, and so on and so forth. Is that all natural too? None of the silver – haired women in my family have lived beyond their teens. Only the dark haired twin survives and their only born when the spells he weaves go awry."

"Your mother ran off with another man, not some imaginary demon," Jonathon shouted angrily. "As for your sister, well the proof of her debauched life was in the pudding." He put his hand in a half circle over his stomach, indicating pregnancy.

Harriet bit her tongue. She could turn this into a row, but what was the point? Nothing would change. Jonathon's stubborn, single mindedness was all he could see. "I know my family's cursed," she replied. "I saw darkness inside my sister that was so cold and foul, it terrified me. Her soul was corrupted; there was never doubt in my mind about that."

Jonathon sat on the edge of the sofa and ran his fingers through his greying hair. His eyes clouded with despair when he looked at Harriet. "Your sister was mentally ill," he said slowly, enunciating every word.

Harriet's eyes blazed fire and she bit her lip to stall an angry retort. He never knew Abigail, yet he judged her on other people's hearsay. She was cunning, callous, and cold almost to the point of freezing. It wasn't natural, but she wasn't insane. Just incredibly evil. As quickly as it came, Harriet felt her anger drained away. It left her feeling tired and emotional. She sighed deeply. They had discussed this over and over again. But it always ended the same. Jonathon's way. Why did she think it would be any different now? "Not everything can be explained away. Some things can't be labelled."

"Harriet, you expect me to believe all the women of your family are cursed, but you're here. Alive and well. You mention an ancestor who became a demon when he died, but there's no proof he existed. We searched the archives, your family tree. He's never been mentioned. Why would he live in a derelict cottage, when he can warm his backside on the fires of hell?"

"Because he wants the women and now, Abbey," Harriet shouted.

"What for? If he's a ghost, what can he offer them? That cottage is probably falling down by now. Be rational. No sane person can be expected to believe your story."

Harriet pulled her lips into a grim line of determination. "So are you saying I'm mad?"

Jonathon stared, his mouth moved to say something, but he stopped himself and looked down at his feet. "No, I'm not saying that."

"Good, because you can't see the air, but you know it's there. I've seen demons use the shadows as doorways to enter the physical world with my own eyes. As for me, I'm still alive because Justin's not interested in rubbish. I'm just a defective over-spill, from his spells. If my hair was silver I'd be dead by now too."

"You're not rubbish. And you're not defective just because you can't have children."

Harriet paced the room, her small, kitten heels clicking angrily on the parquet floor. "Don't you see it's his curse that made me barren? He only lets the silver-haired women have the children. He needs them and I have no idea why. There have been three sets of twins in two hundred years. The other two dark haired ones were barren, insane and died young. I maybe barren, but I'm not insane. So that means something's gone wrong with Justin's curse."

"Oh really," Jonathon replied in exasperation. "And you know that for sure do you? It can't be anything to do with modern living and doctors then?"

Harriet heard the sarcasm in his voice, but continued on. If she could make him believe even a small part of this, at least she wouldn't feel so alone. "Look, think about it. Abbey's past her teens. If she followed the pattern of all the others, she should be dead around sixteen and her daughter being raised by someone else. But she's still here, with us, her family. There is no dark side to her at all. She's the total opposite of all her predecessors."

Jonathon stood up, walked over to the window and stared out into the darkness. "I can't... we can't go down this road again."

Harriet's laugh was filled with bitterness and frustration. He would never believe her. Abbey had to rely on her for protection now. The thought terrified her. If she had to face Justin Montgomery alone, she had no doubt who would win, but she would die fighting. "Oh, we're way down it already, Jonathon. So please, humour me and change the bulb in the night light outside to eighty watts. I don't want the slightest shadow near this house when our daughter arrives."

***

Jonathon opened the hallway cupboard and searched around the darkness for the right bulb. Once Harriet got like this, nothing he said made a difference. Her imaginary family curse haunted her. He had tried to dispel her fears over the years and for a time it looked as though he was winning the battle. At least she stopped jumping at the slightest noise or shadow. But now, because of this damn letter, all her fears about Abigail Cottage were resurfacing. They would lose Abbey for sure if she started going on about curses and demons.

He opened the front door and walked out into the inky darkness with the new bulb clutched tightly in his hand. The night brought a chill to the air, but as it circled him like a snapping dog, he found its coolness refreshing after the oppressive atmosphere of the house. Winter was upon them and it wouldn't be long before it was Christmas. Abbey loved this time of year. It didn't feel like it was twenty-two years ago since he had held her as a squirming baby.

The smile left his lips when the memory of Abbey's sixteenth birthday surfaced. What a nightmare that day was. Harriet had worried herself sick, convinced that Justin Montgomery would come for Abbey. For a few hours, she had even managed to convince him that something terrible was going to happen. He started to look at shadows more deeply, waited for a cold blast of air, anything that signified the demon's arrival. But the day had come and gone without a hitch and he felt angry their daughter's special day had nearly been ruined by Harriet's neurosis.

Jonathon opened the glass door of the outside light and changed the bulb. He flicked on the switch and squinted as the drive lit up as though it had its own personal sunrise. He sighed, filled with deep despair. There may not be such a thing as a curse, but it was ruining their lives anyway. He wasn't looking forward to the night ahead and as he went back inside and climbed the staircase, Jonathon felt old and tired.

"I've changed the bulb," he called. "Do you need me to do anything else?" His voice echoed down the wide hallway and bounced off the closed doors. When Harriet didn't reply, he knew instinctively where she was. He walked into their bedroom and saw her sitting on the edge of the bed, her shoulders hunched and shaking, and his heart ached for her. He had no idea how to console her. The curse was real to her and now she thought a demon was coming for their daughter. How could he argue that logic? He walked further into the room and stood beside the bed. "Please. Stop worrying. I've told you, everything will be fine."

Harriet's face was pale and strained as she stared at him. Her eyes like two flooding pools of misery. "I don't think I could bear it if we lost her," she sobbed.

Jonathon sat down beside her and took her hand. It felt cold and trembled slightly in his. "We've got to put all our trust in Abbey's love for us. We *are* her parents. It may not be by blood, but it's by everything else. That's got to count for something. Now dry your eyes and I'll go down and put the coffee on."

Harriet stood up, her bottom lip quivered as she forced a watery smile. "While you're doing that, I'll go up to the attic. I think Abbey might like to see a few photographs of her real mother."

Holding his wife at arm's length, Jonathon shook his head. "You're her real mother. Don't let anyone tell you otherwise."

Tears ran in rivulets down Harriet's ashen cheeks as she shook her head. "No. I'm just an Aunt who wants to be her mother."

***

Harriet walked through the house and switched on every light she could find. Memories buried deeply in her subconscious resurfaced, and forced her to remember things she had tried hard to forget. Abbey was her sister's child; there was no getting away from that. But apart from looks, she had none of her mother's darker traits. Something had gone wrong with Justin's curse, she just knew it.

She had many rows with her sister. Mainly instigated by Abigail and her selfishness. But one argument had been particularly nasty. It was their fifteen birthday. Harriet grimaced; she could still hear her sister's cold voice ringing in her ears. Abigail's lovely cultured voice was marred with epithets. It was as though someone else was speaking through her.

"You're just angry because I look like my mother. Admit it," Abigail screamed at her father, who stood immobile in the bedroom doorway.

"Stop it, please," Harriet begged.

Abigail ignored her pleas and continued to glare at her father. She pushed her face within inches of his, spewing out her poison, like a snake striking its defenceless

prey. "I don't want your love. In fact, I don't need anything from you."
Harriet saw her father blanch and fought the urge to reach out to comfort him. She
knew that one action of love would drive her sister into a deeper hate-filled frenzy.
She could only stand and watch helplessly as Abigail tossed her long silver-hair in
defiance and strutted around the room like a triumphant peacock.
When their father refused to respond to the taunts, she changed tactics. Harriet
remembered her stomach-churning terror when her sister's sapphire eyes fell on
her. They were cold, emotionless and stripped her bare of courage. She cringed
back into the corner of the room like a cornered fox unable to get away from the
baying hounds. In that horrifying moment she realised her sister hated her most of
all.
"You're not my sister," Abigail spat, her face a mask of contempt. "You're far too
ugly."
Those spiteful words sliced into Harriet's heart. Why did she hate her so much
when all she was guilty of was loving her?
"I am and will always be your sister," she argued, unable to stop the tears
streaming down her face. "But if being perfect means my soul is as black as yours,
then you can keep your beauty."
Abigail sneered; her laugh high pitched and unnatural as she glared. "You'll never
know what it's like to feel adored. I can have any man I want. You're like an old
crow pecking around for crumbs, wishing all the while to be a swan. Well, it'll
never happen. You're ugly and always will be."
Harriet pulled a ragged tissue from her sleeve and dabbed at her eyes. Thankfully,
after that day, her father moved her to another room on the far side of the house.
Abigail disappeared shortly after. Harriet forced the harsh memories to return to the
deeper recesses of her mind. She wanted to remember her sister with love. But,
even after all these years, it still wasn't easy.

***

Abbey ran to her car and fumbled for the keys in her jacket pocket as she went. The
night air was freezing. Its icy tentacles worked through her clothes and weaved
about her naked skin in an icy caress. As she unlocked her car, Abbey caught a dark
flash in her peripheral vision. She spun around, eyes wide, terrified of what she
would see. But all she saw were the shadows on the walls. They were big,
oppressive in their innocuous position and she hated them. Abbey quickly looked
away from the distorted shapes. Fear was a terrible thing. It warped the mind and
made a person think such stupid things. Everything spiralled of control when you
were scared.
Abbey quickly got inside the car and hastily pressed the central locking button.
Feeling more secure, she looked again at the shadows. Some looked as though they
were moving around the walls, while others stayed static, rigidly attentive. Those
she hated the most. It was as though hidden black eyes watched from them. Abbey
started the car. *I've got to fight this*, she told herself. *I won't let myself be like my*
mother.

She drove out of the car park, her lips pressed into a line of determination. As soon as she left a shadow helper stepped out of one of the static shadows. The moving ones grew wider, taller, until they merged with the static ones and became one giant wall of darkness. "We have been commanded to follow," he rasped.

Several shadow helpers scuttled out from the middle of the dark wall, as though a door had just suddenly opened. Once in the street, their dark eyes searched until they saw Abbey's car. Utilising the shadows cast by the street lights, the demons moved in and out of them with great agility and speed, determined that the new queen would never be out of their sight.

Abbey stopped outside her parent's house and got out of the car. She squinted at the bright light beaming down the driveway as she walked up to the front door and rang the bell. Her father answered immediately and Abbey walked in rubbing her eyes as a mirage of bright dots danced in front of them.

"The night light is far too bright," she complained. "You'll have aeroplanes using the drive as a landing strip if you're not careful."

Jonathon smiled wryly as he helped her off with her jacket. "You can blame your mother for that. She thinks we live in a lighthouse."

Abbey chuckled. "I thought she'd be at the bottom of this. Where is she anyway?"

Jonathon inclined his head towards a closed door on her left. "In the lounge."

Her eyebrows drew together in puzzlement as she looked at the door and then at her father. "But it's closed? She hates being in a room with the door shut." All her life her mother insisted the doors to all the rooms stayed open, even when they slept. She had an irrational fear of being locked in. When he offered no explanation, she walked towards it. The house was eerily silent and made the slap of her trainers on the wooden floor sound like an army of soldiers marching across the hallway. Her hand hovered over the round, china handle and she grimaced as a trickle of nervous sweat edged down her back. She had no idea why she felt so worried. This was still her home, she was safe here.

"If you turn the handle, the door opens," Jonathon teased, behind her.

She laughed nervously. "I know," she replied and turned the knob. "I was just thinking how quiet the house is tonight."

"I'll go and make us all a cup of coffee."

Abbey entered the lounge and saw Harriet sitting on the floor with her usually neat auburn hair in complete disarray. Apart from the residue of black mascara, which had left a trail of destruction under her reddening eyes, her face was unusually bare of cosmetics. Abbey swallowed as a knot of fear formed in her belly. This wasn't like her mother, she was always so well presented no matter what time of the day. She saw the old shoe boxes filled to the brim with photographs and curiosity set in.

"What are you doing? It's a bit late in the evening for a sort out, isn't it?" Abbey waited for a response; when none came, she sat on the nearest sofa. Most of the photos were yellowed with age. Some were colour, but a large majority were black and white. She smiled at one of her grandfather looking very young and uncomfortable. But it was the one beside it which caught her eye. She picked it up

26

and stared at it. "Who's this?" she asked and held it out.

The door opened and Abbey smiled uneasily as the pleasant aroma of brandy filled the room. Her father only put it in the coffee when there was bad news.

"Harriet," Jonathon said gently and placed the tray on the small coffee table beside her. "Have you said anything yet?"

Abbey watched, filled with dismay, as her mother jumped as if she had been struck. When her father put a cup in Harriet's hand, it trembled, spilling the contents onto the blue, shag pile carpet. Abbey watched the small, brown puddle settled on the thick weave and knew something was terribly wrong. She swallowed deeply and looked at her father for reassurance. But all she saw in his eyes was fear staring back at her.

Chapter Four

Abbey's confused stare swung between her father and mother. They both looked worried, which scared her even more. "What's going on?"

"I can't," Harriet whispered, wiping the tears from her cheeks. "It's not fair. Why couldn't the curse have died with her?"

"Harriet, Abbey's twenty-two years old. Isn't that enough proof it doesn't exist?"

"What curse?" Abbey quickly interrupted. "What are you both on about?"

"Take your drink," Jonathon stalled, handing her a mug of brandy-laced coffee. "There're things you need to know. Family issues. Your mother and I thought it best that you heard it from us."

Abbey took the cup and held it tightly between her palms. But its warmth did little to ease the coldness creeping around her heart. What family stuff? She knew everything there was to know. Didn't she? "Dad, you're scaring me! Is this about that stupid legacy? If it bothers you both that much, I won't accept it. I…"

"The girl in the photograph you're holding is your Great-Grandmother — Abigail Regina," Jonathon interrupted.

Abbey paused; her mouth still open with a half spoken sentence. She frowned in bewilderment. "Right, okay. I get it. Shut up Abbey," she replied. "So, finally you dig up a relative that I resemble. I thought I was the only silver-haired woman in the family. And we have the same name. How nice."

Harriet passed her another photograph. "Not really, there are many others called Abigail. This is your Grandmother, Abigail Victoria."

Abbey looked at the pictures. They were old. But even though they were faded and yellow, it didn't hide the fact that they all looked just like her.

"Most of my family members died very young. Not more than sixteen years old, some of them. Here's another picture. It's a more up to date."

Abbey took the picture and stared at the two little girls in it. She judged they were about four years old. One had short wiry, auburn hair and held the hand of a sullen-looking girl. She smiled. "Oh my god, that's me, isn't it?" Abbey laughed as she showed her father the photograph. "I don't remember this being taken or the other girl."

"It's not you, dear," Jonathon replied.

Abbey's eyes widened in surprise and she looked at her mother. "Is it you?"

Harriet dabbed her eyes with her tissue, and balled it in her hand. "Yes. The other child was my twin sister, Abigail Hortense."

Abbey sat back in her chair as her jaw dropped open in shock. After all these years, she was only just discovering her mother had a twin. "But you've never mentioned anything about her before."

Harriet glanced at Jonathon, who stared back and nodded. "Abigail… well, she died a long time ago. She was a troubled child." Harriet paused, caught her breath and busied herself with sipping her coffee.

"She caused your grandfather a lot of heartache," Jonathon continued. "When she died, he forbade anyone to mention her name."

Abbey felt her heart go out to the forgotten woman. Was her crime so bad that she had to be banished from everyone's memory? "What did she do that upset granddad so much?"

Harriet took a deep breath and then exhaled. "Abigail had everything. Beauty, intelligence, eyes the colour of sapphires, but it was never enough. Nothing made her happy. Except when she was hurting others."

"Why was she like that? I mean you're not."

Harriet smiled sadly and shook her head. "I don't know. Maybe she's more like our mother than we cared to believe. Gran left your Granddad when she was expecting us, without a backward glance."

"Why? Was he that bad to live with?"

Harriet shook her head. "I don't know. She was only sixteen. Maybe she wanted more excitement."

"Sixteen?" Abbey repeated.

"Girls were married very young back then," Harriet elaborated. "At twenty you were considered a spinster."

"So how old was granddad?"

"You've got to remember people's way of living were different then," Jonathon interrupted.

"He would have probably been in his late twenties," Harriet replied.

"Bloody hellfire!" Abbey choked out, clasping her hand across her mouth quickly. "Sorry, but you've got to admit, that's a big age gap."

Harriet's face flushed slightly. "As your father said, things were different then."

"Mother, we're not talking about the olden days when rich, old men married young girls to sire their heirs. Tongues must have wagged, surely?"

"I don't know," Harriet snapped, and pulled out a clean tissue from the box beside her. "Anyway, it's not important now."

Abbey saw her mother's "discussion over" look and sighed. She would get no more information on that particular subject. Not unless she asked her grandfather. Which took top priority on her 'to do' list next week.

"As a child I thought my father hated us," Harriet continued. "But eventually I realised he was afraid to love us. He suspected that he wasn't our biological father and that we'd be taken from him."

Abbey sipped her coffee, grateful for the brandy which began to spread its warmth inside her empty stomach. "Oh God, how terrible. So why did grandfather take you both in then?"

Harriet shrugged her shoulders. "What else could he do? His wife was dead, her lover had vanished. The only other place was an orphanage?"

"So grandma had another man?"

Harriet shook her head vehemently. "No. It can never be called that."

Abbey glanced at her father, she saw he wasn't going to elaborate and she looked back at her mother. Her eyebrows arched questioningly. "What do you mean, '*it*'?"

"Let's not get bogged down with that, Harriet," Jonathon quickly interjected. "We've more important things to discuss."

"It's important to me. Abbey has a right to know."

"But not now," he warned.

"Okay, as usual we'll do it your way," Harriet snapped. "Your grandfather employed nannies to look after us. We rarely saw him. As we grew up, he seemed to accept me more than Abigail. Maybe because I was closer to his colouring. I had his auburn hair and green eyes."

"So was granddad your biological father then?"

"Yes, we discovered the truth some years later when blood tests became more reliable. He tried to make it up to Abigail for not being there. But it was too late."

"You can't blame her for being angry. After all, there's only so much rejection a child can take."

"I forgave him, dear. But Abigail... well... she just didn't know how. I soon realised that although my sister had beauty, her heart was made of solid granite."

Abbey realised with a start, that her mother's childhood must have been miserable. The total opposite to hers. That explained why she was so protective. "Mother, with your fabulous red hair, emerald eyes and a figure to die for. You're quite a head-turner yourself you know."

Harriet smiled, but Abbey saw it didn't quite reach her eyes. They looked haunted by memories better forgotten.

"I wouldn't go that far, dear. But thanks for the compliment. I once heard my father describing Abigail as a perfect china doll, just like our mother. I was upset, because I knew that I was the one who was left with all the flaws."

"Now you know that's not true," Jonathon chided.

Harriet wiped away a stray tear edging down her cheek. "Abigail had everything. I had nothing, not even her love."

Abbey opened her mouth to argue, but snapped it shut again as her mother continued.

"As the years passed, I realised my father was right. Abigail was like a beautiful china doll. Beautiful to look at, but hollow inside. She only cared about herself. I didn't want to be like that. I was content to be the plain twin that nobody noticed."

"But I look like her, like all of them," Abbey said softly. "Were they all cold and hollow too? Am I?"

Harriet dropped the photograph she was holding and reached up to squeeze her hand. "Don't be silly. You'll never be like any of them."

The simple move of affection did little to alleviate Abbey's mind. "So how many namesakes do I have?"

Harriet's arms dropped to her side. "I've no idea. Abigail's a family name. It spans over two hundred years."

"Two hundred years. And do we *all* look so similar? You've got to admit that it's a bit spooky, isn't it? I mean, it's hardly normal."

"I don't know what the others looked liked," Harriet prevaricated and put the photographs back in their boxes.

"What does it matter anyway?" Jonathon replied. "You're an individual, no two people are the same even if they look it."

Harriet coughed and cleared her throat. Abbey saw she was uncomfortable with the topic and her eyes constantly flicked to her father for reassurance. It seemed there were more family skeletons to come out.

"After a particularly nasty argument with Abigail, Father moved me to my own bedroom on the other side of the house. My sister and I were virtual strangers after that. But I still defended her, despite the names people called her."

Abbey crossed her arms over her knees. "What names?"

"Oh, you know — the names a girl gets called when she is pregnant and unmarried. No one knew who the father of her child was. She never told a soul. But I remember the exact day she told me. I was convalescing after suffering a miscarriage."

Abbey's soft gasp brought Harriet's head up sharply. "It's all right; I'd been married six months by then."

"Married!" she repeated.

"She was nearly seventeen, before you ask," Jonathon added.

Abbey's eyes darted to her mother. "Talk about following in your mother's footsteps?"

"That's enough of that," Jonathon said, jumping to Harriet's defence.

Abbey stiffened at his rebuking tone. She couldn't work out if he was angry or just plain embarrassed?

"I met your mother when she was sixteen and married her five weeks before her seventeenth birthday. So don't go putting me in that child molester package you're building inside that head of yours."

Abbey's face burnt with embarrassment. Was she really that judgemental? "Why did you marry so young?"

"Because I wasn't lucky enough to grow up surrounded by loving parents who catered for my every whim," Harriet snapped back. "I had nothing except the contempt of my sister and the begrudging love of a parent that I barely knew. When I first met your father, I fell deeply in love with him. When I found out he returned those feelings, I grabbed the chance of happiness."

Guilt was a horrible emotion and Abbey was feeling its wrath at that moment. "I'm sorry. I know I'm too quick to judge sometimes. You're right. I can't begin to understand what you went through."

Harriet patted her hand and smiled. "It's all right, darling, don't apologise. It's easy to judge when you haven't walked in the other person's shoes. The same day Abigail told me she was pregnant, she vanished. You can imagine how distraught we all were. Despite the terrible things she had said and done, your grandfather searched everywhere for her.

My father hardly slept or ate for days. When he failed to find her, he hired a private detective. Abigail was eventually found living in the same cottage that our mother had died in. Your grandfather was devastated." Catching a sob in her throat, Harriet banged her empty coffee cup on the table. "After that day, he destroyed everything that reminded him of her."

Abbey put her empty cup down beside it, "do you think she deserved that? Maybe she just wanted to be close to her mother. The cottage was the only place she could think of. Wasn't it a bit run down by then? After all, a lot of years had passed."

"No. It was immaculate. But then it would be. *He* keeps it that way."

"He?" Abbey repeated in confusion.

"The caretaker," Jonathon quickly added.

Harriet smiled sadly. "Is that what we're calling him now?"

Abbey mulled over everything she had heard. Her brows knotted in confusion. "I'm not sure whether I'm pleased to be the black sheep of the family or not," she replied. "After all, I've clearly broken the chain. I'm twenty - two years old and there's not a baby or even a man in sight."

"There isn't a chain to break. It was just a set of unfortunate circumstances," Jonathon said.

Harriet shook her head and dropped a photo of Abigail into the box beside her. "You're nothing like your predecessors."

"Oh, that just means I'm not a wanton woman," Abbey teased.

Harriet chuckled and rolled her eyes. "Heaven forbid."

Abbey smiled back. Maybe this was just an evening of skeleton release. Her parents were just worried it might come out when she received her legacy. "So how old was granny when she died?"

"Seventeen."

"So she broke the chain or curse, whatever you want to call it, too. You did say her predecessors died at sixteen!"

"There was never a curse," Jonathon said gently. "It was a sign of the times. A lot of people died very young back in those days. Why do you think they married so early? We've no real proof the other Abigail's died at sixteen anyway."

"I don't need proof to know what's going on," Harriet snapped. She looked at Abbey and chewed her bottom lip nervously. "I know there's a curse on our family. But it ended with you." she added.

Abbey didn't know whether to be relieved or laugh at the silliness of it all. "Well, at least I'm good for something," she replied.

Harriet's eyes took on an almost dream like quality. She stared into space, her eyes bright with happiness. "Your father and I were so happy when your sixteenth birthday came and went without a hitch."

"Steady on," Jonathon interrupted. "You'll terrify the child. I was never taken in by the superstitious nonsense in the first place."

Abbey frowned. When would her parents see she was a grown woman? "For, God's sake, I'm not a child, neither am I scared of ghost stories. Mother, have you ever thought that maybe the curse isn't real?"

"Oh, I wish it wasn't, but there's more," Harriet quickly replied. "It seems that while all the silver- haired women are fertile, their darker twin isn't so lucky."

"Oh, I see. We're leaning towards the good and evil scenario. This curse sounds more like a bad fairytale now."

"Abbey, your mother and I always wanted a big family," Jonathon continued. "But it wasn't to be. She suffered terribly after the miscarriage. We went to the best doctor in London. But nothing could be done. Her body was just too fragile to carry a child. We were devastated.

But your mother suffered most of all. She sunk into a deep depression. No drugs or therapy worked. I was slowly losing her to a darkness that all the money in the world could never hope to cure."

Abbey listened, not wanting to understand what he was trying to say. "I don't understand," she whispered.

"Twenty-two years ago, an Irishman called Morgan O'Donnell arrived on your grandfather's doorstep with a baby," Harriet continued. "He and a gypsy woman called Rizavoi had taken care of the child, but now they couldn't carry on."

Abbey frowned. "What was the gypsy's name?"

"Rizavoi," Harriet repeated.

That name – she recognised it. The gypsy from the fair told her to remember it. But there must be a hundred gypsies with that name. It was just a coincidence.

"Morgan wanted to marry Abigail, but she refused. She couldn't bear to leave the cottage once she was there and he wasn't welcome."

Abbey grimaced. "I couldn't bear to live in a house that you'd died in."

Harriet sniffed and blew her nose. "I don't know why someone can't knock the damn cottage down."

"I've told you why," Jonathon replied. "It's a listed building. Believe me if it wasn't, I would've bulldozed it myself years ago."

"So was Morgan the father of Abigail's child?"

Harriet shrugged her shoulders. "I think so. Why else would he go to so much trouble to protect it?"

Jonathon coughed, clearing his throat. "Your grandfather was too old to raise a child. He called us and when we saw her, it was as though a light had flicked back on inside your mother."

Abbey could feel her heart thumping against her rib cage. Suddenly there was clarity. When she spoke, her words came out slow and precise. She wanted no misunderstandings. "Was the baby me?"

She saw the look her parents gave each other and every second felt like hours before they replied. She knew the truth, but desperately wanted them to deny it. When their eyes finally locked onto hers, the truth pierced Abbey's heart like a barbed arrow and crushed the breath from her body.

Chapter Five

"Morgan insisted you were called Abigail. After your mother. We respected his wishes, but I was afraid the name would curse you too. So we shortened it to Abbey," Harriet whispered. "As you grew up, it was like I was seeing my sister all over again. I prayed you wouldn't be like her and you never were. From the time of your first smile, you bought sunshine into the darkest places. People loved your calm, gentle nature. I convinced myself if I told you the truth, it would bring back the curse. I couldn't bear to see it ruin your life like it mine and Abigail's."

Tears sprung from Abbey's eyes and she swiped them angrily away with the back of her hand. She couldn't believe that the two people she trusted more than anyone else in the world had lied to her. "But I had a right to know. That's why the solicitor couldn't find me. He was looking for Abigail Moreland."

Harriet nodded. "We just wanted to protect you."

Abbey felt a cold, hard fury whip around her like a tornado. "Protect me! From what? The danger is all in your head." She looked at her father; his expression guarded as he stared back at her. "Why did you let her do this to me?" she said, wanting an answer, but knowing it would never suffice.

"Do what?" Jonathon replied. "Love you? Want to protect you? Okay, what we did was wrong, but we meant it with the best of intentions."

Abbey's laugh was harsh, filled with bitterness. "What was it you always said to me, 'tell the truth and shame the devil'? A nice cliché. But obviously one you don't live by. You only wanted me because I was all that was on offer?"

Harriet gasped. "Abbey, how can you think such a thing?"

"I'm the mirror image of a person despised by everyone. Can you honestly say if you'd been able to conceive naturally, you'd have wanted your horrible sister's illegitimate offspring?" Abbey replied, as her tears threatened to choke her. There could never be a right explanation. She had been deceived in the most cruel, brutal way that could be imagined. It was too late to grieve for the parents she had lost. Abbey wasn't even sure she could. She looked at the two people that she had called her mother and father for twenty-two years, and was filled with disgust. "I have to go." She stood and fled the room before they could stop her. For the first time in her life she felt utterly alone. Now she knew how her real mother felt.

Abbey wrenched open the front door and ran outside, ignoring the hard drops of rain bouncing off her face like miniature pebbles. Her hands trembled as she unlocked her car and got in. The engine roared her anger and the wheels screamed her anguish, as she drove away in a shower of driveway gravel. Abbey squinted through the rain battering her windscreen. But all she saw was the reflection of her own blinding pain in the rear view mirror.

The car sped down the empty road, faster and faster, until it felt as though she was flying through the air like a missile locked onto its target. Then she saw it. A bright, pulsating, white light before her in the road. She knew locked within its depths was sanctuary. No more pain, tears or fear of the unknown. Abbey closed her eyes.

There was no guilt at what she was about to do, just acceptance. The light would take care of her, she didn't need anyone else. A calm blanket descended over her shattered emotions and pushed the pain tearing through her body to one side. She felt as though she was floating. Higher and higher; she knew this was the place where peace reigned and the bitter ache of betrayal could no longer hurt her.

Just as her body relaxed into gentle acceptance of her fate, a sudden heaviness in her lap jolted Abbey back to reality. For a second she thought someone had sat on her. Her eyes flew open and widened in horror when she saw the headlights of another car racing towards her. There was no time to avoid a collision, death was imminent and she froze in terror. Her hands locked uselessly onto the steering wheel as she waited for the impact. To die like this was a sick joke on them all. Where was the dreaded curse now?

When the wheel turned sharply to the left, Abbey gasped in surprise. A scream of terror exploded from her lips as a heavy weight crushed her foot down onto the brake. The car began to aquaplane, rocking from side to side in a crazy, torturous dance, as it hurtled out of control down the road. Her arms flew to her face and she waited for the impact and the inevitable shattering of the windscreen. When the car came to a sudden, juddering halt, Abbey sat immobile. She was still alive!

Her breath came in small, having gasps, until she took a deep breath and forced it back to some sort of normal rhythm. Only then did she feel safe enough to lower her arms. The rain had ceased its relentless battering. Now all around her was dark and eerily silent. Abbey trembled from top to bottom as gut wrenching sobs rose up and ripped through her body. She squeezed her eyelids closed to shut out the pain stabbing into her, but the tears forced their way through her curled eyelashes, running down her nose to splash in little puddles on her jumper. Wave after wave of agony washed over her, until Abbey thought she would drown in her own choking misery.

Abbey had no idea how long the soothing hand had been stroking the back of her head. It took a few minutes for her chaotic mind to register it. She opened her eyes and saw the passenger seat remained empty. Abbey tentatively touched the back of her head and frowned. Something had stroked her hair, she was sure of it.

Abbey leant over the passenger chair and pulled a tissue from her glove compartment. She blew her nose and shivered. As she exhaled, the breath puffed through her lips and turned into little curls of freezing smoke in front of her. Why was it so cold inside the car? Her jacket was at her parent's house and her shirt was way too thin for this low temperature.

Abbey looked at the ignition and wondered in what time, between screaming and stopping, she had managed to turn it off. She turned the key and the engine purred back to life. Her heater blasted out a stream of warm air and the chill surrounding her quickly dispersed. She sat back and, her head cradled on the headrest. Her body felt sore, as though it had been squeezed through a wringer. What was she doing? She had nearly killed herself. Yet minutes before she was so sure the light would protect her.

It was shock, she told herself. *It did strange things to people.* A light can't protect anyone, except in dreams. Abbey put the car into gear and drove off at a slower speed. Half an hour later, she entered her flat and groaned when she saw her answer machine flashing. She threw her keys onto the sofa and sat down on the armchair. It meant more arguments and she couldn't deal with that. All she wanted was a hot shower and her bed. Not that she would sleep. Who could after that shock? *I'll call them tomorrow*, she promised herself, as she got up and padded across the floor. *When my thoughts are a bit clearer.*

Abbey pushed open her bedroom door, relieved to find it pleasantly warm for a change. She peeled off her clothes and dropped them on the floor as she walked into the bathroom. Once showered, she hurriedly dried off and wrapped a towel around herself. The bedroom felt cooler than when she left it and she groaned in frustration. The damn heaters were useless. For once she ignored the shadows on the walls and pulled back her quilt. She dropped the wet towel on the floor and crept naked into her frigid bed. Snuggling down under the thick duvet, sleep came quickly as her body gave way to exhaustion

***

It was in the time between sleep and wakefulness, when Abbey felt the warmth of the quilt slip away. She murmured a soft protest, as her naked body became chilled from the icy air covering her skin like a thick, heavy blanket. But she quickly succumbed to the overwhelming desire to sleep.

Abbey languidly opened her eyes and looked around the dimly lit room. As her eyes adjusted to the soft light, she realised she was standing in a room she didn't recognise. There was no fear knotting her belly as she stared at the gaslights hung on shadowy walls. She saw him straight away. He stood in the shadows staring, as though waiting for permission to approach her. It was then she realised that she was naked. She should feel mortified, yet it felt the most natural thing in the world. Another lamp to her right flickered to life, momentarily diverting her attention. When she looked at the man again, he was gone.

"Where are you?" she whispered.

"I am where you are, my love," a soft masculine voice replied, behind her.

Abbey wanted to turn, but her feet were rooted to the floor, as though invisible chains had manacled them. She stood unafraid, every nerve energised and alive. She could feel his warm breath gently caress the back of her neck. Her skin tingled with excitement. His presence felt familiar, yet remained on the edge of her recollection. "Who are you?"

His voice, a mere echo carried on the whisper of a cold breeze, spoke her name. The sweet scent of roses permeated the air around her. She inhaled deeply and allowed the musky perfume to fill her lungs. With each breath, she felt her body relax more and more until even a single thought became too cumbersome to acknowledge.

Muscular arms encircled her waist and she was pulled into a tight embrace. Still she couldn't turn – and didn't want to. She offered no resistance as she was pulled

36

gently backwards. It felt safe, locked in familiar arms as she floated in a sea of nothing, her body buffeted by invisible waves. Abbey floated down and down, until she landed on something wide and soft. Tiny kisses were pressed onto her throat and she moaned softly as her body crackled to life. When the lips moved down her body, lingering around her breasts, teasing her nipples into hard little mountains, a soft gasp of delight escaped her lips. Every nerve pulsated as her body throbbed with desire. She wanted him so badly, it felt like a physical ache deep inside her. Hands moved, touching probing... needing her to acknowledge them, yet in the far reaches of her mind another voice called to her. It was small, distant, but she heard the fear in it. She struggled through the fog in her mind to make out what it was saying and then she heard the word. Run. But she didn't want to. She was content to be exactly where she was. In the arms of the man who loved her.

When his hand slid up the inside of her leg, the voice in Abbey's head suddenly grew louder. Its urgent caution pushed through the fog of her mind and she felt a stirring of apprehension. She pressed her fingers on the hand. It felt huge, the skin hard and calloused. The sensation startled her and she tried to turn her head and see the face of her lover, but her eyes wouldn't focus and all she saw was his vague shadowy outline. Then slowly, as if someone was pulling back a gossamer veil from her eyes, Abbey saw where she was. The room was shabby, mould settled on the walls like an old friend. Everything reeked of decay. The bed soiled with the seeds of time.

The man who was lying behind her got up from the bed. The hideous shadow his body cast on the wall finally pushed the last vestige of fog from her mind.

She screamed in horror. "No. Leave me alone." A frigid gust of air immediately enveloped her in an icy mantle. She shook as it began to permeate her body, wrapping around her bones in a death like hug.

"You do know me, Abigail. Search deep inside yourself for my name," the man replied.

Abbey frowned. His voice sounded cultured and vaguely familiar. "I don't know you." A foul smell of rotting meat filled the air, becoming stronger with every breath. It filled her nose and throat, choking the clean air from her lungs with its putridity. "Stop. I can't breathe," she gasped. "You're killing me."

Abbey's eyes flew open and she sat up in the bed gasping. Her lungs burned as though they were on fire as she took deep breaths, relieved the air going into her body was clean and fresh. When she regained some semblance of reason, she saw the quilt on the floor beside the bed and quickly reached down. Her whole body shook, chilled to the bone as she dragged it around her. This was by far the worst nightmare she had ever experienced.

Exhausted and scared, she burrowed deep beneath the cover. She was still freezing, sure her veins were full of ice instead of warm blood. She didn't dare close her eyes. What else would come out of the shadows if she did?

***

Justin's black, bulbous eyes flashed angrily as he limped away from Abbey's bed

37

on bowed legs, scaled with age and dirt. She had rejected him and his rage knew no boundaries. He looked at her lying peacefully asleep and his dark eyes hardened. His essence had always calmed the others into submission. They had known him immediately. Welcomed his body next to theirs. So why hadn't she? He grimaced as his loins became unbearably taut with longing. He wanted her so badly. To feel her body crushed against his when he took her virginity was a dream he had cherished since he had first discovered she was untouched. "You should be thanking me," he whispered to her. If he hadn't saved her from the other car tonight she would have been killed and her soul taken before he had the chance to claim it.

"Bring me a slave," he commanded the shadow helper closest to him. Although still in her room, Justin was out of her reality. He was in his, which existed far beneath the astral plane. The dark entity disappeared, returning instantaneously with the soul of a hardened woman, bred in the demon world to please. Justin sneered at her grimy body. After the purity of Abigail, he hated touching something so filthy.

Lowering the woman's unresisting body to the floor, Justin sated his lust only by picturing Abbey's pale, slender body beneath his. His passion mounted as he watched her sleeping in the bed. Heaving and grunting like the animal he had become, Justin released his dark seed into the slave. Sated, he felt little relief from his frustration. He stood up and wiped away the spittle, edging its way down his skeletal chin like a foetid river, on his ragged sleeve. "Leave me," he commanded the woman, who disappeared back into the shadows of the room. He knew it was only Abigail who could take away the emptiness he felt. Only she could make him feel like a whole man again. Justin adjusted his clothes and looked at her. She was so beautiful. So clean and untainted. "Next time things will be different my love," he whispered. But for now he would make sure she was looked after and treated like the queen he knew she was.

Chapter Six

Abbey opened her eyes and blinked several times at the bright light streaming through a chink in her curtains. She rolled over, looked at her clock and groaned. It was ten o'clock. One hour past the time she should have been at work. She snuggled further down her bed feeling like a naughty child. She would ring up the office later and pretend she was ill. Her appointment book wasn't filled with anything important. No one would be bothered about her absence.

Abbey stared up at the newly painted ceiling and frowned as snippets of her nightmare filtered back into her consciousness. She was naked with a man she didn't know. Two things she'd never do. Yet something about him bothered her. She felt safe, yet she was also afraid. What was going on? Her emotions were all over the place.

Abbey slipped out of her warm cocoon and reached for her dressing gown. She yawned and dragged it on. Her eyes were gritty and sore as they flicked around the room. They drifted to her clothes, folded neatly on the chair. She stared, trying to remember how they had got there, when she had dropped them on the floor the night before. Abbey absently touched the towel hanging on the back of the chair. It was dry. Last night it was wet. She had left it beside the bed to put in the wash this morning. Her heartbeat quickened. Something was very wrong. It couldn't be an intruder. They stole things, not tidied them up. On the other hand, she was very emotional last night. Maybe she had done it herself. Her father said that the mind can be a powerful tool when it works against you. She began to think he was right.

Abbey pulled the dressing gown tighter around her shoulders and winced in discomfort. She opened the front and saw a livid purple mark just above her right breast. She lightly touched it and winced. The bruise was raised and if she didn't know better, resembled a love bite.

Abbey chuckled. Unfortunately she had no secret lover. Just a car seat belt. It must have caught her when she skidded in the rain last night. Everything has a rational explanation, she told herself as she marched to the kitchen and filled the kettle. But before it was even a quarter full, Abbey noticed more irregularities. The sink was empty. But she had definitely left washing up in it the night before. The hairs of her neck stood to rigid attention.

"What the hell's going on?" she murmured and quickly turned off the tap. A sudden flash of movement caught her eye and she spun around. Someone was in the room. She could feel their eyes watching her.

"Who's there?" she called. The lounge curtain moved slightly inward and panic rushed over he like a cascading wave. Abbey edged out of the kitchen toward the front door – her only viable escape route. She took small breaths, almost hyperventilating in her urge to try and stay silent. Her eyes were glued to the heavy curtain. It moved again and she caught a glimpse of a black shadow on the floor which disappeared as the curtain settled. She frowned, confused and curious. The shadow was small, hardly human unless the person was incredibly small and squat.

Slightly mollified, Abbey felt braver and peeled herself away from the wall. She cautiously edged her way to the window and quickly dragged the curtain back. She curbed the hysterical bubble of laughter teetering on the edge of her lips when she saw the innocuous plant pot sitting on the window ledge. Had she become so neurotic that she thought a plant was watching her? The window was obviously not fitted properly. Hence the draught that moved the curtain. She shivered, freezing cold again. This was obviously the cause of the temperature drop in the room.

"You're losing it, Abbey," she said as she released the curtain and walked back into the kitchen. The empty sink remained an unanswered question and she purposely ignored the plates, neatly stacked in the cupboard in size order. Like little soldiers standing to attention. Something she never did. Yet it had to be her though. It was the only plausible explanation.

Abbey made a coffee and took it with her to the bathroom. She pushed open the door and stopped, her mouth dropping open in shock as she stumbled back. The crash of her mug hitting the floor resounded like a gunshot in the tiled room. She grasped the door frame for support as her legs threatened to buckle beneath her. "It's not possible," she said out loud.

Her hair products, which up to last night had been spread haphazardly on the window ledge, were now in straight organised lines. Her towels, bundled into a corner, were now folded and stacked in a neat tower of colour co-ordinated sizes. This wasn't her doing. Unless... her mind balked at the thought, but it was the only feasible explanation, she was sleepwalking. It would explain why she was so tired.

Abbey's tense muscles slowly relaxed. If she hadn't enough problems, now she had turned into a sleeping, cleaning fanatic. If only she could be so organised in her waking hours. She stepped over the brown puddle on the floor, careful not to tread on any stray shards of the broken mug, and removed her dressing gown. She waited for the inevitable goose bumps to follow, but this time they chose not to make an appearance. Probably because the room was pleasantly warm. One sudden change she didn't mind. After her shower Abbey felt a lot better. Although sleepwalking wasn't a problem she could ignore, it might be triggered by shock. Her parents' news and she near death crash was bound to affect her – however bizarrely.

Abbey cleared up the mess on the floor and made herself another mug of coffee. She stared at the telephone thoughtfully as she sipped it. If she wanted to move forward with her life, she had to know about her real mother and father. There were still so many unanswered questions. She couldn't believe anything her adoptive parents told her. They obviously disliked her mother and thought her father was a scoundrel for abandoning her. No, she needed an unbiased account of her parents. Making a decision, Abbey put down her mug, picked up the telephone and dialled McKinley and Acorn solicitors to make an appointment to speak about her inheritance.

Once that was done, she rang her office and forced a hoarse whisper and coughed as she explained to Janet that she had a bad dose of the flu. The receptionist was full of concern and told her to get better soon. She didn't feel a jot of guilt as she ran into the bedroom and dragged on a trouser suit. This was the start of a whole new journey for her and she would grab it with both hands.

Quickly securing her hair into a ponytail, Abbey grabbed her handbag and jacket and took one last glance around the room before she left. Everything was neat, tidy and in its place. Maybe sleepwalking had its advantages after all. Half an hour later, she pulled up outside the office of McKinley and Acorn. She checked her watch. On time, with five minutes to spare. Her stomach fluttered nervously as she got out of the car and locked it. Today was going to be monumental. She was about to discover who she really was.

Chapter Seven

"I can't believe my eyes." Alan McKinley shook his head in disbelief. "It's like I'm looking at a mirror image of your mother."

Abbey sat on a black, leather armchair which stood in front of Alan McKinley's huge, antique oak desk. She smiled politely, not sure if she was accepting a compliment or a statement of fact. "Did you know her?"

Alan pushed the papers in front of him to one side. "No, not personally."

"Oh, I thought…"

"I have a picture of her, here" he explained.

Abbey nervously fiddled with her handbag strap as she arranged herself in the chair. "This has all been a huge shock for me. Until last night I believed that my Aunt and Uncle were my real parents."

Alan McKinley's eyes opened a fraction wider in surprise. "Oh, I'm so sorry. I had no idea. Would you like a cup of tea?"

"No, thank you. I'd just like to get on with this."

Alan studied the papers in front of him for a moment before lifting his head. "As you are probably aware, I'm the executor of your mother's will. She's bequeathed to you a sum of money accrued from the sale of her paintings."

"Paintings," Abbey interrupted. "Was she an artist? I had no idea. How many pictures did she paint?"

"Not many, as far as I can tell. The deeds of the cottage are in her name. I have them here. It's a grade two listed building. Over two hundred years old. It yours now." Alan handed a photograph to Abbey. He glanced down the page in front of him. "That's your mother. Your father, Morgan O'Donnell married Aveline Grady - a Belfast woman, after your mother passed away. I believe they have a son."

"So I have a half–brother! Is there anything else you can tell me about my mother?"

Alan put down the paper, took off his glasses and placed them on top of a blue folder. There was something strange about this case. It bothered him as he surreptitiously observed Abbey, amazed at the likeness between mother and daughter.

He was not a superstitious man. Miss Moreland had enclosed the picture of herself so they could trace her daughter more easily. Did she know they would look so alike? Alan swallowed deeply. He had debated for days whether to say anything to his client about what he had discovered about her family. Would it be unprofessional? His job was to execute the will, not to gossip. Most of what he had learnt was superstitious nonsense anyway, but some aspects of it rang alarm bells in his head. Miss Newlands looked an intelligent woman. He was sure she could sift through it all and just be aware of the facts.

"As far as I know, Abigail cottage…"

"You mean the cottage even has my name?" Abbey interrupted.

"Not exactly your name, but one of your ancestors. Lord Albert Montgomery purchased it originally. His surviving son inherited it when they died. I don't think the scandal arose around the cottage until 1814. Would you like me to run through the history of it? It's quite intriguing."

Abbey nodded eagerly. "Oh, please do."

Alan picked up a thin folder and opened it. "It was rumoured around 1814, that Lord Montgomery's son moved in with a woman whom he claimed was his wife."

"What do you mean claimed?"

Alan shuffled uncomfortably in his seat. This was a can of worms he didn't want to open. No one wants to hear their family could be descended from incestuous liaisons. But he had started, so there was no way back now. "It was rumoured she was... um... that he..." Alan coughed to clear his throat, conscious of Abbey's expectant stare. "Well, it was rumoured that his wife was his daughter."

Abbey's face screwed up in disgust. "What?"

"Look, it's all conjecture - Chinese whispers," he hurriedly explained and wished he had just given her the file to read for herself. "Don't pay too much attention to it. You have to remember no records of birth and marriages were ever logged correctly in those days. The dwelling became known as Abigail Cottage shortly afterwards. Maybe Lord Montgomery named it after his wife."

She sat back in the chair, her face a mixture of confusion and doubt. "What happened then?"

"They both died within the year."

Abbey's eyes brightened with interest. "Oh, they died together then?"

Alan frowned slightly. Why did she look so relieved? Maybe she was a romantic and saw it as a great ending for a tragic couple. "Yes, I believe they both died of typhus. I'm afraid we couldn't trace any graves. I assume their bodies were cremated with all the other poor unfortunates who died around that time."

Abbey leant forward in her chair, her eyes wide with intrigue. "Did the child survive?"

Alan smiled. "Mmm... as you're alive and well, I'd say she did."

Abbey flushed a dull red. "Oh. Yes, of course."

"Now there is rather a ghostly tale around Lord Montgomery's son. I thought you might like to hear it,"

Abbey laughed softly. "Don't tell me he rose up from the dead and became a zombie."

Alan chuckled. "Not exactly. It seems that the towns people believed that his spirit came back looking for his family. When he couldn't find them, he cursed the cottage."

"My moth... I mean, aunt, mentioned about a curse. Hypothetically speaking. If he did rise from the dead, what would be the point? What would he do when he found them?"

Alan shrugged his narrow shoulders. "That's a question better put to a psychic. Don't they have ways to get answers from the deceased? Anyway, the curse is supposed to command the women of his baby daughter's lineage to return to the cottage at the age of sixteen."

"Why so young?"

"In 1814 it was probably a good marriageable age. Maybe he wanted to find them a good husband." Alan explained.

"Well I don't think that the story makes sense. But then again, what superstitions do?"

"Ah, but the story doesn't end there. It's said that once the cottage is occupied, Lord Montgomery appears. He makes the occupants fall in love with him and the young women give birth to his silver-haired daughter."

"If it was true it meant all the women in my family are descendants of incest. It's a bit perverse. Who'd spread such an ugly rumour?"

Alan closed the folder. "I wouldn't worry about it too much. He's a ghost and as far as I know they can't procreate."

Abbey laughed. "How on earth did you find all this out?"

"A band of gypsies kept a manuscript about the cottage. Give or take a decade, it's quite up to date. The family raised Justin's surviving daughter."

"So what happened to her?"

"I have no idea. But I expect she went on to lead a productive life."

***

As Alan McKinley sorted though the papers on his desk, Abbey's brain began to fire in all directions. Harriet actually believed this silly curse and it was ruining her life. She felt heavy with guilt. If Harriet was slightly unbalanced after her miscarriage, then this sorry tale would prey on her vulnerable mind. But her father should have done more. Taken her to a counsellor.

The gypsy edge was a bizarre twist. But it did tally in with her message from the Rizavoi, all those years ago. But then again, the sly old gypsy probably knew all about the family curse. She needed to prove to Harriet the curse didn't exist. Maybe then they could start to build bridges between them. It stood to reason that it was the incestuous slip in the family all those years ago which caused the silver-haired women to resemble each other so closely. Not a curse.

But, after all these years shouldn't the dominant silver hair gene have filtered out by now. Unless there was another act of incest. She shook her head, refusing to believe it. Could her grandfather and aunt be responsible for such a thing? She cringed at that thought. It was too terrible to contemplate. Shame riddled her for just thinking it. "Do you know where my father and his wife live?"

"No. It appears they moved around a lot. Now, I'm sorry to rush on, but I have another appointment after you. So let's get on with reading the terms of the will?"

Abbey nodded and steeled herself to hear her mother's final wishes. Despite what everyone said, Abigail Moreland must have loved her. Maybe she couldn't take care of her in life, but she did it in death.

Alan gave a little cough and cleared his throat. "This is the last will and testament of Abigail Hortense Mooreland.

I, of sound mind, do appoint Mr Alan McKinley, or surviving partner in the company, as sole executor of my estate. To my daughter Abigail Mooreland, I leave Abigail Cottage and whatever monies are obtained from the sale of my paintings."

Abbey swallowed the emotional lump building in her throat. She would treasure the cottage. Even though it was probably a pile of rubble by now. It was all she had left from a mother who was banished from the mind of her own family. One day she would restore it. That would be her project. Then Harriet would see for herself there was no ghost, no curse. Just a small cottage, where peace reigned. "Is there anything else?" she asked.

"Well, your mother has made a few provisos. Um… where were we, oh yes.

On accepting her inheritance, my daughter must visit the cottage within two weeks of this will reading and stay for one month. Otherwise she forfeits everything."

Alan McKinley's voice droned on in the back of Abbey's mind as her thoughts raced ahead. Why would my mother want me to stay in a derelict cottage for a whole month? Even if it were possible I can't take that much time off work.

Abbey chewed her bottom lip anxiously. She couldn't bear to lose the cottage. It was like losing her mother all over again and there was her brother to consider. He'd want a share of the inheritance. She wouldn't mind at all. They could get to know each other while they rebuilt it. That's if she could find him. Maybe he still lived in Ireland. She could take unpaid leave. They couldn't complain too much at that offer. Not that she cared. This was a chance to discover who she really was. Would her biological father welcome her? He had abandoned her. "Could you provide me with a map of the cottage's whereabouts?"

"I took the liberty of preparing one earlier." Mr McKinley leaned over the desk and handed her a piece of paper. "If you wouldn't mind signing these papers, I can then complete the formalities."

Abbey stood and scribbled her name on the documents. She picked up a long key and eyed the polished metal in confusion. "Is this the original key to the cottage?"

Alan nodded "I think so. Amazing isn't it? It's weathered time excellently."

"I'm stunned." She inspected it closely. They key looked new, yet the cottage was ancient. "I'll credit your mother's money to your account after you've lived there for the time stipulated. I need your bank details."

Abbey fumbled in her bag for her purse and handed him her bankcard. "Oh, before I go, can you tell me anything about the coin that was in the envelope you sent me?"

Alan shook his head. "No, I'm afraid I can't shed much light on that. Your mother gave us strict instructions to include it in our contact letter to you."

"Oh, right," Abbey said, a little bit disappointed there was no mystery attached to it. "Thank you for seeing me so quickly." She slipped her card back into her purse. Maybe the coin was a keepsake. Something personal from her mother.

"You're very welcome." Alan stood up and extended his hand. "Good luck Miss Newlands and take care of yourself,"

Abbey smiled and shook it firmly. "Don't worry Mr McKinley; I don't intend to become another victim of the Abigail Cottage curse."

Chapter Eight

Alan McKinley watched Abbey leave his office with mixed emotions. He always thought himself a rational man, but aspects about Abigail Cottage bothered him. The private detective they had used to find Miss Newlands had returned with all sorts of tales. The previous habitants were all women and they had all died at childbirth. No one in the town dared mention its name, never mind divulge any information about it. Alan's thoughts drifted back to when Morgan had stormed into his office over twenty years ago.

It was a few days after he had received the will from Abigail Moreland. He begged to see the contents. Alan was appalled at the request. It was a terrible breach of client confidentiality. One he would never be a willing participant to.

"For God's sake man, you don't know what you're doing. If you contact Abigail when she's sixteen you'll sign her death warrant," Morgan shouted.

Alan shuddered, remembering how the tall, wild eyed Irishman, paced up and down in his office like a man possessed.

"I pray to God you never know what it feels like to have to leave your child with strangers, because you're too scared to raise them yourself," he hissed. "That... thing living in Abigail Cottage kills without a conscience. It looks like a flesh and blood man, but he's not one of God's creations. It's an abomination - a murderer of everything that's good."

At first he had thought Morgan was talking about his rival, but as he rambled on he discovered he was talking about demons and people returning from the dead. He was clearly deranged. Maybe over wrought with grief.

"Mr O'Donnell you're asking me to break the law. I'm sorry, but I won't do it. I have a legal duty to carry out the terms of this will."

Leaning over Alan's desk, Morgan lowered his voice to barely a whisper. "Are you a man of God Mr McKinley?"

"I go to church, if that's what you mean," he replied.

"Well, you'd better pray for him to forgive you if you give that child anything from her mother."

Alan shook his head. "Mr O'Donnell, I assure you, I'd never do anything to jeopardise anyone's life."

"Oh, but you will, McKinley. If you track Abigail down and give her that cottage, it's as good as putting a gun to her head and firing it."

"My hands are legally tied. I can't help you, I'm sorry." Alan repeated. He had no idea what was in the will. A covering letter had instructed him to open the brown padded envelope at the time she had stipulated. He had no idea what it contained.

"It looks like I'll be taking matters into me own hands then." Morgan shouted and slammed out of the office.

Morgan's words occasionally came back to haunt him, more so recently, when he had found the key to the cottage inside the envelope. Morgan's death was a tragedy. He heard it was a massive heart attack, brought on by his attempt to burn down the cottage. Why would he do that? Was he filled with so much hate that he would deprive their daughter of her inheritance? Superstition was a terrible burden and Morgan had obviously carried it around with him for years.

Alan sighed as he placed all the signed documentation into a cardboard folder. He had thought it best not to mention to Miss Newlands her father was dead. Sad news like that should come from a family member. He had given this a lot of thought over the last few weeks. He had done the right thing tracing her. Her mother's last thought was of her. A loving gesture from a woman who knew she would not be around for her daughter.

Alan was jogged from his thoughts by a sudden blast of icy air around his legs. He looked down in time to see dark shape rush from under his desk and across the floor. He jumped up and pressed the intercom on his desk. "Mrs Peto can you come in here?"

His connecting door opened immediately and his secretary hurried in.

"I thought I saw some sort of animal rush across the floor and go under the sideboard."

His secretary gave him a strange look as she tentatively bent down and looked. "I can't see anything. It wasn't a mouse, was it?"

Alan's eyebrows drew together in consternation. "No, it was bigger than that. It moved so quickly, I just caught its shadow."

***

Abbey checked her watch as she let herself into her flat. It was already half past two. Time was always against you when you were in a rush, yet plodded on when you were bored. She walked into the kitchen, put her handbag on the breakfast bar and flicked on the kettle. The partners at work wouldn't be too happy about her taking leave at such short notice. But she had to see the cottage. Even if it was a derelict heap. When she returned home, things would be different. She would make a conscious effort to find a new job and a better social life.

She had booked her flight to Belfast on the way home. It was due at six o'clock, which meant she had to be at the airport by four-thirty to check in. Abbey frowned, still unsure about her choice of hire car the other end. A Mercedes was a bit flash. Not her at all really. But the occasion did warrant something more special than a regular, sensible car. After all she was visiting a part of her life she never knew existed. The hire firm said they would send a representative to meet her at the airport with the keys. Why they didn't leave them at the information desk was beyond her comprehension. What if her plane was late and the rep didn't wait? She should have booked a hotel room. It was the sensible thing to do, but clear thinking was not her forte at the moment. Anyway, there was bound to be a bed and breakfast in the town.

Abbey hurried into the bedroom and threw open the doors to her wardrobe. It was the end of September. Ireland would be cold, so she needed warm clothing. She filled her suitcase methodically with her thoughts constantly flicking between her adoptive parents and her natural ones. There was still so much to sort out. Once she had got this over with, she would call her parents. She might be angry and hurt, but she would never abandon them.

Abbey finished packing and winced as the beginning of a headache nagged behind her eyes. She checked her watch. Just enough time for a quick coffee and a painkiller. The loud knock at the door made her pause in mid step. She grimaced. It wasn't the right time to speak to anyone at the moment. When the knock became a continuous rap, Abbey crept across the laminated floor and put her eye to the peep-hole.

Harriet's strained expression stared back at her and Abbey let out a tired sigh. "Not now mother." she whispered and leant against the wall praying that if she kept quiet, her mother might think she wasn't at home. Abbey closed her eyes and prayed she didn't use her key. Just give me a bit more time, she silently begged. Let me work this out my way. After a few more knocks, she heard the rapid click of Harriet's heels as she walked away.

Abbey had no idea she was holding her breath, until it whooshed from her nostrils in a huge rush of relief. The clock on the fireplace waved its arms alarmingly at her. It was nearly four o'clock and she had to leave - now. She called for a taxi and told them to wait for her at the corner of her road. After one quick look around to check the flat was secure, Abbey heaved her case out of the bedroom, shrugged on her denim jacket and skulked out of her front door feeling like a fugitive on the run.

***

The plane was small but comfortable and the tension finally left her as it taxied down the runway. For now she was safe from anxious phone messages and her mother's house calls. The flight was short, just over an hour. She caught the connecting flight, to an airport she couldn't even pronounce, without a problem and as it landed, Abbey felt the first stirrings of excitement.

She shivered as she waited for her luggage to appear on the carousel. The tiny airport wasn't heated and her flimsy jacket was doing little to dispel the cold chill circulating around her. Her luggage came in a flurry of banging cases and bags as though someone on the other side was throwing them onto the carousel. She pulled her bag off, extended the handle and looked around for the exit as she walked through the terminal. Where was the car hire representative? It was too cold to hang around and she would kill of a cup of tea.

Abbey breathed a sigh of relief when she saw a bored looking man, holding a card with her name on it. He wasn't bad looking, she told herself. Then quickly checked her wayward thoughts. This wasn't the time for romantic notions. *You have plenty to keep yourself occupied, Abbey Newlands*, she rebuked herself. Yet she couldn't help but notice the man's coal black hair, pulled back into a neat, wavy ponytail. His deep, rugged looks intrigued her, even though she usually hated men with long hair. For a second she imagined it down, and spread across his wide shoulders in a river of darkness. She blinked quickly to dispel the thought.

Abbey saw his eyes widen as she approached. They were incredible. A deep emerald green that looked too vivid to be real. A tingle of pleasure wandered up her spine when his eyes met hers. She smiled, totally smitten when his face split into a wide, cheeky grin. His teeth were white and straight. Abbey thought of her own silver filled teeth and grimaced. The man was far too perfect to be true. He was probably arrogant and a bore.

"I think it's me you want," she said quickly, trying not to notice the muscles of his tanned arms bulging through his white tee shirt as he extended his hand to shake hers. She refused to be seen gawping and averted her eyes, only to find them drawn to his muscular thighs, encased in tight, black jeans. She groaned inwardly and shook his proffered hand. It felt big, cool, in her small clammy one.

"Tis a fine pleasure to meet you," the man said in a thick Irish brogue. "For a moment there, I thought I was seeing an angel gliding toward me."

His humour jogged her from the discomfort she felt. Abbey rolled her eyes heavenwards in mock irritation. "I've been called many things, but never an angel." It was the first time she had ever heard a full on Irish accent. It sounded musical. As if each word was a prelude to a song. A distant memory of sparkling, green eyes flashed into her mind and she frowned in confusion. "Have we met before?" The question sprung from her lips before she could stop it. She had no idea why she had asked it. They had never met, she was sure of it. But something about him seemed familiar.

Shaun's laugh was loud and raucous and Abbey squirmed in embarrassment.

"I'd be sure to remember if I'd met someone like yourself," he replied. "Me father always swore that the English rose really existed. I thought he was joking, but now…" He paused to stare. "I believe he was right."

Abbey chuckled. He was an outrageous flirt and she should disregard everything he said, but her body had a will of its own and it was taking no notice of her head. It began to tingle and gravitate towards him. He was perfect in every way. Good looking, humorous and something more – what was it? Abbey felt her cheeks flush with embarrassment. He was so damn sexy. She could almost feel his pheromones surrounding her. "Well, Mr um...." she mumbled, realising he had the advantage over her on their names.

"You can call me beloved, honey, or if you'll be feeling a might shy, Shaun." He grinned.

Once again his outrageous sense of humour dispelled her discomfort. "Now that's a tough one."

Shaun's eyes sparkled with mischief. "I've always felt you can get a better feel of a person's nature if you shake their hand."

"But I already have."

"No, you just took it to be polite. Now you have to feel me hand in yours."

Abbey didn't let on she had felt his hand and rather liked it. She took his outstretched hand, and instantly felt a surge of electricity crackle between their palms. "Ouch, that stung." She flapped her hand to dispel the charge. "It must be too much static from the plane trip. I don't usually give people shocks."

Shaun absently rubbed his hand on the side of his jeans. "Oh, I think you do Miss

Newlands."

Abbey let out a high pitched laugh to hide her confusion. It sounded false, yet she couldn't stop it. She was deeply attracted to Shaun. It shocked her. If he kissed her - right now - she would melt like butter. This just wasn't her at all. "I think I'll call you lover... I mean Shaun," she quickly corrected herself, mortified by the stupid slip of her tongue.

Shaun's laugh rumbled around his chest getting louder and louder before it burst from his lips in a rush of air and noise. "Right, lover Shaun it is then," he said and took her case. "That's until you fall foul to me magical charm, not to mention good looks, of course. Then it'll be a completely different story."

Abbey stared after him with her mouth gaping in shock. She wasn't going to be around long enough to fall for any of his charm. Hurriedly snapping her jaw closed, she rushed to catch up. "Do you always flirt so outrageously?" she snapped, irritated for acting like a fool. How many other women had fallen for his banter? The thought suddenly irked her. If she didn't believe she was having some sort of brain storm, she was sure she felt a stirring of jealously at the thought. "If you could hold on a moment, I think you've got a key for me," she said, wanting nothing more than to get a long way away.

Shaun's abrupt stop caused Abbey to bounce off his hard back with a squeal of surprise. She caught the faint scent of soap, as he grabbed her around the waist to stop her from sprawling on the floor. Abbey reached out and gripped his arms to steady herself. She felt his muscles tense beneath her fingers and a shiver of expectancy sent her senses in a new direction. She opened her mouth to apologise, but the words lodged in her throat when his gaze locked with hers. Again, a feeling of familiarity stirred her senses. Very slowly she felt herself drawn towards his wide chest and Abbey's eyes closed as Shaun whispered words in her ear in a language she didn't understand. A feeling of warmth encompassed her as his musical words flowed over her like a cleansing fountain. Somehow she knew that nightmares or shadows couldn't harm her if she stayed exactly where she was. The warmth of his hands filtered though her clothes, making each nerve scream out with longing.

"Excuse me," a petulant voice suddenly complained.

The sharp, rebuking words snapped Abbey back to reality. She pulled back and stared blankly at Shaun, unnerved by the look of confusion in his eyes. He looked shocked - confused as her. Abbey saw an airport worker waiting to pass them with two passengers and a trolley piled high with luggage.

"We don't all have time to waste," a fat, squinty-eyed man declared. His equally rotund wife sniffed and gave them a look of disdain, agreeing with her weasel faced husband.

Abbey quickly extracted herself from Shaun. Her face flushed with mortification at the older woman's condemning glare.

"I don't expect to see such a public display of... well, of inappropriate affection in an airport lobby," the woman snapped as she walked past them. "Come, Wilber."

"Oh, but madam, I've a feeling you don't enjoy any form of affection," Shaun replied with a wide smile.

Abbey smothered a giggle with her hand and looked away quickly.

Wilber took his wife's arm and stuck his nose in the air as though fighting to get way from a nasty smell. "Come Agnes, don't reply and lower yourself to their level."

The airport worker rolled his eyes heavenward as he followed the waddling pair.

"May all your children be leprechauns," Shaun whispered after them.

Abbey coughed to disguise further giggles, which resulted in a hiccuping fit of laughter that she hadn't experienced since childhood. Shaun laughed with her and as their eyes met, she wondered if he felt the strange attraction between them to.

Chapter Nine

Abbey's hiccuping laugher faded under Shaun's scrutiny. His grin was still there, but his eyes held a question. One she couldn't answer, because she had no idea what had just happened either. "I can manage by myself from here," she said quickly.

Shaun winced as if in pain. His wide smile now awkward rather than easy going. "Actually I need to ask a wee favour,"

Abbey sighed inwardly. She didn't want to grant him anything. It was better that she left Shaun and put the madness behind her. "And that is...?"

"In me haste to get here on time, I drove in your car..."

"And...." Abbey prompted.

"I forgot to provide myself with transport to get home. So I was wondering if you could drop me off at the nearest pub. I can ring for a friend to pick me up from there."

Abbey shuffled her feet uncomfortably. She wanted to say no, but how could she without looking bad? "Can't your friend collect you from here?"

Shaun shook his head. "He could, but it'll be a fair old time before he gets home from work. The weather's changing and it'll be colder than an Eskimo's ice pick out here soon." His eyes pleaded. "Have pity. I'm only in me shirtsleeves."

She was cornered. It would be on her conscience if she left him stranded and she had enough to deal with. "I've got a long drive ahead of me as it is. Can't you call for a taxi?"

"We've only got the one hire place in Rossheith and there'll be no cabs to be had at this time of day. I'd be more than grateful to you," Shaun pleaded. "You could stay in the pub tonight and continue on your journey refreshed. They do a good bed and breakfast."

The strain of events and the flight had taken its toll and Abbey knew she was bone tired. The long drive seemed less appealing by the minute. She raised her hands in supplication. "Okay, I give in. But you can drive. It's too dark to check out road signs and I'm bound to get lost."

Shaun's wide grin returned. "That's grand. I've no problem with driving," He picked up Abbey's case. "The pub's a fair skip away and I feel I must warn you that once we leave, we'll be on leprechaun's land. Those little devils are known to spirit a pretty maid like yourself away in a blink of an eye."

Abbey couldn't help but smile and wondered if Shaun had shares in the Irish blarney stone. "I'm a big girl. I can take care of myself."

"I'm sure you can. But you've got me now to take the strain from those pretty shoulders."

Once outside the airport, a strong blast of freezing wind caught her off guard. Abbey gasped, shivering as the wind pushed its way through her clothes and stroked her skin with its icy fingers.

Her teeth clattered together uncomfortably. "Oh my God. It's colder than

Antarctica."

"Winter arrives here with a vengeance," Shaun stopped in front of a sleek black Mercedes.

Abbey tried not to look impressed at the car. As she feared, it was far too ostentatious. She bit her lower lip anxiously and hoped he didn't think she was too flash. But he didn't seem to bat an eyelid as he loaded her luggage.

She got into the passenger side and sunk into the luxurious cream, leather seat with a contented sigh. Now this was comfort with a capital C. When Shaun got in, it felt like the most natural thing in the world for him to be beside her. Her nostrils flared as a familiar scent of his soap, with a hint of lingering aftershave, wafted around the car. The fragrance toyed with her senses and she swallowed deeply and looked out of the window to find a distraction. Anything to take her mind off the fact that his thigh was dangerously close to hers.

It felt like hours before the car moved. She tried to move over to the far edge of the seat, but somehow Shaun's thigh stayed tantalisingly close. Abbey gulped. Maybe this wasn't a good idea after all. In London she would have never given a stranger a lift. Yet again, in London she would not be lusting after a man she hardly knew. Everything was suddenly upside down in her usually well structured life. Too tired to think, it wasn't long before the soft purr of the engine dragged her protesting eyelids down. When she opened them again, Abbey saw it was pitch black outside.

"Finally, Sleeping Beauty awakens," Shaun teased.

"I wasn't asleep, I was resting my eyes," she lied and checked her watch. Fifteen minutes had sped by. She continued to stare out the window. The rolling hills, filled with gold and red winter heather, gave the illusion they were on fire. She looked up into the sky. The full moon in all its glory lit up everything it touched. "No wonder you like living here. It's so beautiful."

Shaun's eyebrow rose questioningly. "And what would you know about me likes and dislikes, now?"

"I'm usually quite good at judging people." Abbey swivelled in her seat to face him. "Now let me see. I bet you're a country boy and you set your alarm just to hear the birds singing in the morning."

Shaun chuckled. It was a nice sound which reverberated in his chest and escaped from his mouth like a warm, afternoon breeze. "Well, if we're talking about judging people, I suppose I should give me own viewpoint on yourself."

Abbey smiled. "Go on then."

"I think you're a country girl, trapped in a big city. You're head strong, hard on the outside, yet soft on the inside. Like a baked Alaska," he laughed at his own joke. "I also think you'd rather be woken up by a dawn chorus than the rush hour traffic."

Abbey opened her mouth to reply and winced as her head snapped sideways with the jerking of the car. She straightened in her seat and rubbed her neck as the car came to a shuddering halt.

"Oh, Jesus, Mary and Joseph," Shaun cursed, banging the steering wheel with his fist.

Abbey stared, unnerved by his sudden show of temper. Her hand reached tentatively for the door handle, just in case he turned into an axe welding maniac after all. When his bow shaped lips formed a wry smile, she relaxed her grip on the door.

"Now some folks would say this is the work of the leprechauns. I bet they plan to steal you away," he said, pretending to look out of the car window for the little people.

"But the real reason is....?" she asked.

Shaun's face flushed a dull red. "We've run out of petrol."

***

Out of the corner of his eye, Shaun saw Abbey slowly reach for the door handle. She looked poised for flight. The thought gave him a painful jab in the guts. Did she really think he'd hurt her? He forced a smile and sighed heavily. "Now don't take this the wrong way." He held up his hand in mock surrender. "But me house is only a lick and a spit away. We can go there and I can get me truck and come back for the car."

Abbey frowned. "I thought we were going to a pub."

"Ah, yes, there was a slight change of plan when you were… um, resting your eyes. The pub was closed so I made an executive decision. Now, don't panic," he added quickly. "Me mother's there and she's the best chaperone a woman could wish for. I can camp on the sofa tonight and you can have me bedroom. It's the least I can do for putting you out." He pulled a wry face and Abbey's lips twitched into a small smile.

"Do pubs around here usually shut so early?"

Shaun's face reddened slightly. "Actually, it never opened. I forgot that William, he's the owner, is away. His brother's wedding so I heard. I couldn't leave you stranded now. Me conscience wouldn't let me."

"And there are no other hotels in Rossheith?"

Shaun shook his head. "Just the one, I'm afraid. We don't get many visitors."

As Abbey remained rigid in her seat, Shaun felt despair. She was a bit apprehensive, he understood that. But couldn't she feel the connection between them? A strange feeling of familiarity, although he was a hundred per cent sure they had never met. Once she met his mother, and realised his intentions were honourable, she'd loosen up. He was sure. "Well, I can see you're not very happy with me grand idea. So now we've a dilemma on our hands. I can't be leaving you here. Those leprechauns will spirit you away for sure. So the way I see it, we'll both have to bed down for the night in the car." He noticed Abbey's eyes grow wider than his mother's china saucers, and inwardly smiled. He punched home with more problems. "Did I mention the temperature at night drops to freezing? You'll need to sit very close to me. Our bodies will need the heat. I've heard of people dying on this very lane in the winter. Froze more solid than ice cubes." Shaun flicked a small lever beside his seat and lowered his chair back. He didn't know whether to be happy or feel rejected when Abbey quickly opened the door.

"If you put it like that, it seems does seem a bit churlish of me not to take you up on your offer," she stammered, getting out of the car.

Shaun reached over to the back of the seat and grabbed a thick, sheepskin coat. He got out of the car and quickly put it on. "Your jacket will give you as much warmth as a fire without coal."

Abbey stared at him and frowned. I thought you said you hadn't got a coat? Just your shirtsleeves you said."

"I swear on all that's holy that I forgot about me old sheepskin," he explained. "I don't usually wear it."

She pulled the thin jacket tighter around her slender body and gave him a dubious glare as she stamped her feet on the hard frozen ground. "I hope your house isn't far, otherwise I'll die of hypothermia before we get there."

Shaun jogged around to her side of the car. "You won't make it ten feet dressed like that, to be sure. Has no one told you about Ireland's winters?" He gave Abbey no time to protest, as he put his arm around her shivering shoulders and pulled her into the soft fleecy confines of his coat. He smiled as she burrowed into him like a little mole. "Are you comfortable, princess?"

"It'll have to do, I suppose," she snapped. "And I'm not your princess."

"Not yet, but one day who knows," he whispered as they set off down the long, dark road.

Every now and then Shaun caught the lemony scent of Abbey's hair. The delicate fragrance tantalised his senses. God, she confused him. He knew her. He didn't know how, but he did. He wasn't one for romantic notions, but at the airport, when they touched, it was as if they were transported back to another time. Where he knew this small firebrand very well. He knew her thoughts, could feel her vulnerability. It was like he had to protect her. But from what? Why she here in his tiny town? How long she was she staying? Did she have a man in her life? He winced at that thought. The thought of someone else's arms around her was unbearable. "Now we're now on closer terms, so to speak," Shaun said. "Do you think you could tell me your name? I can't keep calling you Miss Newlands. It makes you sound like an old maid." He heard a muffled name which sounded like Jodsey and grimaced. How could someone so beautiful have such an ugly name?

***

As the cold nipped her legs, Abbey snuggled deeper into the folds of Shaun's coat. She only came up to his armpit, which was handy right now. What you saw was what you got with him. He didn't appear to have airs and graces and his open nature drew her to him despite her reservations.

Shaun gave her an affectionate squeeze. "I think I'll call you, Josie."

Abbey struggled to breathe under the coat and it didn't help when he squeezed her like that. "MMM uf...." she said, and sneezed as the fleece lining tickled her nose.

Shaun stopped, opened his coat and looked down at her. "You're a might red in the face, Princess. Are you feeling all right?"

Abbey took a deep breath and then exhaled. "I am now. Can you slow down a bit?"

"Oh right, sorry. Now what did you say, Princess? I couldn't hear."

"I said, what's the matter with Abbey? It's a family name."

Shaun eyebrow rose questioningly. "Nothing's wrong with it, 'tis a fine name. Is that what you'd like me to call you?"

She frowned in bewilderment. "That *is* my name."

"Oh, sorry, Princess. Muffled under me coat, I thought you said your name was Jodsey."

Abbey laughed. "What? I sound like a horse!"

"I've got to say that I was thinking along the same lines. I knew you'd have a pretty name. Come on, let's keep moving. I don't know about you, but a hot cup of coffee sounds better than a holiday in Barbados at the moment. Shaun wrapped his coat around Abbey and launched into a loud Irish ditty as they walked.

"That's the worst singing I've ever heard," she complained.

Shaun feigned hurt. "I have to sing. It's the only way to keep the leprechauns at bay."

Snuggled up in her warm, human cave, Abbey humoured him and hummed along as best she could. Then she realised with a start, for the first time in years she felt content. She was having a good time with no frills, no expensive dinners, only her and Shaun walking in the wilderness together.

By the time they reached his house, Abbey was sure her feet had turned to ice. She peeked out through his coat, frowning when she saw the inky blackness of the night. Were there no street lights in Rossheith? Abbey stepped from the warmth of Shaun's coat and gasped as the frigid air almost knocked the breath from her body. She felt as though she breathed in pure frost and her lungs had icicles dangling from them. Abbey impatiently watched Shaun turn the little brass handle on his front door. She couldn't wait to sink beside a warm radiator. "Don't you lock your doors?" she asked, through clattering teeth.

"What for? No one's going to rob us. We're all friends here."

Abbey entered the darkened house and her buoyant mood sank quicker than the Titanic. His mother was nowhere in sight.

Shaun lit a little gas lamp, conveniently placed behind the front door. Once the room became lighter, they both saw the letter addressed to him, propped up on the stone mantelpiece. He picked it up and ripped open the little, white envelope.

Shaun read it and Abbey saw his pained expression. He laughed awkwardly.

"Well, um... It's like this, Princess... Would you believe that me mother has decided, tonight of all nights, to be away helping me cousin give birth?"

Abbey's coral lips formed a silent 'Oh' as she stared back at him.

Chapter Ten

"I'm so sorry," Shaun stammered. "I know this looks more than a might fishy, but I swear on me life I didn't plan it. The last thing I want is for you to feel awkward. I'll be away this minute and get your car, I'm sure I have a can of petrol somewhere. It'll get you to the next town at a push."

Abbey caught Shaun's arm as he moved to walk past her. "It's all right. These things happen. You can't rush out into the cold again. You need a hot drink and some food."

The panic left Shaun's face and he smiled. "Thanks, princess. It's my luck that the first time I invite a lady to meet me mother, she's not here."

How honoured to be the first woman to be allowed into his inner sanctum. The thought appealed to her immensely, if it were true. Not that it mattered, anyway. She couldn't get involved with him. Not when chaos ruled her life. "Don't you have electricity?"

"Not yet. But I'm sure they'll get to us eventually. We live outside the town, so we're mostly self-sufficient. I like it. So much cosier. A nice, open fire, the soft glow of an oil lamp and the company of a beautiful woman. What more could a man ask for?"

Abbey felt her face grow hot with embarrassment. She was trying so hard not to like Shaun, but when his eyes found hers, she was lost in a whirl of different emotions.

Shaun went to the fireplace. "I'd better get this going and warm the place up a bit," he said, taking a small lighter from the mantelpiece. "Me Mother always puts it out. She says it saves fuel. But all it does it make the house bitter cold."

"Do you want me to make a hot drink?"

He nodded."That's a good bargain if ever I heard one." In two strides he was beside her and clasped her hand in his. Abbey felt the calluses on his palms as they rubbed the softness of hers. The friction excited her more than she thought possible.

Shaun led her to a small, wooden closed door. He pressed the latch lever and pushed it open. "I'll show you where the kitchen is." They walked down a short, narrow hallway. Once at the end, she saw another wooden door. Shaun opened it and stepped inside.

The small kitchen was neat and tidy. His mother was obviously a meticulous housekeeper.

"Everything you need is in there," he said, pointing to a cupboard over the sink. "Will you be all right, princess?"

"I'll be fine. By the time that fire's roaring, we'll be drinking a nice hot cup of tea."

"I'll better go and get it started then." Shaun disappeared out of the door and left Abbey to search through the cupboards for what she needed.

Half an hour later, she pushed open the lounge door with her foot, while she balanced a tray laden with food and a pot of tea. She hoped he didn't mind her raiding his mother's larder. But she was famished and he probably hadn't had his tea. She saw him stretched out in front of the crackling fire and smiled. He looked a picture of contentment. An easy man to please.

The flames leapt a little too high for her liking, but then she was used to central heating. Maybe it was supposed to do that. She noticed a brass fireguard, leaning idly against the wall and as she opened her mouth to ask Shaun to put it up, she saw a dark shape slither over the guard and disappear into a dark corner of the room. Suddenly she became aware the room was full of shadows and each one looked to be moving with a will of its own. Abbey recoiled in horror and the contents of the tray clattered together noisily.

Shaun jumped up from his chair. "Oh, sorry, Princess. I didn't hear you come in." He took the tray, placed it on the coffee table and smacked his lips in delight. "I knew you were a woman after me own heart."

Abbey forced a smile. It's okay, she told herself and took a deep breath to calm her jangled nerves. Shaun mustn't know about her irrational fear. He'd think her mad. Even she knew that shadows can't run across the floor.

"What's the matter? You look like you've seen a ghost."

"I'm fine," she lied. "I hope you don't mind me snooping about in your fridge, but I remembered you hadn't had your tea yet." Her voice sounded light, almost natural. If she kept this up, she'd convince herself she was fine.

Shaun patted his flat belly as he took a plate of food. "My stomach and I thank you."

After pouring them both a cup of tea, Abbey took her plate and sat down on the armchair opposite him. It was no good, she couldn't ignore the fire. It looked more ferocious than before. "Shaun, would you mind putting that fire guard up? The flames look very high."

"Anything for you, princess. I take it you city folk are not used to real fires." As he moved the brass fireguard in front of the fire, he paused and looked into the flames. "What is it; what's the matter?" Abbey asked.

"Well, for a second, I thought I saw... no, that's stupid. It's the coal settling. It's your fault," he teased, "You're making me nervous."

Abbey settled herself into the armchair. The material sunk under her weight and enclosed her in its softness. "Oh yes, I've a question for you. What powers the fridge?"

Shaun took a huge bite of his thickly buttered bread and chewed. She knew he was stalling.

"I mean, how does it work without electricity?"

He swallowed his food with a gulp. "Didn't I mention the generator? It must have slipped me mind," he added quickly.

"So you do have lights," she accused. "Your fibs are coming back to bite you. Oh, the gaslight is so cosy," Abbey mimicked an Irish accent.

Shaun's laugh reverberated around the cottage. "I've heard a better accent on a wailing banshee. I didn't lie. Our generator powers the electrical appliances. We save oil in winter by using the lamps for light."

"But it would power the lights?"

"Well, I suppose it would, but…"

In one quick movement, Abbey threw the cushion beside her and hit Shaun squarely in the face. His eyes widened in shock and she chuckled with delight. "That's for all the other lies you told me today."

Shaun put his plate onto the coffee table with deliberate slowness. Abbey eyed him warily. "No one should hit a man while he's eating his tea," he launched his pillow at her.

She squealed as the cushion bounced off her shoulder and shook her plate. Putting down the food Abbey stood up. "Right, that's it, you've asked for this." She reached beside her and took two more cushions from the other armchair. Swinging in all directions, she proceeded to batter Shaun from the sofa to the ground. He put his arms up to cover his head, spluttering as he tried to swallow the contents of his mouth.

"Do you give up?"

"Okay, okay," Shaun put his hands up in mock surrender. "I give up."

Abbey flashed him a triumphant grin. "Ha, now let that be a warning to you. Don't ever mess with me." She turned, with a smug smile, to go back to her chair, when she suddenly felt her legs pulled from beneath her. Crying out in alarm, she crashed down on top of Shaun. "You rotten cheat, I was winning,"

"No, you weren't. I let you think you were. It's a great strategy." He caught her flailing arms and quickly flipped her onto her back; he pinned her lower body to the floor with his. "Don't ever let your guard down, Princess. Otherwise someone will be only too ready to gobble you up whole."

Abbey squealed with laugher and wriggled against her restricting, human bonds. "You're a rotten stinker."

"I'm not. And as a gesture of good will, I'll release your arms if you promise not to scratch me eyes out."

"Okay, I promise."

Shaun slowly released her arm and gently removed the thick hair from her face. In the tussle the restricting band had snapped, spilling it around her head in a silvery pool. "Where are you?" he joked. "Are you under there?"

Abbey found herself floundering in the gaze of his emerald eyes. Suddenly all humour vanished and when Shaun's lips touched hers, she welcomed them with a passion that, up to now, she never knew was within her. As the kiss deepened she felt Shaun undo the small pearl buttons of her shirt. Panic made her stomach roll, but when his hand lightly grazed her naked skin, it faded under the expectant tingle of her body. His hand gently cupped her breast through the lacy material of her bra, sending her swirling her into a vortex of desire. She allowed him to remove her clothes without protest. This time, this moment, this place was right. She knew it, maybe this was what she had been waiting for.

Lying naked in the firelight, Abbey felt the muscles in Shaun's back ripple beneath her stroking fingers. Tentatively reaching lower, she felt his desire for her and gasped.

"You keep doing that princess and I won't be any good to you at all," he whispered. Abbey quickly pulled her hand away. She had no idea what she was doing. Inexperience crowded her thoughts and her desire waned under its heavy weight. As her body stiffened involuntarily, Abbey felt Shaun's hesitation.

"What's wrong? If you want to stop, that's fine with me."

"I... no... I mean." Her face grew hot with embarrassment. "It's just... I haven't..." Her voice trailed off as mortification welded her tongue to the top of her mouth. She heard the soft hiss of Shaun's breath as he exhaled and knew he had understood what she was trying to say.

"Are telling me you've never...?"

Abbey nodded, resisting the urge to grab her clothes and flee. "Is it a problem?"

"Problem?" Shaun repeated. "I'd not call it that. But it's not something to take lightly. Are you sure you want to carry on? This can't be undone, once it's, you know... done!"

"I know that, I'm a virgin not a child."

"I'm sorry, I didn't mean to imply..."

Abbey placed her finger on his lips. The romantic moment was fading fast. If he said anything else it would be gone forever. "You didn't."

"I don't know how we got here, princess. I've never bought a woman to me mother's house, never mind made love to her in it. But this feels right. I know we're moving fast, but don't you feel the connection between us? I don't want this to be a one night stand. It's more than that. I can't explain why, I just feel that you've always been mine."

Abbey understood completely, but rational thought screamed at her to not to be so stupid. They had only just met. But none of it mattered because when she was with Shaun, everything fell into place. "This isn't a big deal," she lied.

"It is to me. Me father told me a story about a race of mythical people who lived in Ireland hundreds of years ago. They said that any man who took a maid's virginity would automatically take her soul into his protection forever. So you see, you're giving me a big responsibility."

"Only if you believe it?"

"That's the thing. I think I do. Don't get me wrong. I'm not innocent when it comes to women, but I've never been anyone's first. It's a big undertaking. I need to know that you're sure."

Abbey wasn't sure about anything. Shaun practically said they would be engaged if they slept together. Not an unappealing thought, but ludicrous all the same. What did she have to lose? Her virginity! She'd lose that some point in her life anyway. "I am sure. Are you?"

"More sure than I've ever been about something in me life. We can have a future together, Princess. I knew that when I first set me eyes on you."

Abbey shivered in delicious abandon as Shaun nuzzled the nape of her neck. Little explosions of pleasure left a trail where his lips were and her back arched, searching for more. His lips found hers and his tongue made sweeping, swirling motions inside her mouth stroking its surface. Desire consumed every part of her and lifted her to a realm where nothing real existed anymore. When his lips moved from hers, her breath came out in urgent gasps. She felt the hardness of his arousal pushing against the entrance of her body and then he was a part of her. The sharp pain which followed, stung for a moment, but as he slowly moved, her body was filled with a frenzied explosion of exquisite sensations. She shuddered in clenching spasms as wave after wave of pleasure engulfed her. Abbey cried out as Shaun convulsed in abandoned rapture. They both rode the wild and wonderful waves of sheer ecstasy until they came to an exhausted shuddering halt. Shaun rolled from her and pulled her close to his side. For a moment they clung together in silence, each lost in their own emotions.

"Are you all right, Princess? Did I hurt you?"

Shaun's questioning voice cut through Abbey languid thoughts. She opened her eyes and smiled. "No. It was perfect. I feel wonderful." Her whole body pulsated with energy. She had never felt so alive.

"The fire's dying out and it'll get a mite chilly down here. Let's go upstairs." Shaun stood and scooped her up into his arms.

She giggled and clung to his neck. "Shouldn't we put out the fire?"

"It'll be fine. The coal's almost gone."

Abbey looked over his shoulder to check and noticed the creeping shadows in the room. She shuddered and nestled closer into his chest. So long as she was with Shaun, nothing could hurt her.

* * *

When the bedroom door closed behind Abbey and Shaun, Adrinia stepped out from the darkest shadow in the room. She stroked a small, dark bundle in her arms, and looked at the hurriedly discarded clothes with a smirk of satisfaction. "You can come out now."

The dark patches on the walls and floor began to grow, until they formed small, hideously shaped beings. "Fisla, bring Justin here. I want him to see his silver-haired saint in action."

"Yes, my queen," a misshapen shadow beside her rasped, and disappeared through a doorway inside another shadow on the wall.

Adrinia stroked Aslow as she walked toward the stairs. "Come on sweetheart. Let's go and watch the fireworks. Justin is going to be so miffed that his little virgin has been deflowered on a dirty wood floor."

Chapter Eleven

Justin Montgomery's bottom lip curled in to a sneer of contempt as he watched Shaun and Abbey. His disgust went deep and tasted like bile in his throat. All his dreams about her purity came crashing down around his ears. How had this happened? She was on her way to him. Her destiny lies in his bed, to feel the thrust of him inside her. Fornicating with a man she barely knew. That was what her predecessors did. She couldn't be like them, he'd never believe it. It must be a spell. Adrinia! This was her doing. Yet, this was too subtle for her. Something else was going on here. A different kind of magic. His dark, bulbous eyes narrowed in anger as he stared at Shaun's muscular back. He's the culprit. The filthy beggar had put a spell on his Abigail, because he knew he'd never get such a prize without it. The thought that she was being coerced made him feel instantly better. Maybe it wasn't a bad thing after all. Everything had a purpose. He needed the child that would be begat this night. After all, he couldn't father one. A nagging thought reminded him that he wanted Abbey more, but he pushed it to one side. He'd have more than enough time to taste the delights her body held. "I'll see you later, my dearest Abigail," he whispered.

***

Abbey frowned, tossing and turning in her sleep. *Shadows surrounded her. Their coldness seeped into her bones. Hands reached out from their darkness. She screamed as they pulled her into their cold, dark hell.*
"Wake up, Princess," a voice urged.
Abbey opened her eyes, momentarily confused at the unfamiliar surroundings. She blinked trying to remember where she was. A light touch on her shoulder sent a wave of panic through her and she cried out in alarm.
"It's all right, princess, you're having a bad dream," Shaun said softly.
His familiar voice immediately calmed her heightened senses and she relaxed against him. "Sorry. It's just a silly nightmare."
"You missed my bird alarm?" Shaun whispered and nibbled at the lobe of her ear.
Abbey rolled over and snuggled up against his chest. "Did I? That's a shame?"
Shaun kissed her neck and throat. "Remind me to wake you up earlier tomorrow."
"What makes you think I'll be here?"
"As the keeper of your soul, I command it."

***

A few hours later, Shaun got out of bed and pulled on a pair of grey jogging bottoms. It felt good to be alive. Abbey came into his life just at the right time. He wanted to settle down. Have a family. Life was strange. Full of twists and turns. "I'll fetch your clothes from downstairs. Then you can dress while I start breakfast." He took one more look at the magnificent woman in his bed, grinned and bounded out of the bedroom. His mother would be in for a shock. She'd be as mad as a box of wasps once she knew Abbey had stayed the night. She was a true catholic, through and through. She didn't hold with unmarried couples sleeping together. But she'd get over it when he told her that he intended to make Abbey an honest woman.

Shaun shivered as he picked up the clothing. The room was colder than he ever remembered. This winter was going to be a harsh one. He quickly banked up the grate and added a few large pieces of coal. It didn't take long for the flames to take hold; in fact, their ferocity surprised him. It must be a new batch, he told himself and jumped back when a flame leapt out and seared the hairs on his leg. "Oh, you bugger," he swore.

Shaun quickly got the fireguard and put it across. "No more of that or I'll install a radiator in and make you redundant." The flames soon died down to a stable crackle and he took Abbey's clothes upstairs. "Hurry up, or you'll freeze. It's going to be a cold one today."

She walked down the stairs half an hour later and saw the pile of crusty toast, homemade jams and butter on the table. Her mouth watered in anticipation. She shivered and rubbed her arms. "Golly, its cold in here."

"I know. It's not usually. I've turned up the portable oil radiator, with the fire roaring like that, it'll soon warm up. It's got a mind of its own today. It nearly ate me for breakfast." Shaun took the cosy off of teapot. "I usually drink coffee, but I find myself drawn to tea since I've met you."

Abbey sat at the table and poured the milk into the mugs. She chuckled softly. "What did the fire do?"

"Me mother must have got new coal. It burns like a demon. The flames reared up like a ferocious lion and attacked me."

"Attacking fire demons, Huh!" she giggled. I'll have to keep an eye on you and that fire."

Shaun bit into a slice of toast. He would never laugh at Rosa's predictions again, '*Your true love will have hair spun from silver thread, her eyes the colour of jewels. She'll fly to you on a giant bird.*' Abbey fitted Rosa's description exactly. But would her other warning fit as well? '*This woman has another interested in her. He is the darkness. Fear is his friend. Despair will be her bedfellow if she chooses him.*' The thought of Abbey with any man made him feel physically sick. He loved her. It didn't matter how quickly it had happened. He had her soul now and he'd never share her with another.

"Shaun, is something bothering you? I know things are happening a bit quickly between us. If you're having second thoughts…" Abbey's voice trailed off.

"Why would I be having second thoughts? I know what's happened is … well, it's unusual to be sure. But it *has* happened and I want you more than any woman I've ever known." Shaun got up and moved beside Abbey. He pulled her gently from the chair and into his arms. "I'll never let you down, you know. I'll take care of you and you'll never want for a thing."

Abbey nestled into his chest. "I like the sound of that."

***

The front door banged and Abbey jumped out of Shaun's encircling arms. She looked toward the noise and saw a pretty, dark-haired woman. Abbey recoiled under her horror filled gaze and looked at Shaun who seemed oblivious to it. She looked back at the woman, but her eyes were now more guarded.

"Good morning to you, Mother. I want you to meet Abbey Newlands. We met yesterday. It's a long story and I..."

"I can't believe I'm away from me home for one night, and you get up to this shenanigan," his mother snapped.

"It's not what you think..."' Abbey stammered.

"I hear there's an abandoned car on the Galgowan fells." She interrupted. "I assume it's this young woman's? Now, unless you'll be wanting to find it with no wheels, I suggest you go and get it. You haven't been working for that hire place long enough to lose one of their best cars."

"It's all right. I'm on me way. When I get back, we'll explain everything over a fresh pot. You must be starving. I hope all is well with the wee baby." Shaun pulled Abbey close to his side and gave her a reassuring squeeze.

"A beautiful boy. They're both grand. But you're right. I'm tired and in need of a hot cup of something." His mother took off her jacket and hung it up on the coat stand. "They'll be plenty of time for talking. Now get yourself off, son. Me and your friend will get acquainted without you clucking around like a nervous hen."

"She hates me," Abbey whispered despondently to Shaun.

He laughed softly and kissed her head. "No she doesn't. Me mother's just been caught off guard. She's not one for surprises. After a cup of tea and a gossip, you'll both get along fine. How can anyone not love you?"

His mother retrieved a floral apron from the coat stand and tied it round her dark skirt. "Are you still here?" She took down Shaun's coat and held it out to him. "Go on, away with you now."

"Do you see how me mother treats her only son?" Shaun laughed. "Pushing me out of the house so she can get you alone and tell you me secrets."

Abbey forced a smile. "I'm sure we'll have a lot to talk about." Or a lot to argue about, she silently added. His mother didn't look easy going or friendly.

"I'll be away then." Shaun let go of Abbey and threaded his arms into his jacket. "Behave yourself, mother. You're making her nervous. After another quick kiss, Shaun ambled out of the house and closed the door with a bang.

Abbey's feet became rooted to the floor and her tongue welded to the roof of her mouth. What should she do? Offer tea? Clean the table? Would that offend her? After all, this was her house. She gulped and forced her tongue to move. "I'm sorry..." Abbey stammered.

Shaun's mother's eyes narrowed and filled with malice. "What do you want? Why are you here?"

Abbey took a step back, perplexed at the fury emanating from the little woman. Surely her staying the night didn't warrant this sort of reaction? "My car broke down and Shaun said it would be all right..."

"I didn't ask why you came to my home, I can see why." She sneered as she looked her up and down. "I want to know why you've come back to Ireland?"

Abbey suddenly understood what was wrong. She'd obviously got her confused with another woman. "I've never been here before. You've got me mixed up..."

"Mixed up," the fiery Irish woman snapped. "Do you have any idea who Shaun is or do you make it a point in sleeping with strangers?"

"No! I mean... I do know..." Her mind raced for the right words. The situation looked bad – she looked even worse. How could she make things better? "I'm on my way to visit... I mean I inherited..."

"I know what you've got, Abigail Moreland."

"Actually it's Newlands. Abbey Newlands, "she corrected. "How do you know my mother's name?"

"I know everything about you. But let me introduce myself. My names Aveline. *Mrs Aveline O'Donnell.*"

Abbey took another step back as she spat out the name like it was poison. O'Donnell. She mulled over the name and then it hit her. It was her father's name. But were many people in Ireland with that surname. "Sorry, I don't understand."

"Let me put it in simple terms then." Aveline picked up a photo on the windowsill and pointed to a man with a full dark beard. He was tall, muscular framed with a mischievous glint in his eye. His arm was clasped around a very young looking Shaun. "Meet Morgan O'Donnell, your father. I'm his widow."

Abbey staggered and clutched the side of the table for support. "His widow?" she repeated. Horror flooded her body. This couldn't be happening. She looked upon the face of the father who'd abandoned her and knew she would never get to know him now. "I didn't know he was dead. I came to see him. To fill in the blanks of my life. I had so many questions."

"That's the least of your problems now. I take it my Shaun's got no idea who you are."

The enormity of the situation floored her. This was a nightmare. Abbey's face flushed with embarrassment. "No, we haven't really spoken about me."

Aveline took a step closer. "How convenient for you."

"I came to find my father and half brother. Not this. Oh, God. What have we done?" The room tilted at crazy angles and Abbey gripped the back of the nearest chair. She had done the one thing she had condemned her ancestors for. The reason why she and Shaun had felt such a deep connection was because they were brother and sister. The horror of the situation gouged into her body and caused physical pain. "When did my father die?"

"Six years ago and he was still trying to protect you!" Aveline shouted. "Your inheritance sent him crazy."

"What do you mean, he died protecting me? He dumped me when I was just a few days old." But he kept his precious son, she thought bitterly.

"Morgan didn't want to leave you. He had no choice."

Abbey laughed, but there was no merriment in the sound. "There's always choices."

"Morgan gave you up because he loved you. There was no other way. You needed protection."

Abbey swiped at the tears springing from her eyes. Now she looked weak in front of Aveline. She hated it. "From what? Come on, tell me. What's so bad that he had to dump me on people he hardly knew?"

Aveline's shoulder sagged. "Has no one told you about the curse that haunts your kind?"

"What do you mean, my kind?"

"The kind who live in that damn cottage and die before their time. The kind whose flawless beauty is a curse. Whose hair is resistant to change or colour. The kind who doesn't care who they hurt. Morgan told me about the demon who lives in Abigail Cottage. It feeds on the silver-haired women and damns their souls to hell. He thought if he hid you away, the beast wouldn't find you. He wanted you to have a good life. Giving you up destroyed him."

Abbey swallowed the emotional lump in her throat. Was she telling the truth? Had her father loved her that much? "He gave me up because of superstitious nonsense."

"It's not nonsense. Do you think he dragged us out here, in the middle of nowhere for fun? I came from a city. I was used to having me family around. I hated the solitude. But I did it for Morgan. He thought if he vanished, the beast might forget you existed too. Then on your sixteenth birthday, he saw the garden of the cottage begin to bloom."

"And…" Abbey snapped.

Aveline gave a wry smile. "It only blooms when the cottage is due to be occupied. Morgan thought you'd come back. He was like a mad man. I begged him not to go there, but he wouldn't listen to reason." Tears slid down Aveline's cheeks. "It's the first time a policeman had ever knocked at me door. I knew what they were going to say. A heart attack, they called it. On the doorstep of the cottage. But my Morgan had never suffered in that way. Strong as a bull in spring that one. The beast in the cottage killed him for loving you. Do you want to know the sick joke? You weren't even there. He died for nothing."

"So doesn't that tell you the curse isn't real," Abbey said more softly. She saw Aveline's pain, so raw and consuming, and wished she could magic it away. "The garden bloomed because someone is looking after it, that's all. It's been held in trust for me for years."

Aveline shook her head. "You stupid girl. It bloomed in preparation for you. ALL the Abigail's are supposed to return when they reach sixteen years old."

"But my mother wasn't sixteen when she went back there. Can't you see there isn't a curse, just tragic coincidence? Next you'll be telling me that my mother's lover was a demon."

"He is," Aveline raised her chin in defiance. "She lost her immortal soul to him, just like you will."

"I'll do no such thing. If you're so superstitious, then you'll know the story of the

Esor. As I no longer have my soul, I've nothing to steal. The stunned look on Aveline's face made Abbey feel better. At least she knew it had been very serious between her and Shaun, however wrong.

Aveline staggered back and made a sign of the cross over her breast. "Oh God," The beast will kill him for sure now."

"No he won't. There's no such thing as ghosts and demons. You're just a lonely widow who's trying to keep her son tied to her apron strings with lies and fables. Shaun's not my brother. I don't believe you. How can something so wrong, feel right in here?" She tapped her chest.

Aveline's emerald eyes hardened. "If you don't believe anything else I've told you Abigail, believe that you and Shaun share the same father. You can never have a life with him. It would be an abomination in the eyes of all that's good. My boy's an honourable man. If he ever discovers the truth about you it'll destroy him. You have to leave. Now."

Chapter Twelve

Aveline's stomach churned with fear. She took no pleasure in hurting Abigail. She seemed nice, not like the soulless creature Morgan had led her to believe her mother was. But desperation had backed her into a corner. She couldn't save Morgan, but she could save Shaun. As soon as she saw the silver hair, her safe world crashed down around her. No one but the cursed women had such a startling colour.

Morgan had shown her a picture of Abigail Moreland. Like this Abigail, she was stunning. She couldn't compete with such perfection. But Morgan hadn't wanted her to. He loved her for herself and told her every day of their marriage. But deep down, she always felt second best to Abigail Mooreland. She couldn't have asked for a better father for Shaun. Morgan had taken him on as his own and their bond had been close and binding. But Abbey must never know that. She had to believe Shaun was her brother. It was the only way to keep them apart.

"I can't leave," Abbey cried. "It would be cruel, especially after…" she paused and shook her head. "I can't."

"Please Abigail, I'm begging you. Don't put Shaun through this heartache. He doesn't know about you. Morgan was worried that he'd try to seek you out and unwittingly lead the beast to your doorstep. We laughed off any rumours our son heard about the cottage. But most of the old ones know about the curse and if they find out about you and Shaun, they'll turn the whole town against us for sure. Shaun will have to leave the home he loves. Will you place that burden on him?"

"If I leave now, Shaun will move heaven and earth to find me."

"Abigail, what you have with him is built on sand. However much you try to hang on to it, the grains will just slip through your fingers. You have to end this. For all our sakes."

Abbey's face collapsed in defeat. Aveline watched the life drain from her eyes, but felt no victory.

"What do you want me to do?"

"Shaun needs to hate you." She saw the look of horror in Abbey's eyes and quickly looked away. "It's the only way. My boy's a stubborn man. He'll love you until the day he dies otherwise. I'm so sorry, Abigail. I wish with all me heart that things were different."

"Do me one favour," Abbey whispered. "Stop calling me Abigail. My name's Abbey."

***

"Where are the two most favourite women in me life?" Shaun called as he burst through the front door. He smile grew wider as Abbey walked slowly down the stairs.

God, he loved every bone in her slender body. Shaun held out his arms to her and frowned in puzzlement when she quickly side stepped his embrace.

"How much do I owe you for getting the car?" Abbey opened her bag and took out a small, black leather purse.

The smile slid from Shaun's face. He felt like she'd just slapped him. Abbey's body looked stiff. Her eyes cold as she stared at him.

"Owe me?" he repeated. "You can't put a price on love, Princess." He moved toward her again and felt panic when she swatted him away like a bothersome fly.

Abbey's laugh was high and brittle. "Oh, don't be silly, Shaun. You can't seriously believe what happened last night was anything more than a pleasant interlude after a tedious journey."

Shaun reeled back in shock. Every word felt like a knife stabbing in his guts. "What are you talking about? We didn't *just* have a pleasant interlude last night. What's going on? Where's me mother? What's she said to you?"

Abbey smiled, but Shaun saw no merriment in the cold depths of her sapphire eyes. "In the kitchen, I expect, pandering to your needs. You really should get your own place. Aren't you a bit old to be a mummy's boy?"

A cold shiver ran down his spine. What happened to the funny, warm women he had left behind this morning? This person wasn't her. "What's wrong, princess?"

Abbey sighed loudly. "Do stop calling me that silly name. I'm no more a princess than you're a saint. You didn't seriously think that we... I mean..." Her laugh echoed mockingly in the room. "I could never live here. Come on, don't look so crest fallen. Even you must admit that it's hardly a town house in the London suburbs, is it?"

Her sarcasm wounded him deeply. She was breaking his heart and didn't give a damn. "Abbey, tell me what's wrong? Has my mother said something to upset you? If she has I'll..."

"No wonder Irish people have so many jokes played on them. You take things far too seriously."

Shaun's hand shot out and grabbed Abbey's wrist to prevent her moving away from him again. He'd never been violent to any woman, but in that moment he could've happily crushed the fragile bones in her hand. "Stop it," he ground out. "This isn't you talking."

"Yes, it is. This is me. Do you love me now?"

"You played me like a second hand fiddle. I take it the virgin tale was a lie too How twisted are you?"

Her sly smile told him all he needed to know. He thrust her from him in disgust. He watched Abbey stagger, feeling nothing but white hot rage as she clutched the chair to stop herself from falling. "I hope the sick game entertained you."

Abbey put her purse back into her bag, which still dangled from her arm like a lost cause. "If you're sure I don't owe you anything, I'll be on my way."

Shaun pulled the car keys from his pocket and threw them at her feet. "You owe me nothing. Just get out. I wish I'd never laid eyes on your devil face."

When Abbey bent down and picked up the keys, Shaun closed his eyes and swallowed deeply as his heart shattered into a million pieces. When he opened them and looked at her face, it held not a shred of remorse. She didn't care how much she hurt him. "I pity the man who has that shrivelled soul of yours. It must be as black as coal dust," he spat. He wanted his words to wound her, like her words had hurt him, but God forgive his stupid heart, he still loved her.

Then, for a split second, Shaun was sure that he saw pain mirrored in Abbey's sapphire eyes. But he had misjudged a lot about her, so he was probably wrong about that too. Every step she took to the front door, took her further away from him and Shaun desperately wanted to beg her to stay. But he knew any pleading would be futile. She didn't love him. "Good bye, princess," he whispered as she opened the door and stepped through. "I'll never stop loving you." How could he? Her face was imprinted on his memory and it would torment him for the rest of his life.

***

Aveline sat huddled on the cold linoleum of her kitchen floor. She rocked as she pressed a red, checked tea towel to her mouth to stifle her sobs. How could she face Shaun knowing what she had done? She heard Abbey's car start and quickly stood up and splashed her face with cold water. Abigail was gone. Now she had to pick up the pieces she'd left behind. Aveline took a deep breath, exhaled and walked down the short corridor to the lounge. Shaun sat at the table, his head resting in his arms and she swallowed the rising lump in her throat. He didn't deserve this. None of them did. This was the demon's doing. He ruined everything good. Aveline walked over and placed a consoling hand on Shaun's back. "I'm so sorry, son," she whispered.

Shaun lifted his head. His eyes bright with un-shed tears had lines of pain were etched around them. "I don't understand. How could I be so wrong about her?"

"It's not your fault, son. Sometimes a person's eyes become clouded through no fault of their own."

"But not mine, Mother. I know what I felt - it was real. I don't care what she says. She loves me. I know it."

Aveline needed Shaun to believe that he was wrong. Abigail was chained to the beast from the day she was born. Nothing could change her destiny. But she could change Shaun's. He would find love again. Abigail Newlands wasn't the only woman in the world for her son.

***

Abbey slowly closed the front door, fighting back the burning tears in her eyes. As she slowly exhaled, it felt that every bit of air was being sucked from her lungs. She was suffocating in her own bitter pain. It was a shame that she was not lucky enough to die from it. Her feet felt encased by lead as she urged them forward. Each step was agony, because it took her farther away from Shaun. Her one consolation was that he possessed her soul, whether he wanted it or not. She needed to believe that they shared that bond. They would always be a part of each other, no matter where they were in the world.

She got into the car and started the engine. Maybe all her family were cursed. Not by a stupid demon, but by the inability to find love and keep it. What were the odds of coming to Ireland and falling in love with your own long, lost brother? Her car tyres screeched out a protest as she sped off - away from the family she had set out to find, away from a man whom she was forbidden to love.

Abbey switched on the radio to quell her chaotic thoughts. Whitney Houston blasted out 'I will always love you' "Typical," she whispered and turned it off. "Bloody typical."

Just over an hour later, Abbey pulled up at the bottom of a steep hill. She saw the little cottage, standing proudly on the top of it. It didn't look half as bad as she had expected. No sign of dilapidation. In fact, it looked in pristine condition. She drove up a winding driveway secluded from prying eyes. The well-kept flowerbeds reeked of expense. The blooms colourful and engaging, yet bizarrely out of season. Much too late for bluebells, yet they grew in abundance. Aveline's words flooded back to her. '*The cottage blooms because it expects you.*' She quickly pushed the thought away. Superstitious nonsense and she refused to be drawn into it.

Abbey pulled up outside the cottage and got out of the car. The wooden front door looked ancient, yet its shiny knocker sparkled in the midday sun. Someone looked after the place. White roses curled around the door, in full bloom. How? It's freezing. They should all be dead. She walked up to the door and cupped a perfect blossom. The soft petals felt like velvet. She inhaled and waited for its heady fragrance. But none came. She sniffed again and realised the flower had no scent whatsoever. She let go of it and frowned. A rose with no scent was a fake. Yet it was very real.

Abbey searched in her bag for the key Alan McKinley had given her. Everything had a plausible explanation. Only silly, superstitious people believed otherwise. The cold metal brushed against her fingers and she pulled it out and inserted it. The lock opened without a complaint and Abbey quelled her nervousness as she gently pushed it open. What did she expect to find, a waiting demon!

She paused on the threshold, uncertainty rippling through her. Then, just when she gathered enough confidence to step inside, a dark shape rushed out and streaked past her feet. It moved so fast that Abbey couldn't tell what it was, never mind where it went. She squealed in fright and jumped back. Her gaze darted in all directions. But whatever it was had disappeared into the flowerbeds. Maybe the caretaker's cat; she told herself and prayed it hadn't left any unwanted surprises on the floor.

She pushed the door wider and groaned when she saw the wooden floorboards. Did no one have carpets anymore? The pale blue Chinese rug, which dominated the centre of the room, brought some comfort. Her heels tapped noisily on the floor as she walked, jarring her over sensitised nerves. The lounge was square shaped. Small, but cosy with its little oil lamps and old fashioned drapes. The furniture looked new, yet everything had an old fashioned air about it. She looked up, relieved to see the ceiling. It had a roof! Everything was perfect as if suspended in time.

A loud click made Abbey spin around. "Hello - is anyone there?" Silence echoed around her. She noticed the closed front door. That's the noise culprit. The cottage was as old as Apollo and probably had a million draughts. Noises were going to be everywhere as the wind whistled through. Abbey shuddered as the coldness of the room seeped though her thin jacket affirming her thoughts. "Why am I condemned to live in cold rooms?" she said out loud and flopped onto the sofa. Its deep, plush cushions immediately engulfed her; like warm, comforting arms on a cold day. She loved squishy furniture.

Abbey settled back and she stared at the long, wooden coffee-table in the middle of the room. A small cut glass vase stood majestically on it, filled to bursting with bluebells. Someone has gone to a great deal of trouble to welcome her. But who? For a second she thought of Shaun, a ridiculous idea. He didn't even know this place was hers. Not that he cared if she lived or died anymore. Her great play acting had seen to that. His face, lined with hurt and disbelief, filled her mind and she shook her head to dispel the image. Then another terrible thought popped into her mind. What if Aveline had lied? She could never believe that. *Only a sick mind could make up such a foul lie.*

She blinked back her threatening tears. It must be the caretaker. Maybe Mr McKinley contacted him about her imminent arrival. As her questions slowly gained answers, Abbey became aware of a faint scent of roses in the room. The fragrance grew stronger with each breath, soothing her jagged nerves. It reminded her of home and her father's coveted rose garden. Maybe living here wouldn't be so bad. The peace and quiet acted like a soothing balm to her aching heart. Abbey yawned. Her eyelids dropped as she tried to focus on one of the small oil fuelled lamps positioned snugly in the corner of the room. Its beauty defied its age. Mesmerised by the small flame flickering inside its little glass home, Abbey watched it dance like a tiny ballerina. Each blink of her eyes became slower and slower as she succumbed to its haunting, hypnotic dance. As she began to fade into a deep sleep, her mind suddenly burst into life as if a switch had been thrown.

She rubbed her eyes and sat up. If the caretaker had a key to the cottage, who else did? Anyone could walk in. Abbey chewed her bottom lip anxiously. She wouldn't feel happy until she had all the keys. Nowadays it's not safe to live alone unless you were secure.

The rose scent in the room faded, as Abbey got up from the chair and walked to the far end of the room; she opened the door and peered down its short corridor. Two oil lamps on either side of the wall burned cheerily away, lighting the way. Yet something about the pretty scene made her shudder. Shadows lined the wall as though daring her to enter amongst them. They were tall; clinging to the ceiling like giant centurions guarding the gates of hell and she had to walk through them to get to her bedroom.

Abbey swallowed and took a deep breath. *I have to do this*, she told herself. *It's time to put all my fears behind me. A new home, a fresh start.* She forced her legs to move down its length, her eyes fixed firmly on the door ahead. One step, two, it seemed like an eternity until she got to three. It felt like eyes were watching her from the shadows and she braced herself for touch of the cold, grasping fingers that would drag at her hair and spin her into oblivion. An icy sweat trickled uncomfortably down her back. Four steps, five steps. Abbey fought the urge to run. Someone was behind her. She reasoned about its impossibility. Seven, eight steps. They were quick ones which bought her right outside two wooden doors opposite each other. Abbey pushed open the nearest one and cried out in gratitude when she fell into a bright little kitchen. Her heart thumped inside her chest as she leaned against the wall, closed her eyes and breathed deeply. She was being silly. No one was outside; no eyes watched her. After a few moments, she opened her eyes as her panic driven breaths subsided. The neat little cabinets around her were suspended on the walls. Like everything in the house so far, they looked new, yet she could tell they weren't. The lemon, chintzy curtains, decorated with a splattering of tiny white flowers, were not something she would have chosen, but they fitted in well and framed the view of the back garden beautifully.

The cooker was a small black and cream Aga. It looked like it heated the house and water. It seemed well cared for, but then such an important instrument deserved nothing less.

Abbey left the kitchen in better control of her emotions. Now the hallway looked much brighter and bigger. The mind had a terrible way of playing tricks on you. If she kept letting fear rule her, she wouldn't get anywhere in life. Abbey opened the other door and her eyes widened. She took a step back, unable to believe the sight which greeted her. The huge bedroom spanned the entire length of the cottage. The delicate queen size bed dominated the room. Its peach, silk drapes, sheets and thick duvet, looked ironed within an inch if their lives. Not a crease in sight. Stunning in its elegance, she felt like a queen. But silk wasn't her favourite choice of linen and she didn't relish the thought of lying within its icy depths.

She stepped into the room. Her shoes sinking into the deep, luxurious weave of the cream carpet. She quickly took them off. Although beautiful, it wasn't very practical. Cream had a way of becoming soiled with just a thought, never mind her feet.

A picture on the far wall caught her eye. She walked over to it and stared. A naked woman leaned provocatively over a bed not dissimilar to the one in the room. Except her drapes and sheets were blood red. Her face was shrouded by a mane of silvery hair, but Abbey knew her eyes would be sapphire blue. Sleek limbs, pale skin glistened with moisture. A soft flush lightly covered her body as she waited – for what? The scene would have been quite sensual and thought provoking if it wasn't for the creature standing behind her.

Half man and half beast with great curled horns protruding from his head, it seemed grotesquely out of place. Its bony, overhanging forehead emphasised its skeletal features as thick lips drew back salaciously. Poised on legs so bowed, she wondered how its clawed feet could support the weight of its body. Its bony hands – encrusted with filth, reached out to grasp the woman's waist. Its eyes, black as coal, bulged with a hunger so raw that Abbey felt sickened. She grimaced with distaste. What sick mind could paint such an atrocity? It had to go and she lifted the picture from its mounting, it was heavier than she thought and as she clutched it to her chest, the barest whisper of her name being called made her pause. She cocked her head sideways listening intently. Every nerve in her body was on edge with fear. She recognised that haunting voice. It had called to her before.

Chapter Thirteen

Abbey waited for the voice to say something else, yet only her own rasping breath could be heard in the stillness of the room. *It's nothing*, she told herself. *I'm just overtired. No one's here.* She refused to start believing in tales and superstitions. When a loud crash reverberated behind her, Abbey screamed in fright and dashed out of the door, dropping the painting on the way. She paused in the hallway. Breathe, she told herself. Calm down. There's a reasonable explanation for everything. Gritting her teeth in determination, Abbey went back into the room. The other painting was lying on the floor. She put a shaking hand to her chest and felt her heart bang against it. There was the explanation. Just a fallen picture.

Abbey picked it up. The woman from the other painting seemed to be depicted in this one too, but in another pose. Now spread across the bed, her eyes were closed, blood red lips pouted, gently swollen as though they were kissed passionately. It looked like the artist had painted this first and set the scene for the second. In the far right corner were three tiny initials. A.H.M. Abbey paused, collating the information. Then it came to her in a sickening burst of reality. It was her mother's initials? So that's why Mr McKinley said her mother's art was an acquired taste.

No one else must ever see these. She would make sure of it. Everyone had a poor opinion of her mother as it was. This would just confirm they were right. She carried them into the hallway and leaned them against the wall. They had to be burnt. It is the only way to eradicate them. She would leave a note for the caretaker to do it. Abbey went back into the kitchen and frowned at the small Aga. She had never used one. Didn't they need to be kept alight? What if it went out? She needed some advice. Abbey prayed the caretaker would hang on and show her the ropes. She felt so utterly alone and a little bit helpless. But she refused to give in to self pity and opened the cupboard nearest to her. A strong cup of tea. That's what she needed to buck up her spirits. She saw the plates stacked neatly in size order, the mugs standing to attention like little rows of soldiers and the memory of her plates stacked in a similar way, flooded back. The thought unnerved her and she quickly slammed the door shut and left the kitchen. Tea could wait.

The one thing she hadn't found was a bathroom. Would a cottage this old even have one? God, she hoped the toilet wasn't outside. The thought of going out into the darkness was terrifying. Abbey went back into the bedroom and then saw another door. It was hidden beside the oak wardrobe. She prayed for a bathroom as she opened it and sighed with relief when she got her wish. A large clawed Victorian style bath, with gold taps, sat begging to be used. She smiled. It was perfect. The sort of bathroom she had dreamt of having since childhood. A china toilet eased her earlier fear. The room was tiled in plain white with a delightful collage of coloured flowers dotted here and there. She closed the door with the intention of having a nice long soak later on.

A few hours later, unpacked and curled up on the sofa, Abbey sipped her tea. The caretaker had thoughtfully stocked the cupboards. She didn't need to shop at all.

The room had warmed up nicely, now she had lit the banked up fire. God knows what she would do tomorrow. She had no idea how to make it up again. There is an art to banking a coal fire. Abbey stared into the crackling flames of the fire idly pondering her dilemma. Again she smelt roses, but she was far too tired to think about where the scent was emanating from. Her eyelids grew heavy, she yawned, put her cup onto the small side table and snuggled deeper into the fluffy cushions, closing her eyes with a contented sigh.

Abbey watched the man step from the shadows. He looked familiar. In the blink of an eye he was behind her. His lips found her bare shoulder and started to lightly nibble it. She swallowed deeply, consumed with a burning need to feel his skin against hers. "I knew you'd come, Shaun," she whispered.

As soon as the words left her lips, Abbey sensed the atmosphere around her change. With every breath her lungs burned, her nostrils filled with the stench of rotting flesh. It gathered in the back of her throat like glue and she retched against its foulness. "I can't breathe," she gasped, "Shaun, for God's sake help me."

Abbey sat up choking and took huge gulping breaths. Tears rolled down her cheeks. Her nightmares had changed and now it was Shaun tormenting her. Abbey wiped her face with the back of her hand and picked up her cup. The tea was cold and unappetising. She thought the cottage would bring her peace. But the nightmares still plagued her, even here. With a heavy heart, Abbey took her cup to the kitchen.

***

When the door closed behind her, Justin Montgomery stepped out of the shadows. His eyes glittered angrily as he stared after her. How dare she think of that idiot when it was he who was loving her. The injustice of the situation infuriated him. Her response to his essence was perplexing. He had chosen a fragrant flower she liked, but as he moved closer to her something happened to counteract it. He angrily kicked the shadow helper grovelling at his feet.

"Why did she have to choose him as her first? Why couldn't it be me?" he moaned.

"Because if you had been her first, your essence would make her womb barren," Adrinia replied. "You know that."

"I don't care," Justin snapped. "I'm tired of being second best."

"Then stop this mad quest of yours. Your wife's soul will never return in those creatures you keep creating."

Justin turned away and looked out of the window. He was so weary of this existence. He needed someone real to love. He wanted Abigail. "Mind your own business. It's nothing to do with you."

"Maybe not, but the way you treat my minions is. Why are you so cruel to them? They only want to serve you."

"I don't care. Their feelings mean nothing to me."

Adrinia gave him a withering glare. "They're only on loan to you. I can revoke their allegiance any time I choose."

Justin spun around. His grin cruel, filled with malice. "But you won't, will you?"

Adrinia moved closer. The room darkened as the shadows surrounding her expanded. "I don't need to be with you. I've ruled the shadow realm for many centuries. I'm used to my own company."

"You pretend you are," Justin snorted. "But it gets lonely at the top, doesn't it? Anyway, your shadow minions would soon be depleted without the bonus of the lost souls I throw your way."

"Don't be naive. I can get more souls in one day than you can supply me in a year. Now tell me the real reason why you're so angry. I might be able to help."

"What can you do? Anyway, it's not one thing."

"Are you still going on about your inability to... um," Adrinia paused purposely, and watched with suppressed humour as Justin squirmed in discomfort. "How can I put this delicately? Your inability to procreate."

Justin's breath deepened as his annoyance grew. "I want a child with the woman I love. Is that too much to ask for?"

Adrinia laughed softly. "You're in love with a dream, not a person. Nothing comes without a price where we exist. You're paying for the crimes you committed when you were Lord Montgomery. You took your daughter as your wife and then gave her a child."

"She wasn't my child." He paused and took a breath. "She's my wife, reborn to me."

"How do you know for sure that she wasn't begat from your seed?"

"Because Abigail and I never... we didn't..." he trailed off, unable to put into words the sexless marriage he had endured with his young, beautiful wife.

"Oh I see. Okay, let's go out on a limb and say she's your step daughter then. You still bedded her. In the mortals eyes that isn't right."

Justin felt fury rise up in his belly, burning his insides like acid. "Who are you to lecture me? You're born from the seed of depravity. That's how all the shadow rulers are begat. From rape and incest."

Adrinia sighed. "Here we go again. Yada, yada, yada. Yes, my mother and her brother begat me. So what? I'm the spawn of darkness. It's supposed to be that way with us. What's your excuse? You create clones of your dead wife from unborn children. Now that is sick. Without the Night Crawlers' spells to transform the child's sex in its mother's womb, you couldn't do half the things you do. But do you know the sickest joke of all? Every time you create one of those silver-haired empty vessels for your wife's soul to inhabit, a darker soul enters them. She's wandered the corridors of death for centuries searching for a fool like you to give her life. Evil spells come with a price. How many times do I need to tell you that?"

"You're a filthy liar. Love has never touched your cold heart and you're jealous that it touches mine."

"Don't presume you know everything about me."

Justin laughed with little humour. "That touched a raw nerve, didn't it!"

"I didn't come here to argue. I need you to see the spells you're using are breaking down. The silver-haired women no longer return to the cottage at the age you first appointed. The dark soul is rebelling. She wants more than the sixteen years you offer."

"It doesn't matter anymore. Because I'm keeping Abigail for myself. Her purity will wash my soul clean of any so called crimes against humanity. Which incidentally, blows your theory of a dark soul inhabiting her clean one, out of the cottage window. Abigail has no stain on her spirit."

"A viper is a viper, whatever guise it might take. Of course she's like the others. You're kidding yourself. The dark soul has become more devious, that's all. Nothing can wash away the stain caused by the murders you've committed in this very room."

Justin shook his head vehemently. "No, it's not all my fault. The women die because their own child steals their souls to survive. My conscience is clear."

Adrinia's laugh was hollow. "You're not listening to me. *ONE* dark soul lives in your vessels. She jumps from one to the other."

"So you keep telling me, but you've never seen her? There's no proof."

"For goodness sake," Adrinia snapped. "I give up. You want the truth, here it is. Lady Abigail Towers, your wife, was the keeper of the darkest soul of all. The Queen of the underworld. She can't return to you ever, because her real soul is entombed for eternity. The queen is now back on her throne. Where she belongs. She wanted to try out a mortal life, that's all. She never loved you."

"You're a filthy liar," he spat, hating Adrinia with every fibre of his being. "My wife was an innocent. Her soul was pure and good. She lost her way that's all. That stinking coven corrupted her."

"Innocent, my shadowy backside. Lady Abigail Towers was a coven leader and fornicated with titled demons of the underworld because she loved to feel them thrusting inside her. As for your second, so called wife, daughter or whatever you want to call her, was probably begat from a union with another coven member. The queen wanted to experience birth. *YOU* were the innocent one, Justin. Led like a lamb to the slaughter."

Justin clapped his filth encrusted hands over his ears. "I won't listen anymore to your filth. You're just a jealous old sow, with no real plane of existence. You're alone and miserable because your ugly and that's why you hide your true form."

"My poor Justin. You were damned the moment you met Lady Abigail Towers. Deep down you know it's the truth. I'm sorry my words hurt you. But I've kept this secret for too long."

"I'll never believe you" Justin replied. "My wife loved me. She would've come back, I wasn't patient enough."

"It's been nearly two hundred years, Justin. How much patience do you have?"

Justin glared at the dark shadow hovering in front of him. What if Adrinia was right? What if his wife's soul was tainted? He couldn't believe it, yet he did have a memory of her cold sapphire eyes freezing him to the bone when he tried to consummate their marriage. The acid words that dripped from her tongue whenever he tried to hold her, filtered through the chaotic realms of his insanity. She had been a hard woman. For all her beauty she was quite untouchable. But he loved her and he thought his love would change her.

But this Abigail was different. Her sapphire eyes sparkled with warmth and life. "Abbey is different from all the others. Her innocence makes her special."

"Oh, it's *Abbey* now, is it? Very familiar and she's hardly innocent."

"I know she isn't now. Thanks to you, I saw that for myself. But O'Donnell was her first. *He* took advantage of *her*. She isn't to blame. So do us both a favour and keep your nose out of my business and that blasted pet of yours on a leash. It almost scared Abbey half to death when it ran out of the cottage. It's always getting in the way."

"That mortal didn't take advantage of your precious Abigail. She opened her legs and welcomed him like a paid whore. I saw her, remember. As for Aslow, he means no harm. But I'll tell him to be more careful if it stops you from glaring at me like that."

Justin sucked in his breath and released it in a furious whoosh. Her condescending manner irritated him beyond belief. "Think what you like, Adrinia. I don't really care. O'Donnell's disposable like all the others."

Adrinia's laugh was high and brittle. "Really! Can't you see that Abigail is actually in love with him? Which, I admit, surprises me. I thought the dark soul was incapable of feeling that particular emotion. But she might have evolved. Anything's possible. If you kill him she might crumble to tiny pieces. Have you ever tried to bed a grieving mortal? Unless you drug her senseless, you'll not get anywhere."

Justin was loath to take her advice, but she did have a point. Abbey was overly attached to O'Donnell. He could feel it. "I'll have her body and soul. Wait and see. We'll be together for eternity, with no barriers between us."

"You're deluded," Adrinia replied.

"Aren't you tired of being alone? I am."

"But you're not alone," Adrinia whispered. "I'm here. Be realistic, Justin. You can't hide your true form, behind an essence spell, for the next fifty years? And what will become of the child she carries?"

Justin shrugged his malformed shoulders. "You can have it. Find it a soul, because I won't allow it to have Abbey's. You've always wanted a mortal child. It's my parting gift to you."

"Oh, I'm sure she'll allow that. Taking a mortals child away is like severing their limbs."

Justin frowned, rolling his eyes in impatience. "Abbey will understand. Love adapts to circumstances."

"You're taking a huge risk. If she turns against you, what will you have?"

Justin watched Adrinia's outline fade away and grimaced. "Not you, that's for sure," he mumbled. *You're one thorn in my side I can't wait to pull out. If my plan works, I'll never have to clap eyes on your dark, soulless form again.*

***

Abbey closed her eyes and relaxed in the bubbles. The bath oil she had found in the cabinet was a godsend. Small things like that were good omens, she told herself. She opened her eyes and sunk deeper, allowing her earlier tension to drain away. A single gas lamp glowed in the corner of the bathroom, it shadowy flame danced eerily on the wall. She watched fascinated as it bent and swayed to an orchestra only it could hear. Had it always been lit? Maybe the caretaker set it on low. Did these things have timers? She was getting to like this mysterious man more and more. He seemed to know exactly what she needed. Right down to the white fluffy towels. Abbey's eyelids grew heavy as she watched the flame. Sleep came before the scent of roses assailed her senses, filling the room, seeping into her every pore.

Abbey opened her eyes. She was standing in a room. It was a dream, she knew it, yet the man standing in the shadows looked real. When his his hand reached out and took hers, it felt warm and soft as it encapsulated hers. Was he the one she had run from for all these years?

His grip felt possessive, yet gentle as his other hand slipped around her waist. He gently pulled her closer to his wide chest. He was naked, but it didn't surprise her. Nestled in the centre of his chest was a thin gold chain. A tiny miniature of her, held in four gold clasps, hung from it. Abbey smiled. He loved her, she realised that now. For years she had run from the one thing she always wanted. Someone to love.

They danced wonderfully well together, as though they had done it all their lives. She followed his steps with ease as others appeared and danced around them. The elegant dancers kept to the shadows, leaving a cold breeze as they passed.

Abbey's heart thumped with excitement or wais it anticipation? She looked up. Now it was time to see the face of the man who had haunted her. He wasn't tall – about five feet nine. Not overly attractive, yet neither was he ordinary. His smile was wide and showed off a perfect line of white teeth. His hair, a shade of chestnut brown, had a slight wave. Expertly combed back and fastened with a silk ribbon at the nape of his neck.

His eyebrows were a little too wide, but they emphasised his soft hazel eyes, which held a hint of gold as they looked at her in adoration. His face was a little too long, but the deep dimple in his chin detracted the attention away from it. His nose was straight. Very aristocratic. Perfectly proportioned to his face. Not a line or wrinkle marred his lightly tanned skin. He looked ageless.

Her searching eyes moved down to his shoulders. She was surprised to see him suddenly dressed. His clothes immaculate, but outdated. The high neck collar of his suit, emphasised the small wings of his shirt collar, turned down onto an expertly arranged peach silk cravat. His aftershave smelt like roses. A scent she favoured most of all.

A gentle tickle on her own legs took her thoughts in another direction. She looked down and gasped at the beautiful peach, silk ball gown she was wearing. Its wide skirt, filled out with stiff petticoats, billowed around her as she danced around a huge ballroom. They wore matching colours. Like a true couple.

The memory of another dark ponytail filled her mind. Her feelings became confused as emptiness crept into her heart. Shaun. How could she forget the man who had taken her soul? The man she loved! Abbey didn't notice the music begin to pick up speed, until everything began to blur around her. Her feet flew around the room, their co-ordination lost in the screech of the orchestra. She looked at the man, filled with confusion and saw his lips were pulled back into a derisive sneer. His eyes black with a rage that terrified her.

"Stop! I can't keep up," she pleaded. The pitch of the music attacked her nerves like nails raking down a blackboard. "Stop. Stop!" she yelled and pushed against the arms holding her. Filled with horror, Abbey's gaze sought the man's, but what stared back at her froze the blood in her veins. The beast from her mother's painting held her. A monster so evil that his mere touch defiled her.

"Let me go!" She screamed, twisting and turning, pounding her fists ineffectually on his rounded shoulders.

But his grip was relentless. His hands, caked with grime, clung to her. His long, yellowed nails dug through the flimsy material of her gown, raking her tender skin beneath. Abbey gagged as the smell of his putrid flesh filled her nose. In a last, desperate effort to break free, she kicked out, but her legs became impeded by the gown, now ragged and stained. Drops of water splattered on her arm and made small soiled dots on her ragged sleeves. She looked up and felt nausea rise into her throat. The beast's thick lips were awash with saliva and it dripped off his skeletal chin onto her.

"God, help me," she begged and closed her eyes, unable to bear the sight of the monster holding her.

"Abbey, listen to my voice. Your fear is playing tricks on you," a familiar voice whispered. "Open your eyes, my love."

Startled by the soft, educated voice, Abbey's eyes flew open. The room had stopped spinning. The music melodious and calm. The scent of roses filled her nose and throat, acting like a balm on her shattered nerves. She looked at the man holding her. "I don't understand," she whispered.

"You don't need to. I'm here to take care of you. Your fears won't torment you anymore," he promised.

Relief flooded through her. She was safe and she rested her head on his shoulder.

"Look at me my love," His whispering voice commanded.

Abbey did as she was asked. When his lips touched hers, she clung to him. Her fog filled mind welcomed his searching lips. She felt herself eased gently backwards, and soon she was floating down to the ground on a pocket of air. His lips left hers and reappeared on her shoulders. They dropped tiny kisses here and there, each one making her body ache with need. His hand, soft and warm, gently caressed her breast, sending her spiralling into ecstasy.

Abbey pictured Shaun's hands removing her gown, easing it over her stomach until it became a silk puddle around her feet. She wrapped her arms around his back and felt his muscles ripple beneath her fingers. She scraped them lightly down his skin and arched her back when his mouth nuzzled the fullness of her breast.

"I love you, Abigail," the man whispered. "You're truly mine now."

The soft words, edged with the sharpness of possessiveness, pierced her foggy mind and bought clarity with it. This time she knew the hard body that slipped between her thighs wasn't Shaun's. The lips that suckled on her breast, teasing her nipples into hard peaks, weren't his.

"Tell me you love me," the man begged.

Abbey felt his hardness pressing at the entrance of a doorway only Shaun had entered; she squirmed away and pushed at his heavy chest. This wasn't right. Not when Shaun still lay in her heart. "No, I can't" she insisted.

"Don't be afraid, Abigail. This is meant to be."

"But I love Shaun, not you," she replied.

Abbey opened her eyes and felt the softness of the bed beneath her. She sat up aware that her damp hair was falling around her shoulders in cold, tangled clumps. Goosebumps peppered her arms and she rubbed them with her hands. The room was freezing. How did she get here? The last thing she remembered was being in the bath. She pulled the quilt over her, and groaned. She was still sleepwalking?

"I bet the bed's soaking wet," she moaned. She touched the material beneath her and frowned in confusion. It was dry. She got off the bed and saw her whole body was dry, yet there was no towel in sight. Abbey dragged on her dressing gown and pushed her feet into her slippers. Nothing made sense. She went into the kitchen and filled a kettle, although she didn't believe tea could take away the cold feeling inside of her. Aveline's words rang in her ears. 'A demon lives in the cottage disguised as a man.' Abbey shook her head. No! She wasn't going to be sucked into Aveline O'Donnell's nightmare. She had enough of her own.

Chapter Fourteen

Abbey carried her tea through to the lounge. She sat on the sofa and her gaze drifted idly around the room. Nothing here connected her to the outside world. Not a television, telephone or a radio. She didn't mind. It was nice to keep the world outside for a change. Her gaze flicked to her watch. Strange how it had stopped the moment she had entered the cottage. There was no clock in the house, so she would never know the time. A pleasant thought. Maybe the cottage was magic in a good way. It wanted her to forget time and its restrictions.

Abbey yawned. Even though she had slept, her eyes still felt sore and scratchy. Maybe she should pay more attention to the needs of her body. If she was tired, why shouldn't she sleep? When she was hungry, she would eat, regardless of the time. How lovely to be so uninhibited. Abbey got up and turned each oil lamp off. When she came to the last lamp, she hesitated. Maybe she should leave one on. Her mother always said to never leave a room in total darkness. "*You never know who could lurk under the cover of it*", she'd say. 'My mother,' Abbey sighed at the thought. She couldn't think of Harriet as anything else.

Abbey watched the remaining lamp cast its shadow on the pale wall behind it and for the first time felt no uneasiness. Tonight the shadows didn't seem to bother her.

***

Justin stepped from the shadow on the wall. His earlier anger was gone, replaced by melancholy as he stared at the closed door with longing. "You're so beautiful," he said softly.

Adrinia moved from the darkest corner of the room and gave an exaggerated yawn. "I don't think she looks any different from the others."

Justin felt anger bubble to the surface. Why did she badger him? Whenever he turned around, Adrinia was there with a caustic comment. "That's because you can't see real beauty."

Adrinia rolled her eyes with impatience. "Here we go again."

Justin's bony, over hanging forehead, creased into an irritated frown. "You've lived too long on the dark side. You've forgotten what it's like to see someone through a lover's eye."

"After all these years you still don't know me, Justin. Just because I dwell in the darkness doesn't mean I'm incapable of feeling emotions. I think you're the one who's sorely lacking in that department."

Justin eyed the shimmering apparition with disdain and pulled his thick lips back into a sneer. "Go to hell, Adrinia."

"I've already been there, my dear," she replied. "Choose somewhere else for a holiday."

***

Aveline placed the fork on the table and listened to the slow rumble of Shaun's truck as it pulled up outside. Since Abbey had gone, her son's happy-go-lucky personality had disappeared with her. She kept hoping his mood would lift. After all, it had been over a month since she'd left. But he stayed depressed and uncommunicative. Winnie Hannagan, from the baker's, told her that Shaun had asked everyone in town if they had seen Abbey. Most of the old town dwellers knew instantly, from his description, who she was. They shook their heads, but the younger ones for a time helped him search for her, oblivious to the danger they were all in. Aveline swallowed nervously. She knew where Abigail was, but wild horses wouldn't drag it from her lips.

Every night Shaun came home drunk and wildly shouted his intent to fly to London and find her. It took all of her cajoling to get him to bed. Then in the morning, they'd sit down to breakfast and act as though nothing had happened.

The door swung open, letting in a freezing wind, as Shaun walked in and hung his heavy coat on the stand. Snow would soon arrive, barricading them in. Maybe that would give him the time he needed, away from the pub, to heal. Aveline turned and pasted a bright smile onto her face. "Hello, son. Has the day been good to you?"

Shaun walked over to the open fire and waved his hands in front of it. "Someone's living in Abigail Cottage."

Aveline bit back her terror. How on earth did he know that? "Oh, and who told you that?" She pretended to brush some imaginary crumbs from the spotless, linen table cloth as if his answer meant nothing to her.

"Mrs Holloman. Not that I believe everything the stupid woman says. Her latest bit of fantasy is that the cottage has come back to life because the demon inside it has been woken. Evidently his true love has returned. Lucky old demon, huh! God, that woman talks a load of old blarney sometimes. Did you know that some folk believe the place is cursed? Mind you, I can't say much, even me own father did. The stupid idiot. Fancy him trying to burn the place down."

Aveline clicked her tongue in annoyance. "I don't know why you bother to listen to that silly old woman. Everyone knows she has frog's spawn for brains. Her endless prattle gives me a headache as soon as I set foot in the bakery." Aveline surreptitiously watched her son's reaction. She and Morgan had taken great pains to bury the past. Now the biggest gossip in town was resurrecting it. Aveline's laugh was high and forced as she straightened the knives on the table. "She loves to prey on peoples superstitions. Next she'll be saying the leprechauns are trying to take over the town."

Shaun's lips tilted into a half smile. "You'd be mad to believe half of what she says. But I might just take a run up there and see who's moved in. The place will be run down and I might get a bit of private work out of it. Let's face it, the weathers turning. I won't be going anywhere soon. It'll shut her ghoulish stories up."

Aveline tried to still her rising panic as she took the plates down from the welsh dresser. Whatever happened, she had to keep him away from there. "Now don't you be wasting good money on petrol to prove any points. Your bosses won't let you take their cars that far anyway. We can't afford for you to lose this job, son. Milly Dawson got it from Mick the owner of Green Acre farm, that he can tell from the ground that it's going to be a bad winter. That generator doesn't run on fresh air and the oil prices will shoot up as soon as the first snowflake hits."

"We'll be fine, mother. Stop worrying. I might have a pick-up near there next week. So I won't be wasting anyone's time or fuel."

Aveline felt the room tilt crazily. The plates she was holding dropped from her hands. Clattering onto the floor, shattering, like her nerves. "Oh damn and blast," she snapped, looking at the china fragments. "The cottage has a caretaker," Aveline lied. "It's always kept well. He'll be kept on by a new owner, I'm sure."

"Oh, right. Maybe someone should tell Mrs Holloman that. It would answer a lot of her, 'who tends the flower beds and paints the cottage,' questions." Shaun looked at the broken china, then at his mother. "Do you want any help clearing that up?"

Aveline shook her head, too scared to look her son in the eye in case he saw her lies mirrored there.

"Suit yourself. Don't dish me any tea yet," Shaun shrugged on a jacket. "I'm away to pick up Rosa's truck."

"But it's ready to be dished now." Aveline complained, irritated at the mere mention of the charlatan's name. She saw Shaun's stubborn frown and sighed as she bent down and picked up the fragments of china. "But I suppose it can keep warm in the oven. Mind you're careful with that old gypsy. She'll con the last penny from your pockets."

"Rosa's not that bad once you get to know her. Anyway, with winter coming I can't leave her with no transport, can I? The fells get a mite lonely in winter when the snow's thick."

"That know-it-all will always get by," Aveline snapped. Probably on a broomstick, she silently added.

"A know-it-all she might be, but I'll tell you one thing, she was almost right about Abbey." He paused, shuffling on his feet awkwardly on the carpet. "Do you think I should keep looking for her? I mean, a person doesn't usually change their whole personality like that. Maybe she's sick or something."

Aveline's heart hammered. She would give anything to say yes. What mother didn't want her child to be happy? But this wasn't a normal situation. If Shaun went to the cottage and found Abigail, that beast would strike him down, like he did Morgan.

She stood and looked Shaun in the eye, silently praying for the strength to tell him yet another lie. "No, son, I don't think it'll do you any good. I... I didn't want to tell you this, but she let it slip about a certain fiancé in London. They were on what she called 'a break' for a few weeks. They're getting married at the end of the year." The pain in Shaun's eyes made her quickly look away.

"I can't believe it," he whispered. "She didn't tell me about him. I mean she was... well, I thought she was..." he paused, unable to carry on.

"Shaun, when people are on holiday they think it's all right to string people along. Abigail was looking to pass the time while she was here. I'm sure she never meant to hurt you this badly."

"But that's exactly what she did do, mother."

Aveline carried on picking up the china. She couldn't bear to see the pain in her son's eyes anymore. "You have to move on, lad. Find a good Irish woman to settle down with." It's all for the best, she told herself. He'll get over her. She heard the front door click and looked up from the floor. Shaun had gone and the only sound she heard was the thump of her own lying heart.

Five months later

Abbey put her empty cup in the saucer and sighed. Christmas had come and gone, the weather had turned bitter cold and she had suffered them both alone. How could she have been so stupid? What a horrible mess. Who gets pregnant the very first time they sleep with someone? Panic made her stomach roll sickeningly whenever she thought about what was growing inside her. Her brother's child.

Terrible thoughts plagued her. What if it was deformed? She remembered reading an article about a brother and sister who had a hideous scrap of humanity because of their incestuous relationship. I have choices. After all, this is the 21st century. An abortion can be done in a few minutes nowadays. Yet the thought of harming her child, conceived through no fault of its own, wasn't something she could ever do. By her calculations, she was twenty weeks along. There was always adoption. She had deliberated on that for days. But the simple fact was she wanted Shaun's child. Even though the consequences terrified her.

She could never go home now. Having an illegitimate grandchild would be bad enough for her parents to take. But if they knew it was her brother's! She couldn't bear to see the shame on their faces. It was better if they never saw her again. But she knew her mother would never entertain that idea. She prayed the letter she had written to them had worked. It said she wanted some time alone. She was going to travel. What she didn't want them to know was that she was here. Her mother would have a fit. *Maybe I can move abroad after the baby's born.* No one must find out her secret, especially Shaun.

Abbey turned to the back of her journal and looked down her 'to do' list. She had already written to a letting agency in London to rent out her flat. Her friend Maddie said she would box up her things for storage. She had posted off a letter resigning from her job. That place she wouldn't miss. Thanks to the caretaker, she didn't have to go out and cause attention to herself. She put the letters in a basket and left on the doorstep with a note instructing him what to do. Such a helpful man, but so elusive. He didn't want to meet her. He kept himself to himself. Not that she minded. It was less explaining on her part. Once she had the baby, she would sell up, combine the money with her inheritance and go.

The caretaker made sure she had groceries delivered to her door. All she had to do was leave the money and a list outside in a wicker basket, she supposed his wife had provided. Tomorrow she would leave a note asking him to knock. He must be paid from her mother's trustees. But she was sure taking care of her wasn't one of his duties. She wanted to thank him. Let him know how much she appreciated his help.

Abbey burrowed deeper into the sofa. For months she had fretted over whether she should tell Shaun about the baby. He had a right to know. Not that she wanted anything from him. She was quite capable of raising the baby alone. But the thought of facing Aveline's scorn, filled her with dread. Abbey closed her eyes, acknowledging the steady thump of a headache. They came frequently nowadays, especially when she thought about Shaun. Abbey allowed her thoughts to drift away and sleep came quickly

Abbey moved her hand and touched the ground. A cold breeze ran its icy fingers along her body and she felt her flesh recoil. "What's happening?" She turned her head and saw the cottage outlined in the darkness. A deeper reasoning told her she was dreaming, yet fear warped any logic. She stared, trying to see through the veil of darkness. No one was there, yet the hairs on the back of her neck stood to attention and told her otherwise. Panic made her heart beat uncomfortably and she placed her hand on her chest to calm the rhythmic ache.

Abbey got to her feet. She felt wobbly, unsure why she couldn't run to the cottage. Fear nagged her like an irritating itch, but the more she hurried the further away it became. The freezing wind whipped by. It was strong, pushing her back, away from safety – away from her home. Huge trees whipped down their branches, slicing the air above her head as though trying to spear her flesh. She screamed when one snagged her hair and tore a piece from her scalp.

Abbey ran until her lungs felt they would explode with pressure. Her legs grew heavy, as though she were carrying a great weight. She stopped, gasping for breath. It was then she saw her grotesquely distended stomach. A sharp stab of fiery pain, spread across it. "Shaun, help me," she screamed into the darkness.

The pain came in waves, with little retribution, until her legs buckled and the ground came up to meet her with a sickening thud. Abbey winced as her body jarred against its firmness. When she saw shadowy figures moving towards her, she almost cried with relief. "Please - someone help me."

"You have the cheek to ask for help with that abomination you carry," a woman's voice replied.

"Why I heard tell it's spawned from your brother's seed!" A man shouted.

Abbey's mouth dried out with terror. How did they know? "It's my child," she argued. "You've no right to condemn me." She forced herself to sit upright and held her head rigid in defiance. "Do you hear me, this is MY baby."

When something warm trickled between her legs, Abbey looked down at the spreading puddle. Another contraction robbed her of coherent thought and she followed a primeval urge to push. This child was arriving, whether it was convenient or not.

"You've committed the worst sin of all," a man's voice condemned.

Abbey knew that she had to get inside the cottage. Once she was there her child would be safe. "Please, help me get home," she begged. When she felt a light touch on her arm, she turned. A grateful smile teetered on the edge of her lips until she saw the furious emerald eyes of her saviour.

"Why did you stay?" Shaun spat.

She desperately clung to his arm "This is your child too."

Hatred stared back at her from the eyes of the man she loved. Abbey's heart sank. Shaun would never accept their child. She was stupid to think otherwise.

"It's no child of mine you carry," he hissed and pushed her hand from his arm.

Abbey wiped away the tears spilling down her cheeks. "Please Shaun. I only have you to turn to."

"Don't look to me for help," he replied loudly. Then his voice lowered to a harsh whisper. "You make me sick to my stomach. The best thing you can do is die with that thing you're carrying."

Abbey stared, stunned into silence. She couldn't believe what she was hearing. The man she loved was filled with so much venom, she barely recognised him. "You don't mean that."

Shaun stood up. "Leave the tramp to her fate," he shouted and walked back into the darkness.

Abbey trembled in shock and pain. Shaun had never loved her. All his talk about taking her soul, loving her, was a lie. She really was utterly alone.

"I'll help you," a voice whispered beside her.

Abbey looked up and saw a pair of familiar hazel eyes staring back at her. Tears of relief flooded down her cheeks. "Thank you. I didn't think you'd come. I haven't been very nice to you." Abbey groaned as another contraction gripped her. "I can't get up," she cried.

The man held out his arms. "Then I'll carry you."

She could feel his muscles tense as he swept her away from the coldness of the ground and into the warmth of his cloak. The sweet scent of roses filled her lungs. This was where she belonged. With a man who truly loved her. She heard a voice call to her in the distance. Its urgency filtering through her pain. "Someone's calling me."

"No one of any importance," her saviour replied. "I'll take care of you now."

***

Shaun lay in bed and groaned. His head hammered mercilessly against his skull as yet another hangover plagued him. He was drinking too much. Every time he went to the pub he told himself that it would be the last, but it was the only way he could blot Abbey from his mind for a few hours. Her face, with their sparkling sapphire eyes, filled his waking moments, until he thought he would go mad with longing. He closed his eyes and winced at the continuous thud. If he didn't stop this, he would go mad. He was tired of being tortured, fed up with chasing a dream he could never have. With one arm thrown across his eyes, Shaun drifted off into an uneasy sleep.

Adrinia stood at the foot of the bed and watched the sleeping man with a dispassionate eye, as Aslow scrabbled about in her arms. With an impatient frown she dropped him on the floor. The small shadow immediately skittered between her feet. "I can see why the slut's attracted to this one, Aslow. I wouldn't say no myself," she whispered. Adrinia ran her tongue over her lips as she took in Shaun's naked torso. For a time, her spell of anonymity had worked on Abigail Newlands. Justin had no hope of finding her. Then he would have eventually turned to her. But she hadn't banked on the strength of his demonic spells or sheer stubbornness. For a time she had debated whether to just kill her, but that would only complicate matters further.

Adrinia watched Aslow skitter around the room and sighed. He had been a terrible nuisance at Abigail's dwelling. For a moment she was sure the silly girl had seen him. But that wasn't possible. No mortal could see what lived in the darkness. If they could, they would never be so complacent about the shadows surrounding them. But all wasn't lost. Abigail's coupling with the mortal had opened Justin's eyes. She wasn't his pure maid anymore.

"Sleep well, my darling boy." She laughed softly. "Ooh, I feel like a fairy godmother granting a wish. Depending on what way you look at it, of course."

Adrinia's shimmering body darkened as she raised her arms up over her head, she parted them and drew a half circle in the air. As she bought them down to shoulder level, she closed her eyes. The darkness that surrounded her began to expand, until after a few moments it had totally filled the room, blurring her outline as she became one with it.

Aslow squealed in terror, and scuttled under the bed as his mistress whispered a dark incantation:

"Open the doorway where darkness reigns.
Let this mortal walk the demonic plains.
Allow him to see where his lover hides,
But stay hidden away from Justin's eyes.
May the pain that grows and withers his heart,
Consume his soul and leave its mark,
No peace will fill this mortal's mind,
Until his one true love he finds."

Adrinia moved her arms and closed the half circle above her head. As the darkness drew back into her body, her outline slowly reappeared. "Such a body, wasted on that slut," she whispered. It would take but a moment for her to summon Samael, the demon of death, to take his soul. She would use it in ways he could never imagine. But for now she needed him on the physical plane. "We'll meet again, Shaun O'Donnell," she promised. "Come, Aslow."

Aslow ran out from under the bed and Adrinia picked him up. "Let us go and watch the show. Starring Justin Montgomery, the slut and the hero, Shaun O'Donnell."

***

Shaun shivered as a biting wind whipped across his naked torso. He shook, frozen to the bone in seconds. It took a few moments to get his bearings. If this was a dream, it was very real. Rosa called them visions. When your spirit walked the land between lives. He looked around. Except for a house in the distance, he was completely alone. Shaun frowned. He recognised it. Abigail Cottage. Why was this place in his vision?

The wind brought with it a murmur of voices. There were people in the distance, shouting something. The darkness around him felt unnaturally thick as he jogged towards the crowd. The wind picked up, driving a relentless force of rain into his face. It took his breath away, obscured his vision until the only thing he could hear was its deafening howl.

As he drew nearer to the cottage, the wind quickly abated, as though someone had thrown an off switch. Shaun stopped and rubbed his eyes to clear the debris. He blinked and tried to focus. He could vaguely make out the silhouettes of people crowding around someone lying on the ground. He ran on, aware that the curtain of darkness was slowly pulling back. He saw what looked like a stage setting. The silhouetted people were inanimate props. The only real person was on the floor and Shaun's throat constricted in horror when he saw it was Abbey.

He sprinted towards her. "Abbey." His desperate cry was drowned out against the sudden howl of the wind, which returned with a brutal force, its invisible hands pushing against him. No matter how he fought against the elements, it was impossible to get any closer. "Abbey," Shaun yelled again, but the wind whipped his voice away, tormenting him with its evil game. Nothing he did made a difference and he could only watch in horror as a monstrous apparition stepped out from the darkness.

Half man and half animal, its clawed feet clung tenaciously on to the end of hideously bowed legs, as it moved towards Abbey. A long hairless tail flicked behind it like a whip, slapping out at the cardboard cut outs. Arms covered in a layer of grey, decayed flesh scooped her up from the floor and encased her in its filthy rags.

"Leave her alone," Shaun yelled. "Abbey, don't let that thing touch you." He ignored the pain burning in his chest from the endless running and continued to battle forward. The beast slowly carried her away and he could do nothing to stop it. A curtain of darkness fell around him, thick and unyielding. Shaun knew that Abbey was lost to him and the thought stabbed into his heart, a piercing wound that he knew could never heal.

"Abbey." His tortured cry burst from his lips and twisted his guts into a spasm of unbearable pain. It took a few minutes to realise he was sitting up in bed. "No. Oh God, please no." Shaun collapsed back onto his pillow. The vision had been sent for a reason. It told him that Abbey was gone for good. Shaun rolled onto his stomach as hot tears poured from his eyes. He buried his face deep into the folds of the pillow to stifle his sobs. "Why did you make me love you?" he groaned out loud. "Well, no more. The torture is over. The visions told me to let you go and that's what I need to do. Do you hear me, Abbey? It's over!"

Adrinia stood in the shadows of the room and frowned. "Oh, you stupid mortal," she hissed. "You're not supposed to give up. You're meant to want her even more."

Aslow squealed as she squeezed him a little too hard in her anger. "Oh shut up. Those damn Spiritual Laws spoil everything. What just happened is called cause and effect, Aslow. With each reaction there is an equal and opposite reaction. Damn it." Shaun just had the latter to what she wanted. If Justin made Abigail hate this mortal, she would succumb to his essence like all the others. Then she would lose him forever. "I thought you were different from the others," Adrinia berated the sobbing man. "Stop blubbering like an infant and make an effort to fight for the slut." She sighed in frustration. "I'll have to think of something else, Aslow. These beings are so weak. They constantly let emotions rule them. We need to take more drastic action." Adrinia mumbled as she and Aslow faded back into the shadow cast by the bedside lamp.

Chapter Fifteen

Harriet sighed and hung up the telephone. Her thoughts were frantic, ranging from deadly calm to near hysteria. "Abbey's renting out her flat. Mary Hobson saw her advertisement on the post office advertising board and wants to know how much the rent is. Her daughter's interested. Why didn't Abbey tell us? "

Jonathon put his cup in the saucer with a clatter. "Stop worrying. She explained in her letter how she feels. We must respect that. She's probably renting to fund her travel expenses. It'll do her good to see the world. It might make her realise how much she needs her family. If you want me to make a few discrete inquiries, I will. But I'm only doing it to ease your over-active imagination."

Harriet paced the room and wrung her hands. She had a bad feeling about this. She didn't believe for one minute that Abbey was travelling. Every instinct inside her screamed her daughter was in the cottage. Now the beast would bend her will to his. Why wouldn't Jonathon believe her? "But she didn't even contact us at Christmas. We've never spent that day apart since she was born. I can't bear it, Jonathon. I can't. What if she's staying in the cottage? The post mark on her last letter was Irish. Think about it Jonathon. If she was there, why would she lie about it? Who's told her to keep it from us?"

Jonathon sighed and pushed his plate away. "I know as much as you, dear. The ball's in her court now. I know it's been a few months, but Abbey's a sensible girl. I think you underestimate her. Anyway, the cottage is probably uninhabitable. You're worrying for nothing."

Harriet stopped her pacing and glared at her husband. "Everything will be pristine, even though it's been empty for years. He'll make sure if it. Don't you understand? It's not about being sensible. Abbey can't fight the hold he'll have over her, no one can."

Jonathon stood up, wiped his mouth on a napkin and threw it onto the table. "I'm not going to have this conversation with you again, Harriet. There's no demon and no magic cottage that's self restoring. A set of unfortunate circumstances created a superstitious curse which has got out of hand."

"Out of hand," Harriet repeated slowly, as if every word burnt her tongue. She shook her head sadly. "You'll never understand. You won't let yourself."

***

Justin admired his reflection. The spell had worked. The man in the mirror was handsome. His clothes elegant. Just like he was before he died.

"Very nice. Going somewhere special?" Adrinia purred.

Justin sneered and turned. "It's time Abigail and I met in person. It will make our bond stronger. I don't like using the essence spell. It agitates her."

"You did this with all the others. Nothing changes. They still end up dead and you'll be alone again."

"Shut your mouth. I told you, this is different."

"At least let me give you a bit of advice then. You're not going to impress her

dressed like you're going to a fancy dress ball. Keep up with the time you're in."
Justin turned back to the mirror. It irked him Adrinia was right. In his haste to get
ready, he had forgotten the year he was entering in to. He looked into the mirror
and willed a gentleman's suit to appear on him. It appeared, fitting in all the right
places. "That's better." He turned and smiled. "Don't wait up for me dear. I'll be
sometime."
Adrinia smiled back. "Don't expect fan-fares and bells, Justin. You're just a
caretaker to her."
Justin walked into the nearest shadow on the wall. "For now, Adrinia," he called
back. "Just for now."

***

Abbey twisted and turned in front of the mirror. She frowned in annoyance. Six
months pregnant and hardly a bump to show for it. Maybe she should go to the
local hospital and have a scan to make sure everything was okay. But they might
ask questions and she had no answers. She absently massaged a little more baby oil
into her tummy. Last night she was sure she had felt a fluttering of movement. She
put her hand on her stomach and gave it a gentle pat. "Come on baby, I want to see
some good healthy kicks," she whispered.
Abbey jumped at the loud knock at the door. The bottle of baby oil slithered from
her hand and dropped onto the floor. She quickly picked it up. No one had knocked
since she had moved in. Why did they now? A tremor of fear ran through her. What
if it was Shaun? Her nightmare was only a glimpse of what might happen if he
ever discovered the truth. At the second insistent knock, Abbey felt her feet freeze
to the floor. Maybe they would go away, if she kept quiet.
"Miss Newlands are you home?" a male voice inquired through the door.
Abbey leant against the dressing table, her knees buckling in fright. He knew her
name. She took a deep, calming breath. It wasn't Shaun's voice. But it did have a
ring of familiarity about it. She straightened, smoothed back her hair, and walked to
the door. Before she could change her mind, she pulled it open.
The man at the door smiled and bowed slightly from the hip in salutation. "Good
morning. I received your note and here I am." His smile was wide, his teeth
impossibly straight, his hair was short. But Abbey recognised him straight away.
"Oh my God," she whispered and took a step back. "It's you." The hero from her
nightmare was standing, in the flesh, on her doorstep.
"Sorry? Is everything all right? Have I called at an inconvenient moment?"
Abbey tried to pull herself together. "Um... yes, I mean no..." she stammered,
kicking herself for sounding like a gibbering idiot. She was being stupid. He can't
be the man from her dream. His dimple was too shallow, his eyes too light, his
smile too wide.
"Yes, it's inconvenient, or no you're not all right?"
Abbey clutched the door. "Oh... God... sorry, I thought you were someone else."
"Ah, well, that'll explain your shocked expression. For a moment I thought you
would swoon at my feet."

Abbey smiled. *Swoon!* Who said that nowadays? He looked a little eccentric dressed in that out dated country gentleman suit, but he seemed friendly enough. She owed him and his wife a great debt of gratitude. "So you're the mysterious caretaker?"

The man laughed. A deep, rich baritone chuckle. Abbey warmed to him instantly.

"Sometimes it's good to cultivate a little air of mystery."

"Well, you've certainly done that." She let go of the door and allowed it to open wider.

"As you've probably gathered, I'm contracted by the estate trustees to keep the cottage in order." He pulled out a plastic card and handed it to her.

She took it and briefly scanned the writing. It confirmed his identification, but the picture didn't do him justice. It made him look older.

"Now you're here, my job's done, but I thought I'd help you settle in first. I know what it's like to be the new person in town. But it's time to say goodbye."

Abbey felt her heart plummet. She had hoped he'd stay on for a while. At least until the baby was born. She handed him back the card. "Oh, I see. Won't you come in? The least I can do is offer you a cup of tea."

She noticed that his eyes crinkle pleasantly in the corners. He had a strange look about him. Not handsome, yet not ugly either.

"Tea, ahh, now that's a beverage I haven't had in a while."

Abbey laughed and stepped back allowing him to enter. "I can't believe that?"

"I've little time for the brewing and steeping of tea."

"You should try tea bags. They're much more convenient than fresh. Take a seat and I'll be back in a jiffy." She closed the door and hurried down the corridor and into the small kitchen. Who made fresh tea nowadays? Then she remembered the old fashion tea caddy in the back of the cupboard. Something told her there would be fresh tea inside it. She wasn't disappointed. Abbey hummed to herself as she warmed the tea pot. It had been so long since she'd entertained; she hoped she hadn't forgotten the art of conversation. After it was filled and a few tea cakes added to the tray, she carried it into the lounge. As she entered the room, the caretaker jumped from his chair and took it from her.

"It isn't wise for you to carry such heavy things in your condition," he said and placed it on the coffee table.

Abbey's breath caught in her throat. It was the first time her pregnancy had been mentioned and she felt a stirring of fear. "How... I mean who...?"

"Your eyes say it all," he replied. "A woman with child always has an inner glow. As though they're harbouring a little secret."

"I'm not harbouring any secret. Just a baby."

"Of course you are," the caretaker contradicted.

Abbey looked at him in horror. Had he heard rumours about her and Shaun?

"The child's sex remains a secret until it's born," he continued. "Although I've a feeling it'll be a beautiful little girl, just like her mother."

Although relieved he didn't know a thing, Abbey suddenly felt shy. She wasn't used to compliments and didn't know how to respond to one. "A girl, huh? Only a scan will reveal that." As soon as the words were out of her mouth she could have bitten them back. If he knew she had no hospital care, he would definitely become suspicious.

"A scan?"

Abbey laughed at his quizzical stare. He had no idea what she was on about. "Oh, I can see you've never had children."

"I don't hold with all the medical ideas nowadays. In the old days millions of babies were born without mechanical help."

Abbey poured the tea through a dainty silver strainer which she had found in the cutlery drawer and handed him the cup and plate with a tea cake on. "Here you go." He took it, his smile wide in appreciation. Abbey felt a tremor of excitement rush through her when his fingers grazed hers. An unexpected feeling to add to her confusion. "You know my name, but you haven't told me yours. I should have read your identification a little better."

"It's Justin," he replied.

Abbey smiled. The name struck a familiar cord. 'Justin' was the name of the so called beast of the cottage. But he didn't look like a demon. It was an old fashioned name. Anyone could have it. She dismissed the thought instantly. "Pleased to meet you, Justin."

"It's unfortunate, isn't it?"

Abbey lowered the tea cake she was about to bite. "Sorry?"

"My name. It's an inherited family name. I can't make up my mind if it's a curse or a blessing." Justin sat back in the armchair and sipped his tea. Ahh, fresh tea. You spoil me."

"A blessing. It suits you." She surreptitiously observed Justin through her lashes as she drank her tea. There was something odd about him. He sat ram-rod straight in the chair, had impeccable manners. Rather like a proper English gentleman taking tea. She liked that it made him different from other men she had known.

"I hope you don't think that I'm too presumptuous, but would you consider staying on a little bit longer? That's if your wife doesn't mind." She added. "I'm sort of resting and I don't feel up to venturing out for shopping, or taking care of the grounds yet. I'll pay you the going rate of course."

Justin put down his cup and drew his eyebrows into a tight frown. "I'd be happy to stay on. I've no family to ask permission from," he added. "It really depends if my landlord will extend my tenancy."

Abbey heart sank. He had to stay, she couldn't manage without his help? "Do you think they will?"

Justin shrugged his shoulders. "I don't know."

"Can you let me know as soon as possible?" She hoped she didn't sound as desperate as she felt

The afternoon flew by. Abbey was enthralled by Justin's quick wit and broad spectrum of interests. If things were different she would be very attracted to her friendly caretaker, despite his old fashioned ideas and dress sense.

"Are you chilled?" Justin asked.

Abbey had barely shivered, but he had noticed immediately. His attentiveness warmed her. "A little. The evenings here get cold so quickly."

Justin got up and added coal to the grate. "The evening is upon us and the fire isn't lit."

"Oh dear, I'm sorry. I don't know how to bank it properly. I shouldn't have kept you so late."

Justin laughed. "You haven't tied me to the chair." He bent over the fire and mumbled something.

Abbey strained to hear. "Are you telling it to light," she teased. "It'll take ages to catch."

The fire suddenly roared to life and Abbey clapped her hands in excitement. "How did you do that? It takes me ages and half a box of fire-lighters to get it going."

Justin warmed his hands over the fire. "I have a knack with them. It just needed cajoling and my lighter. I've enjoyed our chat today."

Abbey stood up. "Would you like more tea?" She hoped he would say yes. She was enjoying his company too much to let it end.

"I'd love some more, thank you."

"Are you hungry?" The words burst from her mouth before she could stop them. She hoped she didn't look too eager. After all, she was hardly in a position to start anything romantic. And Shaun was never far from her thoughts. The thought of him made her feel melancholy and her eagerness to continue the evening waned.

Justin gave the fire a sharp poke before he straightened, "Will you allow me to cook?"

Abbey pushed the dark cloud, hovering over her, to one side. He cooked as well as entertained. A man far too good to be true. "Oh, no. I couldn't impose."

Justin took off his jacket, revealing an exquisitely embroidered waistcoat. Abbey stared. On any other person it would look ridiculous. But not on him. He wore it well.

"Please, it's no imposition. It's not often I get a chance to cook for someone else."

It was on the tip of her tongue to refuse, but she did feel as if her energy was sucked away, like lemonade through a straw. Just one day of not cooking would be wonderful. "If you insist, that would be lovely. Do you need me to help?"

"No. Rest a while. You look tired. I'll have dinner prepared within the hour."

Justin pulled the armchair closer to the fire. "Sit here. The best seat in the house."

Abbey laughed and did as she was told. It was nice to feel the warmth if the fire. She could hardly keep her eyes open. Her nose twitched as the scent of roses lightly invaded her drowsy state. Where it came from she didn't know, but she loved its familiarity. It made the house feel more like a home.

Abbey moaned softly as the fingers of her hand were lightly pressed. The caress was subtle, but her foggy brain registered it instantly.

"Abigail," a voice whispered. "It's time…"

The voice held a haunting command as it filtered through her consciousness. "Time for what?" she mumbled.

"To eat of course."

Abbey opened her eyes and blinked. For a second she was disoriented, as if she had drunk too much wine.

"Hello, sleepy head. Come and eat before it gets cold." Justin stood up, walked to the table and pulled a chair out for her to sit on.

Abbey uncurled from the chair and got up, staggering slightly. Her head was heavy and thick from the nap. "I must have slept too deeply. I feel as if I've drunk a whole bottle of wine. How long have I been asleep?"

"An hour or so."

Abbey sat and Justin moved her chair closer to the table. He certainly was a man out of his time. "Thank you," she said and wished she had on an evening dress instead of tracksuit bottoms and a scraggy t-shirt.

Her eyes widened in surprise at the various dishes on the table. Roast chicken, steaming vegetables and mashed potatoes to die for. Thick gravy in a delicate floral, china jug was the icing on the cake. "My god, how did you manage to make all of this?"

Justin sat and placed his napkin across his lap. "It's not much. It takes a small amount of time to boil frozen vegetables and cook a bit of chicken."

Abbey helped herself to the food. She hadn't eaten so well in a long time. Cooking for one had lost it appeal months ago. The chicken melted in her mouth and the mashed potatoes tasted even better smothered in the gravy. She ate with relish, savouring the frozen vegetables, which never tasted this good when she boiled them.

Justin poured her a glass of red wine.

Abbey shook her head. "Oh no, I can't" She noticed he had hardly touched his food and wondered if she looked like a giant porker tucking in with so much enthusiasm.

"A glass of red wine is fortifying. It feeds the blood," he replied and poured himself a glass. "A toast. To the queen of the house. Long may she reign."

Abbey giggled. "Oh stop it. I'm far from being royalty. Cheers." She raised her glass and tapped it to his. "Thanks for everything."

"You're very welcome, Abigail."

She sipped her wine and enjoyed the warmth it created in her stomach. "My friends call me Abbey," she hoped he took the hint. Abigail was not a name she favoured at all. It never bought her ancestors any luck.

"Then, you are very welcome, *Abbey*," he repeated softly.

Over coffee their conversation was splattered with humour and history. Something, Abbey decided, Justin knew a lot more about than she did. His soft voice had a way of commanding her attention without even seeking it and his gaze caught hers in a lingering entrancement more than once. By the end of the evening, she was smitten with her caretaker. His manners reeked of private education. What amazed her was that he was still single. She sat back in her chair and stifled a yawn. Full and warm - a lethal combination to a pregnant woman.

Justin moved back his chair and stood. "You're tired. Forgive me. I'm inclined to get carried away on subjects that interest me. I'll clear the table and clean up a bit…"

Abbey quickly stood up, hating for evening to end, but knowing it must. "No, I'm not tired. I'll clean up. It's been a lovely evening. I haven't enjoyed myself so much for ages."

"I'm glad. But I insist that I be allowed to finish what I've started." Justin placed the empty bowls on the tray. "Now sit back down and I'll bring you a cup of tea before I go."

"But…" Abbey protested.

"I insist." Justin left no room for her to argue further. "I won't be long. Now please, resume your seat by the fire."

Abbey shrugged and did as she was told. Justin obviously wasn't a man who took no for an answer. She stretched out, kicked off her shoes and wriggled her toes in front of the fire. It had never burnt this well since she had lived here.

***

Once in the kitchen, Justin relinquished the tray with a flick of his wrist. Instead of it crashing to the floor, the whole thing vanished and the plates and bowls reappeared in the cupboard in neat, clean rows.

"Since when are you able to eat mortal food?" Adrinia queried from the corner of the kitchen.

Justin's skeletal features creased into an angry scowl. "What are you doing here?"

Adrinia came further into the room. "That's a nice greeting, I must say."

His gaze flicked to the door, he nodded his head and it closed with a snap. "Go away. The evening's gone well. I don't want you spoiling it."

"It's only your box of tricks and spells that made it so perfect."

Justin glared. "One small sleeping spell, the rest was my gifts. It doesn't count."

"Oh, you're so touchy," Adrinia admonished.

"Abbey needed a little cajolement, that's all."

"Oh, it's Abbey now, not Abigail. You are moving with the modern times. So what are you doing? Courting her? That makes a change. It's usually straight to bed. You must be getting chivalrous in your old age."

"She's not like that. I've told you, she's different. Her nerves are ragged, she needs tenderness."

Adrinia laughed. "Oh come on. Your little protégées are as hard as nails. Please don't tell me that you expect her to fall in love with you without the aid of your stinking essence." She paused when Justin turned his back on her. "Oh, you poor deluded idiot. You really do expect her to fall in love with you, don't you? Can't you see that she's in love with a mortal? How can you compete with that?"

"I don't need to. She's falling for me already. It's only taken dinner and a few compliments."

"You're fooling yourself, you know."

Justin's smile was cold and hard as he stared at the shimmering shadow. "We'll see who the deluded one is." With a flick of his clawed hand, the tray was filled with tea for one. He picked it up and gave Adrinia a sly smirk as he walked out of the kitchen.

"Yes, Justin, we will see," she whispered. "When Abigail's true love comes calling, you'll see who she wants and it won't be you."

***

Abbey sat on her bed and fiddled with her watch. The darn thing still refused to work. Hearing the rattle of cups in the kitchen she smiled. Justin was making tea, so it must be around three o'clock. He said that was the civilized time for a break – in between lunch and dinner. His ideas were so antiquated.

That man had slipped into her life so easily that it was hard to remember a time when he wasn't in it. For the past few months he had been a god send. Justin sorted out her days. Boredom was a thing of the past now. He anticipated her every need, sometimes before she even knew it herself. Good husband material, her mother would call him. Abbey sighed. But Shaun was the one still constantly on her mind. She missed him more than ever.

Justin said her idea to sell the cottage and run, was not a good one. But what if he's wrong? She'd been hesitant to tell him about Shaun at first, but he had a way of drawing things out of her. He did agree on one point. To detach herself more from her parents and just keep in touch by letter alone. Justin's lack of condemnation brought tears to her eyes whenever she thought of it. Deep down she knew he loved her, despite her elephant size. But she couldn't love him back. Not when she loved Shaun so much. She was very fond of him. Some marriages were built on far less and survived, but was it enough for her? She chewed her bottom lip anxiously. She had no idea what to do.

When Justin kissed her, it was nice enough. When he held her in the evening and read to her, it felt right. But there was no passion between them. No spark that made her yearn for more. Abbey stood and pushed on her slippers. Confusion ruled her recently. Her mind, permanently foggy, her thoughts a jumble of passing words. All she knew for sure was that Justin wanted her and all the baggage that came with it. She should be thanking her lucky stars. So why did she feel so worried? A thought nagged her about Justin. Could a man really be so perfect? He had no flaws she could see. She searched for them constantly. But he was always so congenial and attentive.

Justine had packed her away for a nap and said that tonight was going to be special. His expectation weighed heavily on her shoulders. He was going to propose. She just knew it. How could she turn him down? Give up the chance to be a family with a man who truly cared about her?

***

Adrinia looked around the kitchen and grimaced. He was actually preparing lunch without magic. How domesticated. She sneered at the stupid smile on his face. He loved every moment of this mortal existence. It won't be for long. She'd make sure

99

of that. "Well, how's it all going?" she asked and forced herself to sound interested. "We really need to keep in touch. I haven't seen you in days."

"Everything's going according to plan," Justin gloated. "Like I said it would."

"Ah, but you're using the stronger essence. I can smell its magic lingering in the air. What happened to leaving everything to love?"

"Abbey gets confused easily. I use it to help her see what's good for her."

"What about O'Donnell?"

Justin frowned and angrily banged the seasoning jar onto the counter. "What about him? He's in the past. Far from her thoughts."

"Are you sure? Love is one of the strongest emotions to fight."

He threw a dark scowl at the undulating shadow. "Why do you care?"

"Oh, I don't. I'm just making conversation. So tonight's going to be the big night?"

"Yes," Justin replied. "And it'll be perfect."

"Do make sure you're gentle," Adrinia chided. "It's been a long time since you bedded a mortal. I've seen you mounting the slave girls and you don't always have their feelings in mind."

"They're demons bred for such tasks. Don't worry, I know how to make love to a real woman."

"All right, don't get touchy. I'm only thinking of you. She's quite far into her pregnancy. You've never left it this late before."

"Everything will be fine. It's a full moon tonight. It'll give the transformation spell an extra boost."

"Are you sure it'll work? After all, a few months ago you insisted you weren't going to use it on this one. "

"Yes, but I feel I owe you something for your companionship over the years. You need a girl successor, and I'll give you one. That's my gift to you."

"But what if you're left with nothing after all this effort?"

Justin picked up the salad bowl and placed it on the tray alongside everything else. "I won't be."

"And if the mortal finds out about his child and comes here? He won't let them go without a fight."

"Then he'll die." Justin said, adjusting his peach cravat with his filth - encrusted claws.

"But this situation is most unusual. Abigail actually loves O'Donnell. An emotion the others were incapable of feeling. I admit that she does seem to be different from the others. But if the queen isn't controlling her. Who is?"

"No one, you fool. She has her own freewill - a soul. O'Donnell's no threat. Abbey loves me. I can feel her need for me growing stronger every day."

"Oh yes, I'm sure she's like a dog on heat," Adrinia said sarcastically.

"Go away, Adrinia, I've plans tonight and they don't include you spying on us." He picked up the tray and a single red rose appeared in a small crystal vase, on it. "Ah, that's better. A rose for a rose," with a flick of his wrist the door opened and slammed firmly shut behind him.

"We'll see who your precious Abigail wants," Adrinia ground out.

***

Aveline stood in front of Shaun with her hands on her hips. "You've got to stop moping about. It's been months since Abbey left. She'll be married by now and I bet she's not even cast a single thought your way. You're a handsome man, son. Go and find yourself a good Irish girl who'll love you the way you deserve."

Shaun stared into the open fire. He heard his mother's shrill voice invading his dark thoughts, but he didn't want to listen. He longed to forget his silver-haired viper, who slithered into his dreams night after night, but it was so hard. Even though the pillow she slept on had long ago lost the lemony scent of her hair, he still hugged it to his chest every night.

It didn't matter how much time passed, he still loved her desperately. Night after night it rolled around his head, what happened to make Abbey change so drastically? He knew that she loved him. Every fibre of his being told him so. When she intimated that he hadn't been her first, she had lied. Why did she want him to hate her? Because he never would. He had her soul, so he was permanently attached to her, no matter what. He stared long and hard at Aveline. "What did you say to Abbey when I'd left that day?"

Aveline closed her eyes and sighed heavily. "Oh, no. Not this again, Shaun. I've told you a hundred times it's no word of mine that turned her away."

Shaun felt his frustration bubble like boiling water on a stove. "You must have said something," he shouted, banging his fist on the coffee table. "Tell me again. What was said between you?"

"Shaun, we've been through this a million times. I'm tired of your constant accusations. Don't you think I grieve for your pain, son? If I could bring her back, believe me I would. But she's gone and you've got to accept it, because I can't go on being battered by your accusing eyes anymore." Aveline's sob caught in her throat and she reached inside the pocket of her apron for a tissue. "I've lost my husband. Am I to lose you too?"

Shaun cursed under his breath and looked away from his mother's tear filled eyes. He had promised himself, after the nightmare, to forget Abbey. But still she plagued him. "I'm sorry, mother. I don't know what I'm thinking half the time. I know you miss Morgan. He was a good man. I'd never choose a better father. He treated me like his own flesh and blood, and I'll always be grateful for that."

Aveline blew her nose. "He was a good husband and he loved you very much."

"And I loved him. I know I shouldn't keep going on, but I can't help myself. It's like she's cast a spell over me. Do you believe in magic, mother?"

Aveline shook her head. "Please let it lie. You've got to get over this."

"Well, do you?

"I believe there are things we can't begin to understand."

"But isn't that what magic is? As soon as I saw Abbey I knew she was the one for me. I feel like I've lived my life waiting for her. We're meant to be together. I know it."

"It's an evil influence, rather than magic, that holds you trapped. Abbey let you to believe she was something she's not. She'll wreck your life if you let her."

Shaun covered his face with his hands. "Evil can't make something that beautiful."

Aveline knelt down in front of him. Gently taking his wrists, she lowered his hands and looked into his eyes. "Yes it can. Beauty can be manufactured. It traps a person and can make them kill. True beauty lies within the heart. You *will* get through this, son. You and me together. Like we've always done."

Shaun nodded, closed his eyes and took a deep breath. "What would I do without you, mother? There's no woman on God's green earth I trust more. I know you'll never do anything to hurt me. I suppose you're one of the rare ones who has beauty inside and out."

***

Aveline hugged Shaun tightly. No words could hurt her more deeply than those. She fought back her threatening tears. How many times must she pray for forgiveness? It was because of her lies that her son's heart was still beating. Abigail had gone to meet her destiny, like her mother. But it wasn't Shaun's destiny to be bound to her. Oh no. She'd fight to the death to protect him. Aveline kissed his head and got up. "Come on, sit down eat your breakfast. Let this be the start of a new, happier day." She sat at the table and poured them both a mug of tea. "Have you seen the new barmaid in the Clover Inn? She's been asking folk about you for the past few weeks."

A half smile lifted the corner of Shaun's mouth. "Has she now. Perhaps I'll go there for a pint of the black stuff on me way home tonight. I need to return Rosa's truck before she turns me into a frog."

"And how much do you intend to charge her?" It would be another free offering. She knew that for a fact. The old sow was always asking for a hand-out. Her boy was a soft touch. His easy going nature would have him conned out of his underwear if it wasn't for her sharp eye on him.

Shaun sipped his tea. "A fair price."

"I bet she doesn't pay you a penny," Aveline grumbled. "You're too soft with that old con woman."

"She'll pay. Rosa always does, in one way or another."

"It's the other way that worries me. All her hocus pocus nonsense. It fills your mind with rubbish. She's an old witch to be sure."

They ate breakfast in a lighter mood and Aveline felt a dark weight lift from her. The tide had changed and left Abigail Newlands far behind them.

***

Shaun left the house and climbed in to his truck feeling better than he had for months. Was he insane to even think his mother would drive Abbey away? Why would she? She always nagged him to settle down. He would try his best. But his heart would always lie with Abbey. He pulled up outside a brightly painted, old fashioned wagon caravan. He saw Rosa straight away. Wrapped snugly in a blue wool shawl, she sat on its well trodden wooden steps, puffing on a white clay pipe.

102

She looked at him in feigned surprise.

"Oh, tis yourself, Shaun. I wasn't expecting you. Would you be wanting a cup of fresh tea?"

He watched the old gypsy's weather-beaten face wrinkle into a semblance of an innocent smile. She was a sly one. He said he would be back today. "Go on then Rosa, I'll chance a brew with you."

He jumped out of the truck and followed her into the caravan. As usual the place was spotless. He often wondered if she lived there at all. Whatever the time of day he called, not cushion was creased or a vase out of place.

"If its copper you'll be wanting, you'll need more than one cup of tea, boy. For I'm sorry to say the wait is a long one. The King Leprechaun stole me purse last night from right under me nose." Rosa poured the boiled water into a china teapot.

Shaun eyed the two cups already set out. "Oh, I see you were expecting someone then?"

"I've the third eye, lad, of course I expect someone. But an idea did come to me about our dilemma. How about I read your leaves, in exchange for any coin I owe?"

Shaun sighed. He was prepared to haggle over money, but maybe a reading would be better. A bit of good news wouldn't go amiss and Rosa was well known for her accuracy with the tea leaves. "How can I turn down such an offer?" He grinned, taking the small china cup and saucer Rosa offered. "But it does seem a might strange that your third eye didn't see the little people coming for your purse."

"Come on, boy. I'm an old woman. Too frail to wonder on the minds of a leprechaun."

"Ha," Shaun bellowed. "Frail my bare behind. I've seen you chase off people with a broom, quicker than a spring rabbit. Admit it. You're richer than the King Leprechaun himself! And me nothing more than a poor beggar man. Shame on you for taking advantage of me good nature."

Rosa laughed. "Poor in money, makes you rich in love, boy."

"I think I'd still rather have the coins."

Rosa sat down. Her dark eyes stared at him intently. "What ails you, my boy?"

Shaun shuffled uneasily in his seat. Rosa was like a dog with a bone if she thought something was wrong. "Nothing for you to worry your head about. Now leave me to enjoy me tea."

Rosa gave a snort of indifference, but Shaun wasn't fooled. They were closer than friends. She was more like a second mother. They drank their tea in silence, with him trying to ignore her probing stare.

"Come on then. I need to see those leaves while they're still warm," Rosa said and took his empty cup and swirled around the dregs. She quickly up - ended it into the saucer and turned it twice clockwise and then once anticlockwise. Turning over the cup, she peered inside.

Shaun looked at the saucer and frowned. "Most of the leaves are in the saucer," he complained.

Rosa huddled over the saucer. "Hush, boy. I'm concentrating."
He sat back in the chair and allowed her to do what his mother called 'hocus pocus.' When Rosa's hand began to shake, he didn't think much of it. She often did strange things whilst reading the leaves. But when her face took on a grey tinge, he really became concerned. "Are you feeling all right, Rosa?"

***

Rosa heard Shaun's voice in the far distance of her mind, but it was too far away to be intelligible. Her body felt light, her head dizzy, slightly disoriented, which confirmed that her spirit body was no longer on the mortal plane. She had astral projected many times, she knew the feeling well. But on her terms, with her spirit guide's protection. This, she had no control over, or what waited for her. Rosa saw she was standing on a sheer rock precipice, and judging by the tormented screams below, it was the edge of the underworld. The voices of the damned, entombed for all eternity, screeched out their torment in the freezing fog swirling below. Each was willing to kill a mortal if it ended their torment. Rosa shuddered. This was no place for her. It was too dangerous even with protection. Who had brought her here? Not Justin. It didn't feel like a demonic vision. This one had far too much power. Judging by the writhing dark beings around her, the shadow queen had a hand in this. But why?

Rosa pressed her back against the wall. If she fell there was no way back. Flames shot up, like fiery serpents, from the bowels of the earth. They quickly became an inferno in front of her, but she felt no heat. Only a bone chilling coldness that no furs or blankets could mask. Within the flames she watched as shadowy figures danced to a silent macabre tune. It horrified, yet fascinated her. She had heard of the shadow realm, but never experienced it. Now, she was in its heart. The air became suffocatingly thick and Rosa took deep breaths to calm herself. The airless vibration held nothing but evil intent and she wished she had her crystals to shield her from its icy influence. She noticed the shadowy dancers had stopped gyrating and now stood to rigid attention, a prickle of fear raised the hairs on her neck. From the middle of the flames, a clawed foot stepped out. Rosa instinctively took a step back. Attached to the foot emerged a misshapen beast dressed in rags. In his scaly arms he carried a heavily pregnant woman. She was nude, but she wasn't at all perturbed. Everything in a vision was symbolic. Nakedness signified vulnerability.

The woman's silver hair shone through the filth that covered her. Rosa recognized her immediately. Abigail. Which one, she didn't know. So the beast must be Justin Montgomery. A caricature of the man he once was.

"Pleased to meet you Lord Montgomery," she whispered. For two hundred years her family had fought his curse. But no-one had seen him since his return from hell. She felt a moment's compassion. He had paid a high price for the crimes he had committed on the earth. She wished she had the power to end his misery. But purgatory was forever. No magic would change that.

Rosa forced herself to concentrate on the message. She watched Justin put the woman down and hug her possessively to his side. Abigail stood immobile; her eyes vacant. Rosa worked at a furious pace to interpret the vision. He was telling her that he had another Abigail. But how? Morgan's daughter was the final one and she was protected by a shielding spell and an Esor soul.

Rosa frowned. Why was this vision in Shaun's tea leaves? It didn't make sense. Unless... she reeled in horror. He had found Morgan's daughter and bought her back to Ireland. But that was impossible. She would know. But not if the shielding spell had collapsed. Aveline couldn't hold this secret. If she knew, the world would too. Rosa shook her head. It was so confusing, she needed to focus more. She had to work out the message before the vision ended.

This Abigail was pregnant. Nothing new. They always were before they entered the cottage. So this couldn't be Morgan's daughter! The Esor spirit would never allow wantonness. Love had to be in the equation. Rosa sighed. Everything inside her screamed that this *was* Morgan's daughter. If Justin had her, he also held the most powerful soul of all under his spell. If an Esor was corrupted, the cascade of consequence would reverberate throughout the physical and spiritual world.

***

Adrinia stood in the shadows and smiled. The vision had worked. The price for it from Neberius, the Marquis of Hell, was high. He had taken many of her slaves to add to his hellish legion. He was so greedy for power. Easily won over. But it was worth the cost. The old witch was putting two and two together and coming up with the jackpot.

Once she knew that Justin had the silver-haired slut she would do everything in her power to get her back. Abigail Newlands was her cross to bear. She had made her father a promise to protect her; she would never go back on that. Adrinia chuckled. The old witch had been a thorn in her side for years, now it was time to get rid of it. She may be well protected, but Abigail was her weakness. If she got lucky she might be rid of them both in one swoop. When Justin murders Shaun, she would make sure that his precious Abigail saw everything. Her hate for Justin would hold no bounds. That should cure his fantasy of love. Then it would be open season on Abigail, O'Donnell and the gypsy.

Chapter Sixteen

Rosa's fears were confirmed when Shaun suddenly burst through the flames in front of her. Of course it wasn't him really. It was another symbol. But it scared her. To lose Shaun would be like losing a limb. She couldn't let that happen. Rosa watched him try to pull the woman from Justin's arms. He was so hot headed, just like Morgan. Act first and think later. The shadows peeled themselves from the walls and wrapped around him like a seething dark blanket, immobilising him. The beast plunged his clawed hand into Abigail's belly and pulled out an infant. No blood or gore marred the scene. It depicted Abigail as an empty vessel. Which all her predecessors were before the Esor got involved. The child was ominously silent as Justin held it to his bony chest.

His eyes, black as coal, fixed on Rosa's face and narrowed. Wet lips pulled back into a mocking grin, goading her to try and rescue it. "The woman and child are mine," he rasped. "If he tries to interfere, I'll squash him like I did his father."

Rosa felt sick to her stomach. Visions never spoke directly. They were like silent movies you could only watch. This was more like a play, with characters. "I know what you are about queen of the shadows," she shouted. "This vision is your doing, not Justin Montgomery's. What do you want from me?"

Immediately the vision began to fade and Rosa felt herself pulled backwards at a speed much faster than she would have liked. Maybe the shadow queen was angry she had uncovered her little ruse. She had been around too long to be fooled by such a weak ploy. She winced in pain as her spiritual body connected back to her physical one with a hard jolt. She sat, unable to move until the two bodies became realigned with each other. When she was finally able to open her eyes she took a deep breath, exhaling slowly.

"Thank God you're back. You had me worried sick, Rosa," Shaun said urgently.

"I think we've more to worry about than my little jaunt, me boy."

"Why? What's going on?"

"Who's the woman, boy? The one who's stolen your heart."

Shaun looked away and pulled his lips into a stubborn line. "You've been listening to gossip."

"You know me well enough to know I never speak to the Gadjikane or the Foros."

"Oh, hush yourself woman and stop with your Gallic pronunciations of the towns people. Don't you be thinking I don't know that your ears are always flapping for gossip."

"Not gossip, boy. Information that I can use. So tell me, why have I not heard so much as a blackbird's cry about it from you?"

"I met her when you were away on one of your herb gathering expeditions. I'd rather not talk about it. It's done with."

Rosa gave a derisive sniff. "Did she have eyes the colour of sapphires?"

"Do you remember what you said the last time you read my leaves. It's a pity you didn't warn me *against* her." He paused, his eyes narrowing with suspicion. "Have you seen her?"

Rosa's stomach lurched in disappointment. She had hoped that Shaun would say that he didn't know what she was talking about. His last message didn't mention Morgan's daughter. Yet thinking back, it had described her. Why hadn't she realised that? "No, I haven't. Oh Jesus, Shaun. What a mess. Tell me what happened?"

"Rosa, do we need to go over this. I…"

"Yes, we do. How long were you two together?"

Shaun sighed heavily. "Half a day and one night." He laughed, hard and bitterly. "Not quite the romance you hoped for, huh?"

"Did you… I mean when you…" she frowned, unused to being delicate. She always spoke her mind and to hell with those who didn't like it. "Did you take precautions?"

Shaun jumped up. "What? For God's sake, stop woman."

"I need to know. Now stop acting like a coy little boy." She saw the hurt and anger on his face and knew it wasn't her words causing it. Abigail had done this. But why? She didn't have a black soul. It wasn't in her to hurt anyone intentionally.

"Well… no," Shaun stammered. "These things happen… I mean it's not as though we planned it or anything."

Rosa closed her eyes and groaned. It was far worse than she imagined. Abigail's child was Shaun's. "You damn ejit. Haven't you learned anything from me? I explained years ago how to stop a child being conceived?" For years her ancestors had tried to break the curse of the silver-haired women, now she was a breath away from success, he had ruined everything.

"I didn't think to make the herbal tea. Anyway, I'd be proud for Abbey to have my child."

"How long has it been since you last saw her?"

"Look, enough now. I don't know what's going on in that head of yours, but…"

"HOW LONG?" Rosa shouted.

"Six months, three days and… um…," Shaun checked his watch, "Thirty seconds. Is that precise enough for you?"

"Have you any idea where she is?" Rosa saw Shaun's face whiten in pain. Of course he didn't. Nothing would stop him from going to her once he knew about the child.

"Me mother said she probably went back to her fiancé in London."

Her lips drew together in a tight line of annoyance. "Aveline knows about this?"

"Yes, she met Abbey. Now are you going to tell me why you're so interested?"

Rosa shook her head and picked up the cups. "No. You have to go now. I've got one of me headaches."

"Headaches! What headaches? I…"

She pushed Shaun towards the front door. "Don't you be questioning an old lady's ailments, Shaun O'Donnell. You'll get what I owe you tomorrow."

"But I need you to drive me back home," Shaun protested.

Rosa slammed the door behind him. "The walk will do you good, boy" she shouted through it.

She hurried into the kitchen, opened the bottom cupboard and took out a tightly wrapped parcel and thumped it on the worktop. The paper around it was old and crackled with age. Tied in twine, it took a few seconds to cut the threads. Twenty years had passed since it saw the light of day. Passed down from her family, it contained many secret charms and spells from the old days. The pages were fragile and crackled in protest when she carefully turned them. "I need a rescue charm. Something to protect Shaun's child," she mumbled. She clicked her tongue in annoyance and turned the book over. She forgot the spells started from the back of the book and then worked their way forward to the present day. Magic was always so topsy turvy.

"Ah, here you are. She fingered the hand written script. Many thought the gypsies illiterate thieves. But how little they knew. Her great grandmother wrote in beautiful calligraphy. It would put those educated Gadjikane to shame. She quickly got out her oil burner and white candles. After arranging them on the table she lit them and poured frankincense oil into the burner. She needed the help of the spirit world for this spell and the scent of the oil would bring them near.

Rosa sat on the chair. She closed her eyes and forced her mind to still its endless chatter. Then she mentally asked her guide and helpers to draw close to her. She felt the familiar pressure of the spirit world vibrations within minutes and once she was sure they were ready, Rosa spoke the words to the spell in Gallic.

"Bring me a light, for this baby in arms.
Cast out the darkness, which cause is to harm.
I send you protection to wrap yourself in.
To keep you protected from devils and sin.
Let the breath of my ancestors blow away the decay.
And the love of the Esor, protect you this day."

An explosion of light in front of Rosa's eyes caused her to wince even thought they were closed, but she held fast. The white light of protection was powerful. It needed all her concentration. When the light began to fade to a dull glow, she opened her eyes. The candles had almost burnt out and the oil had all but disappeared. The spell was cast – hopefully it would bide them some time.

It was too soon to tell Shaun about all this. He was blinded by love and would react like Morgan had. Without thought or plan. She had to make sure everyone was safe before they faced Justin Montgomery. This time no one would die at his hands, not if she could help it. The only ammunition she had was Shaun. He carried the light of the Esor within him. The one thing that would send Justin and the shadow queen back to the underworld and close hell's doorway forever.

Rosa thumbed through the ancient pages. She had no idea how to waken the Esor light and by the looks of it neither did her ancestors. Many believed they were a myth. But her family knew the truth and guarded their secrets well. Only they can see the chosen ones. Mortals chosen to defend the world if hell's door re-opened. And it was open – wide. Disease, famine, war were all caused by the dark ones manipulating the mortals. It had to stop before the world withered and died.

The spells would help, but they were no match for the shadow queen's power. She had to rely on more up to date things, which were stored away in her head. It was a shame she had no children to pass it on to. Raydean and Hillseth, her ancestors, had seen to that. Because of their rash actions, disaster had descended upon them all.

Having a husband and family would make her vulnerable. Something demons looked for and preyed on. The shadow queen was looking for a weakness in her, but she wouldn't find one easily. She had chosen years ago to never have loved one that could be used against her.

Rosa fingered through the books yellowed pages. She had to make up a talisman for Shaun. He needed all the protection he could get. This was her last chance to stop Justin. In a few more years, she would be too old to fight anymore. She had made a promise to Morgan to keep his daughter safe, she would keep that promise whatever the cost.

***

Rosa pulled her shawl tighter around her shoulders and knocked on Aveline's front door. The wind was bitter, bringing with it freezing misery and she longed for a hot, strong cup of tea to warm her aching bones. But not before her goods were delivered. She had picked and bound together the herbs she needed for Shaun's talisman, under the magic power of a full moon. She was lucky to catch it. The next full moon wasn't due for another month according to her chart. The door opened and Shaun, standing in his boxer shorts, frowned in bewilderment.

"I've made you this," she said, thrusting a small leather pouch out to him "Make sure you wear it around that handsome neck of yours for the next few months."

Shaun rubbed his eyes and yawned loudly. "What… why?"

"Don't ask questions. I'm giving you a gift, boy. If you don't wear it, I'll be mortally offended and might be inclined to put a curse on you."

Shaun took the pouch which was secured with a black bootlace tie. He turned it over in his hand. "You'll curse me for not wearing this?"

"That I will, boy, so take heed."

"Rosa you know what me mothers like. One whiff of curse talk and she'll be after you with a broom." Shaun glanced at the clock on the wall. "It's one o'clock in the morning. What have I told you about roaming these fells alone?"

"Why, do you think I might get lucky, boy?"

"You know exactly what I mean. Look, wait a minute. I'll pull on some clothes and drive you home."

"Away with you," she protested. "I roamed these hills before you were born. Now go back to your bed and stop nagging me like an old woman."

"You'll worry me to the grave with your shenanigans."

"Tis a fine mess you'd be in if it wasn't for me, Shaun O'Donnell. Anyway, only the good die young." She waved a gloved hand in his general direction and disappeared into the darkness.

On the way back to her caravan, Rosa pondered the problems that loomed over all their heads. The shadow queen was planning something despicable in that devilish mind of hers? She had formed an alliance with Justin, that was obvious – but why? Aveline had a lot to explain. She knew the risks involved with having Abigail in her home. She should have told her immediately. Whatever she said that drove Morgan's daughter away must have been good. The girl was obviously in love with Shaun. Her Esor spirit would never let her lie with him otherwise. Rosa sighed heavily. The heavy burden placed on her shoulders weighed her down as she walked. It was twenty years since she and Aveline had spoken. But now the dye was cast, Aveline had to help her. Whether she wanted to or not.

***

Abbey wrapped a large towel around her and left the bathroom, troubled deeply by the unfolding events. Justin had proposed over dinner and she had accepted. He had made such an effort with candles on the table and a wonderful dinner. The ring slipped onto her finger looked antique and stunningly beautiful. It only seemed right she should agree.

But now free from the romance of the evening, her mind regained clarity – and second thoughts settle in to burden her. With Justin everything was perfect. No doubts in that. Moving in together was practical for them both, she had a spare room. Justin was at the end of his tenancy agreement and he visited so much, what did it matter anyway? But now everything felt more real and she wasn't ready to give up her heart. Shaun still had it, whether he wanted it or not. Abbey grimaced as a nagging headache took its discomfort up a notch. It always happened whenever she analysed her feelings for him. A sick migraine appeared that only Justin could cure. She felt like two separate people in one body. One wanted Justin and the other desperately loved Shaun. Abbey sat on the bed and rubbed herself dry. Would he expect anything physical tonight? She tutted, annoyed at her naivety. Of course he would. He didn't see that she was as big as a house. He said a woman who carried a life inside her was beautiful. Anxiety made her heart palpitate. Maybe it was time to let the past go. Justin was kind and honest; she doubted whether he knew the meaning of duplicity. For the baby's sake, she needed to concentrate on building a life. She would write to her parents tomorrow. There was going to be a wedding! It might heal the rift between them too. They didn't need to know Justin wasn't the father.

Abbey looked at her comfy t-shirt nightdress and pulled a face. She could hardly wear that on their first night together. She reached under the bed and pulled out a large square box. A present from Justin a few days ago to cheer her up. But it hadn't, and she had stashed it away after a feigned, delighted thank you.

The nightdress was not something she would wear. The dark brown, sheer material clung to her swollen breasts and dropped to the floor in an annoying muddy looking puddle. But it did disguise her bump beautifully. Maybe that's what Justin meant by cheering her up. You couldn't see through the material, but it gave the illusion that you could.

Abbey slipped it on and then nervously picked at the frill around the neckline to give it more height. It barely covered her breasts. The lace was irritatingly stiff and unyielding. She scratched around it and two welts formed on her neck. She sat at her dressing table and brushed her hair as she mulled over the wedding guest list. Justin never spoke about his family, or where he came from. Come to think about it, there was little she did know about him.

"What are you thinking about that makes you look so serious?" Justin asked, coming further into the room.

Abbey jumped, her brush clattering to the floor. "Oh, you startled me. I didn't hear you come in."

"Let me," he rushed to pick it up. His eyes bright with admiration as he handed her the brush. "The nightwear becomes you. I knew it would. I've made you some hot chocolate with a little added something for your headache." Justin placed the cup and saucer on her bedside table and pulled back the silk sheets.

"Thanks, that's really thoughtful." He always knew when she had a headache coming.

"Are you sure you want me to stay. If you've changed your mind..." Justin paused. His half finished sentence hung in the air like a final declaration.

Abbey licked her lips nervously. This was her ticket out. It was on the edge of them to say yes, she had, when he squatted down in front of her. He placed his hands on her knees and stared, his head cocked to one side. "I know you're worried that all this is too soon. Even I have wondered how this has come about. But I do love you, never doubt that."

Abbey looked away. She couldn't bear to see the sincerity in his eyes. He would be so hurt if she told him how she felt. Awkwardly fiddling with her engagement ring, she fought for the right words. A faint scent of roses drifted towards her. Her nostrils flared at the familiar aroma. His aftershave smelt sweeter than usual. It was a distraction she could do without. As she pondered her dilemma, her thoughts began to lose their earlier urgency. She looked into Justin's eyes, filled with adoration and her doubts began to melt away like snow on a warm day. "No, I haven't changed my mind."

"You do know how much I love you and the baby," he whispered.

Sparkling emerald eyes pushed their way into Abbey's consciousness. She squeezed her eyes closed and willed the image to go away. She mustn't think of Shaun. Not now, not ever. She opened her eyes and looked into his. "Yes, I do. But..."

Justin's lips touched hers in a butterflies embrace. He pulled back. "Shhh. There's no need for more words. We both know this is how it should be. Just you and me."

"And the baby," Abbey added.

He smiled. "That goes without saying." He swept her from the stool and laid her on the bed. His next kiss filled with more urgency. For a second she hesitated, as doubts clamoured back. But they quickly faded, replaced with a great need to feel

Justin's skin against hers. She watched through half closed lids as Justin dragged off his clothes with the eagerness of a teenager. Fuelled with a sudden desire of her own, Abbey felt impatience as she waited for him to come back to her side. The soft whimper beside her went almost unnoticed until it grew louder, more insistent. She turned her head towards the direction of it and she stared, shocked to the core at the woman staring back her. She was stunning, yet her eyes were ugly. Like two dark holes filled with poison. Dressed in a red evening gown, with a crown of what looked like rubies on her head, she looked like a queen. The woman held a dark, wriggling animal, who whimpered to be put down. Abbey sat up and pushed Justin to one side. Her mind was foggy, she couldn't think straight. But her eyes could see very clearly.

Justin sat on the bed beside her. He took her hand. "What's wrong my love?"

"Can't you see her? Look." Abbey pointed to the woman, then stood and frowned at the empty space. "But I saw... I mean...."

"You saw what? No one's here. Just you and me," he whispered.

"No, I saw a woman in a red dress, wearing a crown and holding some sort of animal. She was watching us and her eyes..." she turned to Justin, filled with horror. "They looked so cold and evil."

Justin held Abbey's face lightly in his hands. "Look at me my darling. You're nervous and your imagination is running riot. Remember when you told me how scared you were of the shadows and that you thought they were alive. The mind can play horrible tricks on you. That's all this is, my love. There's no one else here. I promise you."

Abbey opened her mouth to reply and was silenced by Justin's lips. Soon her body began to relax, despite her confusion. The smell of Justin's rose scented aftershave settled her nerves and then all thoughts of the woman evaporated like steam hitting a window. He pulled her beside him and moulded her body to his, deepening the kiss. A tiny voice of protest echoed deep in her mind, but she became too lost in foggy emotions to pay attention to it.

Chapter Seventeen

Happiness rushed through Justin's veins like fine claret as he pulled Abbey closer. He had proved Adrinia wrong, she did love him. Didn't this prove it? He had to use a stronger essence of course, but only because that stupid, shadowy bitch had interrupted them. It had taken every bit of his strength to quell his rage when Abbey had pointed out Adrinia. Hadn't he told her enough times that she was different? Somehow Abbey sensed them in the shadows; he knew that from the irrational fear she had of them. But now she could actually *see* into them too and that spelt trouble.

Justin sighed as Abbey's soft lips opened to his like a flower in bloom. Her response was delightful, like a virgin bonding with her lover for the first time. When her arms threaded their way up his shoulders and pulled him close, his body tightened with desire. But this was no slave beneath him. He had to be careful. This was his future wife. The woman he loved with all his heart. Lost in the moment, Justin stopped using the essence. He didn't need to rob her of thoughts now; she wanted him as much as he desired her. He bathed in delight at her little moans of desire. Her skin felt smooth, soft and smelt vaguely of lemons. It was now his favourite fruit because it reminded him of her. He removed her nightgown with a mere thought and gasped in awe when he saw her naked body. It was perfect. Just as he imagined, despite her rounded middle. Justin reverently cupped a breast and suckled. A small stream of milk filled his mouth and he drank, making loud slurping noises as the nourishing flow became stronger. He didn't want to share any part of her with the child she carried, especially this. If he was lucky, it might die at birth. Plenty of babies did. Then she would be completely his.

*****

A moan of desire escaped through her half open lips as Justin teased her nipples into hard peaks with his tongue and then suckled them like a child. In her fog-filled mind it was Shaun's soft lips exploring her breasts, his hands caressing her skin, his body locked inside hers. She had waited so long for him to come back to her.

When Justin's words of love seeped through her dreams, Abbey started to become more aware who was in her bed. As though his voice had triggered a deeper emotion inside her. Her limbs were heavy, as though great weights pinned them down. With half open eyes, she saw Justin's face wreathed in ecstasy and her spirits sank. Why couldn't it be Shaun?

"No, my love. Let no-one else be in your thoughts tonight," he murmured in her ear.

A new unfamiliar fragrance filled the air. Abbey could feel herself floating in a misty ocean. Its warmth soothed her fears and calmed her wandering thoughts. When Justin's hand caressed her inner thigh, her body didn't tingle with excitement. But she accepted this was how it would be from now on. That thought caused something deep within her to rebel. Was second best the right option? Justin deserved better than that. This was wrong – she was wrong. Panic tightened her chest until she could hardly breathe. She had made a dreadful mistake? This had to end, but, her lips remained silent.

She grimaced beneath his lips, as a pungent smell invaded her senses. The putrefying stench of rotten meat, whipped her breath away. She tried to open her eyes, but they wouldn't budge. Desire still ruled her body, despite her doubts. Every nerve, every cell of her body screamed for Justin, yet her mind refused to be coerced. A light caress on her face stilled her erratic thoughts. "It's all right, my love. You're safe with me," Justin reassured her.

As quickly as it came the stench vanished and once again she could smell the reassuring fragrance of his aftershave. Her panic fuelled fears receded into a dense fog and the tingling of her body increased as Justin gently eased himself into her. Abbey waited for the same ecstasy she had felt with Shaun, but it didn't happen. Justin's lovemaking didn't stir a passion inside her. There were no fireworks, no raw desire gasping for fulfilment. Only a steady rhythm which left her deeply unfulfilled. A silent tear slid down her face. This was all she had left now. A lifetime of pretence.

***

Adrinia stood in the corner of the room and watched the love scene with a dispassionate eye. She could reverse Justin's spell and open Abbey's eyes in a heartbeat, allowing her to see what was really salivating above her. But that would only make him angry and he was so irrational when irked. For the transformation spell to work and change the unborn child into another silver-haired clone, he needs to take his true form. Adrinia chuckled. If his precious Abigail saw what was thrusting into her, she would die from sheer terror.

Her eyes darkened with jealousy as she watched Justin's gentle lovemaking. His grey, scaled skin, which covered his bowed legs right down to his clawed feet, was dry and flaking – yet her fingers yearned to caress it. She watched, catching her breath in longing, as his long tail, coated in callused, sagging skin, swished expectantly in the air. One day it would wave like that when she was beneath him. She accepted Justin's true form as part of him. She loved him for all his faults and failings. With each thrust of his body, Adrinia felt hers pulsate. She would give anything, do anything, to have him inside her cold, aching body. What had been the point of sending the vision to the gypsy, if she refused to tell O'Donnell the slut was at the cottage? He would have raced to her rescue by now and this debacle would not have happened. She would have her revenge on Abigail Newlands. This battle was lost, but the war had only just begun.

***

Aveline set the table for tea and placed the napkins beside the plates. When her front door knocker clanged ominously, she tutted in annoyance. She wanted tea to be special tonight. Shaun had turned the corner, she was sure of it. "It's open," she called impatiently.

"You'd better see who's waiting on your step before you invite them in," Rosa replied.

Aveline's hand came up and clutched her throat in panic. That was a voice she hoped never to hear again. She nervously wiped her hands on her apron and opened the door. She stared at Rosa, her chin jutting out defiantly. "What do you want?" she hoped her inhospitable attitude would drive the gypsy away. Rosa's taste in clothes hadn't changed much. She still wore a gaudy woollen shawl and an old fashioned calico dress that reached to her ankles. Her hair style was the same, greyer maybe, but still pulled back into a tight bun. The same gold hooped earrings dangled from her ears. She had lost count the amount of times she had itched to drag them out and pummel the old witches face into the ground.

"Well! Are you going to ask me in or keep me waiting here so I freeze to death?" Before Aveline could reply either way, Rosa pushed past her. Her eyes darted around the room. "Ah, so you still have Morgan's cross on the wall."

"Of course. He made it for the family. Why would I not have it on show?"

"Still as feisty as ever, I see. Now don't be getting all defensive. I've not come here for a fight."

Aveline didn't believe that for a second. The old witch was always up for a row. "What do you want?"

Rosa slowly sunk down onto an armchair and held her arthritic hands towards the open fire. "Ah, that's better. She turned her face, now flushed with heat and nodded to a vacant chair. "Sit yourself down then. We've things to discuss before your boy comes home."

Aveline perched herself on the edge of the sofa. She swallowed her irritation. "We've nothing to discuss."

Rosa screwed her face up with impatience. "Ah, but we have, to be sure. We both know what's occurred in this house and its put Shaun in great danger. If we're not careful he'll end up the same way as Morgan."

"What do you mean by that?" Aveline swallowed and felt the cold hand of dread squeeze her heart. Did she know about Abigail? Pray God, she didn't.

"Your boy is in love with Morgan's daughter and don't you be telling me otherwise, Aveline O'Donnell!"

Aveline's heart sank like a stone. Just when Shaun had moved forward, the old cow was going to dredge it all up again? "I've sorted that mismatch out already. Shaun's forgotten about it now. Don't you be going through other peoples dirty washing, Rosa Rizavoi."

"Did he forget about his child as well?"

Aveline gulped. Her stomached rolled sickeningly. A baby! No, it was too cruel – too terrible to contemplate. She was lying, because her nose was out of joint because she didn't run to her about Abigail. "What baby would that be?"

"Your grandchild, of course."

Aveline jumped up, her face twisted in anger. "You're a wicked liar. My Shaun's fathered no child."

"Yes, he has and deep down you know I'm telling the truth. I've no need to darken your doorstep otherwise. You should have told me Abigail was here. I could've done something, maybe even prevented the child being conceived."

"It could be anyone's. You know how the curse works. They copulate with anything that moves."

"But Morgan's daughter isn't cut from the same mould as her predecessors. I read Shaun's tea leaves today. Someone sent me a very powerful vision while I was doing it and it wasn't the beast from the cottage. They wanted me to know that Shaun's the father of Abigail's child. So even if you don't believe it, a demon does and you know what that means."

"Oh, God no," Aveline sank like a deflated balloon into the nearest chair. Her hands shook as she covered her face. This was her worst fear. No mortal can fight demons. They always win. Hell was on their side. She lowered her hands and stared at Rosa. If she maintained it wasn't true, the demon might believe it too. "Think about what you're saying. Abigail and Shaun are brother and sister. They'd never commit such a sin."

Rosa clicked her tongue, her stare hard and narrowed. "Oh, hush. You know as well as I there's no blood relationship between them. You've begun to believe your own lies. Shaun said that Abigail told you she was to be wed. Don't you think it's a might strange that she'd say that after she'd just climbed out of your son's bed?"

"They lie. You know that. This is none of your business. You've no right…"

"*Right*?" Rosa repeated. "I've got every *right*. My family dedicated their lives to this damn curse and I gave up the chance of having a family of my own. I promised to protect Abigail Newlands and I never go back on my word. Now you tell me the truth. Did you tell Abigail that she had bedded her brother?"

Aveline's glare wavered under Rosa's scrutiny. To hear her dreadful lie repeated back, made it sound even more terrible. She looked down and smoothed out her apron.

"Your silence says it all. Why? Why would you say such a terrible thing? Doesn't Morgan's love for his daughter mean anything to you?"

"That thing isn't my husband's daughter," Aveline cried. "She's…" she paused and search for a word that described Abigail properly. "Not real… not human as we know it. My son is flesh and blood. I have to protect him."

"You're so wrong, Aveline. We made sure Morgan's daughter is real flesh too."

"We?"

Rosa frowned. "Me and Morgan, you silly ejit."

"Then why does the demon call to her? You can't change what's to be. She'll always be cursed."

"You'll lose Shaun. If he ever finds out…"

"He'll never know if you keep that big mouth of yours closed."

"But Justin will come after him. It's inevitable. Shaun needs to be prepared for that. Only his sword of light can protect him now."

Aveline's brow wrinkled in confusion. "His sword of what?"

Rosa sat bolt upright in the chair. Her gaze unwavering. "That's something else we need to discuss. Shaun's a chosen one. A mortal picked by the Esor to carry the weapon of light. The only thing which will destroy demons."

"You're mad. My boy has no such thing. He's just a simple man."

"Oh shut up and listen, woman. Abigail has a pure Esor spirit. I should know. I put it there. If Justin corrupts it, hell will have a foothold on the Physical and Spiritual plane."

"Now I know you're mad. You'll never convince me that Abigail has an ounce of goodness inside her." Aveline got up and walked over to the fire. She held out her hands to the dancing flames. They were big tonight, crackling in the grate, yet she felt no warmth from them. Rosa was bringing nothing but a cold chill of trouble to her door. A hot lump of coal jumped out at her feet and she quickly stepped back from its searing heat. Aveline frowned, annoyed it had marked the rug. Damn coal kept spitting out recently. She used the scuttle and threw it back. The flames reared up and consumed it instantly. "You'll be telling me that the coal's alive next."

"Coal is only food for the flames," Rosa replied. "Fire demons have masters too. They don't burn so calmly for everyone. Otherwise there would be no need for firemen. Aveline, there are things Morgan never told you about his daughter. We didn't think it was necessary at the time. But the tide has changed and it's blowing nothing but trouble our way. It's time you knew everything.

I discovered long ago that the cursed women were inhabited by a soul so dark that it had no feelings except that to live. It fed off lust, malice and anger. All the silver-haired women died at child birth because the dark soul jumped from body to body. You know a mortal can't live without a soul. The moment Abigail O'Donnell came into the world, I used a shielding spell to prevent the dark one from entering her. The last time one of my ancestors used it, it fought a demon who brought pestilence to London. The black plague. She sent it straight back to hell. It's a very powerful spell. When the black soul was banished, I prayed for a good soul to take its place. One that would allow the child to evolve. My prayers were answered by the Esor. A tribe long forgotten, whose King used the universal power of love to rule. They allowed one of their people to blend with Abigail. I assumed that broke the curse. But now I realise some part of her is still bound to Justin. The Esor soul will try and protect her, but Justin's spells are strong. If he corrupts her and the child, the higher spheres of pure spirit will be tainted. They are all linked you see." Rosa shook her head. "Where will our souls go when we leave this life, if that happens? Abigail fell in love with Shaun and he loves her. Together they are a formidable force against the dark powers. They can close hell's door for good. Think about it. No more wars, disease or famine."

Aveline snorted and pursed her lips in disbelief. "I don't believe your silly story for a minute. Shaun's my flesh and blood. I'd know if he was special."

"Then tell me this. Has your boy got a birth mark shaped like a flower on his body?"

Aveline's stare widened. How did she know about that? "So what if he has?"

"All the chosen ones have the same mark. It's called the Fleur-di-lis. It's the symbol of goodness. The mark of the Esor. Abigail has it too. See the bigger picture, Aveline. Shaun and Abigail met, against all odds. Fell in love and conceived a child all in one day. You must know that's not normal. They came together because they had a commonality, the power of good.

Together they've conceived a child so pure and powerful, that its birth will help to heal the earth and repair the damage the dark ones have done. It's time we stopped running away from this. We need to fight back. But we can only do that if Abigail and Shaun are united."

Aveline felt sick to her stomach. The woman was mad. Rambling on about swords, pure spirits. Good fighting evil. God was in charge of all that, not them. "You're not the Almighty, Rosa. Only he is in charge of such things. My family have suffered enough? I'll not put my Shaun in Abigail's path."

"Have you had your ears closed?" Rosa snapped. "I'm here to help Shaun, not hurt him. I believe those two can win this fight."

"No. Leave us be. Take your madness and drown in it."

"It's not your choice to make. In the next few days the child will call to Shaun from its mother's womb. It's instinctual to go to a parent for help."

Aveline swallowed convulsively. Her throat felt like it was closing - suffocating her. If Rosa told Shaun any of this rubbish he would go to the cottage for sure. Her lies would be uncovered. He would hate her.

"As far as I'm concerned Shaun and Abigail are brother and sister. How they feel and what they did together was wrong. So let it lie, Rosa. Stop interfering."

"Are you going to say that to Justin Montgomery when he knocks at your door?"

Aveline eyed the wooden cross over the fireplace and quickly made the sign of a cross over her breast. "Morgan made sure he can't enter this house."

"That won't help you. The charm placed on that was the same one protecting Abigail from Justin. If it's failed her..." Rosa looked at the cross ominously.

"It'll protect us. I have faith."

"Your faith won't keep demons away."

Aveline glanced at the clock on the mantelpiece. Shaun would be home at any minute. Rosa had to go. "I need time to think. It's a lot to take in."

"How much time? The danger to your boy increases with every minute that passes."

Aveline paced the floor, agitatedly wringing her hands. "I don't know. I'll come to you next week and we can discuss it again. Now please go. Shaun will be wanting his tea."

"Next week's too long," Rosa replied. "You must come at the weekend. We need to work out a plan of action."

"All right," Aveline conceded.

Rosa stood and wrapped her shawl around her. "I'll be waiting. Don't make me come to you again. I won't be as polite next time."

***

Rosa felt a pinch of worry as she walked home. She hoped there were no fire demons hiding in the flames of Aveline's coal fire. They were the most discreet

118

spies a demon could use in a mortal's home. And they could be commanded to flare up and consume a whole city, never mind a house. Aveline's rooms were too dark. She needed to use a brighter light to keep the shadows away. But she won't listen. The stupid woman refused to believe what was staring her in the face. Rosa sighed as she trudged over the uneven ground of the fells. The wind held a chill to it tonight. It made her bones ache. She shuddered as it bit through her woollen shawl and she pulled it tighter around herself. Rosa made a mental note to light her gas burner instead of her candles when she got home. No demon was going to watch her from the shadows. Her back ached and her bones felt older than Methuselah, yet it didn't stop her picking the wild fennel she needed. Her herb cupboard was almost depleted. The cold weather made it harder each year to go out and harvest them. She needed chamomile, nettle, crab-apple, fennel and chervil. If she searched the lower fells, she might find at least some of them.

Rosa looked up at the half moon hovering over her head, like a huge, silvery balloon and tutted. The herbs were most powerful when picked under a full moon. But that isn't due for ages and she needed them now. She crossed a narrow wooden bridge. It creaked its complaints at the intrusion and bowed under her slight weight. One day it would break and send her plunging into the river below. Wouldn't that be a sight to see? The local gypsy floating dead, with her skirt around her ears. Rosa chuckled at the headline. It would be the only time her skirt was up so high.

She scanned the area for the herbs. Age might be upon her, but her eyesight was as good as anyone half her age. She saw the nettles and walked over to the small bush. As she bent over to put the small leaves into her leather pouch, Rosa paused. She straightened and watched a dark shape dart into the shadow of the trees. It wasn't an animal. She recognised the misshapen shadow that scuttled away. It was a shadow minion. She frowned and stared hard into the darkness. A trickle of apprehension followed the line of her spine and she reached into her pocket and pulled out a large quartz crystal. "I ask thee crystal to give me protection," she whispered. Immediately a white light enveloped her. It expanded upwards and outwards, like a giant bubble encircling her as she walked. Rosa's voice was calm and firm when she called. "What do you want, Queen of the shadows?"

The shimmering outline of a woman stood outside the perimeter of the light bubble. Rosa's gaze locked with hers. She knew not to look away. Dark ones thrived on fear. The woman's eyes turned black with fury, before she turned and disappeared into the nearest shadow cast by an oak tree. Rosa released her breath, unaware she had held it. A visit from the shadow queen herself. That madam was out to cause trouble. She had a heart colder than Jack Frost's. No mortal or demon was safe when she was around.

Rosa's arthritic bones pained her considerably by the time she got home. It had taken all night to gather her herbs. After her encounter with the Queen, it was imperative she had everything. Dawn broke over the hills and the damp, morning mist began to lift, which meant she could dispense with her dome of protection. She put the crystal back into her pocket and mentally thanked the crystal for its protection. As the dome of light vanished, Rosa saw a dark shape lurking around her front door. "Who's there," she shouted, taking out a pouch of cayenne pepper from her pocket. Some of that thrown in the eyes would make a robber run quicker than a jack-rabbit.

"It's me, Aveline. Where have you been? I've been waiting here for ages."

Rosa slipped the pepper back into her pocket and clapped her hands together to get rid of the residue. "I needed some herbs."

"But it's five-thirty in the morning. What time did you leave?"

Rosa smiled. Leave! That's a joke. She hadn't even been home yet and every bone in her body was reminding her of that fact. "What's wrong, Aveline? Is Shaun all right?"

"Of course he is. Why shouldn't he be? He left early to go on a breakdown recovery. I need you to answer some questions."

Rosa sighed as she walked up the steps to her caravan. She wanted her bed more than a chat. "You'd better come in," she said and pushed a long, steel key into the door.

"You need a more secure lock than that."

Rosa grimaced. The key was old, rusted around the sides, but it worked these last thirty years. "I'm as safe as I'll ever be." Once inside she hurried to light the oil lamps, turning the flames up high.

"This place is a fire hazard," Aveline said. "Why do you need so many lamps, anyway?"

Rosa ignored the barbed comment. "I don't want any dark corners in here. I need to make something and I don't want shadowy eyes to see its secret. Do you want tea?"

"I need answers not a drink."

"Well, I do. So you'll have to wait," Rosa placed the kettle on her tiny stove. When she had made her tea she sat down opposite Aveline and reached for the clay pipe, which lay on the table. She lit the tobacco inside it and puffed on it thoughtfully.

"What do you know about that cottage? I mean about the demon that supposedly lives there?"

"You mean Justin Montgomery," Rosa replied.

Aveline nodded. Rosa sipped her tea and sighed as the warmth of the caravan and drink, eased the pains in her joints. "Fourteen generations of my family have fought to free the silver-haired women from their curse. Journals, long since gone, listed everything they have tried. It named every man the demon has killed. Many of them the fathers of the silver-haired women."

Aveline shuddered and pulled her coat tighter around her. "Morgan never told me much about it."

Rosa sucked on her pipe and blew out a cloud of smoke. "The wind's changed. The Shadow Queen's appeared and that means trouble."

Aveline grimaced and waved her hand in front of her face to disperse the smoky cloud heading toward her. "Shadow Queen? Oh no, don't you be making up stories now. I want facts."

"To know them you need to believe the unbelievable. Justin controls the mortal women by using a mind essence. It's derived from an ancient spell which was once used for calming the anxious by apothecaries in the eighteenth century. But it was used for evil and now the essence is tainted. It bends free will. The women don't even realise it's happening to them.
It blinds their senses with a sweet perfume. Takes pain from their heart and makes them believe the darkest lies. It works especially well on the vulnerable," she added with an accusing glare. "To you and me it smells like the foulest scent imaginable. Think rotting meat and you'll not be far wrong." Rosa chuckled at Aveline's disgusted sneer. "It's the stench of pure evil. If you ever smell it, run for your life."
"Oh hush with your horror stories. You don't scare me."
Rosa saw the fear in Aveline's eyes. Nothing stayed hidden from her. "Justin's power to control Abigail's mind gets stronger as she grows more dependent on him. She needs to be fully under his spell before he can get to her child and drive out its soul."
"Why drug them? How is he able to harm something so pure?"
"Because to bed a human, Justin has to revert back his true form." Rosa saw Aveline's look of confusion. "He's a demon. His form too hideous to take in."
"But how do you know all this for sure? Journals can be exaggerated."
"Because I've seen Justin in his true form and I'll tell you something else, I'd rather be dead then have that foul monster humping me."
Aveline sniffed disapprovingly. "There's no need to be crude."
Rosa smiled inwardly. How Aveline ever got pregnant was beyond her. The woman acted more frigid than a cold snap in winter. "So far I've managed to put a cloak of protection around the child, but it won't last for long."
"Who is this Justin Montgomery anyway? Why is he doing this?"
"Justin is a weak man, born into a rich life. He married Abigail Towers to get himself an heir. But all he got was a bundle of trouble. His wife was the high priestess of a witch's coven. When she became pregnant it would be a holy miracle if it were Justin's child. But the fool was so blinded with love, he believed anything she said. When she died in childbirth, he went insane with grief and believed her daughter was his wife reincarnated."
"He did what?"
"The child inherited her Mothers silver hair and beauty, so he thought his wife's soul had gone into her and returned to him," Rosa explained.
"The man is an ejit," Aveline replied.
"The foolish or naive have no protection against the powers of darkness. The child grew and became as devious and twisted as her mother. She fed Justin's madness. Spent his entire fortune. He had no choice but to sell his family home and live in Abigail cottage, a small house his father had brought for a mistress years before."
"She could have been his daughter," Aveline argued.
"Could, would, should, they're all words. They both died of typhoid. A member of my ancestors rescued their new born daughter. By the time they realised the child

was cursed, it was too late."

"So they had a child together as well?"

"Yes, but I don't believe it was Justin's either. Her name became well known with the gardener, stable lads, anyone she fancied. She was her mother's daughter and they cast her out of the band at sixteen, when one of her many conquests left a present in her belly. She had nowhere to go except back to the cottage of her birth."

"So let me get this straight. Justin uses spells to make them all look identical."

"He makes them look like his wife so when her soul returns to the vessels he's provided, she'll look exactly the same."

"Oh my God, it goes against all that's natural?"

"But his wife can't return, even if she wants to. She gave her soul up to the devil years before. A dark one ruled her body. But sometimes the curse falters and twins are born."

Aveline jumped as one of the oil burners suddenly flared up beside her.

Rosa paused, her eyes darting around the room for a moving shadow. She looked at the flame in the oil lamp, but she couldn't see a fire demon. They were safe - for now.

"In magic there's always a yin and yang – cause and effect," Rosa continued. To everything there is an equal and opposite effect. Abigail's twin is the good to her evil. There are only three sets to my knowledge. The dark haired ones are barren and never find their place in life. They suffer with madness, die young, except one. Morgan left his daughter with that twin."

"So one twin keeps the soul she was born with?" Aveline replied.

"It looks that way. But even they are tainted."

"What I don't understand is why Abigail Moreland returned to the cottage. Morgan loved her and their child."

Rosa relit her pipe. They were about to travel down a rocky road and she wished she didn't feel so weary. The web of lies unravelling required explaining in detail. She had to break a promise. One she vowed to take to the grave. "She fled to the cottage because I told her that I knew her child couldn't be Morgan's. That dubious honour belonged to William O'Hara." Rosa watched Aveline's face turn chalk white.

She stood, her lips pulled into a sneer of disbelief. Her emerald eyes flashed angrily as she buttoned up her blue, wool coat. "You're nothing but an evil old woman. You're sick. A wicked liar."

Rosa hated to see such raw pain. Aveline didn't deserve it. "I know this news pains you, but I knew for sure the child couldn't be his. Morgan was sterilised by the mumps when a teenager. He came to me for a cure. But no charm can put back something robbed by illness. I told Abigail that I would not hold for her taking Morgan for a fool. I convinced her to leave and then discovered that he'd known all along. But he wanted the child and the family it would have given him."

Aveline collapsed into the chair like a rag doll that had lost its stuffing. She laughed hysterically, but it soon changed to loud bitter, choking sobs. "You're telling me that Morgan died protecting another man's bastard."

"We both know he'd have done the same for your son as well."

"Don't you dare compare my circumstances to that... trollop."

"I'm just saying that Abigail filled Morgan's empty life. He knew about the curse, but believed the power of his love might break it. But it didn't. I promised never to reveal his secret and he took the child, when her mother died, believing he could raise her. But the curse haunted him. So he gave her up and I made a shielding spell around her. We need to stand together, Aveline. Just like Morgan and I did. Otherwise if Justin doesn't get Shaun, the Shadow Queen will."

Chapter Eighteen

"So you're telling me that Morgan gave his life protecting that... that whore's child." Tears streamed haphazardly down her cheeks as she shouted. "That means he lied to me for years."

"He didn't mean to lie. Sometimes emotions bind you as securely as rope. He loved the child as a father should."

Aveline pulled a tissue from her pocket and scraped it across her reddened eyes. "I'd better get back. I need to get the breakfast ready before Shaun gets home."

Rosa looked at Aveline's white face. She was in shock. Nettle tea would help with it, but she wouldn't drink it. "You'll need to bring Shaun tonight. He needs to know what's going on."

"Not tonight, I want to get my head around things. We'll come at the weekend. I'll let myself out."

Rosa watched Aveline leave with a heavy heart. Lies always led to heartbreak in the end. Why couldn't people be honest with each other? She picked up her clay pipe. After re-filling it she went outside, lit it and sat on the steps. The morning air held a freezing chill and she shuddered. She was getting too old to live in the wide open spaces. The winter snow cut her off for days sometimes. Maybe she would think about moving closer to town this year. The thought irked her considerably. Old age was a cruel enemy. Rosa sucked on her pipe and blew out a stream of smoke. She watched the small white clouds float upwards, eventually disappearing like misty shadows into the sky. Aveline had no intention of bringing Shaun to her. She knew that and gazed resolutely heavenwards. "What can I do mother?" she whispered. "There's no place on this earth that Aveline can hide her precious son. The demons *will* find him." The thought sent a shudder of apprehension through her as she watched the sun rise like a giant flame coloured football. Rosa sucked on her pipe. "It's a hard task you've left me, Morgan." She watched another cloud of smoke spiral from her mouth. She stood and winced as her bones creaked in complaint. The protection amulet she made for Shaun would not be enough to save him from the shadow queen once her wrath was stirred. She needed a stronger protection spell. Rosa sighed, resigning herself to a long morning without sleep. This damn curse has taken over her life for too long. She needed to end it. Once and for all

***

Shaun opened the door and squinted at the bright light emanating from within. "Mother, are you having trouble seeing or something."

Aveline looked up from the sofa. When Shaun hadn't come home for breakfast she had imagined the worst. His call of explanation thankfully shelved her worries. That old witch had rattled her with her lies about Morgan. The curse was on the silver-haired women, not her Shaun. But that old gypsy was never going to rest until she had unsettled them all. She looked up and feigned surprise. "Oh, you're home. Is it that time already?"

Shaun's eyes went to the dying fire. Shaking his head, he walked over to it and picked up the poker. "Mother if you let the fire burn this low it'll go out and the whole house will turn into a refrigerator." He prodded the ashes and added fresh coal. It quickly picked up and began to crackle. "That's better." He warmed his hands on the leaping flames. "So are you going to tell me what's on your mind?"

Aveline hated the tears that spilled down her cheeks like rapid rivers of misery, yet she couldn't stop them. Why did this have to happen now? They were just getting back on track and now that meddling gypsy was ruining everything.

Shaun quickly crossed the room and hugged Aveline to him. "Hush now. What's upset you so much?"

"Oh, tis a poor sight I must look lad," she sniffed and pulled away. "I've been thinking about your father and I've got myself all upset, that's all. Now don't you be worrying your head about me." She managed a watery smile and dabbed her eyes with a tissue. "Look, I've been thinking. What do you say about a little holiday in Scotland?" Aveline saw the dour look appear on Shaun's face and held his arm before he could turn away. "Your Aunt Josie would love to see you. She'll be forgetting what her nephew looks like before long."

"Mother, Scotland's a beautiful country, but Aunt Jo lives in the part the devil carved out for himself. I hate it there. Why don't you go on your own? You two don't want me tagging along at your heels like a little lapdog."

Aveline felt panic stir her already churning stomach. She had to convince him it was a good idea. "I don't want to go alone. I'd like to take a holiday with me son. Is that too much to ask for? All I'm asking is a few days from your precious time. I don't think that's too much to give?" She watched his face blanch at her words. He didn't deserve her sharp words. But it was all for his own good. Rosa's words came back to her. '*Emotions can bind like rope.*' She was playing on her son's emotions, but what else could she do?

"Okay, calm down. If it means that much to you, I'll come. But don't expect me to enjoy it. Aunt Jo's forever trying to fix me up with friends who look like their related to the Loch Ness monster."

Aveline felt a stirring of excitement. The sooner they left, the less chance that old witch had to cause trouble. "I'm sure you'll enjoy the break once you're there, Shaun. You've been working too hard. I'll pack tonight and book us a flight for tomorrow. I'll go into town now and use Mrs. O'Hara's telephone."

"Hold on, I can't go now. I thought we'd leave in a few weeks."

Aveline shook her head. "No! I want to go now. I told you..."

Shaun held up his hands in supplication. "Okay, Okay. We'll go tomorrow if that's what you want. I'll have to go and tell me boss. He's not going to be happy, I can tell you."

Aveline wanted to shout for joy. Rosa would be waiting a long time before she got the chance to ruin their lives

***

Shaun opened his eyes and blinked into the inky blackness of his bedroom. He squinted to see the luminous arms of his alarm clock and sighed. It said half past two. Whatever had disturbed him was quiet now. He closed his eyes and turned over in his bed. The room was freezing and he shivered as he pulled the quilt up to his ears. As sleep stole over him, he heard the faint sound of a baby's cry. His eyes snapped open and he sat up listening intently. Last year a child was abandoned on Mrs. Donavan's doorstep. She had not discovered it until the morning. With the winter bringing its freezing chill, no infant could survive a night outside.

The baby's cry came again. Soft, yet insistent – demanding attention. He left the warmth of his bed and shivered as the frigid air embraced his skin. It was ridiculously cold. He touched the radiator, expecting it to be off, but it was on and very hot. He shook his hand quickly to dispel the sting of the heat. "At least one thing's warm in here," he mumbled and stepped into the hallway. Another, more insistent cry from the baby, sent him hurrying down the stairs. When he got to the front door, his fingers trembled as he fumbled to unlock the two stout bolts. Who would do such a thing? What drives a mother to abandon their own flesh and blood when they are at their most vulnerable?

"What's going on?" Aveline asked from at the top of the stairs.

Shaun struggled with the last protesting bolt. "Mother can't you hear it?"

Aveline hurried down the stairs and placed her weight against the door, making it easier for him to slide the old fashioned bolt across. "Hear what?"

"A baby's cry. Don't you remember the one left on Mrs. Donovan's doorstep last year? I think someone's left one on ours. Quick, move out of the way, it could be dying of exposure out there."

Shaun threw open the door and gasped as a blast of frigid air pushed its way into the room. They both peered out into the darkness. "I can't see anything." He went outside and quickly became engulfed in the inky darkness.

Aveline held her robe tightly to her throat, "Shaun, come inside before you catch your death, boy. You've been dreaming. There's no child out there."

Shaun came in rubbing his arms vigorously. "I know what I heard. It sounds silly, but I feel like the baby was calling out to me." He shut the front door and Aveline quickly shot the bolts across.

Her hands trembled as she put them inside her pockets. "It could've been one of the gypsy women out with her baby. The fells are awash with them this time of year. They wander around under the moon collecting herbs and plants."

"I suppose so. You'd think they'd have more sense! Fancy taking a child out in this weather. It's pure madness."

"It's not up to us how people live their lives, son. I could do with a cup of tea. Do you want one?"

Shaun nodded and walked over to the fire. Prodding it with the poker, it quickly sprung to life. "My God. That coal burns well. I've never seen the fire so fierce. Here, take this." Aveline tossed a thick dressing gown, hanging on a hook at the bottom of the stairs, at him.

Shaun caught it and pulled it on. "Thanks. I'll need to check the heating tomorrow. My room is colder than the Antarctic, I think my radiator might be on the way out."

***

Aveline walked into the kitchen as sickening dread washed over her. Rosa said the baby would call out to him. She shook her head. No, it was ridiculous - an impossibility. The cup rattled on the tray as Aveline's shaking hands carried it through to the lounge. She smiled gratefully when Shaun jumped up to take it from her. But her smile quickly changed to horror, when a flame leapt from the grate like a huge fiery serpent and hit him square between his shoulder blades.

Pushed forwards from the force of the blow, Shaun fell, sending tea and cups crashing to the floor. Aveline watched the snake-like flame writhing over her son, leaving smaller flames behind as it slithered along. She screamed, rushed forward and pulled the blazing material from Shaun's back, as he got up and beat at the flames with his hands. When they too caught alight, his agonized cries tore through Aveline's own. She grabbed a chair throw and tried to smother the flames, but they fought back, tearing through the thick wool, even more ferocious than before. Aveline screamed as her son became a human torch before her eyes. The hissing tendrils of heat reared into the air as though they had a life of their own, and fought any attempt to extinguish them. She beat at them as they fed voraciously on Shaun's flesh, leaving not one piece of skin untouched.

"Help me," she screamed, knowing that her pleas were futile. No one would come. The nearest house was five miles away. Aveline watched Shaun crumple to the floor covered in a seething carpet of blue and yellow flames and threw herself on top of him, uncaring what they did to her. But it was an impossible task to beat them out. Even when he ceased to writhe in agony, Aveline continued to beat at the flames, because if she stopped, she would have to acknowledge that her reason for living was dead. Her arms were like dead weights hanging at her side, when the flames finally gave up their prize and leapt back into the fire. Aveline sat back on her heels. Pain, unlike anything she had experienced before, pierced her body like darts. Her eyes raked Shaun's body as she searched for life. But not a flicker in his lifeless body gave her hope.

The strong odour of baked flesh filled the air as she cradled his head in her lap. Aveline kissed his blackened face, so badly devoured by the flames, it was beyond recognition. "My beautiful boy," she whispered. "My beautiful, beautiful boy. I'm so sorry, son... I'm so sorry."

She rocked to and fro looking accusingly at the huge cross on the fireplace wall. "Why didn't you help him, Morgan? Why didn't you look after him the way you did Abigail?" Tears poured down her cheeks and Aveline closed them, praying that death would come and claim her too.

It took a few moments, before she realised that a gentle force was pushing her backwards. She opened her eyes and tried to see through the veil of mist clouding her eyes. But all she could make out was a faint bubble of light around Shaun. She held on to him tightly. "Leave him alone. I won't let you take him. Not while I have breath in me body. You've taken his life, isn't that enough?" But the white light continued to grow and push her away. The force was gentle yet insistent and

Aveline had no choice but to let him go. Shaun then became encapsulated in a translucent dome of rainbow light. Aveline felt her limbs grow heavy as the light pulsated like a giant heart. Inside the dome a figure formed. "Leave him alone," she screamed, before darkness pulled her into its merciful oblivion.

Aveline blinked several times before the ceiling came into focus. It took her a few seconds before reality hit her. "Oh God, Shaun," she cried and dragged herself over to where he lie. She rolled Shaun's lifelessly body over and cried out, shocked to the core. Naked as the day that he was born, Shaun's skin was pink, healthy and perfect. No blackened skin or burns marred his body. She put her ear against his chest, held her breath and strained to hear a heartbeat. The sound of the steady thump sounded like a choir of angel's singing. "My beautiful boy," she crooned.

Shaun's eyes fluttered open. "What... what happened?"

Aveline rested back on her heels as he rolled onto his side and sat up. "You had an accident, son,"

"Did I? Oh yes, the flames. I was on fire." He checked his arms and legs, patting his torso, his eyes filled with confusion as he looked at Aveline.

"I managed to pull the robe off before the flames got to your skin," Aveline quickly added. "You passed out. Probably from shock." She forced a smile onto her frozen lips. He had to believe what she was saying. He would never believe the truth. Morgan had sent an angel to heal him.

"Me, faint!" he repeated incredulously. "How did it happen? I wasn't near the fire." Shaun cupped his head in his hands, "God, me head's pounding like a steam train." He got to his feet and swayed like a drunken man. Aveline flew to her feet to steady him.

"Don't fuss, mother, I'm fine," he said, rubbing his arms. "It's freezing in here and me dressed in my birthday suit isn't helping. Did you have to take off all my clothes?" He pulled another throw from the armchair and secured it around his waist as he walked slowly back to the fire. He picked up the poker and moved to the coal bucket.

Aveline watched filled with horror. "No, don't touch it," she shouted and ran to the table and grabbed her crystal vase. Upending it onto the fire, she watched with satisfaction as the fire crackled and hissed angrily, before a thick acrid smoke filled the room. Shaun coughed and flapped his arms about like a giant windmill. Aveline's eyes smarted, but she refused to look away until she was sure the flames were dead.

"What did you do that for?"

"I never want that fire lit again. Do you hear me? I'll never have an open fire in my home for as long as I live."

"That's a bit over the top isn't it? You've had a nasty shock, that's all." He placed his arm around his mother's shoulders. "Come on, we'll make a pot of tea. It's not every day you save your son from death and then watch him faint like a girl."

Aveline helped Shaun pick up the broken china and her resolve hardened even stronger than before. When they left this house tomorrow, they would never set foot inside it again.

Chapter Nineteen

Abbey forced her reluctant muscles to move and got out of bed. She reached for her dressing gown and grimaced as she slid her arms into its towelling sleeves. Justin's lovemaking had left her feeling shattered. She should feel relieved about her decision. It was a step forward. No more looking back. Yet she didn't. She had the chance to erase Shaun from her mind once and for all, but last night only seemed to make things worse. Abbey placed her hand on her stomach. The baby was quiet today. She looked forward to its fluttering movements in the morning. Walking into the bathroom she turned on the taps. Even the noise of water hurt her head. Her mouth was dry, her throat parched and sore. Maybe she had a bug coming. She certainly felt unwell. A gentle ripple across her abdomen diverted her thoughts. "So you've over-slept little one," Abbey whispered, patting her stomach. "I hope you feel better than me this morning."

***

Justin stood, his hands locked behind his back, spine stiff and upright as he glared out the window of the lounge. The night had not progressed well. Abbey's indecision troubled him. He had to use the full power of the essence. Something he had never done before.

"What's the matter, Justin? Your frustration fills the air like a brewing storm," Adrinia asked.

He closed his eyes and sighed deeply at the sound of her irritating voice. The way she appeared from thin air was getting on his nerves. "Nothing," he growled back.

"Yes, there is. Everything will be all right you know. You're only nervous because you've never used the transformation spell this late before."

Justin turned and opened his eyes. Hatred spewed from their dark depths at the shimmering darkness before him. "You don't know anything about how I'm feeling."

Adrinia moved closer and he shuddered as the frigid air surrounding her enfolded him. "Then tell me."

Justin sighed. He felt weary. The emotional weight on his shoulder felt heavier than usual. "It's just... well, if only... oh, what's the use in trying to explain anything to a cloud of vapour? You've no soul, no feelings for anything warm and real. You can't possibly understand how I'm feeling" He turned back to the window, feeling the dark clouds of loneliness descending on him like great winged vultures. He would do anything for Abbey. She had to love him back. Nothing else would do. Her purity cleansed him – made him feel like a real man again. Something he had not felt in a very long time.

***

Rosa winced as she rewound the coarse bandage around the burns on her hands. The fire demons had put up a ferocious fight last night. She winced as the burns pressed uncomfortably against their bindings. She had not protected herself fully from their venom. Time was of the essence. A spell would have taken too long.

Shaun was lucky. The stupid boy had not worn the talisman. Lucky for him, Morgan's cross had amplified Aveline's screams. What was left of the protection spell around it brought a vision to her while she had slept. A glimpse of Shaun's burning body was all it took to waken her astral body and send it hurtling to him. It was a dangerous feat and one she used only in extreme emergencies. But she had no choice if she wanted to save him.

At Aveline's house, there was no time for shock at the devastation around her. Calling for the light of protection from the spirit world she forced the fire demons to relinquish Shaun's unconscious spirit. She still felt the sting of their fierce heat on her hands as she had tugged him away from them. Rosa bit her lip anxiously as she secured the bandage with a pin. The fire demons were sent to take his spirit - but to where? Worry pricked her like a blunt needle. She used the Esor light within Shaun to help her. If she hadn't, the fire demons would have them both now. She could not fight them alone. The power of it was awe inspiring. His badly damaged body was lost to her capabilities as a healer. But with the light, her gift was amplified tenfold. Rosa's heart fluttered in panic. Shaun needed to know the truth now. He had to learn how to gain control of the lights' power before he faced Justin a second time.

She looked at her burnt hands and her brow wrinkled in confusion. The astral body should not be able to be harmed by that of the physical world. But somehow fire demons had the power to create havoc on any plane. It was bad enough the damage they did in the physical world, they could kill millions by a single sweep of their fiery tails. Their knowledge of destruction was phenomenal.

Rosa swallowed the herbal, painkilling tea she had made. She grimaced at the bitter after taste. None of them were safe anymore. Whether they be mortal or spirit.

***

Adrinia, hidden in the shadows cast from the ancient trees surrounding Rosa's caravan, trembled with rage. She wanted to strip the skin from the witch's withered body and feed her spirit piece by piece to the lowland dwellers in the darkest regions of hell. But she needed her for the time being. Something inside Justin had snapped – again. His sanity was questionable at the best of times. But his actions last night were born more from desperation than madness. Why did he send the fire demons to kill Shaun O'Donnell? Unless he finally believed his precious Abigail still pined for her mortal lover. Thankfully the gypsy has saved the day. Unlike her minions who were tardy in protecting the mortal. Their punishment did nothing to appease her anger. Banished, to burn for a few hundred years in hell's fire. It was nothing. The sentence did not fit the seriousness of their crime. Her plans were almost ruined. Abigail had to see, with her own puppy dog eyes, the destruction of her lover at Justin's hands. Then this sorry mess would be at an end. But it is not going to happen anytime soon. O'Donnell and his wretch of a mother had fled the proverbial coop. Now it was down to her to drag them back.

Adrinia absently stroked Aslow as her outline began to dissipate. "Shaun O'Donnell will rue the day he messed with her. She would make sure of it.

***

Shaun looked out from the fourteenth floor walkway and sighed. The Red Row flats hadn't changed at all. They were still grey and depressing. Every spare bit of wall was emblazoned with the same worn bits of graffiti, with new bits added here and there. He frowned as an ugly, concrete factory chimney in the distance belched out its polluted residue into the smog-filled skies. The few trees, which managed to survive in the filthy air, looked old and worn out with their struggle to exist. Shaun closed his eyes to blot out the depressing scene. The distant call of a bird momentarily made him forget where he was, and he took a deep breath, grimacing as the scent of stale cooking greeted his nostrils. He opened his eyes and saw a black cat rummage inside a bin bag it had clawed open. It looked painfully thin and neglected. How can people bear to live so squashed up - suffocating each other with their unhappiness?

He needed the wide-open spaces of the fells, like a flower needed water to survive. His spirit would shrivel up and die if he stayed here too long. Shaun glanced at his mother. She looked much better today. The deep frown lines marring her forehead of late were nearly gone. Her smile brighter, without an edge of nervousness. Shaun's meandering thoughts took another direction when his Aunt Jo opened her front door and emitted a wild screech of delight. He submitted to her bear hug and wet sloppy kisses with a fixed smile. Although she lived in Ireland until the age of six, her broad Scots brogue belied it. When she finally released him and moved onto his mother, he noticed a small boy behind her. He looked about five years old. Yet his eyes seemed older as he gazed curiously back at him. Shaun smiled. He was a cute little chap, with a shock of red hair that looked as though it would light up even the darkest of nights. He squatted down in front of the boy. "Good morning. And who might you be me fine fellow?"

The child's head cocked to one side as his freckled face creased into a frown. "Och, dinna ye talk funny,"

Before Shaun could answer, the door behind the small boy opened and the child was scooped up into the arms of a young woman, whose face rapidly turned pink. "Douglas McCloud, ye' apologise for yoor rudeness this minute,"

Shaun stood up and smiled. The woman had the same fiery hair as the boy, except it was a mass of curls winding down her shoulders. The smattering of freckles around her small button nose, gave her an elfin appeal. She was tiny. Barely five feet tall.

"Don't be making the boy apologise for his honesty. He's right, I probably do sound a mite strange to him. I'm Shaun O'Donnell." He held out his hand, and the woman put her son onto the floor to shake it.

"Pleased tae meet ye, Shaun. My name's Jessie McCloud and this wee chatterbox is my son Douglas. We live next door."

Shaun tried not to stare at their pale complexions and care worn faces. A few weeks on the fells would a healthy colour to their cheeks and remove those dark circles from beneath Jessie's eyes. But not everyone was as lucky as him to have such a beautiful home to go back to.

"Oh, I see you've introduced yourself, Shaun," Josie said, standing beside him.

"Do you want tae come we' us tae the park?" Douglas piped up. He looked at Shaun and waited.

"Och Douglas, ye canna go askin' things like that. Shaun's not here tae see us. He's here tae see Josie and he's probably tired from his journey."

"Och, dinna worry about that. A short trip tae the park won't hurt a big man like him." Josie replied

Jessie pulled her reluctant son to the front door. "No, it's fine. It's actually his nap time,"

"Och, I dinna feel tired, mummy."

"Do I get a say in this?" Shaun interrupted, noticing the child's immediate look of expectant hope. "I'd like very much to go to the park with you and your mother, Douglas. That's if she doesn't mind. It'll save me having to listen to these two gossiping." He gave the child an exaggerated wink and smiled.

"Well, if yoor sure." Jessie stammered. "But dinna moan tae me aboot' being tired later, Douglas. I'll go next door and get our coats."

***

Aveline chuckled. "That's quick work. Josie. My Shaun didn't stand a chance against that onslaught."

Josie's smile faltered. "That was more for Jessie. The poor wee lass needs a bit o' fun in her life. She's nae been well."

"What's wrong with her? She looks fine enough."

"Cancer," Josie whispered the word, as if saying it out loud would make it worse. "She's had treatment for months. Now it's all over, she's finally beginning tae get a wee bit o' colour into her cheeks."

"But she's got a fine head of hair. I thought chemotherapy made you lose it."

"She's had radiotherapy. It's different. I dinna ken the ins and oots of it. Jessie isn't one tae let on much."

Josie picked up the kettle and poured the hot water into a china teapot. "Anyway, ye dinna come tae hear this. Tell me, what's bought you tae me in such a hurry?"

Aveline sipped her tea as she thought about what to say. She couldn't tell her sister the real reason she was here. It was too unbelievable for her ears, never mind someone else's.

"After Morgan died I thought I could cope with living in the cottage without him, but I can't. There are too many memories." Aveline watched Josie's face for any sign of disbelief. When none came, she continued. "I want to be closer to the only family I have left - you. We're not getting younger. A person needs family around them in their old age." Aveline squirmed uncomfortably under Josie's puzzled stare. It wasn't all lies. She did miss her.

"Aww lass, I dinna ken ye felt that way. But ye always tol' me ye loved the wide-open spaces of the fells, and living here t'would be like binding th' wings of an eagle. And there's Shaun tae consider. He'll nae make a good city dweller. He's one o' nature's free spirits."

"People change," Aveline sipped her tea. "He'll adapt."

Josie shook her head. "Not the Shaun I know." She sat down opposite Aveline and took her hand. "Look, I dinna ken what's wrong with ye lass, but I know yoor not telling me th' whole story. But I can wait fer that. Until ye feel more ready to confide in me. Now, where ye thinking of living?"

Aveline bit back her discomfort. Josie's kind heartedness never failed to move her. Lying to her made it even harder to bear. "I was thinking of this block. I saw a for sale sign on the tenth floor."

Josie picked up her mug and sipped her tea. Her forehead wrinkled in thought. "I can see ye'll nae tek' any advice from me tae change yoor mind. So let's drink up and we'll go down tae have a look at it. Willa has th' key. It's her brothers flat. He's moving in with his girlfriend. At sixty two years of age you'd think th' man t'would know better."

***

"Douglas, ye canna go that high laddie, ye'll fall off," Jessie winced as her son sailed through the air on the small plastic swing.

"You've a fine boy. I wouldn't mind having a son like him one day." Shaun sat down on a patch of grass, which they both had meticulously checked for dog's excrement. He looked around and felt sadness. The park was a pitiful excuse for a playground. A few swings and a dirty slide. It did nothing to inspire a child's imagination. Earlier he watched Jessie painstakingly search the ground around the play area, before she allowed Douglas to enter, in puzzlement. She explained that drug addicts came at night and left dirty needles. Horror and disgust prevented him from commenting. Even the grass, yellowed and dry, was barely able to keep itself alive. Shaun swallowed back the yearning for the lush greenery of home. Only two weeks to go. He could stomach it for that long.

"Josie talks about ye a lot. From what I hear, yoor' a real heart breaker," Jessie teased as she lowered herself on the ground beside him.

"Me, breaking hearts?" Shaun shook his head. "Tis a terrible lie you've heard."

She chuckled as her gaze constantly flicked around the play area. Shaun wondered if she expected her husband to storm over. After all, she was in the park with a stranger. "Look, I hope me coming along doesn't cause you any problems with your husband."

Jessie frowned. "Och nae. Dinna fash yoursel' Douglas's father died afore he was born."

"Sorry, I didn't mean to pry. Anyway, I'm guessing that you've a whole army of admirers."

"Och, well, I dinna ken aboot that. Douglas teks up all o' my time nowadays."

Shaun watched Jessie's face flush a dull red. It clashed with her hair, but made her strangely prettier. Her eyes reminded him of the colour of grass. That dark, vibrant green that came in spring. A sudden flash of sapphire eyes filled his mind and his guts contracted in despair. Would Abbey's face never leave his thoughts?

Depression settled around his shoulders like a damp cloud. Nothing in Scotland would lift his spirits and he felt sorry for Jessie. She would have to endure his bad company. "Well, you never know what path the leprechauns will lead you." He stood and forced a smile. A few months ago he would have asked her out, but now his thoughts were filled with Abbey. It made him miserable, but what could he do? Jessie quickly got up as well. "We dinna have leprechauns in Scotland."

Angry at himself for being poor company, his voice came out clipped and hard. "I'd better be getting back. No doubt me mother will be waiting to drag me here and there."

"Hold on, we'll come with you. It's way past Douglas's nap time anyway." Jessie called to her son and clicked her tongue when he conveniently ignored her. "Och that laddie is a wee devil. I'll be back in a minute."

Shaun watched Jessie walk away and as he followed, a sudden flash of movement to his left caught his eye. He turned to see a streak of black burst from the bushes. It rushed towards him, gathering speed with every gallop. His body tensed to jump out of the way, but it suddenly veered to the left and vanished into a nearby bush.

"What the hell," he mumbled, and hurried over to where it had gone. It was like no animal he had ever seen before. He pulled back the leaves. Confusion wrinkled his brow. Nothing was there. It was too quick for a dog and too big for a cat.

"Shaun, what air ye doin'?" Douglas called, racing towards him.

Shaun straightened. "I think I'm looking for a needle in a haystack."

Douglas peered into the bush. "Och, ye'll nae find needles in there. Maw puts them in th' bin afore I can go and play."

Shaun sighed and ruffled his hair. The child thought he meant drug addicts' needles. What a shame his innocence was blighted by such a harsh reality. I tell you what. How about you show me where your favourite burger shop is. I could eat a horse between two slices of bread."

Douglas laughed loudly. "I'd like tae see that. Can I sit on yoor' shoulders, Shaun. I can point oot th' way better."

"Now that's a mighty good idea. Climb aboard." Shaun hoisted up the squealing child and looked at Jessie, remembering that he hadn't asked her if it was okay to go for a burger. "Would you like to come with us, Jessie?"

"Come on. We're goin' tae have a burger."

"But I thought ye wanted tae go back, Shaun."

"It's not only a woman who has the prerogative to change their minds, you know," Jessie laughed and fell in step beside them. "It dinna look like I've a choice."

Douglas clapped his hands in excitement and bounced up and down. "Great. Come on horsy. Giddy up. Can I come tae yoor house in Ireland, Shaun?"

"Och, where've ye hidden yoor manners?" Jessie chided. "You canna go inviting yourself tae someone's home."

"Of course he can. Think of yourselves both cordially invited to me humble abode anytime you have a mind to visit."

***

135

Adrinia picked up Aslow and frowned in annoyance. "What have I told you about running about in the daylight? Justin's right. You're becoming a liability." Her eyes narrowed suspiciously as she stared, hidden by the shadows of the overhanging trees, at Shaun walking with Jessie. Mortals were so unpredictable. He was supposed to be pining for his beloved Abigail! She clicked her tongue in annoyance. It didn't look like he was missing her. "I don't like the way this is heading, Aslow. I don't like it at all." Adrinia re-materialised back into the cottage and immediately searched for Justin. Recently she could sense his turbulent emotions in every room. It surprised her that he was capable of such deep feelings. A demons heart seldom cared for anything except its own welfare. It gave her hope. One day he would care about her like that.

Adrinia absently stroked Aslow as she went into the lounge. The bitter taste of jealousy stopped her in her tracks at the romantic scene which greeted her. Justin sat at Abigail's feet, his eyes sickeningly wide and adoring. He read from a book of sonnets. Anger fuelled her bitterness deeper. He had never read anything to her. Even when they were bored out of their minds. That book was her favourite. It was not to be shared with that slut. Adrinia's breath came in small gasps of pain. Only Justin could hurt her like this and that meant he had power over her. She didn't like that feeling either.

"We need to speak to Hacate, Aslow," Adrinia whispered. "She may be a demonic goddess, but she sure knows her witchcraft and I need a spell that will drag Shaun O'Donnell back here quicker than you can say 'fires of hell'."

Chapter Twenty

"What did ye think of th' flat? Are ye going tae buy it?" Josie asked.

"It's got potential," Aveline replied, half heartedly. It was nothing like her spacious home in Ireland. How would she survive shut away in such a tiny place? But she'd find a way, if it meant Shaun would live. "I'm sure once me own bits and pieces are around me, it'll be more like home."

"Maybe ye can convince yourself o' that, Aveline. But who's goin' tae do th' same fer' yoor son?"

Aveline sighed, and sunk further into the sofa. Shaun would take a lot of persuading. He won't like losing his inheritance or living here. "I'll not mention anything yet. Let him get the feel of it here first." She ignored her sister's questioning frown and knew, deep down, that once Shaun discovered her plans; there wouldn't be a safe place to run for cover. His hurt and anger would be like a box of fireworks exploding in all directions.

***

Douglas moaned, lost in a deep sleep as Shaun carried him. He waited patiently as Jessie fumbled in her pocket for her key to her front door. The day had turned into a great adventure for them all in the end. It felt nice to have his thoughts taken up by someone other than Abbey for a change. The door swung open and Shaun followed her down a small dark hallway. She opened a door to his left and they walked in. Douglas gave a little moan of protest as Shaun laid him on the bed. Jessie quickly removed his trainers.

"Go back tae sleep." She kissed his cheek, covered him over and followed Shaun from the room. "Tea or coffee?" she whispered, closing the door behind them.

"Whatever you're having. I'm an easy man to please."

Jessie shook her head and smiled. "Somehow I dinna think ye 'air. Now go and meke yourself comfortable in th' lounge while I put th' kettle on."

Shaun watched Jessie move down the hall. He liked the way her slender hips swayed as she walked. Her small waist, nipped in by a wide belt. Ahh, if circumstances were different, he told himself. But they weren't, and she wasn't Abbey. Unfortunately that was who he wanted. He walked into the lounge and paused. The room was tiny, with hardly a stick of furniture, except for a large armchair and an unsteady looking wicker table. He swallowed his homesickness as remembering his cosy lounge with its coal fire. With one chair in the room, Shaun had no choice but to sit on it. He felt the cushion sink under his weight. A few pictures of Douglas decorated a mostly bare, cream wall and on the other side of the room was a giant poster of a cartoon character he didn't recognise. Jessie came into the room carrying two green mugs and Shaun jumped up, conscious that she had nowhere to sit.

"I added milk and sugar," she said handing him a mug. "I forgot ye may not like it th' way I do."

"Tis fine the way it is." He shuffled awkwardly on his feet. One chair, two people.

A conundrum he wasn't sure how to acknowledge.

"Sit yourself down then. I'll nae bite you," Jessie sat down on the floor and pressed her back against the wall. "So, how long will ye be stayin' next door?"

Shaun sat down, relieved the decision where to sit had been taken from him. "If I know me mother, it'll be a week or so."

"Och, dinna sound too enthusiastic."

Shaun sipped his coffee. It tasted bland. He missed his regular, fresh brand. "What can I say? I'm dependent on the whim of a woman."

"Douglas will be happy tae have ye around a wee bit longer."

"Only Douglas?"

Jessie opened her mouth to reply and snapped it shut when a loud crash came from the kitchen. She jumped up and Shaun followed. When his foot crunched on something hard, he quickly stepped back.

"Och, no. I dinna understand. How did my pasta can jump off th' work surface? It's always pushed up tae the wall so Douglas does nae get his hands on it."

Shaun shook his head. "Looks like leprechauns work to me."

"Och, away with ye Shaun O'Donnell. Ye probably brought th' wee folk with ye. Go and sit yourself down while I clear up the mess."

"I'll help, I'm house trained you know."

Jessie began to sweep. "You'll nay do such a thing. Go away and be a good guest."

Shaun laughed and went back into the lounge. His breath pressed from his lungs in alarm when he saw the outline of a woman in the semi lit room. Half hidden by the evening shadows, she was almost invisible "What the…" he murmured. He saw something darker squirming in her arms and stepped closer. "And you are?"

"Who is who?" Jessie asked behind him.

Shaun felt his heart jump into his mouth as he turned. "Her." He pointed to the woman, but the space where she had stood was empty. "I could've sworn… I mean, I know I saw a woman holding an animal in the corner of the room."

"You couldn't have. Not unless th' leprechauns 'air playing tricks on ye as well."

Shaun smiled. Now he felt foolish. Maybe he was more tired than he thought. Rosa said the mind could play horrible tricks on you. "I'll have you know, the king leprechaun is my best friend. His band wouldn't dare mess with me."

"I'll have tae tek' yoor word fer that," she giggled and sat back on the floor.

Shaun sat down and picked up his coffee. He sipped the tepid brew and pushed the strange apparition to the back of his mind. Tomorrow he'd be rested and all this silliness would fade away.

"So tell me about Ireland. Is it really all green and full o' fairies?"

"Of course. The birds sing in the morning and the soft whisper of an evening breeze meanders across the hills carrying with it the scent of wild flowers."

Jessie gave a big sigh and stretched her legs across the floor. "It sounds beautiful. Your accent's fascinating. Has anyone told ye that? You meke each word sound like a musical note."

"Then on that note, I'll take me leave," Shaun replied. "I've had a great time today, thanks for including me."

Jessie stood and walked him to the door. She opened it. "Goodnight Shaun. Don't be a stranger now. You're welcome tae drop in anytime."

He stepped outside. A smell of stale chips assaulted his senses. He grimaced with disgust at a pile of cold ones thrown on the landing. "I might just take you up on that offer. Being locked away with me mother and Aunt Josie isn't much fun."

***

"Aboot time, laddie. Th' wanderer returns," Josie teased.

Shaun walked into the small lounge. "You shouldn't leave the door on the latch around here, mother. You're not at home now."

"Have you been with Jessie all this time?" Aveline asked.

"It's only nine o'clock. I didn't leave here until two."

Josie laughed. "Do ye want a cup o' tea, Shaun afore I go tae me bed? I've been up since six and canna keep long hours anymore."

"No, I think I will away to me dreams as well. It's been a long day."

"Jessie's a bonny lass, inst she?" Josie probed.

"Yes, she is. But, before you start matchmaking, I'm not looking for romance."

Josie got up from the chair and stretched. "I wouldn't dream of interfering lad. Are ye comin' up, Aveline?"

"Yes, I'll leave me son to his dreams." Aveline stood on tip toe to kiss Shaun's cheek. "She's a lovely girl. You could do worse," she whispered.

"Stop it. Jessie's merely an oasis in a parched desert. She takes me mind off... well... things." The innuendo lay in the air like a heavy blanket.

"You never know what's around the corner son. Give her a chance."

***

Shaun banged his empty mug down on the kitchen worktop in frustration. "Mother, it's been eight weeks. I know you've been ill with a fever and too weak to travel, but now you're saying you need more time here because Aunt Josie is feeling poorly. How much longer do you want me to stay? I've lost me contract with the hire company and I have to get back and find some winter work. We need the money."

"Ssh, your Aunt's still asleep," Aveline whispered.

"I want to go home, mother. I'm suffocating here." He ran his fingers through his hair in agitation. "I was thinking of asking Jessie and Douglas to come back with us for a holiday."

Aveline looked away from Shaun's pleading eyes. He had not softened to Scotland at all and Jessie still remained nothing more than a friend to them both. Her stomach rolled sickeningly with nerves. "Son, you know I've only ever wanted what's best for you. Now you need to know what's best for me."

Shaun pulled out a chair and sat opposite her. "What might that be?"

"I'm going to buy the empty flat on the tenth floor." Aveline watched Shaun's face whiten with shock.

"Have you gone mad?" he said, slowly enunciating every word. "You don't need to buy one of these rabbit hutches to be near Josie. You can visit anytime. Stay as long as you like."

Aveline picked at a thread on her cardigan. This was her only chance to win Shaun over. He had to stay. For his own safety. "We can't go back, son. The cottage holds too many memories for me. I thought we could have a fresh start here." Aveline felt her heart sink at the horror in his eyes.

"You can't be serious? I'd shrivel up and die if I had to live in one of these tiny boxes. The air's polluted and the animals are the sorriest excuse for beasts I've ever seen in me life. There's nothing here for me or you."

"I can't help how I feel, Shaun. I need to sell the cottage to buy the flat."

"You can't do it. It's me home too. I want me children to grow up there. I don't want to be looking out for needles and dogs muck whenever I take them out. " He squatted down on his haunches and took Aveline's hands in his. "Tell me what's wrong. Why are we really here? Whatever it is, I'll sort it out. I promise you."

Aveline shook her head. "Some things just can't be put right, son."

Shaun dropped her hands and stood up. "If you think for one minute that I'll stay here, then you've lost your mind."

"Please. Try and understand."

"Fine, have it your way. Sell the cottage, if that's what you've a mind to do. But I'll not stay here. I'll go back to Ireland and I'll rent a place until I can build me own home. One you can't take away on a whim."

Aveline turned to the kitchen door when it slowly creaked open. Douglas's tearful face stared back.

"I dinna mean tae listen. But maw told me aboot our holiday. If you sell yoor home, I won't get tae see the king leprechauns house and the fairy glen."

Shaun glared at Aveline. "One thing you'll need to learn, Dougie, is that when I promise we'll do something, we do it. You'll see all those things and more. So don't you be worrying your little head about it. Now off you go and find your mother."

Douglas nodded and hurried down the hallway sniffing loudly.

Shaun shook his head. His breath ragged with anger. "I never thought I'd see the day that me own mother behaved so selfishly."

"You can't go back to Ireland, Shaun. Who'll take care of you?"

"Not yourself, that's for sure." He angrily kicked his chair across the kitchen floor, before he stalked from the flat, banging the front door closed behind him.

Chapter Twenty-One

Harriet tied up the last black bag for the charity shop and heaved it across the room. She heard the click of the front door opening and glanced at the carriage clock on the mantelpiece. "Is that you, Jonathon?" she called. "You're home early?"

Jonathon hurried up the stairs, into the bedroom and held out a plain brown folder. "I've got news about Abbey."

Harriet's heartbeat quickened as a sick nervousness crept up to her throat. Abbey's short note had hardly told them anything. But she could sense that something was wrong and the only thing keeping her away was Jonathon. "Is it from the private investigator?"

"Yes, but I don't think that you're going to like the news." Jonathon gave his wife the folder, and sat down on the freshly made bed.

Harriet sat beside him and opened it. The first thing she saw was a blurred picture of Abbey. It looked like it was taken through a window. When she read the report beneath it her worst fears became a horror filled reality. Abbey had moved into the cottage. The investigator mentioned a man was with her as well. But they were unable to get a picture or establish his identity. She guessed why. You couldn't take a picture of a demon. They have no physical form. "Oh my God, she's pregnant." Harriet looked at her husband, her eyes wide with terror. "He has our daughter, Jonathon. Now do you believe me?"

"Don't be silly, Harriet. Can't you see what's in front of your eyes?" he tapped the page impatiently. "That's the real reason Abbey's not been in touch. She's in trouble and thinks we won't be happy about it."

Harriet banged her fist on the folder. "No, no, no. That isn't the reason. She's following the same pattern as the others. He… that thing, has her in his grip. He's manipulating her. Cutting her ties with us and anyone else who cares about her."

"So you're saying a demon made our daughter have sex with a man to get him a baby. Don't be ridiculous."

Harriet waved the folder in the air. "This proves it. Our daughter is going to die, Jonathon. We've got to do something - before it's too late."

"You're blowing this out of proportion. Abbey's living with a man, so what! There's nothing macabre about that. If you rush to Ireland with this half-cocked idea of yours, we'll lose her for sure. We need to tread carefully. Maybe invite them here for the weekend. Let her see that we're not angry."

"You're not listening. You never do. That thing isn't a man. It's not human in any way. And it's going to kill our daughter and leave us hell's child to raise."

***

Abbey absently rubbed her stomach as she stood in the garden taking deep breaths of fresh air. As the baby grew, she lost weight. Justin cooked amazing meals, but she had no appetite. Her memory lapses worried her the most. It wasn't natural to lose track of whole days. It was all right Justin telling her that lots of women give birth without outside intervention, but she suspected a lot died, too. He mentioned that he'd read somewhere that changing hormone levels sometimes caused memory problems during pregnancy. That answered one question. But now she was hallucinating too?

She kept seeing the dark outline of a woman in the cottage. But only in the evening, when the shadows were at their darkest. Maybe, like Justin said, it was a trick of the light. But it bothered her a lot. Abbey tilted her face to catch a few rays of the sun as it peeked out behind the grey clouds. Ireland seemed to stay in a perpetual state of rain. Every day was miserable. She shivered and hugged her arms around herself. The frigid air refreshed her dulled senses. It was nice to get out into the open. Justin's sweet scented aftershave followed her everywhere in the house. Recently she began to feel suffocated by his attentiveness.

He had begun to change. It was almost as if he had a split personality. One moment he was funny, kind, very good company and then an angry, petulant and needy man appeared. Abbey sighed, hating the self imposed isolation she had brought on herself. Her thoughts moved to Shaun. What was he doing? Did he still think of her? Abbey watched steam pour from her mouth and nose. It curled upwards drifting towards the sky. Free. Like she wished she was. How did her life become such a mess?

The morning breeze brought the scent of wild, winter flowers. Shaun would know straight away what flowers created such a wonderful scent. He was a true child of nature. The wide open spaces were as essential to him as the air he breathed. A small cluster of tiny white flowers caught her eye in the far corner of the garden. How they managed to push their way through the frosty ground, she didn't know. They looked tired and ragged. How she felt. The garden had looked so pretty when she'd first arrived. Now it seemed as though an invisible hand was crushing the life out of anything that dared to look beautiful.

"Abbey, come inside," Justin's sharp command filtered through her rambling thoughts.

She turned and saw him frantically beckoning to her. Why didn't he come out? He never set foot outside anymore, preferring to have food delivered. They were like hermits squirreled away from the outside world. She took one last look at the garden, watched the sun disappear behind another grey cloud, and sighed as she headed back to the claustrophobic walls of the cottage.

Once inside, the door slammed so violently behind her, Abbey cried out in alarm. "Do you have to do that?" She snapped and watched in bewilderment as he angrily twisted the key in the lock and put it into his jacket pocket.

"I didn't give you permission to go outside."

Abbey saw the anger blazing in his eyes and felt a stirring of fear. Here comes the other Justin, the man she began to hate. He was irrational, sometimes bordering on deranged. Suddenly a life with him in the cottage wasn't so appealing. "I wasn't aware that I needed your permission to visit my own garden." She raised her chin defiantly and held his glare. This was still her house and he could leave if he didn't like what she did.

With his eyes bulging in anger, Justin banged his fist down on the kitchen worktop. "I told you never to leave the cottage. You must obey me. Do I make myself clear, madam?"

Abbey took a deep breath to quell her rising fury. These constant battles of will with Justin weren't good for her or the baby. *"Obey you!* Since when did you become my lord and master? I can go into my garden whenever I like. This is my house, not yours. Do I make myself clear?" She saw the glittering anger in Justin's eye quickly fade. Instead a flicker of fear emerged. "What are you afraid I'll do out there?" she probed.

"I'm not the one who needs to be afraid." His voice was low, a whispered threat held in the air unclaimed, and it made the hairs on her neck stand up in alarm.

Abbey took a step back. "Why do I need to be afraid?"

Justin reached out and lightly caressed her cheek. She flinched, unable to bear his touch.

"I'm sorry, my love. My fear for you makes me shout in anger. You're carrying your brother's child. If someone should see you outside and tell him you're here, it would bring disaster on all our heads. He would not bear the shame well. The people in this town are small minded. They won't understand your mistake in judgement. They might harm you and the child to hide the shameful act. They protect their own here."

Abbey shook her head. No way would Shaun hurt her. He was a gentle man. "You don't know him like I do. He's not like that." Even though her dream had told her otherwise.

"Trust me when I say that people, when whipped into a frenzy, are capable of any atrocity. They live by their own rules here. Why do you think I no longer go out? Too many questions are being asked about you."

Abbey instinctively put a protective arm across her stomach. "I can't believe that Shaun would harm our child."

"Oh, my poor love. I've tried so hard to protect you from the truth. The last thing I want to do is hurt you in any way"

"Tell me. What's happened?"

"Last month, when you were napping I went out for supplies. Rumours immediately attacked my ears. I won't speak of their vileness, but I did make a point of finding out who was spreading them. It's your brother. His lies are vicious. Slanderous to the fullest."

Abbey clutched the table for support as her legs threatened to collapse beneath her. Devastation seeped into every part of her body. "What exactly did he say?"

"It's not pleasant, my love. Are you sure you want to know?"

Abbey nodded. Unable to trust herself to speak.

"He's told people how... um, how can I put this? That you're loose with your morals and are of very low character. There is more, but I refuse to repeat such wickedness. I wanted to protect you, Abbey. That's why I was angry at you for going out. I couldn't bear for you to hear such hurtful lies from someone else. I know now that I should have told you straight away. I'm so sorry."

Abbey quickly sat before she fell. So Aveline's plan to make Shaun hate her had worked. He believed her lies and now they came back to haunt her. She had to make things right? "It's not his fault, Justin. It's mine. I let him believe that I..." she paused and took a deep breath. "I should have told him the truth straight away. I've got to find him. Explain that he's the father of this child, whether he likes it or not. He has a right to know."

Justin dropped to his knees in front of her and took her hand in his. "If I thought it would make a difference I'd take you to him myself. I love you, Abbey. I don't want to lose you, but I also want you to be happy. But you can't make this right. He's married. An Irish girl I'm told. They're expecting a child. If you tell him the truth, you'll ruin a lot of lives. The repercussions will be catastrophic."

Abbey had no idea she could feel such deep, painful despair. Shaun was married - so soon? Then he hadn't really loved her at all. A dull ache began to form behind her temples. She couldn't think straight. In the back of her mind, she harboured a slim hope that she might have a chance to make things right between them. Now that was gone, she was filled with agony. Tears spilled down her cheeks and when Justin folded her into his arms, she clung to him. He was so kind. She felt terrible for all the bad thoughts she had about him. He loved her, despite her failings. She was blessed to have him in her life. His sweet smelling aftershave filled her nose and throat and she welcomed the calm it brought with it.

***

Adrinia was incandescent with anger. Not one spell had worked on the Shaun to bring him back. And it was all because of that old gypsy. Her spells shielded him. She was getting help to boost her powers, but from who? Justin's moods annoyed her. He was like a man possessed when it came to that trollop and she had to keep pretending she cared about his woes. "What's all this conscience rubbish going on with you, Justin? I can't remember you having such an emotion before. You've lied to Abigail about her precious beau, so what?"

"Oh, shut up, Adrinia. It's my fault she was so upset in the first place. She went into the garden and you know I can't go out there now. What if someone sees her and reports back to O'Donnell? "

Adrinia clicked her tongue in irritation. "Stop worrying. If he comes, deal with him like you've always done in the past. Anyway, you can go out into the garden, you chose not to."

"You know the spell I use to keep this shape doesn't work properly outside the cottage anymore. It's taking everything I have to hold this dump's illusion in place."

"I warned you that nothing works forever. You need to get rid of the mortal. I told you that months ago."

"I can't, not yet. She still feels something for him. If she had even an inkling I'd hurt him..." Justin paused, his breath rapid with agitation. "I don't want the child to come early and kill her."

Adrinia smiled in the darkness. "So she still loves the mortal then?"

"NO," Justin roared. "Abbey loves me. She's just confused at the moment. The pregnancy is taking its toll on her. The brat is sapping her strength."

"You've changed these past few months, Justin. You're weak. Next, you'll tell me that you love her," Adrinia said, daring him to admit her worst fear. Why did he need that fragile, ugly creature, that he had to drug to get into his bed, when he could have her, willing and very capable of satisfying his every need?

"It's none of your business what I feel and the only one changing around here is you. You're like a vine, clinging to me everywhere I go. I know you watch me from the shadows. Do you like to watch us in bed, Adrinia? Do you wish when I suckle on Abbey's soft, round breast, that it is yours?"

Adrinia was grateful that Justin couldn't see the flush which stained her cheeks. He was right, she did want him. Every time he made love to that trollop, she wished desperately it was her. His madness fuelled hers. She needed that unpredictability to fill the dark void of her existence. "Justin you're being ugly again. You really must reign in that temper of yours. I understand that you don't want to lose this child after all your hard work."

"You don't see it, do you Adrinia? I don't care about the baby."

"Don't care?" she repeated. "But that's all you've gone on about for years. How much of your soul have you bartered off to obtain spells to change the infants in the womb to look like your wife?"

"My priorities have changed now."

"Change them back," Adrinia snapped. "You can't expect her to love your true image. Get a grip of yourself Justin, and look in the mirror. You're not the handsome man you once were. No one on this plane of existence would accept your true form now. You have to let this stupid quest go, otherwise it will destroy you." Adrinia materialised back in the shadow realm, boiling with rage. Aslow ran to greet her and she absently picked him up, pushing back her jet coloured hair which spilled down her narrow shoulders and across her voluptuous breast to her waist. She rested Aslow on her rounded hip, and he burrowed against her small waist, made smaller by the laces of her corset. A flush of anger stained her high cheek bones and gave her skin a fevered look.

In her mortal life the members of her coven had coveted her beauty – worshipped it. Yet in the mortal world, she could only exist as a vaporous cloud. Her vanity was now used as punishment against her. She may be a queen, but of what? A realm that no one could feel, see or touch. Loneliness ached in her body every day. If only Justin loved her enough to become her king. Then he could enter her world and see her beauty and know that she loved him deeply. Tossing her hair back defiantly, it was down to her to show Justin the error of his ways. Their constant bickering was fuelled by her desire and frustration.

"Come, my pet. We're going to catch a cat and let it loose amongst the pigeons."

***

Jonathon stood in the hallway, tapping his foot impatiently. "Come on Harriet, we'll miss the flight."

Harriet pulled on her black leather gloves as she hurried down the winding staircase "Okay, I'm coming,"

They got into the taxi and she checked her bag for the tickets and passports. "Right, I have everything we need. Did you book the hotel?"

Jonathon nodded. "But it's nothing special, a double room in a local pub."

Harriet's eyes widened in disapproval. "A pub? Oh, really Jonathon. Couldn't you get anything better? I don't want my clothes to smell of beer when we meet Abbey."

"No, I can't. It's a small town and they don't cater for visitors."

"It will have to do then. We need to get her out of that cottage before she gives birth, otherwise we'll lose her forever."

Chapter Twenty-Two

"Aveline, ye dinna look well lass. I hav' nae seen ye tek' a bite tae eat in days. What's going on?" Josie asked.

Aveline pushed the cold toast around her plate. "Nothing. I'm fine."

Josie heaved a sigh and sat down on the chair. "I dinna ken ye and Shaun ignoring each other is normal?"

"It's complicated, Josie."

"Then explain the uncomplicated version."

Aveline's mouth tightened into a stubborn line. Shaun was doing a good job of shutting her out of his life. She expected him to be angry about the cottage sale. But his silence and condemning looks were hard to bear. So much bothered her now, she was lucky if she got an hour of sleep a night. God forbid he should go back to Ireland. Who would help him if the fire demons come again? Maybe it was safe now. The demon probably has Abigail under his spell, so Shaun offered no threat. Part of her wanted to save the child – her grandchild, but how could she? Nothing can fight evil as powerful as that. Shaun wasn't going to budge. He was heading back. She had already made up her mind to follow. But now she had to somehow find a way to keep Rosa's mouth shut.

"I've been thinking, Josie. I might forget me plans and go home. I don't know what I'm thinking. Shaun will never settle here and I don't want to live the rest of me life without him in it."

"That'll be the first sensible thing you've said since we got here. You had me worried sick, mother," Shaun said from the doorway. "I didn't want to leave you all alone, but you gave me no choice. I hoped your good sense would eventually prevail. Jessie said it would and that you might be having a woman's crisis, whatever that is. I had to be patient. Well, you've really tried me patience. I'm almost a martyr. Has the crisis passed? Can we go home now?"

Aveline swallowed the aching lump in her throat. Terror consumed her as she forced a smile. "Yes, son. Me crisis is over." But hopefully yours in not beginning, she silently added.

"Then I'll tell Jessie to pack. Their coming for a well deserved holiday."

Aveline watched excitement light up Shaun's eyes. Maybe there was hope for him and Jessie after all.

***

"Is this too short?" Aveline asked, plucking at her dusky pink skirt. She had bought it on a whim, now she wasn't so sure of her choice.

Josie put down her hair brush and looked her up and down. "No, it's only a wee bit above yoor knee. Mind you, if I had legs like that I'd show them off too."

Aveline shrugged on the matching jacket over her white lacy top. I look like a dog's dinner," she complained.

"Och stop it, you look fine. Is Jessie ready yet?"

"Yes. They've got so much luggage Shaun's ordered them a separate taxi."

Josie's chuckle was halted by a soft tap on the door.

"Mother, can I come in?"

"Yes, Shaun. Your aunt and I are as decent as we'll ever be," Aveline said, smoothing on a pale pink lipstick.

Shaun opened the door and heaved in a suitcase she didn't recognise. "Oh no, not another one. How long are they staying again?" She secretly hoped it was for good. But only time would tell about that.

"I know. What with Jessie taking her entire wardrobe and Dougie insisting he can't leave one toy behind, I'm expecting the plane to fall over with the amount of luggage we're putting on it."

Douglas stood outside the front door with a bright green rucksack on his back that bulged out in all directions. "Are we goin', Shaun?" He hopped from one foot to the other, barely able to contain his excitement.

Shaun laughed. "We'd better wait for your mother."

"I'm here," Jessie called from next door. "I'm locking up."

She came out and stood beside Douglas. "How do you like my travelling outfit?" She spun round and her dark green, gypsy style skirt billowed out around her like a balloon. "Will I blend in with the natives?"

"Maybe with the leprechauns, although I've given you fair warning about them." He winked at Douglas, who giggled. "Mind you, the fairies might put up a good fight for you too. They collect beautiful things."

Jessie's cheeks dimpled at the compliment. "It's so nice of you and Aveline to invite us. I can't tell you how excited we are."

"You're more than welcome. You know that." Shaun pushed a chocolate bar in Douglas's hand. "Eat it in the taxi when your mothers not looking! Now hurry up you two, the car will be here in a minute. I'll meet you both at the airport."

Jessie kissed Shaun on the cheek. "You really are a kind man,"

Aveline smiled and pretended to busy herself with straightening Douglas's rucksack.

"Look Aveline. I've had my nails done especially for the trip," Jessie held up a fine row of French polished nails.

"Ooh, I'm jealous," Aveline teased.

Adrinia's eyes narrowed in fury as she watched from the shadows of the walkway. Mortals were so fickle. Where was his love for Abigail now? So this was her replacement, was it? Not if she had her way.

Aveline heard the ambulance siren wailing down the road, as their taxi turned off for the airport. She shuddered. That noise always spelt doom, even when the occupant wasn't dead. It didn't seem right for them to be so happy, when a poor soul was suffering somewhere else. At the airport, Shaun unloaded their luggage while she waited for Jessie.

"You did tell them to wait at the main entrance, didn't you?" she queried.

Shaun checked his watch. "Yes, mother. They've probably got held up in traffic. Did you see it building up before we turned off?"

Aveline opened her mouth to reply and was cut off by an anguished shout behind her. She turned and saw Josie running towards her with tears streaming down her face. "What is it? What's wrong?"

Josie took a deep breath. "Oh, Aveline."

"What is it? For God's sake tell me."

"I was travelling behind the taxi when th' car came oot o' nowhere. The driver couldna' avoid it. Oh, Aveline, it crashed right into Jessie and Douglas."

Shaun dropped the luggage and stared at Josie. "Where?"

Josie pulled out a tissue and wiped her eyes. "Down the road. The police wondna' let me near, so I've come straight here."

"Is she hurt? How's Dougie?"

Josie shook her head. "I dinna ken. The police wouldna' let me near them."

Aveline had no time to respond. Shaun took off down the road and she followed, cursing her stupid high heels for slowing her down. "Please God, let them both be all right. Don't let them be badly hurt," she prayed. By the time she rounded the second corner, Aveline felt her lungs burning with exertion. She stopped, breathing hard and tried to take in the pandemonium around her. Fire engines, ambulances and paramedics littered the carriageway; she could barely see what was going on. A taxi lay on its roof as if a huge hand had flipped it over. Luggage spilled out into the road and she watched as a snowy length of ribbon blew along the road as if trying to continue with its journey. She looked for Shaun and saw him kneeling on the side of a grass verge. When the paramedic left his bike and walked over to him, Aveline felt her heart miss a beat. Why was he so still? She hurried over and got there as the paramedic walked away. It wasn't until she stood behind Shaun that she saw the reason why he hadn't moved. A silent scream of horror filled her head, blotting out her cry of anguish, as a ragged piece of green skirt, lay like a final epitaph, in the gutter beneath a white ambulance blanket.

Aveline told her legs to move; yet they remained unresponsive, rooted to the spot. When they finally responded, she jerked forward like a puppet, as if someone else was pulling the strings. She sank to her knees beside Shaun. He held a small hand with a pretty French manicure and a sob burst from her frozen lips.

"The paramedic said that Jessie won't be here for long, they need a different ambulance to take her away," Shaun said woodenly. "He said she wouldn't have suffered. It was instant."

Aveline hadn't felt such raw pain since losing Morgan. It burned the back of her throat like acid, killing any words of consolation tumbling around in her mouth. Tears poured from her eyes as though a dam had broken and washed everything good from their life. She wanted to remove the cover from Jessie and see her beautiful face one last time, but there was so much blood and she was too afraid at what she might see.

"It's better if we don't look at her," Shaun said, as if reading Aveline's thoughts.

"It's not fair, mother. It's bloody not fair. What did she do to die like this?"

Aveline had no words that could help. No prayers of solace. She shook her head and laid her hand on his shoulder. "No, it isn't bloody fair, son."

"Where's Dougie?" The words burst from Shaun like a shotgun round. "He mustn't see his mother like this." He gently tucked Jessie's hand beneath the blanket and looked up and down the road.

Aveline scanned the area for any sign of a boy with bright red hair. "I don't know. Maybe Josie has him."

The same paramedic as before came running towards them cutting of any further conversation. "Look, I'm sorry tae interrupt ye, but we've a wee laddie still in th' wreck and he's asking for Shaun. Would that be ye, sir?"

"Yes. Where is he?"

"Shaun…" Aveline said grabbing his arm. "Tell him…" she paused as tears poured from her eyes, "tell him I'm waiting for him out here."

He squeezed her arm softly and ran with the paramedic towards the overturned car.

"The wee laddie is lying between th' back and front seat. I dinna think he was wearing a seat belt, so he's got significant crush injuries."

"What do you mean by *significant injuries*? He'll be all right, won't he?"

The paramedic refused to meet Shaun's inquiring eyes. "We're doing all we can to stabilise him. The fire crews are going tae start cutting away th' side door. Ye need tae keep th' lad calm. It'll be noisy fer him."

Aveline watched as an ambulance, like no other she had ever seen, pull up beside her. It was black and 'Private' was written in white capital letters down its side. The windows, except the window screen, were blacked out. She got up from the floor when two men, dressed in the green uniform of an ambulance crew, got out and opened the rear doors of the van.

One of the men walked up to her and touched her arm. She saw his eyes were grey, like the sky just before it rained. They looked kind. He would take care of their Jessie. She knew it.

"It's okay, we'll tek good care of her," he said softly.

Another man pulled out a stretcher and Aveline heard a soft whoosh as its wheels lowered onto the floor. This ambulance was not for the living. This took the dead and today it was taking Jessie. She watched the men gently lift her onto the stretcher. Their respect was genuine and heartfelt. Somehow it made a difference. Jessie looked so small on the wide stretcher. Barely breath and bones held her together in life, and now there wasn't even that. As they wheeled her away, Aveline caught a glimpse of Jessie as the blanket partially slid away. Her face broken and bloodied, held none of her earlier prettiness. Eyes open wide in death, stared at her almost accusingly. She gasped, shaken to the pits of despair, and quickly averted her eyes.

***

Shaun looked at the taxi, crushed like an old tin can, in horror. It was a wonder anyone survived the wreck.

"The fire crew is gang tae cut off th' driver's side o' the door and try tae get the seat oot. Th' laddie is lying in th' rear on th' cars roof, trapped under th' back of th' front passenger seat. I need ye tae speak tae him through the rear window. We've got most of th' glass oot and I've put a blanket down. It's not a safe area. But the wee lad's so scared. He needs a face he recognises."

Shaun took off his jacket and lay on the ground as close to the car as he could. He inched over it and through the back window. He could see Dougie's mop of red hair. The paramedic had somehow plugged a drip into his small arm and the transparent bag was hooked above his head.

"Dougie, it's Shaun," he said softly.

"Och Shaun, th' man cut th' sleeve of my new jacket and shirt. Maws gang tae go mad when she finds oot'," he sobbed.

"Don't worry about that, I'll buy you a fine new suit when we get to Ireland."

"Can you buy maw a new dress too? When th' men took her away she was asleep. She dinna see it's all torn. There was so much blood, I dinna ken where it was from." Dougie began to sob. "Och, my arm hurts. The doctor said th' pin in my arm would make me feel better. But it hasna worked."

Shaun inched further into the car.

"Ye canna go any further, it's too dangerous," the paramedic warned, placing a restraining hand on him.

"I can't leave him all alone. He's just a wee boy," Shaun replied, his voice filled with anguish.

"Go on then. Don't let him touch the drip."

Shaun nodded and crawled further into the car. "Now I don't want you to be moving about like a wriggly snake," he said to Douglas, trying to make his voice sound light. "The firemen will get you out soon enough."

Dougie's face screwed up in pain. "But th' pin hurts. Everywhere hurts."

Shaun's thoughts scrambled to find away to take his mind from the pain. "You're being such a brave boy that when we get out of here, I'm going to buy you the biggest hamburger and chips you've ever seen."

"And maw? She likes burgers. Do you think th' fairies will still wait fer me at your hoose, if it teks me and Maw a long time tae get better?"

Shaun took a deep breath to steady his voice. For the moment it was better to let Dougie believe his mother was hurt. There would be time to tell him the truth later. "Oh, I think they'll be kicking their heels in anticipation."

A cough shook the child's body and he cried out with pain.

"And I'm even sure the leprechauns will let you into all their secrets," he added quickly. "You know what? I bet you'll be the one who finds the lost crown of the king leprechaun."

Shaun watched with concern as Dougie's face grew paler with each passing second. "I'll tell you a little secret," he carried on. "I've an idea where the crown is. When you're feeling better we'll put our heads together and make a plan to get it." He blinked back the tears threatening to spill down his face, when he saw a trickle of blood seep from Dougie's lips. "He'll be so grateful when we give it back to him. I think he'll make you an honoured leprechaun."

Dougie smiled. "I'd like that." He took a shaky breath, exhaling slowly. "I'm so tired. Do ye think I can hav' a nap?"

Shaun felt the pressure of another body edge beside him. "They're starting to cut away now," the paramedic whispered. "How ye doing, son?" he reached out to gently take his wrist. "His pulse is weak," he whispered. "Keep him talking. That's all you can do."

"How long until they open this tin can?" Shaun snapped. "What's taking so long?"

"Look, yoor doing great," the paramedic replied. "It won't be long now." He moved back and left Shaun with Dougie.

"There's going to be a little noise. Don't you be scared now, I'm here," Shaun gently grasped the boy's fingers. They felt so cold and small inside his.

The paramedic stood up and signalled for the Chief fireman. "We need tae get a move on. The laddie's gang tae go and I dinna want him goin' in there."

"No hope at all then?"

The paramedic shook his head.

The fireman raised his hand for the others to begin cutting. "We'll move as quickly as we can."

"Dougie, can you hear me?" Shaun called softly.

"Aye, Shaun, but I feel strange. Like I'm floating away."

The noise was deafening as the fireman cut into the car. The paramedic pushed his way down the side of Shaun. "How ye doing laddie?"

"Dougie says he feel strange."

The paramedic felt the boy's pulse again.

"What's wrong?"

"You need tae understand, the lads injuries are very severe," he whispered. "His pelvis is crushed and being held together by the seats. When we move him, I can't stop the internal haemorrhaging. No one can." The paramedic left the words he couldn't say hanging in the air.

Shaun felt as though he had been punched in the stomach. Bile rose in his throat and he swallowed it down. Dougie wasn't going to make it either. He was going to lose them both.

The paramedic shifted his position. "I'm so sorry."

"How long?" Shaun whispered.

"When he's moved, it'll be a couple of minutes."

The sun suddenly streamed onto their faces as the bottom of the car came away from its mountings. Shaun clambered over the seats with the paramedic and placed his hand on the small of Dougie's back. "Some men are going to move the seat next to you. Squeeze my hand and it'll be over in a jiffy."

Douglas squeezed and cried out with pain as the seat came out in one swift movement. The paramedic felt the child's pulse again and shook his head at Shaun. Lying beside Douglas, one arm around his shoulders, Shaun forced his voice to be jovial.

"Hey, Dougie, you'll never guess what that doctor just told me."

Douglas turned his head and stared at Shaun. "What did he say?"

"He's told me there's a gathering of fairies outside and they're demanding to speak to you. They want to help you search for the king leprechaun's crown."

"Do they know I'm hurt?"

Shaun swallowed the aching lump in his throat. "Of course. But don't worry about that. They'll fix you up and make you well with their special fairy dust. You'll be in their fairy glen tonight dancing around their fire." He watched a small smile flit across Douglas's lips as they began to whiten.

"Can maw come too? Will she dance with me?"

Shaun nodded. "Of course. In fact she's already there waiting for you."

"Are ye coming? We canna go wi' out ye?"

"I wish I could. But this trip's just for you and mummy. But I'll keep me eye on you, never fear."

"I'll be good, I promise. I canna wait tae see th' crown and tell maw about the gold…" Dougie's voice trailed off to a soft murmur.

"Sleep now, and when you wake up, all the pain will be gone."

"Okay. I'll see ye later then."

A soft sigh floated through his parted lips and Shaun knew he gone. "Goodbye, my wee little man," he whispered, as tears streamed from his eyes and puddled on his arm, forming a pool of misery.

Chapter Twenty-Three

Aveline wiped a tissue across her eyes. They felt sore and scratchy. She looked around the small church and counted eight people. That included her, Shaun and Josie. Not much of a turnout for Jessie and Douglas.

"Ye did a wonderful job organising this," Josie whispered to Aveline. "Th' flowers are beautiful."

Aveline's eyes lingered on the two coffins lying side by side. "They deserve the best."

"Aye lass, they certainly do. How's Shaun doing? I've nay seen hide nor hair of the lad since the accident."

Aveline watched Shaun standing alone in the front row. He stared at the coffins, yet she knew it wasn't those he was seeing. This past week she feared the vacant look in his eyes. He seemed no longer inside his own body. "Not that well," she admitted.

Josie sighed. "After th' funeral I think ye should go home. The poor lad's mind needs tae heal and he canna do it here."

She nodded. Shaun had taken the deaths very hard. How well would he fare at home?

"I ken something else is going on back home, Aveline, but I canna help ye, if you dinna tell me what it is. Ye hafta sort it oot'. If ye stay here, Shaun's spirit will die," Josie added.

Aveline lightly touched her sons arm. He looked at her and she frowned at the void in his eyes. Was that in his heart too? "Come on, it's time to go, son."

He looked at her in confusion. "Where are we going?"

"Home. Back to Ireland where we belong," Aveline replied.

***

Rosa put the smoky quartz crystal in her pocket. Her legs momentarily felt like lead as its energy grounded her. Satisfied all the crystals were now around the caravan to ward of psychic attacks from the Queen and Justin, she made herself a strong cup of tea. They would not get her without a fight. As if she didn't have enough to do, now with the added burden of Abigail's parents arriving in town. If they took it upon themselves to visit the cottage and see their daughter, it would be disastrous. Justin would attack. No one would escape his wrath if he felt threatened. Rosa sat on her sofa and puffed thoughtfully on her clay pipe. No news from Aveline or Shaun in eight weeks. The thought bubbled anger inside her. How dare they leave their problems to her! "Oh mother," she mumbled in between blowing out curls of white smoke. "What a task you've left me."

Justin and Adrinia forming an alliance. Who would have thought it! Those two couldn't trust themselves, never mind each other. She only believed it because her spirit guide told her it was true. The queen is a cruel wretch, without an ounce of mercy running in her frozen veins. It was written that she was beauty personified, yet on the earth plane she can only appear as a dark vaporous cloud. A fitting punishment for one so merciless, Rosa decided.

She drew deeply on her pipe once more and felt the smoke hit the back of her throat. She coughed, bringing tears to her eyes. The damn pipe would be the death of her. A tap at the door brought her out of her melancholy thoughts.

"Who's there?" She was in no mood for small talk today.

"It's me, Aveline O'Donnell."

Rosa smiled with relief as she got up and hurried to unlock the door. By the time she pulled it open her smile was gone, replaced with a reproving glare. "So you're back then?"

Aveline pulled her coat closer around her body. "I didn't come here to argue. Can I come in?"

Rosa saw her red eyes and haggard face and took a step back from the door. Trouble was brewing and she hoped Shaun wasn't part of it. She needed him more than ever now that Adrinia was involved. "You're always welcome here. You choose not to visit."

Aveline stepped in and glanced around. "Are you alone?"

"Of course. At my age the only thing warming my bed is a water bottle. Sit yourself down and I'll make some tea. You look like you need it."

"Thanks. I know you're angry that I took Shaun away, but after the angels saved him from the fire, I…"

Rosa gave a sharp laugh. "Angels? I've never been called that before."

"I didn't call you an angel. I mean the one…"

"Who saved Shaun from the fire serpent," Rosa interrupted. "That was me, Aveline. Even the Lord himself heard your screams for help that night."

"You," Aveline repeated incredulously. "That's impossible. I saw the angel in a dome of light bending over my Shaun's burnt body."

"You saw me in my astral form. I'm the one who pulled his spirit back from those devils." Rosa held up her hands, showing the new, pink skin where her blisters had been.

"It couldn't be you."

"Oh, you never believe anything until it pokes you in the eye," Rosa snapped back. "I had to use the Esor light to help me. It's no longer asleep inside him, Aveline. It's awake and churning out enough energy to raise the dead. If he had worn the protection pouch I'd made him..."

"I threw it away. I thought it was one of your spells to keep him here. I don't know what this light is that you keep going on about, but it didn't help Jessie and Dougie."

Rosa paused, her hand in mid air with a spoonful of sugar. "And who might they be?"

Aveline dropped on to the sofa and pulled a tissue from her pocket. "I'd better start at the beginning."

Rosa bought the cups of tea over to the table and sat down. By the time Aveline had finished, both their teas were untouched and cold.

"The trip was doomed to fail. It was no accident what happened to those poor mites," Rosa said picking up the cups. "They are casualties of war. Shaun is wanted back here and they thought Jessie and Dougie stood in the way."

"No, it was a car accident. There's no magic in that," Aveline said.

Rosa poured the tea down the sink. "I don't believe in accidents as far as your family and Abigail are concerned. This has the stench of evil all over it. Accidents can be manipulated, you know. Even you said the driver of the other car kept babbling on about how his car had steered itself."

Aveline sneered. "The ravings of a stupid, drunken man."

"That's what you and everyone else will think. We always choose to believe the plausible."

"But Justin should be happy that Shaun's interest is elsewhere."

"If we were dealing with him, I'd agree. But he's in league with the shadow queen and that changes everything."

Aveline pulled her coat tighter around her body. "Shaun's hardly slept a wink or taken a bite to eat in days. He hasn't spoken a word since the funeral. I think he's gone mad with grief."

Rosa's hopes plummeted. This couldn't have come at a worse time. Shaun was now vulnerable and in no condition to use his light to self heal. "The mind can be a terrible weapon when it turns against you."

Aveline dabbed at the tears running down her cheeks. "What can I do? I want him to be safe,"

Rosa reached for the grey woollen shawl hanging on the back of the chair. "Come on. We've no time for tears. Shaun needs us." She opened a cupboard and took out different crystals which she pushed into the deep pockets of her dress.

"Thanks. I know we've never seen eye to eye, and I doubt if we ever will, but we both love Shaun and that can't be a bad thing." She walked out the front door before Rosa could reply and left the cold, evening air to enter. Rosa shuddered, unsure if it was the draught causing it or the thought of what would happen if Shaun had lost his mind. She didn't have the power to fight those two alone. They walked across the fells in silence, giving Rosa the chance to mentally contact Tessa, her spirit guide. She needed her advice and protection if she was going to bring Shaun back from whatever dark place he was in.

Aveline paused outside her front door. "He won't speak. All he does is stare into the fire. I begged him not to light it, but he ignored me."

Rosa nodded and followed her inside. She felt a gentle tug on her heart when she saw him. His dramatic weight loss had aged him and, his once mischievous, emerald eyes were marred by black circles.

"My God, Shaun, its hot enough to bake bread in here," Rosa took off her shawl. Delving into her pockets she took out a handful of crystals and placed them around him.

"What are they for?" Aveline questioned.

Rosa placed a milky quartz crystal on the arm of the chair beside Shaun. "This one will help me unblock his energy centres and reduced his anxiety." She placed another clearer crystal on the other arm beside him. "This Aqua Aura quartz will help the angels to heal him. I'll put the smoky quartz at his feet to ground him. This one," which she took almost triumphantly from her pocket, "is for me. Selenite, to help me speak to and hear Shaun's tortured spirit. You really should learn about the crystals, Aveline. They'll do you a power of good and might even curb that temper of yours. Now fetch me a stool so I can sit in front of him."

Aveline pushed a wooden foot stall at her. "It's all I have that's low."

"Then it will do. Now, I'm going to sit here with me eyes closed. It's called a meditative trance. So don't touch me or speak and don't make any sudden noises unless you want me to drop dead."

"What if you don't wake up?"

"Then Shaun and I will stay here, until our flesh rots and bones crumble," she said adamantly. Then, seeing the fear on Aveline's face she relented and smiled. "Don't worry yourself, I intend to come back *with* Shaun." Clasping the Selenite, she closed her eyes and allowed Tessa, her spirit guide, to lead her astral body into Shaun's mind.

Tessa was a nun in a previous incarnation and she always appeared dressed in the dark robes of the convent. Her quiet, yet strong presence comforted Rosa. On this perilous journey it was good to have someone trustworthy by her side.

"We are going to a place you've never been before," Tessa warned. "It's where the higher self lies."

"You mean the conscience," Rosa asked.

"No. Above the rational mind and below the soul realm is an intermediary plane of consciousness. Let's call it the intuition. Although God and the soul are the truly creative agents of the universe, the process of creating begins with the intuition and then moves to feeling, responses, images and shapes. It is a key to initiating the creativity within - your higher self."

Rosa frowned. "I'm not with you, Tessa."

"Think of your spirit and soul as Yin and Yang. The soul is receptive, the spirit active. The spirit is that which incarnates and your soul oversees the incarnation and gathers all the experiences, it then processes the information for evolution.

Your spirit self sends the information it learns through the stem of your being - soul. When your soul feels that you've gained all the knowledge you require, your spirit will merge with it and progress to a higher realm."

"But what's that to do with the higher self?"

"It's your point of reasoning. If it's not balanced and in harmony, everything else goes haywire."

"Oh, I see. So the light within Shaun is the energy left behind by an Esor spirit, and now activated, it's unbalancing his energies?"

"Yes. At the moment, you need to concentrate on Shaun. His emotions are at war with each other. His subconscious is ruling coherent thought and you need to deal with that. I'm going to send healing colours to aid you.

His heart energy centre is closed. So I'm going to fill the space with green and pink to revive it. The throat is blocked, so I'll fill it with blue. When it begins to work, he will be able to communicate what he is feeling. Apart from that there is little more I can do."

Rosa swallowed her apprehension. "Tell me this, Tessa. Once Shaun has used the Esor light for the right purpose, will it leave him?"

"No, it will rest where it is, giving Shaun a brighter light to guide him through life."

"And Abigail?"

"I can't say what will happen. Her spirit is severely compromised."

"Okay. I'm ready. Let's get this over with."

Tessa led her into a dark and silent place. Rosa felt the oppressive atmosphere locking her in. "I can feel his unhappiness covering me like a blanket," she whispered.

"You're going to feel everything he does, Rosa. We are in the confines of his mind. You need to keep yourself grounded. If you begin to feel overwhelmed by his depression, visualize the crystal you left at Shaun's feet. I will send energy through it to you, combined with its own energy, it will give you added strength."

Rosa opened her mouth to reply and realised that she and Tessa were no longer alone. Milling around them were shadowy silhouettes that looked like men.

"Walk past them," Tessa whispered. "They are the shadows of Shaun's thoughts, wandering around aimlessly. Usually there are too many to count. An active mind has over a million different thoughts in a day."

The further she walked into Shaun's mind, the more Rosa felt his depression weighing her down. She visualised the smoky quartz at his feet and drew its energy into her solar plexus. A wave of heat coursed through her, pushing aside his negativity. She walked past his thoughts and felt their cold despair cover her like sticky cobwebs. Depression is a terrible thing to witness, but when seen from this angle it was very daunting - even for her.

Rosa carried on walking through the darkness, occasionally bumping into a stray thought, and just when she believed that she would never reach Shaun's higher self, an agonised scream filled the air. "Did you hear that?" Rosa whispered.

Tessa nodded. "That's Shaun grief. The emotion is locked away deep inside his mind. If he doesn't acknowledge it, it can't be released. He won't heal."

"The poor boy. No one should suffer such despair."

Tessa stopped and pointed. "We're here."

Rosa looked up the length of the biggest brick wall she had ever seen. "What is that?"

"This is what he's locked himself behind. When mortals erect this wall in their minds, it can take a life time to break it down."

Rosa lifted her chin in defiant determination. It wouldn't take her a lifetime. The grief and tears binding it together were still fresh and it meant the cement was still wet and vulnerable. "How do I get in?"

"You have the power to make your own door," Tessa replied.

"A door. How can I do that?"

"The mind is a wondrous tool. Forget your mortal body and all its boundaries. This world is ruled by thought and logic."

Rosa immediately thought about soaring over it like a giant eagle. But she suspected that Shaun would only make it taller. She stared at the wall and visualised a wooden door with a small, round, china handle. It shimmered for a few seconds and resettled back to bricks. She looked at Tessa for guidance.

"I never said getting inside would be easy."

Concentrate, Rosa, she told herself. *You're stronger than this wall.* She visualised the door again and the wall shimmered under her penetrating gaze. She could barely contain her excitement when it appeared. She reached for the handle.

"Be careful when you enter," Tessa warned. "I can't come any further with you. There are spiritual laws that even I must abide by. I'm not allowed to influence free will in the physical world. But because you're astral projecting, the rules don't apply to you. Remember, a closed mind is capable of locking you inside with it."

"I'll heed your advice. Thanks for your help, dear friend. You've taught me a lot over the years, but this is exceptional. Is there no end to what I need to learn?"

"Of course. You have your own free will. You don't have to keep seeking knowledge."

Rosa smiled. "Ah, but I do. You can never know too much."

"Then I'll be here to teach you."

"I'll see you later, then," Rosa placed her hand on the china handle. It felt hard and cold as she twisted it and pushed open the door. The heat, as she stepped through, almost took her breath away. It dried her mouth, melting her tongue to her teeth. The door slammed shut with a finality that made her jump. She watched it shimmer and turn back into the impenetrable wall. Now she was locked inside too. But not for long. "It's time for me to gather your thoughts together, Shaun O'Donnell," she whispered into the darkness. "Where are you, boy? I know you're here." she shouted.

"Of course he's bloody here," a disembodied voice shouted back.

The voice sounded like Shaun's, yet it was so hard and unforgiving, Rosa was in two minds. "That's not the Shaun I know."

"I'm part of who he is now," the voice barked.

Rosa strained to peer through the blackness, but she couldn't see through its thick veil. "What do you mean, who he is now?"

Maniacal laughter echoed around her. As it was made up from more than one voice she deduced it must be a chorus of all his erratic emotions.

"You'll know me as anger. I'm in charge now," another voice snapped.

Rosa grimaced, not if she had her way. She had to get these in order so Shaun could tackle them and move on with his life.

"Who else is in here?"

"I'm here, but I want to be alone," answered a softer, more reasonable voice.

Rosa watched as a dim glow appeared to her left. A wooden, hard-backed chair appeared first and then Shaun materialised on it. He sat with his head resting on his arms, which were folded onto his knees; he didn't acknowledge her presence.

"Hello, boy, it's good to see you." Rosa moved closer. Showing his true spirit self was a good start. "I've come to help you find your way back."

"I don't need any help. I like it here," a voice shouted out.

Rosa knew she was going to have to reason with every individual emotion. A daunting prospect. "I know what happened is a terrible thing, but giving up won't take your pain away. It just prolongs the agony."

"No! If I stay here I don't have to remember," anger shouted. "Pain can't touch me here."

"But it will wait for you. You can't escape it any more than I can. We all have to face pain at some point in our lives. Without it, how can our spirit grow and evolve? We have to take the good with the bad, lad."

"I can't go on," said a softer voice she instantly recognised it as grief.

"Yes you can. I know you, Shaun. I've suffered too in my life. If I can survive it so can you. Fight back. Let me help you knock down this wall."

"NO," anger responded, like a sharp crack of a whip. "I've had enough. NOW LET ME BE." The voice thundered in the air, bowing Rosa's shoulders with its terrible weight.

"Then I'll stay here with you. I'll give up my life to stay in this miserable place. Because you're worth it."

"I don't want you to stay," grief replied.

"And I won't return without you. I need you Shaun."

"The wall's too big to climb," fear whispered.

"Go away, fear. There's no place for you here. Listen to me, Shaun. You can't live life and not lose someone you care about? Love is a complex emotion. You'll be lead in many different directions with it."

"I don't want to be lead anymore," grief replied.

Before she could retaliate, the wailing she had heard earlier began again. As it grew louder and louder, Rosa covered her ears, but she couldn't shut it out. "Shaun, stop this. Talk to me, boy."

But the terrible screaming continued. It was as if all his emotions cried out at the same time. Was this the true sound of madness? "Shaun, listen to me," she shouted. "You've a flesh and blood child. Your one night with Abigail produced more than love."

"LIAR," anger roared.

Rosa imagined a cloak of light around her for protection. She could feel the violence emanating from the emotion and she didn't know if it had the power to actually hurt her. "Shaun O'Donnell, you've known me many a year. Do you think I would tell such a lie? You heard your child crying out to you! Remember the night a child's cry woke you up and you went outside to look? Your mother said it was a gypsy with her child on the fells. It wasn't. It was your child calling out to you because it's in terrible danger.

Ask your mother if you don't believe me. Aveline knows everything. She told you a terrible lie, boy. But it was done from love, not malice. She wanted to protect you. But she can't fight demons and the fire serpent almost killed you. You didn't faint that night, Shaun. You DIED, and I bought you back."

"If what you're saying is true, what can I do? I couldn't help Jessie and Dougie," fear replied.

"But you did. You couldn't fix his broken body, but you sent his spirit happily onto the other side where his mother was waiting. You let him die without fear. That's something only a few are able to find when the time is upon them. Your child needs you. Otherwise it'll die and its spirit will be used as a slave in the underworld. Knock down this wall, Shaun. Come back to the living and to those who need and love you."

"I don't know how."

Rosa's head snapped around to the chair and saw Shaun looking at her. She reached out and took his hand. It felt cold and lifeless inside hers. "I'll help you. We'll bash this down together and we'll get your child back. Now concentrate on my voice. Close your eyes and imagine you're bathed in a sea of white light. Feel its gentle warmth on your skin. Can you feel it, boy?"

Shaun nodded.

Now stand up and walk forward. I've got your hand. You're safe with me. See the white light in front of you? Follow it. You're nearly home, my boy. Now walk forward."

***

Adrinia watched Rosa from the darkest corner of Shaun's mind. It was so easy to get into a mortal's conscience when it was corrupted by futile emotions. Thank goodness she didn't have any. Except for the one keeping her at Justin's side. "That's one problem solved, Aslow. I began to think the stupid mortal would lock himself in here forever." She absently stroked her pet. It was so easy to manipulate mortals. A push here, a shove there. They really should not be let loose behind the wheels of moving objects. Cars. I do love the sound of them smashing together. We did him a favour getting rid of them. Clinging little vines, the pair of them. "Now O'Donnell knows the trollop carries his child, he's going to race to the cottage like a knight on his gallant steed." Adrinia chuckled. "Abigail will fall into his arms and Justin will kill him in an instant." Jealousy was dangerous to a rational mind, never mind an insane one like Justin's. "That should just about make his precious Abigail hate him forever, Aslow. Then he'll turn to me for comfort." She smiled, pleased with her plan. All she had to do now was sit back and wait for the show to begin.

Chapter Twenty-Four

Aveline sat on the edge of the sofa and stared at Rosa, too scared to blink in case she missed something. She quickly glanced at her watch. Five hours had passed with Rosa not moving a muscle. Shaun's face remained impassive. She leaned closer to see if she was breathing.

"Can you remove your hot breath from me face?" Rosa snapped and opened her eyes squinting against the bright light of the living room.

Aveline yelped in shock and fell back into the chair. "Jesus, Mary and Joseph, you almost gave me a heart attack. What happened? Is Shaun all right?"

"Yes, he's back with us. But it's been hard. I had to tell him about Abigail and the child."

"Oh no, you didn't."

"I had to. Otherwise he'd have stayed locked in his mind forever. Don't look at me so accusingly. You've only yourself to blame. When will you learn that you can't run away from your problems? They follow you or wait for your return. Shaun will sleep now. His spiritual centres are open and Tessa is healing them. When he wakes, give him a bit of scrambled egg and toast. His stomach won't take much else. I'll return in the morning."

***

Rosa pulled her shawl tighter around her shoulders as she followed Aveline to the door. Her bones ached and her temple throbbed with fatigue, but she could not rest yet. She had to drive into town. Abigail's parents need to know what was going on too.

"I'll not say sorry for trying to save me son," Aveline said defiantly as she held the front door open.

"Then apologise for those who got tangled up in your misplaced loyalty," Rosa snapped as she walked out. Her stubborn refusal to see sense would kill them all. So deeply entrenched in her thoughts on the walk home, Rosa almost missed the person lurking outside her front door. She quickly ducked behind a tree and reached into her pocket for a handful of Cayenne pepper. "Who are you and what do you want here?" She called.

"My name's Jonathon Newlands and…"

"Oh, tis you," Rosa stepped out from behind the tree and clapped her hands together as she walked towards him. A cloud of pepper followed in her wake.

"Do we know each other?"

Rosa dug into another pocket and pulled out her door key. "Not exactly. But we will." She opened the door and went in.

Jonathon stood on the threshold. "I was told you know everything that happens around here."

"Don't stand letting in the cold, shut the door and seat yourself," Rosa replied.

Jonathon entered the caravan and hovered near a chair. "Do you know anything about Abigail Cottage? My daughter's living there with her um... well, a local man

I think?"

Rosa's gaze held his. She searched his aura for subterfuge, but saw none. He had no idea about Justin. "What's it got to do with me?"

"My wife insisted that I speak to you about the cottage. I'd rather go and visit our daughter like civilised people, instead of creeping around behind her back like criminals."

Rosa flicked on the kettle and prepared her china pot for tea. "Do you know your daughter carries a child?"

"Yes, I do. That's why we're here. Her mother and I are taking her home. Harriet, my wife, isn't happy that Abbey's so far away. She needs proper medical care."

"I understand your concern and I also know about your daughter. Her baby's father is a good lad. He comes from a fine family. I've just come from his house."

Jonathon smiled. "Oh, right. I'll tell my wife that. She's convinced that Abbey's living with... oh well, it doesn't matter now."

Rosa shook her head and poured the hot water into the pot. She popped in two tea bags. "I didn't say she's *living* with the child's father."

Jonathon's smile slipped from his face. "I don't understand. You said the father is a good lad. Has he abandoned Abbey because..."

Rosa clicked her tongue in disapproval. "No, Shaun would never do that. He didn't know the child existed until today. There are things that need discussing about your daughter and the cottage. Bring your wife here tonight. I'll explain everything then. Tell her my name is Rosa Rizavoi. She'll recognise those words."

"My wife is very vulnerable at the moment. I don't want her head filled with any hocus pocus."

Rosa poured the tea into the cups. "I'll not play games with you, or bandy around the houses. "Your wife is the twin of Abigail Moreland. She's barren. You raised a girl child fathered by Morgan O'Donnell. I suspect your wife's tried to tell you about the cottage and the curse it holds, I also suspect that and you won't listen. But hear me. If you want to save your daughter and her child, return at seven o'clock."

"How do you know about my family? My wife?"

Rosa laughed softly. "I know everything about your family. Now go. Follow that path all the way to the end. It'll take you back to town." She walked past Jonathon and opened the front door. "Two hours, mind. Not a minute later or you won't see my face this night."

Jonathon nodded and walked out without a word. Rosa went back to her tea and poured one cup down the sink. She just had time to smoke her pipe and enjoy her tea before holy hell broke loose.

She looked out of her window at five to seven and smiled when she saw two dark shapes hurrying around the elm tree. She returned to the table and picked up her pipe. Striking a match she lit the end and puffed on it thoughtfully. She had to convince them not to go to the cottage. The woman will listen, she understood everything. But the man... he was stubborn like Aveline.

A light tap at her door came, Rosa placed her pipe into a glass ashtray on the table and got up to open it.

"I'd just like to say that I think this is ridiculous," Jonathon protested.

"I know your name," Harriet whispered. "Abbey told me that when she was at university you read her palm."

Rosa smiled and opened the door wider for them to enter. "That honour goes to me Mother, God rest her soul. Come in. I'll make some tea."

They stepped inside and sat down while Rosa busied herself with the kettle.

She felt their gaze boring into her back; their impatience surrounded her like a cloying scent. "When's the last time you heard from your daughter?"

A long silence followed before Harriet replied. "It's been about eight months. We had… a family misunderstanding."

Rosa walked over to the table, carrying the teapot, two china cups and matching saucers on a brightly coloured tray. She saw Harriet's surprised expression and swallowed her irritation. "What are you expecting, cracked mugs and crystal balls?"

"Of course not. I was admiring your china. It's exquisite."

"It was my mothers." She poured the tea and sat down opposite them. "We've a lot to discuss, so we'd better get on with it"

Rosa saw Harriet's eyes widen. She could see fear in their depths. A meal most demons would relish.

"You know who's in that cottage with Abbey, don't you," Harriet asked.

Rosa nodded. "Of course and so do you."

"Oh, come on," Jonathon interrupted. "I'd rather you didn't feed into my wife's fantasies."

"It's fact, not fantasy. Whether you chose to believe it or not is up to you. It's more..." Rosa paused, her face alert to the sounds coming outside the caravan. She hurried to open it. "Oh, not now," she mumbled. She pulled it open and stepped hastily back as Shaun ploughed through it. "Good evening to you, boy. I didn't expect to see you up and about so soon." Rosa saw the rage darkening his eyes. He remembered her words. A good sign that his mind had healed, but bad for all of them. Shaun was hurt and angry. He wasn't going to listen to reason. Aveline appeared moments later, her face the colour of ripe cherries.

"I'm sorry, Rosa," she puffed, holding onto the door frame while she caught her breath. "He woke up a short while ago and began shouting about Abigail and the baby. Then he ran outside. I've chased him clear across the fells. He's gone mad! You said he was all right."

"I said he will be fine. I didn't say he won't be as mad as hell," Rosa replied.

"Is it true? Is Abbey carrying my child?" Shaun shouted.

"Calm down, boy. Save that anger for when it's needed. Can't you see I have guests? Let me introduce everyone," Rosa edged forward, pulling Shaun with her. "Meet Abigail's parents, Jonathon and Harriet Newlands. This poor excuse for a man is Shaun O'Donnell, your grandchild's father. He doesn't always look like this, he's been unwell. And this woman," she tugged Aveline from behind Shaun's wide body, "is his mother, Aveline O'Donnell."

"O'Donnell," Jonathon replied.

"Yes, Morgan O'Donnell's wife," Rosa explained.

The crack of a china cup smashing to the floor drew everyone's gaze to Harriet.

"Oh, God no," she gasped. "That means Abbey's carrying her brother's child."

There was a moment of deathly quiet before a loud tempest of voices erupted.

"Quiet," Rosa pleaded. "No one can understand a word that's being said."

"Morgan's my step-father," Shaun replied quickly. "Isn't that so, mother?"

Aveline swallowed, her eyes bright with tears as they met her sons.

"It's time the truth came out, Aveline," Rosa replied.

"I did it for you, son. I couldn't lose you to that beast as well. Anyone would've done the same if their child was in danger."

Shaun's face held a mixture of bewilderment and confusion. "Rosa said you told a terrible lie. What is it?"

"I… well…" Aveline stammered.

Rosa knew she would never be able to finish her sentence. She was too afraid of losing the one thing she was driving away. "Your mother told Abigail that you were her half brother,"

Shaun staggered back as though he had been hit with an invisible blow. His face drained of colour, leaving his eyes to blaze their anger. "No, you wouldn't do that to me. You promised nothing from your lips sent her away."

Aveline's long dark hair acted like a curtain, obscuring her face as she hung her head. "I did it for you, son. To save your life."

"I trusted you. You know Abbey means everything to me. Is her marriage one of your lies too?"

Aveline nodded and Shaun's face twisted into an angry sneer. "You evil… rotten…"

Rosa touched his arm lightly. "Shaun, calm down. Words spoken even in anger cannot be taken back. If your mother hadn't sent Abigail away, you'd be dead now."

"Hold on, I don't understand," Jonathon interrupted. "Is Morgan O'Donnell the father of Shaun and Abbey or not?"

"No," Aveline said softly. "Morgan took my Shaun as his and Abigail isn't his blood daughter either."

Harried dabbed her eyes with a tissue. "Oh, what a mess."

"You could've told me, Mother. Given me a chance to make up me own mind. Losing Abbey ha tortured me for months. You know that, yet still you stood by your disgusting lies."

"I did it to protect you, Shaun," Aveline sobbed. "Don't you understand? Abigail isn't yours to love. Her destiny lies in that damn cottage with a monster for a lover."

"Oh, stop with all that rubbish," Shaun sneered. "You ruined me life because of a fairytale that's been around since I was a boy?"

"It's not a fairytale," Rosa interrupted. "Everything you've heard is the truth. A demon does live in the cottage and he's in league with another even more dangerous one now. They've already attacked you once."

"Attacked? I remember now. You said I died." He pointed at Rosa accusingly.

"You did, boy. I dragged your spirit back from the fire demons. Justin wants you out of the way and he will succeed if we're not careful."

"So if you're saying the stories are true about that cottage, then you..." his finger moved and pointed at Aveline, "would condemn your own grandchild to be raised by strangers. Because no women survive childbirth there. Don't you care about anyone except yourself?"

"Of course I care, "Aveline shouted, brushing her tears away with an angry swipe of her hand. "But the demon won't allow Abigail to stay with us. She was on her way to him when she bumped into you. If she doesn't return to the cottage, the beast will come here and kill us all. You've got to believe, I had no choice."

Shaun's bitter contempt was laced in his hollow laugh. "Believe you? You've got to be joking. I'll never forgive you for this. Not until the day I die."

"If you want me to say that I'm sorry, Shaun O'Donnell, then you'll find yourself waiting a long time. I'd do it all again if I had to. You would do the same for your child." Aveline opened the front door and walked out quietly closing the door behind her.

Shaun rushed over and threw it open. "I'll rather cut me own tongue out than speak to you again." he slammed the door closed.

Rosa felt his pain as if it were her own. Being let down was the worst agony of all. "You mustn't blame your mother for trying to protect you."

Jonathon stood up. "I'm sorry to interrupt, but all this demonic rubbish has gone far enough." He looked at Harriet. "It's too late to visit now, but we'll go to the cottage first thing in the morning. We'll bring Abbey home and we can talk about child access then."

Rosa opened her mouth to protest and snapped it shut when she saw a shadowy form materialise in the corner of the room. "I know you're here, Adrinia, I can see you," she shouted. "You'll not learn any secrets hiding there, now be gone and leave us alone." Rosa reached into her pocket, took out a small blue Chalcedony crystal, and threw it into the corner of the room.

Harriet ducked down. "Oh, my God, she's throwing rocks at us."

"What is it, Rosa? What can you see?" Shaun asked.

"It's not a rock," Rosa corrected. "Chalcedony protects us from psychic attack."

The shadow shimmered for a second and vanished. Rosa laughed. "Ha! My crystal grid around the caravan is working well. No demon can sneak in unnoticed with that on our side. The shadow queen is here, listening to us argue like children," she turned to Jonathon. "Whether you believe about the demons is of no consequence now, she knows you're here. You need to protect yourself."

Jonathon took a step forward. "This is…"

"Shut up, Jonathon, and sit down," Harriet demanded. "And if you love our daughter as much as you say, sit down as well," she barked at Shaun.

Both men sat down quickly.

Rosa hurried to turn up her lamps "We need to keep the room bright. Adrinia will return. I'm sure."

Harriet turned to Jonathon, her eyes condemning. "Haven't I said all along that something unspeakable lurks in the shadows?"

"The shadow demons are a formidable force," Rosa agreed. "You're right to fear them. Now, Adrinia is interested in you, Shaun. But I don't know why yet."

"I can't see why we can't just go to the cottage and get Abbey?" Shaun snapped.

"Oh, for God's sake," Harriet interrupted. "Don't you listen? The demon wants my daughter more than anything. He won't give her up without a fight."

Shaun shook his head. "Come on, we're all rational people. It's all just superstitious nonsense."

"Then why did Morgan bring Abbey to us?" Harriet questioned. "He became a good father to you, didn't he?"

Shaun shrugged his shoulders. "Maybe he couldn't cope with a newborn."

"No," Rosa replied. "Morgan knew the beast would come after her. I placed an invisibility charm on Abigail to hide her from dark magic. Justin murdered Morgan when he tried to burn down the cottage on Abbey's sixteenth birthday. He knew it was the age when Justin would call to her."

Shaun sighed. "So that's why he did it. He was a damn fool to believe such nonsense."

"You're the damn fool," Rosa snapped. "You must open your mind and believe that everything isn't just black and white. Otherwise you'll lose your child and Abigail for sure."

Shaun heaved a long sigh. His rigid shoulders sank. "Okay, you win Rosa. I've had proof in the past of your special gifts. If you tell me this curse is real. I'll believe you. But I'll not give Abbey up because of it?"

"Then we must fight for them, boy," she replied grimly.

Chapter Twenty-Five

Abbey lay in bed. Her eyes were closed, but sleep eluded her. She needed to speak to Justin about his moods. Although his easy going nature was still there, recently a more sinister side of him had started to emerge. She could see his eyes, literally bulging with suppressed rage sometimes. He was on edge and on more than one occasion she had heard him arguing with himself. His vile mumblings shocked her. It was not something she wanted her child to hear. The bedroom door opened and Justin came in. She heard the rattle of a cup in its saucer and sighed. He thinks tea is the solution to every ailment. Abbey opened her eyes as he placed it on the bedside table. As he bustled around the room, she found herself inspecting him more closely.

His clothes became more outdated daily. She accepted his eccentricities. But today it irritated her. She wrinkled her nose in distaste, as a waft of his sweet scented aftershave filled her nostrils. The smell made her feel sick to her stomach some days. She sighed. Why did she feel so melancholy? She had everything she needed. Justin sat on the edge of the bed. "What's the matter, my love? You're staring at me so strangely,"

"Was I?" she feigned ignorance. Dressed in his long brocade dressing gown, he looked like he belonged in a museum. She forced a smile and sat up. "I was just wondering where you buy your clothes. Take for instance your dressing gown. It's finely made." She opted out saying it was very old fashioned. She much preferred to see Shaun in his boxer shorts than Justin in that heavy, ankle swinging curtain.

Abbey saw Justin stiffen. His smile was wide, yet it didn't quite touch his eyes.

"I'm sure you're not interested in where I shop."

Abbey swallowed her irritation. The way he assumed everything started to annoy her too. "Tell me about your family. Do you have any brothers or sisters?"

Justin got off the bed and made a great pretence of tidying the covers. "My, so many questions, what's brought all this on? You need to rest, not clutter your head with so much nonsense."

"It's not nonsense to want to know more about the man I live with. I came here to learn more about my mother, but I haven't discovered anything except stories about a silly curse. Have you heard about the story connected with this cottage? It's about a demon who lives here and kills the women who are mad enough to fall in love with him."

Justin laughed. "Yes, I know the tale. It's superstitious nonsense."

Abbey sipped her tea. "I know. I think I'd have met the demon by now, don't you? But what I'm driving at is how little I know about you."

Justin took a towel out of the cupboard and walked over to the bathroom. "All you need to know is that I love you. Now, come on, I'll run you a bath. Time to soak away all those questions. I've found a particularly good Shakespeare passage. I think you'll enjoy listening to while you're relaxing."

Abbey grimaced. She was beginning to hate Shakespeare. The endless passages bored her to tears some nights. "If you don't mind, I'd prefer just to soak. My head aches a bit."

Justin came out of the bathroom. "You usually like me reading to you."

"Not today. I'd rather be alone." She got out of bed and hurried to the bathroom before he could reply. She shut the door and leaned against it stroking her stomach as the baby kicked.

"I'll be outside in case you need something," Justin called through the door.

Abbey closed her eyes, sighed and wished for home, to be with her parents.

***

"Oh dear, it looks like your essence is beginning to overwhelm her, Justin," Adrinia said from the far corner of the room. "I did say it would if you used the full force of it too often."

"You'd love that to happen, wouldn't you? It's the pregnancy making her snappy. I don't use the essence to bend her will anymore. I know she loves me. I'm using it to calm her. She's nervous about the birth."

Adrinia's derisive laugh echoed around the room. "You really believe that she loves you! You're a fool, Justin."

"I don't remember asking you for an opinion."

"There was a time when you valued it."

Justin's tail swished in the air as he hobbled to the bedroom door. "Abbey and I are fine. Don't you think it's time you paid more attention to those in your own realm?"

"Are you telling me to leave here for good?"

Justin smiled. "Let's say you won't be invited to our wedding,"

Adrinia ignored the hurt prickling her skin. "Do you think after two hundred years, you can just discard me like you would an old book?"

Justin's smile grew wider, showing off a row of rotting teeth. "Consider yourself well-read and placed back on the shelf." He laughed heartily as he left the room.

Adrinia raised her hand and slammed the door shut behind him. "On the shelf I may be, Justin Montgomery, but well-read? I don't think so. Revor, Revor!" Impatience made her voice sharp.

A shadow helper immediately materialised in front of her. He bowed low. "Yes, my queen."

"Bring Shaun O'Donnell here. Use any spell, potion, whatever it takes. But get him here – tonight. I want to see Justin suffer the agony of rejection when his precious Abigail falls into the arms of her lover."

"I'll have to ask the Soul stalkers for one of their spells," Revor said. "They'll ask a high price."

"Give them anything they want."

"They'll want something *you* value, my queen. What shall I offer?"

Adrinia tutted with impatience. What did she have of value? Souls were cheap and plenty, they wouldn't take them. Jewels were of no use. Soul stalkers existed in that fragile time between evening and dusk. When mortals were easy to pick off.

No. It had to be something that could disappear with them when night fell. Adrinia looked at Aslow, lying contentedly at her feet, and smiled. Maybe they would like a pet. Soul stalkers loved to torment things and Aslow was becoming a dreadful clinging nuisance. It would please Justin to know he was gone. He hated Aslow. "Take him. They won't say no. The thought of being able to endlessly torment something will thrill any demon." She nudged the sleeping shadow pet with her foot. "Sorry my dear, but nothing lasts forever."

Revor bent down and picked up Aslow, who struggled fiercely in his arms. "I'll carry out your commands immediately."

Adrinia frowned as Aslow's terrified howls echoed around the room. "Goodness me, so much noise. How am I supposed to think," she waved her hand dismissively at Revor. "Well, go on. What are you waiting for?"

***

Rosa put a tray on the table with a fresh pot of tea and a few hurriedly made sandwiches. "Help yourself," she said. "It's going to be a long night."

Shaun filled his cup and took a sandwich. "So, what happens now?"

She opened her mouth to reply, only to snap it closed again. "Hush boy, listen." She sat in the chair rigid with concentration. "Can you hear it?"

"Hear what?" Harriet interrupted.

Rosa put her finger to her lips. "Shhh."

Shaun sat up, dropping his sandwich. "I can hear a baby crying."

"Tis the cry of *your* child, Shaun." Rosa took a sandwich. Food always helped her think. Something to do with chewing relaxed her. But before it got to her mouth she cried out, blinded by a terrible pain that ripped through her head like a knife through paper and sent her reeling backwards.

Shaun jumped up and caught her before she fell onto the floor. "Rosa, me darlin', what's the matter?" He carried her to the small cushioned sofa and gently laid her on it.

Rosa felt nothing except the sensation of flying through the spiritual ether. Her astral body raced down a spirit path on a vision quest of someone else's making. She had no control, no way of fighting - the pull was too strong. She had to obey or die trying to fight her way back. Tumbling through the ether with no crystals to guide or protect her, Rosa felt battered by a multitude of vibrations that belonged to those who resided in the lower astral planes.

Just when she thought she would never stop, Rosa came to a shuddering halt. Her feet sank into a deep weaved carpet. A soft moan drew her attention to the huge bed dominating the room. It was beautiful. Draped in peach silk, with matching covers. The room was perfect in every way. Right down to the matching peach curtains on the windows. In the centre of the bed was Abbey. Bathed in perspiration, moaning in pain, her silver hair plastered to her face as she struggled with labour pains. Rosa jumped when a door to her left opened. She took a step back, momentarily forgetting that she was invisible. She saw Justin enter and dab at Abbey's face with a flannel.

"You're doing well, my love," he murmured. "It won't be long now." Justin turned his head and Rosa gasped as his dark eyes bored into her. His smile sent a chill of fear through her body. "You've lost, witch. They're both mine now."

Before Rosa could utter a word, she was pulled back. Her body screamed in protest as she sped quickly through the ether. The pressure was too much and she knew her death was imminent. Sorrow enveloped her like a shroud. All the deaths of the women he touched, her own friends and family he had murdered, her own wasted years of trying to put right a terrible wrong, had culminated to this final act of treachery.

"Rosa, me darlin'. Come on, wake up."

The anxious voice's filtered through to her consciousness in a bleary haze. A soft pressure was beneath her and moved her hands. She felt cushions and opened her eyes. She blinked and tried to focus. Her body felt battered and sore, but definitely alive. Rosa saw Shaun's panic filled eyes and smiled. "Don't look so worried. I'm not dead yet." Her mouth felt dryer than the desert as she struggled to sit up. "Fetch me a drink, boy. My body feels like an empty water bag." She took the glass of water handed to her and drank thirstily. Almost immediately her body came back to life. Water held a life force that people rarely tapped into. She was grateful for its strength now.

"I think she should see a doctor," Jonathon said. "She's obviously got health problems."

Rosa sat up. "None that a doctor can cure."

"What happened? What did you see?" Shaun asked.

"Your child's coming. The beast is tending Abigail as we speak. We've run out of time, boy. We need to go to her now. If she gives birth in that cottage we'll lose them both."

"No. Abbey mustn't die," Harriet cried half hysterically. "Jonathan, we can't lose her."

Jonathon put a comforting arm around her shoulders. "Abbey isn't going to die. Not when she has so many people who care about her."

Rosa saw the desperation in his eyes. Finally, he believed! "Help me up, boy." Astral travel took a lot out of the physical body. Sometimes it took a full day to recover from it. But there was no time to recharge her batteries. She had to rely on the spirit world to give her an extra boost. She looked at Harriet and then Jonathon. "You two go outside and get in me truck. Shaun and I need to gather some things and we'll join you."

Rosa opened the bottom cupboard. She took out a variety of crystals and filled her pockets. "Shaun, get my trolley from behind the bedroom door. We can load the big ones inside it."

He hurried to do as he was asked. With the giant crystals in the trolley, Rosa opened the top cupboard and took out a handful of dried sprigs. She put them inside the trolley. "I think that's it."

Shaun pulled the trolley towards the door. "I hope you know what you're doing."

Rosa gave him a huge bag of salt. Worry nagged her. The demons were strong to pull her into that vision. What if she was too old to fight them? The doors of hell were swinging wide open. There was so much evil spilling into the physical plane, it would take a miracle to banish it. "I need to tell you something before we go. It's important, so listen well. You have the power to defeat Justin and the shadow queen. You have a gift. It was given to you by the Esor. It's a powerful weapon, Shaun. One that can close hell's door forever and put an end to Justin's curse. There's no time to explain everything, you'll have to trust me, boy."

"And you're telling me this now!" he replied. "How does it work? What do I do?"

"If you concentrate on saving your child - the light will come. You'll feel its energy in your solar plexus." Rosa pointed to the middle of her stomach. "It'll feel like a great pressure building inside you, but don't be afraid, it's part of you. It can do no harm to those who are pure of spirit. Your own thoughts will bring it into the open. Like a beam of light streaming from your body. It's very powerful, so be accurate in your aim. It uses your body's energy to power it, so it won't last for long. It'll remove any evil in its path and close the demonic portal which has opened under the cottage."

Shaun shook his head. "But Rosa, the Esor aren't real. They're myths."

"They are *very* real, Shaun. Things exist on this earth that would make your hair curl in fright. Just because you can't see it, it doesn't mean it isn't there. Everything we do tonight depends on you believing in your gift."

"I'll do me best. You've never done me a wrong turn, Rosa. So I've no reason to distrust you now. However irrational you sound."

Rosa smiled. "You're a good boy, Shaun. You're the closest I'm ever going to get to a son. I love you dearly. But now you need to trust my words more than ever before. Can you do that?"

"Of course."

"Your child is the most important person of all. No matter what, she has to survive…" Rosa wondered if his fragile heart was able to stand losing Abigail. In every battle there were casualties and she suspected Morgan's daughter would be a major one. Her body was already corrupted by Justin. No spells or magic could reverse that. But she would leave a wonderful legacy. The Esor spirit would continue its journey within her daughter, free of Justin and his curse.

"Are you telling me to let Abbey die?"

"You won't be able to stop the events unfolding, boy. Your daughter can't survive without a spirit and Justin's spell has driven hers out. The Esor will move from Abbey to her as soon as she enters the world. We both know a mortal being can't survive once the silver cord that binds their spirit to them is severed."

"Don't ask me to give her up, Rosa. I can't do it. Not again."

"This is our last chance to break the curse. If we fail, we'll condemn others to the same fate as Abbey. Including your own daughter."

"You can't ask him to give up on Abbey," Harriet said from the doorway. "You've got to save her, Shaun. I'm begging you…"

"Stop it," Rosa shouted. "Do you think any of us *want* to give up on her? We've no choice. But the child will live. That's all we can hope for."

***

Abbey closed her eyes and allowed the warm water to sooth her jagged nerves. She never thought her life would end up such a mess. Mr. McKinley's words floated through her dark thoughts. *'The ghost of a man lives in the cottage and makes women fall in love with him.'* She smiled at the ridiculousness of it. Maybe Justin was the ghost. He fitted the criteria. A man out of his time. She sat up, suddenly less complacent. Was it really possible? Justin never went out, wore out of date clothes and read sonnets. What modern man did that? For a moment her heart raced in panic. She mentally shook herself. What a stupid thought. Ghosts were vaporous – he was as real as her. But she had seen a ghost. A woman whose eyes held so much hate. But Justin said she was hormonal and seeing things. One thing she did know for sure was that she no longer wanted to give birth at the cottage. A sudden uncomfortable tightness in her abdomen jolted Abbey from her thoughts. She waited for it to pass. Then as it did, a stronger pain ripped through her body. She screamed when a pinkish hue began to colour the water. Another pain quickly followed and she gripped the edges of the bath. Abbey vaguely heard the bathroom door burst open and then she was lifted from the water. Paralysed with fear, she clung to Justin's neck.

"It's all right, my darling. I'm here. Don't be afraid. The child arrives a little early, that's all." He laid her on the bed.

"I can't have her here," Abbey moaned.

"Of course you can, my love. This is what we planned."

Abbey groaned as another pain ripped through her. She turned her head and her eyes widened in fright. "The ghost is here, Justin. I can see her."

Justin turned and glared at Adrinia. When he turned back to Abbey, all trace of his rage was gone. "Calm yourself, my love. There's no one else here."

"Justin, I can see a woman behind you. She's got dark hair and she's wearing a long red gown. You must be able to see her."

"Perhaps the pain is making you hallucinate. Be assured there's no one there." He pointed to reiterate his statement.

In that instant, Abbey realised that Justin could see the woman. He had pointed directly at her.

***

Justin left the bedroom and hurried to gather fresh towels. Soon it would be time to reveal the truth. He had a reversal spell that enabled Abbey to live once the child was born. The child would die because of it, but it didn't matter. It was a small price to pay to get what he wanted.

"Justin, she saw me in my true form," Adrinia said incredulously. "No one on this plane has ever seen me before."

Justin frowned in irritation as he gathered the items he needed. "Leave us. Adrinia. Can't you see I'm busy?"

"I'm not going anywhere. You promised me that if your wife didn't return this time, you'd give up this stupid quest. Maybe then you'll see me as…"

Justin threw the towels on the chair and spun around. "As what, exactly? Don't you see Adrinia that you're the darkness I run from. The cold vapour that surrounds you chills me to the bone. I need the warmth of a mortal beside me. Not a cold bodied, hard hearted bitch like you."

"You've no idea what I can offer you, Justin. I'm more than what you see here. Return to the underworld with me. Let me show you the woman I am."

"Haven't you understood anything? I don't care what you look like. You've no idea what love is. You use things until they out live their usefulness. Like that pet of yours? How did you repay his faithfulness?"

"And you think you're so innocent," Adrinia sneered. "Look at yourself. Why do you think you've returned looking the way you do? It's because you're corrupt in spirit and soul. But I don't care. I don't need a spell to help me accept you."

Justin sneered as he looked her up and down. "I don't want your acceptance. I love Abbey and we *will* live as man and wife on this plane, and when she dies, we'll go to the underworld together."

Adrinia's bitter laugh bounced off the damp, crumbling walls. "Have you looked out of your front window recently?"

Justin picked back up the towels. His eyes narrowing suspiciously. "No. Do I need to?"

"Oh, yes, I think you should."

Justin walked to the window and pulled back the curtain. He dropped them again with a shrug of his shoulders. "Why should I be bothered about mortals? I can swat them like bothersome flies. Now go away. Annoy someone else."

"Aren't you worried about breaking your precious loved one's heart if you kill the man she *really* loves?" Adrinia moved closer to Justin. "For goodness sake think about this for a second. This plane of existence has never brought you happiness alive or dead. It's time to leave it behind."

"Not without Abbey," Justin growled. "I can be the man I once was with her at my side."

Adrinia sighed. "You'll never be that man again. He's dead and all that's left behind is the tattered pieces of his damned spirit."

***

Abbey groaned as the pain began to build yet again. Agony seared her body, electrifying every nerve, every muscle until they screamed in protest. She couldn't bear it. "Shaun," she screamed and realised, despite everything, he was the only one she wanted by her side. When heard Justin enter the room, she was filled with dismay. She didn't love him; he didn't belong in her life. "I need an ambu…" The words died on her lips when her gaze locked with monstrous, black eyes. She screamed, as a beast, dressed in rags, shuffled towards her on bowed legs.

It reached out a filthy, clawed hand towards her. "What's the matter my love."

Abbey cringed back as the stench of rotting flesh filled her nostrils. Recognition widened her eyes. The monster in her mother's painting stood before her and he spoke with Justin's voice.

She scrambled further up the bed, until the oak headboard dug painfully in her back. "No." Her scream bounced off the walls, hurting her ears as realisation hit home. The stories were true. Justin was the demon and he would kill her like he had done to her predecessors. To her own mother!

She arrived so blinded by hurt and fear that she allowed this… whatever he was, to ingratiate himself into her life. He made her feel that she needed him, when all along it was him who needed her. Now it was too late. Her child was going to be born and she would die, never knowing it.

Chapter Twenty-Six

"Quickly, Shaun, pass me the grounding crystals." Rosa grabbed the salt bag and made three big circles in a line, about six feet apart. She saw the dying flowers at the edges of the drive and felt hopeful. Justin's powers were weakening. He couldn't even keep up the pretty cottage illusion anymore "I know this looks primitive," she whispered to Shaun as she took the crystals from him. "But I haven't got time to prepare anything else. I thought I had a few weeks until the birth. "But salt rings work very well." She took out a long piece of white chalk from her pocket and drew a strange symbol in each circle.

"What are you doing?" Harriet whispered. "Shouldn't we go inside?"

"I'm with her on that," Shaun agreed. "It's pointless doing all this witchery when we can go up to the cottage and get Abbey."

Rosa stared, hardly able to believe what she was hearing. Hadn't they listened to a word she had said? Her lips pulled into a tight, angry line. "What's wrong with you two? Didn't I tell you that the beast will kill you if you go in unprotected? Am I talking a foreign language? Or would you like me to dig up Morgan's body for you to see what Justin Montgomery does if he's crossed?"

Shaun shook his head. "Okay, Rosa. Don't get yourself in a state. We're only saying..."

"Don't say anything more! Haven't I got enough to worry about without you two acting like ignorant vigilantes?"

Harriet took Shaun's arm and pulled him back from Rosa's angry glare. "Maybe she does know what's best."

"And sort that husband of yours out," Rosa snapped again. "He's standing around like a wet weekend. Tell him to get into a circle if he values his life."

Rosa saw the look of panic on Harriet's face and sighed. Fear was making her bark like a rabid dog. It wasn't their fault they didn't understand how dangerous evil could be. They were all in peril, every minute they stood in the open unprotected.

"What exactly do you want my wife and I to do," Jonathon asked. "I really don't think that standing in a circle..."

"Then don't think. I need you all to listen to me words."

"We've been listening for the past hour."

"But you're not hearing me. These four salt rings will protect our physical bodies and spirit. Evil cannot enter these rings of light. But if you step outside you will die. I can be no clearer than that."

"Don't you think this is a bit theatrical?" Jonathon replied. "We're going to look very silly if Abbey's... erm... friend comes out and wants to know what's going on."

Rosa swallowed her harsh retort. The man was so closed-minded he was almost automated. "Oh, he'll come out all right. But be assured he isn't her friend and he won't be asking what we're doing."

"For God's sake, Jonathon, do what she tells you," Harriet replied. "If it gets Abbey out of that damn cottage, we'll stand in these until morning. Now come on," she pushed her reluctant husband into a circle.

"You'll need one of these." Rosa placed a Smokey quartz crystal at Jonathon's feet inside the salt ring. "This is a grounding crystal and it'll keep your spirit firmly where it belongs." She handed Harriet one for her circle, and then handed her another crystal. It fitted into her palm with its tiny crystal towers pointing upwards to the darkening sky. "This is a clear quartz. When I tell you, hold it up for as long as you can."

"I can feel it moving," Harriet said incredulously.

"It's resonating," Rosa replied, pleased the crystal had activated so quickly. "It will act as an extra energy source should Shaun need it. If you think it's buzzing now, wait until later."

"What about me?" Shaun asked. "I'm still not sure how to use this special power I'm supposed to have."

Rosa chewed anxiously on her bottom lip. No crystal would help him. He needed to trust in his higher self. "Stand in the circle, boy. Look within yourself for the light. It's all about visualisation. Think of a round, whirling, energy ball and it will form. I'm going to call on the spirit realm for help. We'll need them to keep the shadow demons at bay, while you try and close down hells door. The vortex has been here for two hundred years, so it's very strong. You'll need all your strength Shaun, and any reserves." Rosa quickly kissed his cheek. "Don't expect me to do that again, it's for luck. Whatever happens, boy, you must stay in the circle. Do you understand?"

Shaun nodded. "What happens if this special light doesn't work?"

Rosa smiled wryly. "Then I'll see you in hell."

***

Shaun felt ridiculous standing in the salt circle. If Abbey came down the drive now he would die of shame. He wanted to bash the cottage door down, punch whoever Abbey was with on the nose, and drag her home. Yet something about Rosa's insistence kept him there. People from the town feared her strange ways. But he never did. Yes, she was a sly one and never paid a coin for anything if she could get away with it. But she wasn't a liar and she didn't make up stories. He valued her friendship and trusted her advice. So he had to trust her now. Shaun looked at Rosa and his mouth gaped in shock. He could hardly see through the hundreds of little flashing lights which surrounded her. Each one had tails of grey mist. They looked like little tadpoles floating outside the circle. One of the lights moved inside Rosa's circle. It shimmered as its tail of mist grew and took the form of a nun. He looked at Jonathon and Harriet who also stared in wide eyed fascination.

"Harriet, hold up your crystal," Rosa shouted.

Her arm immediately shot up. "It's vibrating," she said excitedly.

"Hello Shaun," a soft voice to his left greeted him. He turned and stared into the deep, blue eyes of a nun. "Yes... I mean hello. How did you get...? Rosa said nothing can enter the circle," Shaun stammered.

"Only those with evil intent will be kept out. I'm Rosa's spirit guide, Tessa. I believe she's told you about the light within you."

"Yes, but she hasn't told me how to use it."

"The light cannot be touched by evil. If they step into its auric field they will be immediately sent back to where they came from. You don't have to do anything really. Just think of a bright light expanding here." She pointed to his solar plexus, the point just above his stomach. "Expand its width in your mind and then visualise it beaming from your body in one long stream of white light. Think of it as a giant broom. The evil it touches will be swept away. The dark ones will have no choice but to retreat in the end. Once they do, use it to close hells door."

"But I thought all this was to save Abbey and our child. I don't hear their names being mentioned at all."

"I know Shaun, but you have to realise that you hold the mortality of the world in your hands. We asked Rosa not to mention what would happen if the doorway does not close. It is a weighty secret she has kept for many years. If we fail tonight, demons like Justin and Adrinia will surface everywhere. Plagues will start again, wars will increase in ferocity, famine will never end and fires will devastate the lands. This plane will not survive such chaos."

"I won't let Abbey die," Shaun said stubbornly. "I don't care if I have to fight the whole of the demonic nation. They won't take her from me."

"It sometimes takes great personal sacrifice to win a war. Rosa gave her whole life fighting this one, and you might be pressed to choose too. Make it the right choice, for all our sakes. Now I must go and prepare. I may be a sister of Mercy and unable to fight, but nothing says I can't coordinate the battle. Take care of yourself and good luck."

Shaun watched Tessa fade into a tiny light with a misty tail. It hovered for a short time and then whizzed off into the sky. "I'll make the right choice, Tessa. But if I have to go to hell to get Abbey, I will."

***

Abbey felt her stomach lurch in fear as she looked at Justin. "What are you?" she whispered, hurriedly dragged her dressing gown over her naked body.

"Oh dear, it looks like she can see the *real* you, Justin." Adrinia laughed. "Where's the love in her eyes now?"

"SHUT UP," Justin yelled, and wiped the fetid spittle away from his chin with a filth encrusted sleeve. "I don't understand. How can she see me?"

"Because I made it possible. You won't listen to reason. So what about fact. Look at her face, Justin. She's repelled by you. While I, on the other hand, accept you are, what you are."

"But I don't bloody want you. I've only put up with you because the lowlanders will only trade with me because they think it will ingratiate themselves with you. You're nothing but a thorn in my side, Adrinia. An itch I can't scratch."

"Oh, am I? Then I might as well tell you that it was me who brought the mortals to your front door. Face it. Your hold over these silver-haired trollops is at an end.

What will you do now? Eternity is a long time to spend alone."

Justin threw his head back and laughed manically. "But I won't be alone, I've got Abbey."

"She doesn't want you," Adrinia screamed.

"She does. Once she gets over the shock she'll realise I'm the same person I always was. We can't live here of course. Now we're parting company the lowlanders won't provide me with spells to keep the cottage from crumbling. I'll take her home to the underworld. With me."

"You can't take a mortal there."

Justin's eyes glittered insanely as he smiled. "Yes I can. I've got a spell which allows her to exist wherever I want her to."

A strong wind blew in from the shadows on the wall, fuelled by Adrinia's murderous fury. She pointed to Abbey, who sat in wide eyed terror on the bed. Paralysed with fear. "Does she look like she wants to stay with you?"

Justin looked at Abbey and continued to smile. "She just needs time to adjust."

"And you think she'll *adjust* with her lover outside the door, do you?"

Justin's growl of rage rumbled in his chest like a bowling ball thundering down the alley. When it exploded from his mouth in an animalistic roar, he lifted his clawed hand and, by a mere thought, sent Adrinia flying through the glass window. "I asked you to leave," he shouted after her. "Now I'm helping you."

As the dampness of the cold night air settled around Abbey like a freezing cloak, she shuddered.

Justin's eyes, filled with rage, softened. "Are you cold my love? Don't worry. I'll get you a few more blankets."

***

Abbey pulled her legs up and away from Justin's filthy hand as it moved to pull a cover over her. She couldn't think through her mind numbing terror, how to get away, or even if she could. The row between him and the woman terrified her. She must have been the one he had mumbled the vile things to. Why did it take her so long to figure it all out? "What do you want from me?" Chaotic thoughts raced through her head with no firm direction.

"Want? Why nothing, my dear. Your love is all I need. Now let me seal this window." Justin flicked his clawed hand in the air and frowned. He did the same motion again and sighed. "Oh dear, it looks as though Adrinia's playing silly games and blocking my powers. Never mind, I'll have to do it the hard way. I'll get those boards from the cupboard in the kitchen. They'll do for now. And then we'll have to get a move on, my love. It's time to leave this place. I've got so much to show you. Our new home awaits."

Justin hobbled out and Abbey took a deep breath and released it in a shaky hiss. She had to think. First of all, she had to get out of the cottage. Just because she was in labour it didn't mean the baby would pop out right now. As if to purposely contradict her, Abbey writhed as an excruciating contraction took over her body. She gasped and squeezed her eyes tightly closed. Tears of pain streamed down her face, but she stayed silent. Nothing must bring that monster hurrying to her side. When the contraction passed, she opened her eyes and felt a trickle of sweat leave a cold trail down her back. Nausea bubbled up into her throat and she swallowed. She had to regain control of herself.

Abbey reached for her nightdress on the floor and quickly pulled it over her head. It didn't warm her, but being covered made her feel safe. Now she had to find a way out – quickly.

Chapter Twenty-Seven

Abbey got off the bed. Her legs felt stiff, her body heavy as she stumbled to the window. She looked at it in despair. The gap was so small, but she needed to squeeze through it. Adrinia's words came back to her. '*Her lover's outside.*' Did she mean Shaun? Her heart raced with excitement. If he was, he must know about the baby. Why didn't he come and get her? Mr. McKinley's words suddenly flooded back as a chilling reminder. 'The silver-haired women all died in childbirth.' Was Shaun waiting for her to die so he could get his child without the embarrassment of explaining the truth? Abbey's resolve hardened. 'I'm not going to die,' she told herself defiantly. 'I'm going to break this cycle of death and raise my child.'

Abbey gasped as another wave of pain engulfed her. She gripped the window ledge as a primeval urge to push robbed her of further thought. The pain passed slower this time and Abbey steadied herself against the wall. Horror struck her hard and low. The baby was coming now. There was no time to get out of the cottage. When the next contraction came, Abbey pushed. When it passed she released the breath she had held and edged her way to the bed. She lay down as another contraction came. "Come on, baby. Hurry up, she ground out. If she gave birth before Justin came back, she might have the strength to get out of the window. Abbey bit down on her pillow and bore down with every ounce of strength she had.

The pressure between her legs was immense – more painful than she could ever imagine. Tears rained down her cheeks as she pushed again, determined they both would live. With one final push, Abbey felt her child slide from her body. Her eyes went to the door, it remained closed. Whatever was keeping Justin occupied, let it be for a few minutes more. Abbey lifted the baby and placed it beside her on the bed; she felt the placenta leave her body and quickly ripped a ribbon from her nightdress to tie off the cord. Frantically wondering what to do next, she remembered her manicure scissors in the drawer beside her. She took them out and cut the baby's cord, praying hard it was the right thing to do. When no scream of pain came, she wrapped the baby in her dressing gown and suddenly realised it had not uttered a sound.

Abbey quickly pulled off a pillow case and wiped its face. "You will not die. Do you hear me?" As if it was complying, the baby slowly opened its eyes. Abbey smiled as emerald green eyes watched her intently. "Hello," she whispered. "I'm your mummy."

She opened the dressing gown and tried to clean the baby as best she could with the pillow case. "You're such a good gir...." She paused. "You're a boy." The shock hit her like a thunder bolt. She had a son. Not a silver haired girl. The curse was finally broken.

She kissed his smooth forehead. A small gurgle of response bubbled up from the baby's throat. "You are a very special little man."

"I'm sorry it's taken me so long, my love. I've had to sort out a few..." Justin stopped, mid sentence, as his eyes fixed themselves on the bundle in Abbey's arms.

"No, it's not possible. The child cannot be born. I haven't done the reversal spell yet."

Abbey saw the fear in his eyes and held her son tighter to her chest.

Justin dropped the boards in his hands. "Give her to me."

Abbey scooted over to the other side of the bed "Get away from us."

"But you don't understand my love. Your daughter's dead. Let me get rid of the body and then I'll run you a nice bath. I have a special sonnet you might like to hear."

"My son and I are fine."

"Son" Justin repeated. "A boy child? But that's not possible? Show him to me now." He moved closer to the bed, his arms outstretched.

Abbey clutched her son tighter and knew, with a sinking heart that she would never make the window. With slow, reluctant hands she unwrapped her son.

Justin stared, his eyes narrowed in fury. "What an ugly child. We'll give him to Adrinia. That will satisfy her bad temper. She's always going on about wanting a male heir for her god forsaken throne."

Abbey wrapped up the baby and held him close. "I'll never give him up. You will have to kill me first."

"You're tired and emotional my love. Let me sort everything out, like I usually do."

Abbey forced a smile onto her stiff lips. He was mad. But was he deranged enough to think that she would go along with him? She needed time to get herself together. To plan their escape.

"You're probably right. But I'd like to clean us both up first. Adrinia won't want a dirty heir, will she?" Abbey slid her legs off the edge of the bed and headed for the bathroom before Justin could argue.

"You go and have that wash and I'll tell Adrinia the good news." Justin called after her.

Abbey's legs shook with every step. Her head spun wildly and it was all she could do to concentrate on reaching the bathroom door. She pushed it open and leaned against it, snapping it closed. She sank to the floor as her strength ebbed away. Her son felt like lead in her arms as she battled to hold him. If there was a way out, she no longer had the energy to find it. But she would save her son. Adrinia would never get him.

The sound of an almighty crash in the bedroom sent Abbey scrambling to her feet. She pressed her ear to the door. Maybe Adrinia wasn't as pacified as Justin hoped. A variety of screams filled the room and she realised there were more than two demons outside the door. She quickly locked it and crouched by the sink. Over Justin's bellow of rage she heard wood splintering, glass breaking. She expected the door to cave in and her son to be snatched from her arms. "God help us both," she whispered and tearfully kissed her sons face. "I'm sorry, little one." It took her a while to realise how silent it suddenly became outside. She slithered on her bottom to the door and listened.

"Abbey, are you in there?" The voice of a woman, with a soft Scottish burr, whispered through the thick wood.

Abbey gasped in terror and looked around the room for a means to escape. The window looked big enough to squeeze through, but not holding her son.

"Abbey," the voice called again. "I ken you're scared, lass, but I've not got th' time tae gain ye trust. The beast is being kept occupied in th' lounge, but it will not be fer long. You hav' tae come with me."

Abbey put her back to the door. "Who are you?"

"My names Jessie. A friend of Shaun's. It's okay, he knows about everything."

Abbey bit nervously on her bottom lip. "What do you mean he knows everything?"

"He knows about his daughter and th' curse and... well... that yoor living wi' th' beast."

The word daughter confirmed to her that Shaun didn't know everything. But he knew enough. But how? "But I didn't know Justin was..."

"I ken that and so does he," Jessie interrupted. "None of this is yoor fault. You've been manipulated by not only th' beast, but by others too. Shaun will explain everything once we get ootside."

Abbey felt consumed with fear. Confusion clouded her thoughts. If Shaun knew the truth, he should be outside the door, not this woman. Something wasn't right. "I'm not going anywhere with you. Leave us alone"

"Maybe you'll trust me then," a soft voice said beside her.

Abbey yelped in terror and jumped sideways clutching her son tightly to her chest. As her heart pounded in fear she stared at the person beside her. She recognised him straight away. His face burned into her mind through a picture held out to her. "Dad!" she whispered.

Morgan O'Donnell smiled. "Hello Abigail."

"But you're... I mean..."

"Dead? Yes, I am. But I'm still your father. I don't care what anyone else says on the matter, you're my daughter. I've always loved you."

A small, red haired woman suddenly walked through the door. "Sorry to disturb ye both, but we have a situation ootside. Ye'll probably find this hard tae understand," Jessie explained, "I dinna want tae walk straight in and frighten ye, but ye father had other ideas."

"Mum, can I come in too?" a small voice pleaded outside.

"Aye," Jessie called back. "She canna be no more shocked than she is already."

Abbey watched in stunned disbelief as a small boy came through the wall and took Jessie's hand. "This wee laddie is Douglas, my son," she said ruffling his red curly hair.

"Hello. Is this th' lady the gypsy told us aboot'?"

Jessie nodded. "Aye, son."

Abbey took a deep breath. She couldn't take it in. First monsters, now ghosts, what more could she expect?

"Ye need tae trust me and yoor father. The beast will be back and then we'll nae be able tae help ye."

Abbey tried to keep her mind focused on what Jessie was saying, but her voice started to recede into the background. Blood pounded in her ears and the room tilted into a crazy angle. She grabbed the sink with one hand to support herself.

"Och, you're bleeding, lass," Jessie gasped.

Abbey stared stolidly forward, doubting whether she could follow Jessie's horrified gaze. But she felt a pool of warmth around her feet and knew it was her blood which warmed them. "Maybe the curse isn't entirely broken after all."

"It will be if I know my son," Morgan replied. "He's waiting for you, Abigail. All we've got to do is get you both outside."

Abbey fought the nausea rising in her throat. The energy drained from her with every drop of blood that hit the floor. "Why doesn't he come for us then? Why does he send you?"

"Technically speaking he doesn't know I'm here. He sent Jessie."

"Shaun canna tek a step inside here," Jessie relied. "This is the beast's domain. It's where th' doorway tae hell lies open. Here th' beast is protected by shadow minions. Once yoor outside, Shaun can use th' light of th' Esor tae save ye and the child. Now come on Abbey, we need tae go."

"But... I don't..." Abbey stammered.

"There's nae time fer any more talking. If ye dinna come, ye'll bleed tae death where ye stand," Jessie interrupted, "Then yoor spirit is trapped with Justin forever. Along with yoor child's."

Abbey let go of the sink. "Okay. How do we get out?"

"The only way oot' is though where th' window used tae be. We'll help you. Once we're clear, Shaun will do the rest. Run towards him and don't stop for anything."

Abbey looked at her son, who had somehow amongst all the chaos, managed to fall asleep, and felt her heart contract with pain. There was no way she could make it. She was dying, it was obvious from the haemorrhaging. The thought brought a sense of calm, enabling her to think straight. She might be half dead, but her child would live if she let Morgan take him.

Abbey raised her son to her lips and gently kissed his brow. "Go to your daddy little one. He'll look after you now." She held the baby out to Morgan. "Take him. Tell Shaun, I love him and that I'm sorry for everything."

"Nay lass," Jessie replied. "We canna leave you here. Come on, ye can mek' it. I'll help ye."

Abbey shook her head. "Thanks, but I won't make it. But at least something good will come out of this. It wasn't all for nothing."

"Abbey," Justin's panic stricken roar reverberated around the cottage. "Where are you?"

"Please Dad. Don't let those monsters take my baby. Jessie can't do it alone, she has her own child to protect."

Morgan took the child. "I'll come back for you. I promise."

Abbey nodded, not believing for one moment that he would be able to. You can't defeat destiny, and it was hers to die in this god forsaken hole. "Go," she hissed.

"You can lower the baby out of the window to Jessie."

"I'll give Shaun your message," Jessie said and grabbed Douglas's hand. They disappeared through the wall and Morgan climbed onto the sink and lowered the child down to her.

"I'll be back," Morgan said and disappeared through the wall.

"ABBEY," Justin shouted and pounded on the bathroom door.

I'm coming," she called and opened the door. She bit back a scream as Justin loomed over her. His dark eyes bulging with fury. What crimes could turn a man into such a monster?

He looked at her empty arms. "Where's the child?"

"Someone took him," she lied. "They said Adrinia had…"

"That was quick," he interrupted, "Mind you, she was never one to miss an opportunity. You look pale, my love, is everything all right?"

Abbey looked down at her nightdress, now clinging to her like a crimson second skin. "Yes, everything's fine now," she whispered.

Chapter Twenty-Eight

Justin scooped Abbey into his arms before she could protest. The stench of rotting flesh filled her nostrils as her face pressed into his barrelled chest. She pushed against him and turned her head, but her strength ebbed with every beat of her heart.

"Oh, my poor love," Justin cooed sweetly. "Sometimes, after childbirth, a mother bleeds and it can't be stopped. But don't be afraid. It only means you'll leave this mortal existence a little earlier than planned." He tenderly laid her on the soiled bed sheets and rested his bulk beside her. "Now close your eyes, my love, and when you open them again, this terrible day will be over. There is so much for you to see and experience. You'll have the finest slaves. A beautiful home where I will love and cherish you for eternity."

Abbey closed her eyes to blot out the terrible sight of Justin salivating beside her. This 'terrible day' was a day she would remember forever. She had a son. A big beautiful boy, with his father's eyes. From all the chaos and terror, something wonderful had happened. After seeing her father and Jessie, she realised that death wasn't the end, it was the start of a whole new journey. Justin couldn't hold her forever. Eternity was a long time and she would fight him every minute of every hour. She would find her way back to her son and she will make sure he was safe from monsters like Adrinia and Justin. Her body felt cold and heavy. Was this how it felt to die? No pain, no fear. Only a hollow feeling of regret, which dragged her down into the waiting darkness.

***

"I need tae go back fer her," Jessie yelled, handing the baby to Rosa.

"You can't," she tucked the child inside her voluminous coat. "Look around you. The battle's begun. The demons are defending the doorway too fiercely. You'll never get past them now and you have your own child to consider."

Rosa saw the look of horror on Jessie's face, as the ground split open before them and dark, shadowy demons poured from the earth like liquid poison. She quickly pulled Jessie and Douglas into the safety of her circle. "The demons are more than capable of taking you to the underworld and using you as slaves. You must get to safety. You've done all you can here." She squinted through the thick dust clouds caused by the rift in the ground. "Tessa, Tessa, where are you?"

Her spirit guide appeared by her side. "I'm here, Rosa."

"Take the child to safety. If something happens to us you know what to do."

Tessa nodded and took the silent baby. "God be with you, Rosa. Have faith. Good always prevails in the end."

"It had better," Rosa replied, "because we are going to destroy that cottage. Even if I must pull it down with my bare hands."

"But what aboot' Abbey? She's still in there." Jessie shouted over the loud wail of demonic voices.

"I know. But if we don't close hells doorway now, it'll open too wide. There'll be demons, worse than Justin, coming through it then. The child is the catalyst to all this. His birth ends the curse. It is a boy isn't it?"

Jessie nodded, and pulled Douglas closer to her. "Aye, how did ye know?"

Rosa smiled. "The child was protected from the beast by a stronger magic than mine."

"Whose? Maybe they can help us?"

Rosa shook her head. "That particular spell was cast a long time ago. The Esor have done all they can, it's up to us now. I told Shaun from the beginning that he would lose Abbey." She looked at Shaun. Now encased in a brilliant white light, he looked bigger and stronger than ever. "If we win this fight, the child is the balm that will heal his grief. Now get to safety. This battle's going to get a lot worse, before it gets better."

***

Jessie was filled with despair. In death she was reunited with Dougie's father again. The greatest love of her life. But Shaun would lose his and never find her again. The least she could do was giving him Abbey's final words. Jessie grabbed Douglas and dragged him over Shaun. The light around him was so bright that she could hardly see him inside it. "Shaun," she shouted, just outside the perimeter of the light. "Shaun." Jessie saw his eyes widen in shock at the sight of her. The bright light dimmed quickly and disappeared back inside his solar plexus.

"Jessie, is that you?" Shaun said incredulously.

Douglas grinned. "Hello Shaun,"

"Oh my God, Dougie."He moved to step out of the circle.

Jessie put her hands up to stop him. "No, Shaun. Ye canna come oot of there. You'll be killed fer sure."

"What… I mean… How?"

"It's amazing isn't it? I've been afraid o' death all my life, only tae discover that it's a whole new wondrous world. Thank ye fer everything ye did for Douglas. Because of ye help he slipped from one world to th' other without fear. He came tae me and his dad filled with excitement aboot fairies and finding a leprechaun's crown."

"His dad! So you're all together now?"

Jessie nodded. "Aye. We're a real family now and you have a son of your own too."

Shaun's face split into a wide grin. "I've got a son! How do you know? Where's Abbey, is she all right?"

Jessie felt the guilt of leaving her behind weighing heavily on her shoulders. Morgan did go back, but she didn't hold much hope of him getting her out. She decided not to mention it to Shaun. "I'm sorry, Shaun. I tried tae get Abbey oot, but she was too weak from th' birth. She gave me yoor son and said tae tell ye that she loves ye and she's sorry for everything. You canna fight that monster. He wants Abbey fer all eternity. He'll do anything to keep her."

Shaun's lips pulled into a grim line of determination, "He's not going to get her. Abbey *will* live and we'll raise our son together."

Jessie turned and saw that the shadow helpers were ferociously fighting the people from the spirit realm. She had to get Douglas to safety.

"Go now, Jessie. It's not safe. Thank you for saving me son. "I'm glad you're happy."

"Good luck, Shaun. I hope your son brings you as much happiness as mine brought me."

***

Shaun watched Jessie and Dougie hurry away, with a sense of satisfaction. So it was true. You never really lose the ones you love. He looked at Rosa, whose hands moved like lightening as she used various crystals to send out energy vibrations to the spirit people. His light was supposedly amplified by the crystals that Rosa had placed inside his circle. She said eventually they would be like fully charged weapons. When they begin to resonate, it was the signal that the doorway was collapsing. But how could he do it with Abbey trapped inside? Shaun knew the crystals were charged enough to emit a burst of energy that would carve a pathway between the fighting demons and protect him. It should give him enough time to get Abbey out and get back to the circle.

"I'm sorry, Rosa. But I can't let her die," he whispered and closed his eyes. A burst of light encircled the crystals at his feet. They lit up like a lighthouse beacon and sent a pulse of light out into the night. The demons leapt out of the way, shrieking in terror. Shaun sprinted from the circle. He felt the shadow demons grab his clothes and pull him from the protection of the light. He punched at their grasping hands, fought to stay in the light, but there were too many of them. Wrenched sideways in a powerful grip he could not get out of, hope of escape seemed impossible. Then suddenly he was free, and encased in a thin skin of glowing light.

 He looked at Rosa and saw her hands move, as if she pushed something invisible towards him. This was her doing. "Thank you, my friend," he whispered, before propelling himself through the front door in one almighty crash of splintered wood.

The momentum of the door crashing open sent him sprawling along the wooden floor of the lounge. When he hit the opposite wall, his breath exploded painfully from his lungs.

"So, the knight in shining armour has finally arrived. It's about time. Where's your mighty steed?"

Shaun jumped to his feet. He scanned the room, but he couldn't see the owner of the voice. "Who's there?" he shouted, "Show yourself, demon."

"Mmm, that's not a very nice hello, Shaun O'Donnell, where are your manners?"

He watched as a woman stepped out from the shadows of the room. She was stunning. Her dark hair shimmered down her back, like a lake of glossy oil, stopping at her tiny waist. But it was her eyes that gave away her true identity. Black as night and twice as evil. "Where's Abbey?" he demanded.

Adrinia yawned and idly inspected her long red nails, "Oh, that silver-haired bore. She's down the hallway, the first door on the left. She's busy. Dying takes so long. It's quite tedious to watch."

Shaun wrenched open the door nearest to him and raced down a narrow hallway.

"Give Justin my love." A mocking laugh followed Adrinia's floating command.

Shaun crashed through the door and saw Abbey sprawled on a bed. Her face looked as pale as the white pillow she lay on. The same beast that haunted his dreams leaned over her, touching her with a filthy clawed hand.

"Get away from her," he snarled.

Justin's head snapped up and his lips pulled back into an enraged sneer. "I knew I should have got rid of you in the beginning. You're too late. Abbey has left the building." He sniggered at his own joke, his eyes bright with madness.

Shaun staggered back, filled with a gut wrenching despair. Then he saw the slight flutter of her eyes and knew that the beast hadn't won yet. "Abbey will never be yours. I have her soul. You'll never get any part of her if she dies, because her spirit will return to her soul." Shaun fervently prayed that the myth was true. That a virgin really can relinquish her soul to the man she gives herself to?

Justin stood up and slowly came around the bed. "Liar! I control the destinies of all the women who enter here."

Shaun immediately felt a strangulating pressure around his throat. He closed his eyes and visualised the energy ball. It came instantly. Whirling around like a tornado in his mind, releasing the grip on his throat. "Maybe it's not so easy to kill me after all." He glanced at the bed and met Abbey's stricken gaze. He smiled at her reassuringly and turned back to Justin. "Your reign here is over. There will be no more Abigail's for you to curse. Go back to where you belong and leave us in peace."

Justin dragged his tattered sleeve across his chin to wipe away the saliva edging down it. "I'm going. I have all I need."

"NO! You came back to claim your rightful wife. Abbey isn't that woman."

"I know that. She's better." He raised his hand as though saluting an invisible commander and Shaun flew through the air. The breath whooshed from his body as it was smashed against the opposite wall.

"Shaun," Abbey cried weakly. "Justin. Leave him alone. I'll come with you," she pleaded. "Please, don't hurt him."

Justin pulled his thick lips back into a hideous grin. "It's all right, my love. Let me deal with this. Loose ends need to be tied. Once he's dead, we can get on with our lives."

Shaun felt the pressure around his throat build again. This time it was stronger, more choking. Through the haze misting his eyes, he saw the woman from the other room directing her malevolent glare at him. He realised she was killing him, not the beast. She wanted Abbey to think it was Justin. It became harder to visualise the energy ball, above the loud thunder of his heartbeat. He was dying and he cursed himself for being so weak.

"Oh, no you don't, yer damn bitch," a voice shouted.

Shaun felt his throat released and he quickly sucked in air as a body sailed past him in a tangle of legs and arms. As it thumped against the dressing table with a sickening crunch, he saw it was the woman who was killing him. Wild eyed and furious, stood his mother, with half the wooden cross his father had made for the house. Justin lay on the floor, the man who put him there turned and faced Shaun.

"Mother, father is it really you?"

"Yes, it's us, son. Rosa told me that devil woman would materialise into human form tonight, which means she can be touched with the cross your father made for us. So consider yourself touched," she yelled at the unmoving Adrinia. "We have half each".

Justin stood up. "You're nothing but bothersome parasites."

The cross ripped from Morgan's hand and flew across the floor. Before Shaun could do anything it smashed across Aveline's shoulders. He watched his mother crumple to the ground like a broken puppet and felt a white hot rage course through him. Morgan's pain-filled cry echoed in his ears as Shaun dived at Justin. They both crashed to the floor, clawing and punching, both knowing they were fighting to the death. Shaun buckled under hands which pounded him like shovels and then it abruptly stopped. Through the blood running into his eyes, he saw Justin writhing on the floor, screaming in agony. His mother, battered and bloody, propped up by Morgan grinned at the empty brown pouch in her hand. "What did you do?"

"I've no idea. Rosa said I was to throw it at the beast and it would make him weak. Tie his hands and feet with this while you can." She pulled out a long strip of twine and held it out to him.

Shaun shook his head. "That won't hold him."

"It will. Rosa said it's woven from fairy thread. It's stronger than chains and will give us time to get out of here."

Shaun saw the wide gash on Aveline's head. "Mother, you're hurt."

"I'm fine. A bang on the head will knock some sense into me. I'm sorry, son. I made a terrible mistake. I never meant to hurt you or Abbey."

Shaun took the twine and bound Justin's hands as Morgan tied his legs together. "Let's get out of here. We can say sorry later."

As they finished tying Justin, Shaun watched in horror as Aveline lifted from the floor as if an invisible hand had dragged her up. Her face turned scarlet as she gasped for breath. Shaun saw a shimmering darkness in the place where Adrinia had fallen. "Leave her be. She's no threat to you."

"Hey demon, look what I've got," Morgan yelled.

Adrinia materialised, her eyes black with rage. Then Shaun saw his father throw a lace handkerchief. As soon as it touched her, the material changed into a giant cobweb. Screaming in outrage, she fought the sticky threads and Aveline dropped to the floor in a heap at Shaun's feet.

"Quickly, son, get Abbey," Aveline rasped. "Rosa's magic won't hold them for long."

"Where are your minions now, Adrinia," Justin roared. "Call yourself a queen."

"They're outside trying to stop you being buried, you idiot," Adrinia retorted.

Shaun picked up Abbey. He carried her to the window and waited for Aveline. "Come on, mother. We have to go."

Aveline shook her head. "No, son. Me and your father need to stay. It won't take them long to escape. Get back to the circle and finish this once and for all. We'll be fine. Rosa's given me a few more tricks. I'll see you outside."

Shaun shook his head. "But mother... I can't..."

"Yes, you can. Only you can stop this. Rosa's cloak of light will protect you. Go, send these monsters back to hell."

Shaun cried out in pain as claws shredded the flesh of his calves.

"You're not taking her anywhere," Justin growled.

"Let him go," Aveline screeched and threw a brown pouch, filled with herbs, at him. Justin roared and rolled over to try and escape the tiny flowers which tumbled out on him. The stench of burning flesh filled the room. Aveline pushed Shaun to the window. "Leave son, while you still can."

Shaun looked at Morgan. "Make sure you get her out."

"I'll do me best, son."

Shaun climbed out of the broken window with Abbey held tightly to his chest. Pushing through the fighting mass of good battling evil, he ran as if hells dogs were snapping at his heels. Demons clawed at his clothes, hair and face, but they were unable to hold on for long. Rosa saw to that.

Abbey lay deathly still in his arms. She neither moved nor made a sound as the demons tried to rip her away. He knew she needed medical help, but there wasn't time. If he didn't shut the doorway, she was as good as dead anyway. He saw his circle, but it looked surrounded by dark writhing shapes. He realised they were guarding the ring so he couldn't enter. A dark arm came out and hit him square in the face. Shaun's knees buckled and he fought to hold onto Abbey.

"Here, give me your hand."

Shaun looked up and saw Tessa holding her hand out to him. He took it and was immediately transported to the circle.

"Thank you," Shaun said gratefully,

"I've a few tricks up my sleeve still," she said and disappeared back into a misty tailed light.

"I'm going to put you on down me darlin' " He knew it would be hard for Abbey to stand. But if she lay down, she wouldn't have the protection of the circle. "Can you stand beside me?"

Abbey's eyes fluttered open and she nodded. Soaked in her blood, he looked over at Rosa and nodded his thanks. His mother must be out by now. It was time to send those devils back to hell. "Hold on to me, Abbey. Don't let go." He closed his eyes. Immediately a bright beam of light burst from Shaun's solar plexus and cut straight through the warring fighters.

***

Rosa watched the column of white light shoot out into the night. It travelled in a straight line towards the cottage. Then, like a great piercing lance, it embedded itself in the front of it. Immediately the cottage began to creak and groan. It bent and swayed as though it was made from rubber. Bricks fell from the eves, tiles rained down from the roof, windows splintered as it started to implode. The noise was deafening, like a great thunderclap in the air. The whole building folded as if it were sucked downwards, disappearing into a wide void that opened below it. The beam of white light went into the opening, sucking the surrounding demons with it. In a matter of minutes, all the dark entities were being, pulled into the hole, they screamed and roared. Clinging onto the spirit people, dragging some down with them. When the light retreated back into Shaun, like a wounded bear roaring in pain, the earth began to rumble and move, slowly healing the gaping wound left by hell's doorway. The screech of the demons became muffled as the ugly gash in the ground healed. Then there was silence.

Rosa stepped out of the ring. "It's all right, it's over," she said to Harriet and Jonathon. "You can come out now."

Harriet flew from the circle with her husband in hot pursuit. "Abbey, Abbey," she cried, in time to catch her daughter as she collapsed.

***

Shaun opened his eyes. His body felt like someone had squeezed through a wringer. "We did it, Abbey" he whispered. When no reply came back, he looked to his side and saw the woman he loved so desperately, being cradled in her mother's arms. He dropped to his knees and gently gathered her up. Her face was white as the snow on the fells and her lips held a bluish tinge that made his heart contract in fear. "There's so much blood," he said to Rosa, who knelt down beside him.

She put her shaking fingers onto Abbey's neck.

"I'm so sorry, boy. You did your best."

"No! This isn't how it's meant to be," Harriet screamed, weeping into her husband's arms. "Please, bring her back. You know magic, you can heal."

Rosa shook her head. "I can't. Once the spirit has left and the silver thread is severed, mortal life is gone forever."

Shaun hugged Abbey to his chest and gently rocked backwards and forwards. "I did what was asked of me, Rosa. Is this my payment?" He squeezed his eyes tightly closed, but his tears pushed through and ran down his face, marking his agony for all to see.

"Shaun. Shaun, look at me."

The soft insistent call of his name pulled him momentarily from despair. He opened his eyes and saw Tessa standing in front of him. Beside her stood Abbey. Gone were her blood soaked clothes. Instead she wore a sky blue dress that skimmed over her hips and puddled around her feet like fresh water. Her silver hair shone like a halo around her shoulders as magnificent sapphire eyes held his gaze. "Hello, me darlin'," he whispered.

"Shaun, do you remember when Abbey entrusted you with her soul?" Tessa asked.

He nodded. "How can I forget the best day of me life?"

"A spirit returns to its soul when it leaves the physical body. Abbey can't return to hers because you have it."

Shaun stared, shocked to the core. Can it really be true? "Are you saying I really

192

do have Abbey's soul? Where is it?"

"It's beside yours. Now listen closely. You can give her soul back and allow Abbey's spirit to join it, or for this one time only, it is possible for you to ask her spirit to go back into her physical body. Her etheric, silver cord is still unbroken."

Relief pushed away Shaun's earlier despair. They had a second chance. Yet something made him hesitate. Rosa told him that everyone on earth had free will. It was God's gift to them. It gave them humanity. Who was he to tell her spirit to do anything? He wanted her back more than anything else in the world, but she must want to return too. He looked at Abbey. "What do you want, Princess?"

"She can't hear you," Tessa replied. "Abbey's half way between worlds. She can only project what she feels through vibrations."

Shaun looked into Abbey's eyes. He saw so much love, it made his throat constrict with emotion. She did love him, he was sure and there was her son to consider. She would want to come back for him. "I want you to come back to me and our son," he whispered. "Come back me darling. Let us be a real family."

It happened so quickly that Shaun could not take it in. One minute Abbey was beside him and then she was gone. He looked at Tessa. "Where is she?"

"In your arms Shaun," she replied softly.

He looked down and saw Abbey in the same blue dress. Her face held a gentle flush, her hair shone brightly as if just washed. She looked peacefully asleep. "Wake up, me darling," Shaun whispered.

Her eyes fluttered and Harriet gasped and clung onto Jonathan's arm. "Abbey's awake, look she's all right."

Abbey opened her eyes. "Shaun... I..."

"You sure know how to scare a man, princess," he interrupted. He saw her eyes widen and become fearful. "What's the matter princess? You're safe now. You've nothing to be scared of."

She struggled to sit up as tears spilt down her cheeks. "Shaun, our son. Where is he?"

Aveline walked out from the trees. Beside her strode Morgan with a wide smile and carrying something wrapped in Rosa's brightly coloured shawl. The bundle in his arms let out a loud yell. "Who wants to meet me Grandson," he said proudly. He gently handed the child to Abbey. The child's cries instantly stilled.

The breath caught in Shaun's throat and took away any words that made sense as he gently pulled back the blanket. "He's got me eyes."

"Look at all that dark hair," Harriet squealed in delight.

"Shaun, isn't he beautiful," Abbey said. "Maybe if we went away, lived a new life where nobody knew us..."

"It's all right, Princess. We don't have to run away. We can be a family, here or wherever you want. Me mother told you a terrible lie out of fear. She thought that if you stayed with me the beast in the cottage kill us all. I'm not your brother. Morgan's my step-father. Our son's not blighted in any way. He's made from pure love - our love."

Abbey gently kissed her son's head. "I knew it. Nothing this beautiful could be made from anything so ugly."

Morgan looked at Shaun. "A parent will go to any lengths to protect their child. Remember that son."

Harriet knelt beside Abbey. "I thought we'd lost you. I've spent my life being afraid for you. We should've told you the truth earlier, but…"

"Mum, it's all right. I acted like a spoilt child."

"No, not spoilt," Jonathon interrupted. "You're just headstrong like your moth… I mean… like," he stammered.

"Like my mother," Abbey finished for him and looked pointedly at Harriet. "I've got all the parents I need on this earth plane and the bonus of an extra father in the spirit world. What more can a girl ask for?"

EPILOLGUE

Five months later

"What I don't understand Rosa, was how could Shaun's body harbour such a wondrous light without me knowing about it?" Aveline handed the old gypsy a cup of tea.

Rosa sighed. "Aveline, when are you going to stop harping on about it? Accept the impossible and you won't go wrong. That's what my mother always told me. Have you worked out how to make that herbal poultice yet? I don't know why I chose you as my protégé. Your mind's always wandering down paths that don't concern you."

"Because I've a new daughter in law to pass your knowledge on to," Aveline replied looking pointedly at Abbey.

Shaun placed his cup on the coffee table. "I don't understand half the things that have happened. But I'm glad it's all over. The demons are back where they belong, hells door is closed and Justin Montgomery is out of the way for good. You know, I still I think I preferred you with silver hair," he said to Abbey.

"I rather like it auburn," she said, and patted her short bob into place. "Anyway, you married me for better or for worse. So get used to it."

The front door flew open and Harriet came in pushing baby Morgan in his new buggy. "My, it's windy out there. We were practically blown around the town. Your father's parking the car. I must say Ireland has spectacular views. We could see for miles once you get to the top of the hill. Is that one of your carrot cakes I smell baking?" she asked Aveline.

"Of course. I couldn't have you staying with us without making your favourite cake for supper."

"Remind me to take you to Harrods for afternoon tea when you come to visit us. They do a wonderful fruit scone. Delicious with jam and cream."

Abbey cuddled under Shaun's arm as the babble of her extended family faded into the background. She knew she had made the right choice to live in his mother's cottage. Morgan had returned to the spirit realm. She felt blessed to have met him, even if he wasn't her real father. It was a comfort to know that he was still out in the ether, looking after them. Life could not be any better.

She was glad Aveline convinced Rosa to have her caravan outside. Not that she stayed in it much nowadays. Her rheumatics preferred the warmth of the cottage and as much as she'd hate to admit it, she knew that Rosa liked the company too.

Harriet took Morgan from the pram and settled him in his baby bouncer. Morgan Jonathon O'Donnell gurgled happily, content to sit and watch the pretty lady waving to him from the shadow of the lamp beside him.

The End